The Oyster Pirates

+ + + + + + + + + + +

Jim Walker

BETHANY HOUSE PUBLISHERS
MINNEAPOLIS, MINNESOTA 55438

Oyster Pirates

Cover by Dan Thornberg,
Bethany House Publishers staff artist.

Published by Bethany House Publishers
A Ministry of Bethany Fellowship, Inc.
11300 Hampshire Avenue South
Minneapolis, Minnesota 55438

Printed in the United States of America.

Library of Congress Cataloging-in-Publication Data

Walker, James, 1948–
The oyster pirates / Jim Walker.
p. cm. — (The Wells Fargo trail ; book 6)
ISBN 1-55661-701-1 (pbk.)
I. Title. II. Series.
III. Series: Walker, James, 1948– Wells Fargo trail ; bk. 6.
PS3573.A425334O97 1996
813'.54—dc20 96-25283
CIP

In the midst of the story,
this book is about redemptive friendship,
the kind that builds up another
in spite of his or her faults.
Lifelong friends do that.

This is why it is dedicated to my friends
Noel,
Mark,
Bruce,
Mike,
Rob,
Dave and Steve.

Thank you, guys.

JIM WALKER is a staff member with the Navigators and has written *Husbands Who Won't Lead and Wives Who Won't Follow.* He received an M.Div. from Talbot Theological Seminary and has been a pastor with an Evangelical Free Church. He was a survival training instructor in the United States Air Force and is a member of the Western Outlaw-Lawman History Association. Jim, his wife, Joyce, and their three children, Joel, Jennifer, and Julie, live in Colorado Springs, Colorado.

CHARACTERS

+ + + + + + +

Zachary Cobb—Undercover agent and bounty hunter for the Wells Fargo Company. Zac is growing reluctant to take assignments for the company as his relationship with Jenny Hays, his long-time sweetheart, grows more serious.

Jenny Hays—Zac's sweetheart. She has come to terms with Zac's job, refusing to pressure him further. A patient woman, Jenny loves Zac very much and will not allow herself to think about changing him.

Skip—Zac's ten-year-old charge. Skip's parents are deceased, and Zac is trying, although not very hard, to find any living relatives who will claim the boy. Skip feels very much at home with Zac and looks to him as a father figure.

Jack—A boy of ten pulled from the waters of San Francisco Bay with the body of his dead friend. Jack is an oyster pirate and a thief. He lives in Oakland with his prostitute mother and survives by his quick wits and fast feet.

Steven Van Tuyl—The skipper of the *Delta King*. Captain Van Tuyl is an old hand on the river, a man of experience and leadership.

Rance McCauliff—A professional gambler who plies his trade on the riverboats of the Sacramento River. The man's nature is shady and his contacts suspicious.

Dennis Grubb—A pilot on the *Delta King*. Grubb has a great deal of experience in the river and is known to navigate in the fog by the "feel" of the boat on the river.

Manny—A river pirate with a sordid reputation. He has been raised in a God-fearing home, but has long since left his roots to seek his fortune among the worst of society.

William Page—A doctor from Sacramento who is fulfilling his agreement with a missionary brother to care for his niece.

Mary Page—The daughter of medical missionaries in India. She is entering college and has little experience with handling the kind of men she meets after her kidnapping.

Colonel Princeton—The leader of the band of river pirates. Princeton is a Confederate veteran with a grudge. He is brilliant in his planning and ruthless with men.

Robert Blevins—A wealthy farmer and merchant. He is bent on controlling the trade in the Sacramento River and is the financing and intelligence behind the band of pirates now terrorizing it.

Hattie Woodruff—Zac's aunt. Hattie is a crusty veteran of the gold fields. Profane and harsh, she has a reputation as a scrapper.

Aunt Mamie—Blevins's aunt. Mamie cares for the riverfront mansion and oversees the entertainment of infrequent guests. She comes from a well-do-to family and has East Coast breeding and manners.

Cliff Cox—An agent for Wells Fargo. He maintains his position in the company by way of marriage.

Russ Korth—Henchman of Colonel Princeton. The man is quick on the draw and has a desire to prove himself with every man he can find. His rival in the group of brigands that report to Princeton is Manny.

PART 1

THE BOYS IN THE BOAT

CHAPTER 1

+ + + + + + +

ROBBIE PULLED AT THE OARS while Jack stripped off his trousers. The bell on the buoy clanged with each swell. The fog made going difficult, but the tide was out, and if they were going to get at the oysters, they would need to do so within the hour.

Robbie continued to pull toward the sound of the bell. He leaned back and strained his wiry body, tightening it against the black, glassy water. If they could find the ringing floater, they knew where to go from there. They had been to the oyster beds a number of times. The bar of sand jutted out from Alameda and pointed straight at the lights of San Francisco.

Oakland and the two boys' homes, if you could call them homes, lay at their backsides. The shanties they occasionally slept and ate in were nothing more than rickety shacks on the backs of derelict buildings. The slightest spark would set flame to much of the part of Oakland they lived in.

There was one good thing, though; if Jack and Robbie stayed out all night, no one would care. There would be no questions. Jack's mother was what they called a woman of easy virtue. He had heard the term and seen her smirk many times when she used it. The man they were living with now was not his father. Rarely had Jack seen the man "out of his cups," as they said. Jack had never seen his real father and didn't know who he was. He doubted his mother did either.

Stealing oysters from the beds of other folks seemed to be the only way the boys could make do for themselves. They were both too lazy for selling apples on the street and too proud to beg. Jack had used what he'd come up with the week before to buy some food and the dark wool sweater and cap he wore. Even in the summer, the chill on the bay went right through to the bone. There had even been some usable pearls that fetched more in the way of money than copper coin. His mother had taken those, but with the money from the oysters and the pennies he'd already saved, he had bought the sweater from a sailor who needed a drink. It was a fine one, too, all ribbed and scratchy.

Jack pulled off the sweater and folded it carefully as he watched Robbie bend back on the oars. Robbie was older, even if he wasn't smarter. He said he was fourteen, but Robbie was never sure of much, even his own age. Jack knew he himself was ten, though. His mother had been almost sober when she had him and even remembered the day—maybe not the exact day, but at least the month. The San Francisco Bay was too chilly for Jack to stay in the water for long, but it would be long enough. He leaned over the side and ran his hand in the water.

"That is cold," he said.

"You the one that's got to go," Robbie said. "You knows that. I can't swim a lick."

"I'll go, all right. T'ain't rightly deep 'nuff over them beds for a body to do much in the way of swimmin'. I can feel them oysters with my feet when we gets over the place."

"How you go and put yer head down there in that water, I'll never know."

"T'ain't hard none. You just can't go to thinkin' 'bout it much. Just do it and do it real quick like. That water's too durn cold for a body to get much in the way of greedy on one night. With this here fog, we ain't likely to get old man Riley comin' after us."

"I seen his new skiff yesterday," Robbie said. "It sure is pretty like, painted yeller and green. He gots two sets of oars on it and mounted hisself a four-gauge shotgun on the bow. It be a fearsome sight, that thing."

Jack looked overhead. The stars blinked through the low fog on occasion, and behind Robbie, Jack could just barely make out the lights of the big city. "With this here fog, I don't think we're gonna see old Riley."

"You better hope not. That man catches us, we is dead."

"Who'd ya get the boat from tonight?"

"Old Bill give it to me. 'Course, fer fifty cents I can't rightly call it givin'. At what we gots to pay out just to do this, you better reckon on bringin' up a bunch of them rocky boogers from down there."

"You ever think much abouts what yer gonna be when you get all growed up?" Jack asked.

"Nah, can't rightly say as I have. Mostly I guess I'm just too taken in with the notion of how hard it be to grow up at all."

Jack shivered, his bare skin shaking in the fog. "I been thinkin' about being a pirate when I gets able, a real pirate, not just a boy one."

Robbie continued to pull on the oars. The sound of the bell was getting closer. He chuckled. "You is so fulla them dreams and stories of yourn. When you sets me down and tells 'em, I faint lose all sight of things."

"Did I tell you the one about the green dragon?"

Robbie grinned. "Only about ten times. That's one of my favorites, though. How you come up with stuff like that?"

"It just comes." Jack waved his hand over his head. "Out of the top of my noggin, I reckon. That preacher on Fourth Street been teachin' me how to read a mite. The more I read, the more of them stories rattle 'round inside my brain." He bowed his head. " 'Course, he makes me read a mite in that there Bible of his, but I don't mind it too much." His head jerked up and he smiled. "You know there was this one man that lived way back then in Bible times that killed hundreds of soldiers with nothin' more than the jawbone of a donkey."

"Go on!"

"No, I ain't funnin' you none, and if it t'weren't so, then the Bible wouldn't have it writ down in plain words."

"Why didn't they just shoot him?"

"Silly! Such folks didn't have no guns way back there in Bible times."

Robbie dipped his paddles deeper and pulled. "Wish we wuz back in them times. Don't think Riley could chase us down with no jawbone."

"Naw, I reckon not. He ain't gonna be 'round, though." Jack looked out over the water. The fog continued to roll in, deep clouds of gray that hung just over the black water. "Would you be out here if'n you wasn't hungry?"

"Naw, I'd be curled up next to that stove of ourn."

The buoy came into view and Jack pointed at the red-and-white bobber. Candy stripes twirled up the white marker, and on top of it, a brass bell produced a sharp, crisp ring with each movement of the waves. "Won't be long now," Jack said.

He picked up a large basket with several tears in its sides and lowered it into the cold water. "Got to soak this here thing first off. Don't want it floatin' away from me." Taking a line from the bottom of the boat, he secured it firmly to his thin waist and poked the other end through a hole in the basket.

Robbie lifted the left oar out of the water and pulled hard with the right, spinning the dory around. The gentle waves thumped on the side of the little boat, hitting it with crisp thuds that echoed out over the water.

Several minutes later, the boys reached what they figured was the spot over the oyster beds. Jack picked up the long pole they carried and pushed it down into the water. "It's plenty shallow 'nuff here," he said. "If this ain't it, it's durn close."

"Then, you best get over the side and go to feelin' fer them things. That there tide ain't a gonna stay down fer very long, ya know, and I don't rightly favor spendin' too much time awaitin' to see if Riley and his fellers is indoors by the fire like you say you'd be."

Jack stared at the cold black water, took off his cap, and edged over the side, plunging up to his thin chest in the brine. The sudden shock of the cold water took the breath out of him. He wanted to double up with the shivers right then and there, but he started moving his legs and feeling the dirty bottom with his bare feet.

Robbie spun the boat around and pointed toward the faint, fog-dimmed lights of San Francisco. "You oughta skinny over there a ways. I thinks we is a little off." He leaned over to catch Jack's eye. "Don't you go to steppin' in no hole, though. All I could do is listen to you gurgle, and I don't much wanna hear that. 'Sides, I can't rightly set store in losing the only pirate I ever knowed."

Jack waded through the chest-deep water, wiggling his toes in the loose mud as he moved his feet over the silty surface. The waves lapped against him, spraying salt water into his face and curly black hair. He continued to dig with his toes in the muck until at last he felt the first of the rocky, precious cargo. "I got 'em," he yelled out.

Robbie swung his head around, looking at the dark shore behind him. "Pipe down, mister pirate man. Old Riley coulda heard you from that big feather bed of his'n."

Jack waited for a set of waves to pass over him and then stooped down into the water, bracing his face against the cold current. He waggled his fingers through the dirt and brought up a handful of the oysters, piling them into the basket. Again and again, he plunged into the dark, frigid water, each time scooping up a fistful of the shellfish. With his basket full, he surged toward the dory and slung the pile of shells into the bottom of the boat. "I-I-I-I'm just good fer a few more, then I gotta get outta here."

"We ain't got us a whole lotta time. B'fore you knows it, that tide's gonna sweep you away. You best be on with it."

Jack shivered.

"I gots me some gin back to the house. That'll warm yer innards up when we get ourselves back."

Swinging his arms against the incoming waves, Jack moved along, feeling for the beds. Down he went into the brine, again and again. When he had another full load of oysters, he moved back to the dory. Robbie pulled it closer. The current fought him from staying in place, and he kept the oars churning. He was unable to stop and simply float the dory where Jack worked, but he did his best to shorten his friend's trip back to the boat.

Jack threw the oysters into the wooden boat. A series of thuds echoed across the water as they hit the bottom. Suddenly, staring back into the darkness, Jack's eyes widened.

"What is it?" Robbie asked.

"We got to get!" Jack said.

Robbie swung his head around; through the fog, they could see a faint light over the water. The glow of the lantern was mystical, like an angel hovering in the fog over the dark water, an angel of death. The sound of dipping oars floated out over the bay. With each sound of the oars, the angel drew itself closer.

Jack piled himself back into the boat and onto the sharp oysters. Robbie began to spin the oars, first clipping the surface of the water in panic and then feeling the bite of the wood against the water. Shivering, Jack pulled on his trousers. He shimmied the heavy black sweater on and then crushed the cap onto his wet hair. Fumbling in the darkness, he wrestled the beaten brogans onto his feet. "Can't leave these," he said. "You reckon it's Riley?"

"I reckon," Robbie said.

"You better pull then, and real hard."

"If'n it be Riley, there ain't no outrunnin' that there skiff of his. 'Sides, he'll have at least two growed-up men pullin' on them things."

"We just better get off'n these beds and hope they don't see us."

Jack flipped over on his belly and scooted toward the back of the dory. He continued to watch the dim light as it came ever closer. Moving back, he edged up next to Robbie. "They is coming on fast. We're gonna be catched."

"That man ain't gonna catch nobody, I already heard him say that. He's gonna shoot us down. We'ze gonna be afloatin' out here come mornin', no questions, no bother."

Jack reached into his belt and pulled out a knife.

"Now what is you gonna do with that? You ain't no pirate yet, and we sure as blazes ain't got no cannon to spit at them, but they has, I done seen it. And the thing is this, they can hear our paddlin' same as we can hear theirs."

"Maybe we'd best leave the boat and go over the side," Jack said.

Robbie pulled the oars hard. He shook his head. "Like I done told you, I can't swim a lick. 'Sides, with that tide coming in and us moving offa the beds, we is way over our heads now. We gots to shake them in the fog or die like good boys. You best be a praying to that God that helped that man with the jawbone, 'cause right now we is the dead donkeys if'n you don't."

"Don't rightly know what the preacher would say 'bout that. Two thieves prayin' to escape? That might not go over so well in a prayer."

"Then, you hang on. If them folks gets close enough to shoot, you might just be better off in the water. Leastwise you can paddle in the stuff. Me, I'd just as soon die up here wheres I can breathe."

"Want me to pull on them oars a spell?"

"Here, you take the one over here. We can put two arms on each one, I reckon. That might help us a smidgen. You watch me and pull when I pull."

Jack scrambled onto the seat and, taking the oar, began to strain against the water. Both boys moved forward in unison and, arching their backs, raked deeply at the sea. The ghostly light edged ever closer through the fog, like a giant, hungry sea bird swooping down on a small, struggling creature. They could see the faint outline of the men in the skiff, pulling hard and in their direction. At the bow of the boat, beside the lamp, a man stood next to a mounted swivel. The boys' eyes widened as they rowed. This was the man who would try to kill them.

The man stood erect and swung the big gun in their direction.

"Heave to!" he shouted. "Heave to or I'm gonna shoot you down. This here is our beds you're on."

Jack and Robbie stared at each other and continued to row in unison.

The man crouched down over the gun and fired a blast. The boom echoed over the bay and a shower of buckshot pelted the water at the stern of the slower dory.

Jack picked up the knife and stuck it back in his belt.

"We is done fer, sure 'nuff," Robbie said. "You best go over the side and leave me be."

Jack kept up the steady pull on his oar. "Hush yer nonsense talk," he said. "I ain't about to leave you here to face them folk."

"If'n you don't, then yer gonna die with me. That's all there is to be said about the matter. They ain't about to take us back to no jailhouse. We'ze gonna be feedin' the fish."

A large bank of fog moved over the water and surged at the scattered mist. Jack saw it first. "Looky over there," he shouted.

"Hike up yer oar a mite," Robbie said. With Jack's oar momentarily out of the water, Robbie dug hard, spinning the dory around and pointing it at the heavier vapor. "All right now, pull for it," Robbie said.

The two boys strained hard for the bank of fog, and the trailing skiff changed direction, moving swiftly to overtake them. The men in the skiff angled toward the small dory, dipping the oars vigorously into the murky brine. It would take a few minutes to get into the stuff, the boys knew that, a few minutes they might not have. The man at the bow shouted once again. "Heave to or I'll cut you down right where you are."

Jack could feel the increasing wetness on the back of his neck as they drew close to the heavy fog. It didn't help to watch the unearthly light as it came closer and see the man at the bow as he squinted down the barrel of the big shotgun.

Once again the big gun boomed. A piece of lead bit savagely into Jack's arm and spun him aside. Grabbing the fresh wound, he sat back up. Robbie was twitching in the bottom of the boat, writhing like a fish on the end of a skewer. Jack quickly let go of the oar and dropped to his knees beside the boy. "Where you hit?" he asked.

Robbie turned over on the scattered oysters. Jack could hear the rough breathing and the bubbling sound coming from the boy's chest as he spoke. "I'm laced up the front pretty good. I ain't a gonna make it."

The heavy bank of fog swept over them, turning the air around them into a murky gray. Jack slipped his hand over Robbie's mouth and leaned next to his ear. "Shhh, we're in it now," he whispered. "Don't make a sound."

The dory drifted silently, and Jack could hear the skiff as it paddled nearby. The oars of the men worked the water and one man began to shout. "I think I got 'em. They got to be close. I know I winged 'em bad enough to take them off their oars."

"Then you be piping down," another man yelled. "With all the noise we're making, we couldn't hear them if they was right on top of us. Ship them oars and hold her steady."

In unison, the men lifted the oars from the water. Jack could hear the water as it dripped from the smooth surface of the men's paddles. They were close. The way his heart was beating, they might even be close enough to hear that. He clung to Robbie and kept his hand over the boy's mouth. Whispering in his ear, Jack spoke ever so softly. "They're close by. We can wait 'em out. Just hold on. I'll get you back home."

Robbie blinked his eyes, and Jack could see tears forming in them. The boy shook his head at Jack slowly and deliberately.

"Better pull a mite," one of the men shouted. "That tide will be drifting them back toward Alameda. We best turn in that way a bit. If we don't find them shortly, we can swing on back toward the docks. They got to come in. I tell you, I hit them pretty bad."

Jack lifted his head. He saw the dim light in the shrouded fog and heard the men's oars go into the water once again. If they turned too quick, they would be on them, and he knew it. He didn't know how to pray, just silently plead with someone or something he knew little about. He looked down at Robbie. Maybe it wasn't right to ask about himself, but favor might be shown for a friend.

"Are they going?" Robbie's raspy voice asked the question.

Once again Jack lowered his head next to Robbie. "Yeah," he whispered. "They might be going over the top of us, though. I can't rightly work on them oars, they'd hear us fer sure. All I can do is hope the tide don't carry us right into them, hope and pray a bit."

"I ain't never prayed afore," Robbie grunted.

"Me neither. Ain't sure how to start."

The boys listened to the sound of the skiff's oars. Each dig at the water sent shivers of doubt up their backs. There could be no predicting where Riley's boat would turn, nor if it would be back. The wet fog hung over them like a blanket from God, a soft covering of tender mercy, gently caressing them and causing them to feel warm in the midst of the nighttime chill.

As time passed, the sound of the oars drifted off. It was only a matter of time before Jack and Robbie found themselves alone with only the sound of the waves lapping against the sides of the dory. The boat swung gently to the side and creaked as it moved.

"We'ze in the current now," Robbie croaked. "They'll be no rowin' against it, 'specially not you by yerself."

"Then we'll just go 'round to where it takes us."

"Where it takes you. I'm done for." Tears fell down his cheeks. "I ain't gonna ever see the sun again."

"Sure you are. Don't go to talkin' nonsense."

"I got me some pieces of antler bone in my pocket. Shined 'em up pretty good like. I wants you to have 'em. There's a real pretty agate in there too. When you look at it, you can think about me." Robbie closed his eyes.

"Now stop all that dead talk, ya hear? When I get you back to the docks, I'm gonna find you some good liver and fry it up fer you. You'll be fit in no time."

There was no answer from the boy, only silence followed by the plaintive moan of a foghorn.

CHAPTER 2

+ + + + + + +

THE SUN WAS BARELY UP when Zac picked up and shook out his napkin. Even though the fog on the bay would keep the sky dark for hours yet, the hotel dining room was filling up with merchants and bankers. It was not the sort of place where Zac could feel comfortable. He sat stiffly in his polished dining chair, his little .45 bulging beneath his dark blue suitcoat. No matter what his dress, the man still couldn't give up the gray cavalry hat. He always wore it with pride, as if clinging to a cause he still believed to be right. The hotel had cleaned and blocked it the night before, but it still looked out of place, in Jenny's thinking.

"Hattie will meet us when we dock?" she asked.

Zac pointed with his knife at Skip's eggs. "You'd be well advised to not let those things run cold." He nodded slightly at Jenny. "Yes, and the woman's never been known to be late, unless it's on purpose, especially when it comes to the opportunity of giving me grief. So, I expect she'll have been there for some time before we pull into Sacramento."

Jenny knew that Zac was right when it came to his aunt. The old lady seemed to take special pleasure in pushing Zac in directions he didn't want to go. She smiled and took a dainty fork full of grits. "Maybe she's too excited about coming to San Francisco to stop to worry about your singleness."

"That ain't likely, and with you standing next to me when we pull in, she's gonna be on me like a duck on a June bug."

"I'll do my best to keep her off you. Besides, I don't even want you." Her smile grew larger.

Skip broke open a steaming biscuit and piled orange marmalade onto its insides before cramming it into his mouth. The sticky substance ran down the sides of his cheeks.

"You'd think we never fed you at home," Zac said.

Jenny reached over and tousled the boy's blond, straight hair. "He's just growing, that's all. I bet he's plenty excited about that boat ride, too."

"Yes'm, I am," Skip said. "I ain't never been on a big paddle-wheeler before."

"There, you see," Jenny said. "If you don't bother about his table manners at the hacienda, why should a hotel with a tablecloth make any difference? None of us care about people in boiled shirts we'll never see again."

She could see the notion about impressing the swells made Zac brace. It was something he'd never let into his head. She smiled at his obvious discomfort. Suddenly, he returned her smile.

"I can see it's my manners that are in question here, and I guess you're right at that."

They had finished their breakfast, and Zac was lingering over coffee with a lit pipe when Henry Wells walked up to their table. The man's shining blue eyes were offset by the shock of white hair and full, rounded, snowy beard that framed his face. His prominent nose and the wrinkles that ran from his eyes showed him to be a man who seriously surveyed his books, often by dim lights. His jet black suit was set off by a carefully starched white shirt and pressed tie. "I was hoping I'd find you here, Cobb."

Zac motioned toward the empty chair at the table, and without being asked, Jenny poured the man a cup of coffee from the porcelain pot on the table. "Why don't you go and look over the lobby," Zac said to Skip.

Without a word, the boy shot to his feet and out the crystal-lined doors into the lobby. Wells nodded a thank-you to Jenny and, taking his seat, sipped the coffee. "Thank you," he said.

"Don't thank us," Zac replied, "Wells Fargo is paying for this."

Wells took a long sip and grinned. "Of that I'm quite aware, and I suppose we are mighty happy to do it."

"Now, what's so special about this short load that you sent for me?"

Wells set down his cup and, pushing it away, hunched forward, elbows on the table. "We've been getting grief from some people who want to control the shipping from Sacramento, and it's business we've had since we've been here. Now, I can't say for sure, but a bad batch of river pirates have been operating in the Delta ever since we were challenged, and this is a shipment we just can't afford to lose."

Zac leaned back and puffed on his briar pipe. "What's so special about this one?"

"It's over half a million in gold, that's what. The army is giving us a small group of soldiers to help, and I have one of our agents in Sacramento to accompany it, but I'd feel a lot better having you riding along with it. You've never lost a shipment for us yet, and there's been plenty that you've gone out of your way to bring back."

"That's just my job."

"Yes, and right now I need a man who knows how to do his job. You'd be surprised, Cobb, at how very few men actually take the trouble to do what they're paid to do."

Jenny reached over and patted Zac's arm. "Mr. Wells, you couldn't have come to a better man. When Zachary here has work to do, he lets very little get in his way."

Zac looked at her carefully. There was something about the way she said it that was meant to be more than a compliment.

Wells folded his hands. "I don't believe I've had the honor of meeting this lady, Cobb."

"This here is Jenny Hays, a friend of mine and Skipper's," Zac said.

"Pleased to meet you, ma'am. It's about time our associate here had someone in his life to take the edge off." He cocked his head at Zac. "And such a pretty someone too, I might add." He lightly brushed back his white beard and gave off what for Henry Wells could be interpreted as a smile.

"That she is," Zac replied. "Miss Hays works right hard at keeping me on my best behavior. I have to make sure I hold my knife and fork right proper like."

"Good for her. I've always said that it was the women who did more at taming the West than any collection of Bill Hickoks could ever have done." He picked up his cup for another slurp. "You just keep all that thankless work up there, Miss Hays. All of San Francisco will thank you for it someday. This man of yours is going to make his mark, mark my words."

Wells pulled out three steamboat tickets and laid them on the table, along with an envelope filled with cash. "Here's what you required, Zac, and I'm happy to pay it for the peace of mind. I couldn't do this with every delivery, mind you, but until we see some resolution of our problem, it will buy me a good night's sleep."

Zac picked up the bundle and shoved it into the pocket inside his jacket.

"The tickets are for the *Delta King*, as fine a boat as ever ran the river. Captain Van Tuyl is a personal friend of mine, and he will show you every courtesy. I even have the two staterooms you required. They were hard to come by, but it's worth it to the company."

Zac nodded and puffed smoke. "Coming from you, Mr. Wells, I'd say that was quite a sacrifice."

"You seem to be worth the investment, Cobb—a mighty steep one, but so far worth every penny. It will sail within the hour, and I have the porter ready to take your bags and get you a cab to the docks." Wells got to his feet and dropped his napkin on the table. "I expect to see you back in San Francisco in three days' time, along with our gold."

He bowed slightly at the waist toward Jenny. "It was a distinct pleasure in meeting you, Miss Hays. When you get back to San Francisco, Mrs. Wells and I would look forward to the pleasure of your company for dinner at our house." Brushing the coffee wetness from his beard, he ran his hands down the lapels of his suit and tucked his thumbs in his suspenders. Once again, a faint smile crossed his lips. "And you can bring your hardworking but disagreeable friend here with you."

Watching him walk away, Zac took out his pipe and tapped its remains into the half-full cup. "He's a nice enough man when you get him out from behind that desk of his."

"I think he's splendid."

Within the hour, the cab had pulled up next to the docks, and Zac and Jenny watched Skip run up the gangplank to the *Delta King*. His eagerness and enthusiasm would have been hard to quibble with. The white boat was trimmed in red, its delicate latticework making the paddle-wheeler look like a triple-layered wedding cake, thick on the icing. The men on deck were swinging a large carriage on board with the help of booms and pulleys. Others transferred cargo to the main deck by way of a second catwalk.

Zac stood beside the cab and took the bags the driver handed down. He squeezed the leather bag containing his sawed-off shotgun under his arm and picked up the carpetbags containing his, Skip's, and Jenny's things.

From the docks one could see a misty forest of masts that melted into the shroud of fog on San Francisco Bay. Their bare black masts and rigging appeared to form a ghostly village of leafless trees and spider webs that melted into the murky gray. Hundreds of ocean-going ships lay at anchor long after their cargo had been deposited. Each ship had the same story, a long voyage ending in San Francisco and a crew that wanted to search for gold. It was the thing that made the streets of the city an unsafe place for any man over the age of nine. Roving gangs of kidnappers prowled the streets, searching for members of the next reluctant crew, a crew that could once again free a ship to set sail.

The gangplank had a give to it as they walked up its length, and on the other side of the rails, a mate was checking names off the passenger list. "I take it you're Zac Cobb, and that boy belongs to you."

"He does."

The man craned his neck up and called out to the pilothouse on top. "Captain, he's here." Turning back to Zac, he checked off his name. "Captain Van Tuyl wanted to show you 'round on his own. He's on his way down."

Moments later a short, stocky blond man scurried noisily down the wooden stairs. His dark blue coat was ringed with gold piping. The coat looked as if it had been slept in, and the white shirt underneath it was wrinkled and streaked with sweat. The man held a large gold watch, its heavy gold chain trailing to its moorings on his scratchy belt. Upon seeing Jenny, he dropped the watch in his coat pocket and doffed his black cap. He stuck his hand out in Zac's direction. "Steven Van Tuyl," the man said. "I'm the master of this vessel."

Zac set down his bags and shook the man's hand.

"Henry Wells has told me about you, and from what he says I was expecting the fire of Moses and the thunder of Elijah."

"I'm afraid all you're getting is a rancher come up from San Luis. I work for Wells Fargo only on occasion."

"Well, those occasions must be something to curl a Chinaman's hair, to hear Henry tell it. You've saved that man a pretty penny, and you know how pretty Henry's pennies truly are."

"Yes, I do. Allow me to introduce you to Miss Jenny Hays."

"Pleased to meet you, ma'am. I didn't know our unnamed passenger would be a lady, and such a pretty one at that. I think you'll find your room more than adequate, however."

"Thank you, Captain. I had no idea this ship would be so large."

"Boat, ma'am. The *Delta King* is a big old boy, but he wouldn't last long as a ship outside the Golden Gate, I'm afraid. We do have accommodations that you'll find quite comfortable, however, and I have all of you at my table for supper."

A man in a black broadcloth suit walked up the gangplank, and the captain's demeanor suddenly shifted. "I see you're with us again, McCauliff."

The tall, lanky man stopped and loosened his tie. His black hair, plastered to the sides of his head, had the shine of bear grease, and he gave off a faint aroma of lilac water. "That I am, Captain, earning my living on this river, the same as you. I pay my passage like any other passenger."

"You can make money on the river to your heart's content," Van Tuyl shot back, "but if I don't find what you're doing to my liking, you won't be able to do it on my boat. Am I making myself understood?"

"Perfectly."

The man tipped his hat to Jenny and swaggered away.

The captain watched his walk and grunted. "Professional gamblers; they're same as rats in my book, filching what don't belong to them and taking up space to boot. 'Course with him, I don't lose a room. He stays at the tables night and day. I hate his type, though. What I want is happy passengers, not ones that get to where they're going dead broke. I've never caught him cheating, but he wins too steady like to make what he does something a body could call honest."

"Lots of people think the best way to come by money is to take what doesn't belong to them," Zac said. "That's the kind of attitude that keeps me in business, I'm afraid. If McCauliff there can teach them that hard work is the only way to make a living, then I'd say more power to him."

The captain scratched the back of his neck. "I suppose that's the long view of it. I'd just as soon, though, that he set up his school somewheres else. I like happy paying passengers." He paused, then swung his hand around to the walkway. "Why don't you let me show you to your cabins. You'll need to put your things away and might like to make yourselves comfortable. Ma'am, you just might want a washbasin to freshen up a mite."

"Thank you, Captain," Jenny said. "That's very thoughtful of you. I wouldn't want to get too comfortable, though. This is my first time on a boat like this, and I'd like to see the bay."

"You won't see very much, I'm afraid. This fog has got things pretty well hid. It'll slow us down a mite, to boot. But you're welcome to stand up on deck and watch the wetness go by."

"Thank you. I'd enjoy that."

"Well, I'm sure you'll soon find out that on this here bay a body has to admire the sea at a respectable distance. When we heave away, we'll be in the chop and our decks don't hold much back. You'll be able to get yerself closer on the river."

Zac dropped his upper lip and let out a shrill whistle. It was a talent he had picked up long ago, and one that could call a cab in any city of the world. At this point, however, all he wanted was Skip's attention. The boy had gone up front to the hurricane deck, and the whistle stopped him cold and spun him on his heels. Moments later he joined them and trailed the group to the back of the boat.

"I have adjoining cabins for you folks," the captain said. He unlocked the first of the doors and gave the key to Zac. Pushing it open, they stepped inside. There was barely enough room for all of them, but the bunk beds made any sleep they might want workable. A dresser contained a washbasin and a pitcher filled with water. "You are next door, Miss Hays. It's a mite fancier and with a bit more space to spare."

After putting their bags down and locking their doors, the three of them continued with the captain on his tour, finishing in the pilothouse on top of the boat. Two plain-dressed men with caps stood to attention as Van Tuyl introduced them. "These are my pilots for this trip, Dennis Grubb and Wes Lansing. They spell each other to keep fresh. They know this river better than any, even when it changes during the rainy season."

"My," Jenny said, "you two have important jobs, then."

Grubb smiled at the attention and seemed to stand even straighter. "Yes, ma'am. These channels are narrow and a body has to keep track of where he is. It would be easy to get lost in that Delta, if we should venture in there."

"But we won't," Van Tuyl added.

In a short time, with the tour ended, the three of them stood on the bow and watched the *Delta King* begin to navigate through the fog. With each minute that went by, the fog grew heavier. "Is it always like this?" Skip asked.

"Well, you know it can get this way down our direction," Zac said, "but the fog isn't near as heavy, and we don't have it so long."

"It's kinda spooky," Skip said. "Like dead men's breath."

"I suppose a body could let their imagination run away with them out here, but let's hope our Mr. Grubb up there doesn't let it happen with him."

"No," Jenny said, "I should say not."

"Can I go and look around some more?" Skip asked.

"Yes, just be careful you aren't a pest. Men are working here, and I suspect with this fog, they'll have to be keeping a sharp lookout. We've been away from the dock for a spell, but I think they're all still pretty busy like."

The engines chugged slowly, and the sound of the water pouring off the big stern wheel created a steady noise that could put a man to sleep standing at the rail. A shrill whistle blew from a pipe at the pilot's cabin. It brought all their heads around.

"What's that?" Skip asked.

"I suspect that will continue," Zac said. "They want to make sure that if there are any other boats around they know we're coming. Sounds like a wise thing to do. We wouldn't want to catch anyone by surprise, now, would we?"

"No, I reckon not."

"All right, Skip, you can look around, but don't get too close to the rails. If you fell over, we might not find you in this fog, and that water's plenty cold."

As the boy walked away, Jenny shook her head. "I suppose caring for someone makes you think all the time."

"That it does."

She took his arm. "It makes you think about nice things too, though, doesn't it?"

"I love him. I didn't want him, but right now I wouldn't want to lose him."

"Then, you haven't been able to find out if he still has living relatives?"

Zac looked off into the fog. "No. The company is still working on that, but I must admit I hope they aren't looking too hard."

"What if they find someone who wants to take him?"

"I suppose we'll have to deal with that when we're staring it in the face."

She gripped his arm tighter. "I hope they aren't successful with that little mission. I'd hate to see what it would do to you."

"It would leave a big hole inside. But I'm more concerned about what it would do to him. Right now, I'm all he's got, and the kid's not wise enough to know what a narrow spot that puts him in."

"I understand how he feels. I care about you, and I guess that puts me in the same place. I'm old enough to know better, but I'm right there, all the same."

He leaned down to kiss her but suddenly snapped his head up. "There's a boat out there!"

"Where?" She looked around.

"Out there." He pointed through the fog.

In the distance they could see the faint outline of a small boat. As they watched it carefully, it was plain to see that there was someone moving in it. Whoever it was began waving his arms at the approaching paddle-wheeler."

High overhead, the shrill whistle blew several short blasts.

"I think they've seen whoever that is," Zac said. "I just hope they don't run him down."

CHAPTER 3

+ + + + + + +

THE BIG PADDLES REVERSED THEMSELVES, stopping the drift of the *Delta King* in the fog. All the while, the whistle overhead continued with a loud, continuous blast, sending its steam out into the foggy air. Several of the crew made their way to the bow near where Zac and Jenny stood, and Captain Van Tuyl and Skip joined them minutes later. The little captain waved his arms at the men to get them to back away and give him a better look.

The *Delta King* was a boat built for river travel, its waterline all too close to the choppy waves of the bay to make standing there long something anyone could take comfort in. It allowed for a good look at whatever it was they came across, but on a windy day with the waves high enough, it was far too good a look. The sea would tend to wash over the deck, sending sheets of salt water lathering over the polished wood and making sleep on deck for those who couldn't afford the price of a stateroom a wet impossibility.

A small dory with a boy in it bounced on the waves. Captain Van Tuyl leaned over the rail, soaking his pants from the knees down with the chop that hit the steamer's platform. "Yer a hazard to navigation," he called out. "Back yerself away!"

"I ain't no hazard!" the boy screeched. "I'm lost in the fog, and my friend's got himself kilt."

Jenny moved closer to the captain for a better look. "Has that boy got someone in the boat with him?" she asked.

"You alone?" Van Tuyl yelled.

"Naw. Like I says, Robbie's here with me, only he's dead."

Van Tuyl leaned back. "I can't be stopping to take no-account, nonpaying passengers on."

Jenny leaned forward and put her hand on the captain's shoulder. "Captain, we can't leave that little boy drifting out here in the fog with the body of his friend. It wouldn't be Christian."

Without responding, Van Tuyl waved at several of the deck-hands. "Bring 'em on board. We'll keep the dory as payment. If the boy's right and his friend is dead, wrap the body in a tarp and lash it aft to the deck."

One of the hands threw a line to the boy, and the captain cupped his hands to his mouth and shouted, "All right, boy, you latch on and come aboard when we're ready for you."

The boy caught the line and, tying it to the bow of the dory, began to scoop up oysters and stuff them down the front of his sweater. As the men hauled the dory closer, the sight of the small boy and his distorted figure in the black sweater was almost comical. Van Tuyl leaned back and growled at Zac and Jenny. "The boy's an oyster pirate, probably got just exactly what he had coming."

"He's just a boy," Jenny said. "Small, cold, and all alone."

"Yes, just the kind I'll be chasing in ten years," Zac murmured.

On deck, the boy started to shake; he wrapped his hands around his thin body while pushing and adjusting the cargo under the sweater.

Jenny took her shawl and placed it around him. "You're freezing," she said. "We've got to get you out of those wet things and get something hot into you."

The boy watched as the men lifted the body from the bottom of the boat. He screeched out at them, "You be careful. Handle him real gentle like." Looking up at Jenny, he wiped tears from his eyes. "Robbie's the only friend I gots. We lives over in Oakland."

"Your parents will be worried," Jenny said.

"T'ain't likely," he replied. "Got no folks to speak of. Got a ma, but she's gonna be too drunk to know or care where I am." He held on to his overstuffed sweater. "She'll miss what I'm bringin' in afore long, though."

"We can't be carting this kid over to Oakland," the captain said. "We've lost enough time already. That other one's headed for Potter's Field, but we got no time for that, either."

Jenny looked up plaintively at Zac, her blue eyes glistening in the mist. "He's Skip's age," she said, "and just as lost and alone as a body can be."

Zac straightened himself up and looked down at her. "Well, I'm not starting a home for wayward boys, but he can have my bunk until we think on what to do with him." He looked at the flustered

Van Tuyl. "Captain, we'll put the boy in my cabin. If one of your men can scare up some small old clothes, we can get him somewhat warm and dry."

"All right, Cobb, I'll leave him to your charge, you and Miss Hays here. But take my advice, this boy is no good. He'll only bring you trouble. You better have anything of value with you at all times." Looking out at the ghost ships through the fog, Van Tuyl added, "What this boy really needs is two years of going 'round the horn on one of those. A little hard work makes a thief grow up fast."

The boy continued to shiver, holding on to his overstuffed sweater. He ventured a bold glance at the captain. "I gots some oysters I could sell you."

The captain was taken aback at the brazenness of the remark. "What makes you think I'd care to buy those things you've stolen from somebody else's beds?"

The boy drew himself closer to the captain, glaring into the man's eyes. "I can't just leave them be. Robbie got himself kilt for this here stuff. 'Sides, if'n I don't sell them, they'ze gonna stink somethin' awful."

"We'll deal with that when we get you warm," Zac said.

"This kid's real trouble," the captain stressed. "Nothing good can come of him, you mark me on that."

Skip had been silently watching the exchange, and Jenny caught his eye. "Come on, Skip. You come with us. You two boys can get to know each other after we get our young friend here warm."

Back in the cabin, with fresh clothes on and the oysters in a bag, the boy began to talk. The pot of hot cocoa did wonders for his spirits, and he was quickly devouring the biscuits and honey that sat beside it.

"We wuz plumb lucky to make it into that fog last night or I wouldn't be here now no ways. Old man Riley's skiff was on us so fast—scared the dickens out of us."

"I wouldn't call what happened to your friend very lucky, son," Zac said.

The boy continued to cram the hot biscuits into his mouth. He spoke in a stifled voice, trying hard to get out the words from around the warm obstruction. "My name's Jack and, mister, if'n you knew where we lived and what happens to us all day long, you might say Robbie wuz the lucky one and I wuz the jinxed kid."

With that, Jenny put her hand on Zac's arm and gave him a

pained glance. "What does your father do?" she asked.

"Don't know who he is, never seen him. Near as I can tell a pa ain't good for nothin' no ways. I ain't never had one, and I'm working out okay."

"It's plumb providential you're alive," Zac commented, "but I wouldn't call that working out."

"Well, I ain't much worse off fer not having one. Robbie had himself a pa that he knew, and he didn't make out so good." Jack slowed down on the biscuits and held the one in his hand away from his mouth. "What's gonna happen to him? We gonna bury him at sea?"

"I shouldn't think so," Jenny said. "Your friend deserves a Christian burial."

"I don't rightly know if Robbie was one," Jack said. "He was born in America, and I guess it makes him one same as the rest, but I ain't never heard him talk about it or pray none. He ain't near like the preacher I knows back in Oakland."

"A man's faith doesn't depend much on where he was born," Zac said, "or who he was born to. It's a thing of the way a man lives and the decisions he makes. My own father told me that, many times."

"You was lucky," Jack said. "Havin' a pap that could talk to you and tell you what he thought with his head cleared up is somethin' I never known about before. That preacher man talks to me, but it's something he's paid to do, I think."

"Well, we're talking to you and feeding you, to boot, and nobody's paying us," Zac said. "Before we're through, I've got a feeling we're the ones that'll be paying."

The boy's eyes strayed to the dresser in the cabin, where he spotted the leather-bound book *Ivanhoe.* He jumped down from the chair and picked it up. "This here a real book?"

"Yes," Zac said. "A real good book."

"What's it about?"

"Knights in shining armor and ladies that need their help."

"Tarnation! For real?"

"Real enough to make a good book."

"Do you read?" Jenny asked.

"That preacher taught me some. I been reading his Bible from time to time. I likes them old stories about giants, swords, oceans splittin' in two, and men that make miracles."

"Well, nobody's payin' that preacher friend of yours to teach you to read," Zac said.

"No, I reckon not," Jack replied. "I really likes it, though. Can't much understand all them thees and thous in the good book, but I likes them stories. Stories take a body to places he ain't never been to before, but I'm gonna go someday." He puffed his chest. "I got myself some stories to tell too."

"I'll just bet you have," Zac replied.

"We'd love to hear them sometime," Jenny said. She nudged Skip.

"I started to look this boat over before we came up on you," Skip said. "When you finish the biscuits, we could both go look around."

"I seen myself boats before, but I'll go with you. There might be somethin' we come up on."

"You just make sure that whatever it is you come up on," Zac said, "gets left right where it lays. Do I make myself clear?"

\+ + + + +

Hours upstream, in the marshes of the Delta, three men poled a small boat toward a dock. Blackberry bushes grew around the stream, their height reaching upward of twelve to fourteen feet. The rambling underbrush kept the small shantytown that surrounded the dock almost invisible to the naked eye until the boat pushed itself up to the rickety landing.

The three men jumped off the boat, dragging a well-dressed man after them. They were followed by an attractive brunette whose hands were tied behind her. The men helped her out of the boat and snickered as they forced her onto the well-worn dock. "You behave yerself, missy, or you'll pay."

Scattered, weather-beaten shacks with peeling paint and rotting boardwalks made up the village. It looked to be a ghostly, abandoned burgh, except for a small funnel that belched smoke into the gray foggy mist from a dilapidated two-story farmhouse.

The men pushed their captives in the direction of the house, where a stumpy man sitting on the porch with a shotgun in his lap got to his feet. The man's long, curly black hair fell to his shoulders and lapped over a bright red silk shirt. A glowing orange scarf was tied around his waist and hung down the side of his brown trouser legs.

The leader of the small group held up one hand in greeting. "Hey,

Manny, we got ourselves somethin' pretty special here, a fancy doctor and his right pretty niece. He was carryin' lots of cash, and we figure them both to be worth plenty of coin."

The brightly clothed pirate scratched his stubbled face, tracing his finger down a long scar that ran the length of his cheekbone. His flattened pug nose sat perched between two shining brown eyes. "I don't know that Colonel Princeton is gonna be all that happy with you three goin' off on your own and doing what you please. He's inside, and you had just better wipe them grins offa them faces of yours before he sees you."

The three of them pushed their captives forward and cautiously wiped their feet on a haggard mat before entering. Persian rugs lay scattered haphazardly over the worn wood, as if thrown by someone in a hurry. Soft oil lamps glowed beneath heavy green-glass globes, sending shadows flickering across worn, peeling wallpaper that pictured lovers walking hand in hand under numerous cupids with drawn bows. Overstuffed furniture, still showing a faded reddish color, sat around the room, and green curtains streaked with white and yellow from years of wear covered the windows.

Behind a massive oak desk, a broad-shouldered man worked on a set of books. He scribbled beneath the dim light. His shirt was a bright white, and his tie dangled on either side of an open collar. On the back of his chair, a gray officer's coat hung, its gold braids tattered and discolored. With his head bowed over his books, it was hard to miss the plumage of gray hair that blossomed out of the midst of what was otherwise dusty brown hair. A salt-and-pepper beard surrounded a lean and angular face. Lifting his eyes from the books, he got to his feet. "What is this?" he asked.

The leader of the group of brigands squeezed his hat in his hands and stepped cautiously forward. He produced a small burlap bag and dropped it on the edge of the man's desk. "These be some folk we took on the road this morning, a Dr. William Page and his niece. I think you'll find their poke to yer liking, and I'm a reckoned we can fetch a pretty penny for 'em up in Sacramento. That's where the man says he's from. He says he gots some people up that way too. That's why we didn't just slit their throats where we found 'em."

"You should have done just that!" the man exploded. He rounded his desk and walked toward the group, his bright blue eyes glinting like shooting stars across a dark sky.

The pirate holding the girl shoved her forward. "But looky here,

Colonel. This one's a real looker. To leave her back on the road would be a real waste. Don't think the boys 'round here woulda taken too kindly to losin' some nighttime entertainment."

With sudden force, the big man knocked the pirate to the floor. The sound of the concussion echoed in the room. "I'm the one that says what my men will find their pleasure in, not you, not ever."

Pointing his finger at the leader of the group, he drove his point home. "This operation requires only one person to do the thinking, and that is me. Y'all spindly brained hooligans aren't capable of doing one iota more than I tell you. Do you actually think you could have kept us out of the papers and away from the law or worse, the army, these last two years? I think not. If I allowed you to roam the countryside and sidewind anything you chose to strike at, we'd have been swinging on the gallows long before now."

The girl twisted at her bindings and wrestled against the distracted pirate. "You let my uncle and me go," she demanded. "We are people unused to being treated in such a fashion."

"You see," the colonel said, waving his hand at the three men, "they've seen me and all of you. They've been to our headquarters. They know where we are."

The man on the floor got to his feet, rubbing his chin. "Colonel, we brought them up by boat. Ain't no way they could find us here."

The colonel paused, then abruptly pivoted and returned to his ledgers, murmuring under his breath. He removed his cufflinks, dropped them on the desk, and then rolled up his sleeves. "I'll give you credit for at least one modicum of thought, then, but I rather doubt you could even manage the decent delivery of a ransom note, and we have bigger fish to fry here. It wouldn't be worth the hazard. Now, y'all three take them out to the smokehouse and lock them up. We will dispose of them later. There are some deep places in that river out yonder. I am expecting our benefactor any minute, and I wouldn't want him to catch the slightest whiff of your stupidity. We are privateers on this river, not thugs and kidnappers."

A short while after the three had taken their captives away, Manny stuck his head in the door. "He's here, Colonel. His carriage is coming down the road."

With that, the colonel got to his feet and closed his ledger. He fastened his cuffs and tied his tie securely. Shrugging on his officer's coat, he buttoned the row of shiny brass buttons. Walking calmly to the ornate buffet at the side of the living room, he produced two sparkling sherry glasses and a crystal decanter filled with amber liquid. He watched the carriage with its two pair of blacks pull up outside and poured the two glasses half full. Reaching into a humidor, he took out two stout cigars.

Manny opened the door for the visitor. The rotund, short man with his wine-colored waistcoat and polished boots walked into the room, tracking the mud picked up from the carriage to the house onto the Persian carpets. He had a slight smile and his clean-shaven face glistened with fresh cologne, carrying with it the scent of lilacs. He tugged at the fingers of his black gloves, removing them and then slapping them to the palm of his hand. "Princeton, I have the news we've been waiting for," he said. "Wonderful news."

The colonel held out the glass of liquor and motioned toward two massive chairs and their adjoining intricately carved tables in the front room.

Taking the glass, the man raised it high. "This news is going to make you a rather wealthy man, Colonel Princeton. I promised you that when we made our arrangement two years ago, and now, by Jove, I intend to deliver. A Blevins always keeps his word."

Princeton had never seen the man in such good humor. He was like a child looking under a Christmas tree, his face animated and the rosy luster to his cheeks a genuine flush of excitement, not a spotting of face powder. "Do you mind if I know what we're drinking to, Robert?"

Blevins raised his glass. "My dear colonel, we are drinking to a crippling blow to the Wells Fargo company. I intend to drive their stock even lower with this thing and buy them up ten cents on the dollar. The news will shock the financial world."

"And just how do you reckon to do that?"

Blevins smiled, a big grin from behind the glass held to his lips. He swigged down the alcohol and smacked his lips. "I just love that Mississippi drawl of yours, Colonel," he said, holding the empty glass away from him and staring at its coated but suddenly empty lining, "and this Kentucky liquor. It makes my mind drift back to the good times I had on the bluffs over Natchez, good times with friends in their fine houses."

"You will find that many of those places are in ashes today, Robert, with those friends of yours buried out in back of them."

"Yes, I know. They fought for their consciences during that war while I and others like me made money, lots of money."

Princeton picked up the decanter and refilled Blevins's glass.

"I think when I tell you what our prize is, Colonel, you will be even more eager. You will truly have an opportunity to strike a blow at the blue-coated army you hate so badly." He gestured over to the chairs. "Perhaps you had better sit down. This is going to take the wind out of your sails."

Princeton took his seat, and Blevins's gaze drifted to the crossed foils that adorned the mantel above the smoldering fireplace. He walked over to it and lifted one of the blades from position. A swishing noise sang out as he swung it in a figure eight. Lunging forward, he tested his reach. "Fine steel, Colonel. I did tell you I was a fencing champion back East, didn't I?"

"Yes, and I've seen you use one before. You remember?"

"Yes, I do. Our friend from Spain. He did rather fancy himself good with one of these, didn't he?"

"And you left him in shreds, as I recall."

"He survived."

"With a few noticeable memories for his trouble. I always preferred the saber, myself."

"Yes, Colonel, a brutal weapon of war, not the sort of tool one would find in the hand of a gentleman." Taking a few more swings, he stood upright and balanced the weapon. "The *Delta King* is our target, Colonel. It will be your largest prize to date. It will be in Sacramento tomorrow and return on Thursday. You haven't much time to get ready for it. It will take all the manpower and ingenuity at your disposal."

"That boat is a big one."

"Yes, and it will carry a small contingent of troops on board, a squad of six men as I am given to understand." He held the sword at his side and smiled. "A gold shipment that Wells Fargo is responsible for will be on board that trip back to San Francisco, a half a million in gold bars. You may have whatever else of value that you find. There will be liquor supplies, cotton, and a shipment of rifles bound for the Presidio. I will pay you for half the gold in currency. That much gold would be impossible for you to deal with, and your men can't spend gold bullion, in any event."

"And you expect this to break Wells Fargo?"

Blevins grinned. "Precisely!" He swung the blade back and forth, then lunged at the imaginary opponent in front of him.

Princeton picked up one of the cigars and bit the end off, spitting it into the fireplace. "I have just under thirty men, Robert, and I wouldn't want to use anybody that I couldn't trust on a strike like this, so I can't expect more help than what I already possess." He struck a match and lit his cigar.

"That is your problem, my dear Colonel. Our arrangement is the same as always. I supply you with the information and sell whatever you take. You keep half the cash that is taken, and I give you political support. That will be a hard thing to do, where this is concerned, but I will be working on a smoke screen. I believe I have just the candidate to take the blame."

"And who might that be?"

"Their best agent, a Mr. Zachary Cobb. They have sent him specially to guard this shipment along with two of their other agents, one of which belongs to me. The man is notorious, but I don't want him harmed." He smiled. "In fact, I intend to make quite a large deposit into Cobb's account in San Francisco tomorrow morning. It will look very suspicious. I have friends in the police department who will be glad to find every reason in the book to throw suspicion on our Mr. Cobb."

Choosing one of the cupids on the wallpaper, Blevins launched himself forward and skewered the angel through the heart. He stood back to attention, dropping the sword to his side. "Then I will own Wells Fargo."

CHAPTER 4

+ + + + + + +

ZAC AND JENNY WALKED OUTSIDE to once again stare at the foggy bay. They'd be moving into the mouth of the river soon, and both wanted to see just how well the pilot managed the big boat in the thick pea soup. "I think we'd better move to the other side," Zac said. "It's always best to keep the wind out of your face."

The two of them strolled around the aft section of the boat, where they spied the carefully wrapped corpse of Jack's friend, Robbie. They stopped and studied the small package, a boy who had barely begun to live and now was gone. Zac walked over and crouched down next to the boy's body, inspecting the lashings.

"I think it's terrible to shoot a small boy like that, even if he is stealing from you," Jenny said.

"Oysters are those men's livelihood, hon. Nobody takes kindly to somebody taking food from their table."

"Maybe so, but it's cowardly, all the same."

Zac nodded. He brushed the wetness from his full mustache and got to his feet.

"The loneliness of that boy Jack and what he must go through to survive makes me feel sad and almost helpless," Jenny said. "That's something I hate to feel. I suppose I've always liked to believe that there's something to be done about almost anything, but at times there just isn't. Sometimes a person can only watch and cry silently."

"Part of what's happened to that boy has nothing to do with his own choosing, and then part of it is just that. That boy wrapped in that tarp back there would still be on the streets if those two hadn't taken up with the notion of stealing other people's property. The men I go up against have guns and mean to kill me, but years ago they just intended to take something they didn't work for."

"I suppose our problems start in childhood," Jenny said.

"Yes, I think so. It's why children are so precious and why I want to make sure Skip gets every chance at being cared for."

"Sometimes a child can be cared for too much," she said.

The thought stopped him. "What do you mean?"

"I mean there are times that a child can be cherished far too much by someone that disappears, someone that can't finish the job they start out to do."

Zac stopped walking. He stood and looked at her, a slight frown on his face. "You're talking about the danger of my job and the fact that Skip depends on me."

"No, I wasn't thinking about you at all."

"You weren't?"

"No. You know, in the years you've known me, Zac, you've never asked me anything of a personal nature." They continued their walk.

"Personal?"

"Yes, personal. You don't know much about what I'm like on the inside. What my fears are. What makes me the way I am."

On the leeward side of the boat, Zac stopped and took her hand. "I know all I need to know about you, Jenny. I can tell who you are just by watching you and the way you care about other people."

"And that might just be more than enough for all your men friends, but it isn't for me. A woman wants no surprises. I wouldn't want you to discover something someday that you wouldn't like about me. I know you seem to be a man who despises weakness, and I want you to know that I have them."

"We all have them."

"Yes, but these are mine, my own set of faults. They belong to me and me alone. If you don't know where my weaknesses and fears are, then you don't really know me, and I want you to know me."

"Look, Jenny"—Zac stared deeply into her blue eyes—"you know I'm a very private man. I always have been. I suppose I've always thought that if there was anything you wanted to tell me, you'd come 'round to it." He bowed his head, taking his eyes off her. Then once again looking at her pretty face he said, "And I suppose I always knew that the more I knew about you, the more you'd want to know me."

"Somehow, I knew you'd say that. Well, maybe not say it, but think it all the same."

She began to walk, and Zac caught up with her. He took her arm and stopped her. "I'm not saying I don't want you to know me, Jenny. Maybe I'm just not sure of how I look at myself."

She looked at him, and he turned his head away, gazing off into the thick fog. "I do all the things in life that my folks trained me to hate. What I do is a dirty business. I seem to violate the Ten Commandments for a living." He looked back at her. "I reckon I just don't have a very good handle on how I feel about what I am and can't rightly tell you something I'm not comfortable with my ownself."

"Maybe that is why I'd like to share more of what I'm like with you. You're so locked into that violent world of yours that the thought never occurs to you that other people may be in pain too."

He bowed his head. Jenny could tell that she had hurt him. She put her hand on his arm. "Zac, all there is to know about you, I love. It makes me want to know more, though. I won't hold you to telling me anything you'd feel more comfortable with keeping to yourself. You need to know that. I won't be pushy."

"I know. You never are." He held both of her hands. "All right, anything you'd care to tell me, I'd like to hear."

"There's so much I'd like to say to you, but I do want to know more about you. I know you feel uncomfortable with what you do in your work and, given the nature of the job, that comes as some relief to me." She looked up into his soft brown eyes. "But there are times I get the feeling that it goes deeper than that. It's almost as if there are things inside of you that you carry around, dreams you'll never be able to have, grief you can't share."

"I suppose it goes back to something I don't think I can ever be."

"And what would that be?"

"A man like my father, a good man."

"You *are* a good man, Zac."

"Not like him I'm not. He was a decent man, a farmer, no fool notions about changing the world and righting all wrong, just a good husband and father. I guess growin' up I never realized how good he really was. When I came back after the war and found my folks both dead and buried out back of the place, I learned things standing over my pa's grave that I'd never known about him before."

"What things?"

"People found out I was there and they came, all sorts of people. People told me how he helped them when they were sick and couldn't get their planting done. One man told me how my pa gave him clothes that he knew my father could've worn himself. Just left them on his porch to save his pride. Another woman that was a widow lady told me how he'd brought her money for years, money we could ill afford to lose. When she'd try to refuse he would just say, 'we got plenty.' That man was just that way, as good a man as ever lived."

"And you don't think you can ever be that way?"

"No, I've seen too much of the rottenness of life. That boy we took in today—frankly, I want nothing to do with him. The boy's a thief. I'm not sure he'll ever change. If he is the way he is, my time and effort are wasted on him. I've seen his kind grown up. It's taken all the moonglow out of my eyes about children and I suppose robbed me of a generous spirit. I feel bad about that. Sometimes it's better to be taken advantage of than be jaded and hard inside."

"But you care about Skip."

Zac smirked. "Yeah, now I do, but that wasn't my choice, either. You see, I seldom go out of my way to concern myself about anybody. I mind about him, but that's because I felt to blame for him being an orphan. I do what I'm supposed to do, whether I feel like it or not. It's only after I start to do what I need to do that the feelings come. You're not like me, Jenny. You really do care. I can see that."

"Yes, I do. But there are times I need to be cared for and times I don't feel that anybody does."

"Jenny, everybody thinks highly of you."

"That dead boy back there, all cold and alone, and his friend, all fatherless and uncared for—sometimes I feel just like that. I go about my business, but I'm alone too. I'm independent, and I like that part about myself, but sometimes I feel like I'm so independent because there's no one for me, no one that I can completely trust. If I don't act like I need it, then I won't ever be disappointed."

"Jenny, you know that if there's ever anything you needed, I'd be there."

"Yes, I know, but how would you know what that was? I mean, if you don't really know me, how can you know what I really need?"

"All right, I want to know. You tell me."

She paused and turned her head. Taking her hands free from him, she leaned over the rail and watched the water cut by the bow of the boat. The engine chugged and the sound of the water pouring from the paddle kept the noise at a constant roar.

Zac edged up next to her. "I really want to know, Jenny."

"All right." She looked back at him. "I'll tell you how I feel. You know that I was only ten when my father died."

"Yes."

"And that my mother had her hands full with trying to care for six children, all younger than I was."

"Yes."

"Well, my father was special to me. He cared for me as if I were a china doll in a glass case. When he passed away, there was no one left to care for me in the tender way he did. My mother was just too busy with survival. I had to learn fast to look after others."

"And you still do that. I've seldom met anyone since my mother that looked after people they didn't need to like you do."

"I do care after people, but the people who love me back all die. My father died. My fiancé died. And you . . . you . . ." She gripped the rail tightly. "You try your darndest to get killed."

"But, Jenny, you always seemed to hold up with what I do. Oh, I know there's been times, but—"

"Yes, I do," she cut him off. "But deep down inside, I'm still that china doll that longs to be admired and looked after. I feel very fragile at times, but I can never let it show. Sometimes I feel like that doll, just gathering dust, all forgotten and all alone. I make myself busy in that glass case of mine, but still inside, I'm behind the glass, looking out on a busy world, longing for someone to take me out and love me."

She brushed back a tear from her eye. "Zac, there are many times I cry in my room at night. I cry when no one can see me, and then I get up in the morning and scrub my face so I can look perfect, like nothing ever happened, like I don't ever feel a thing."

Zac blinked. This woman who loved him had made herself very vulnerable to him, like a bird at his windowsill with a broken wing. He ran his hands up her arms and held her steady. "You know," he said, "with us telling each other these things about our lives, we can never be the same."

"I know, and I don't want to be the same. I want you to either take me out of my china cabinet or just walk away and leave me"—she turned and looked back at the stern of the boat—"like we left that boy back there. What I don't want is for you to just stand here and look through the glass."

"Jenny—"

She put his hands up to his lips and stopped him from speaking. "Stop right there. You've wanted to say it before, and I haven't let you. I won't stop you now, but I don't want or need your pity."

"I feel no pity for you."

"Then, I want you to say whatever it is you've thought about saying for a long time, not something that I've managed to coax out of you here and now. I respect you. You use that wonderful mind of yours silently when you play the violin. Many times as I've watched you play for me, I've imagined what it is you're saying to me with it. You have your own mind, and I want you to use just that."

"Jenny Hays . . ." He seemed to stumble for a moment over the words. "If all the women in the world were lined up from end to end, I'd walk right up and pick you. I love you."

He leaned over and ever so gently kissed her lips, a soft, warm kiss, pulling her close to him.

"Ah—hemmm." The sound of a man loudly clearing his throat snapped their heads around.

Behind them, a tall man in a brown suit stood looking very uncomfortable. His eyes squinted out from behind the lenses of his glasses and his thin lips were drawn. "Excuse me," he said, "but are you Zac Cobb?"

Zac backed away from Jenny and raised himself to his full height. Even then, he was looking up at the gangly man. Zac seemed slightly flustered. Jenny thought that just at that moment he looked for all the world like a small boy stealing a pie from his mother's windowsill. "Yes, I'm Zac Cobb."

The man extended his hand. "I'm Cliff Cox. Mr. Wells sent me to work with you."

Zac ignored the gesture.

"I know you normally work alone." The man dropped his hand. "Mr. Wells made that perfectly clear to me. He also told me to expect you to be unfriendly."

"He's right, I do work better alone. I find it easier to worry about the people I'm chasing when I don't have to clutter my mind with protecting the people sent to help me."

"Yes, that's exactly what Mr. Wells said. In fact, I believe those were the very words."

"He's heard them enough. You'd think the man would have them straight by now."

Cox smiled and dipped his head slightly. "Mr. Wells doesn't miss much. Well, he said you already had company on this trip"—his eyes flashed at Jenny—"so he couldn't see that one more would make much difference. He thought I might come in handy for you too. I know quite a bit about these river pirates he's so concerned about. I've been on the case for over a year now."

Jenny stepped forward. "Mr. Cobb forgets himself," she said, nodding. "I'm Jenny Hays."

"Pleased to meet you, ma'am."

"Well, Cox, if you're so good and you've been looking into this for over a year, why aren't those men behind bars?"

"We've never been able to catch them in the act, but it hasn't been for lack of effort."

Zac stuck his hands in his pockets. "Sounds like a great deal of wasted effort to me. What makes Wells put up with someone who doesn't deliver results?"

Cox put his hand to his mouth and cleared his throat. "I guess some might say it's because I'm married to Mr. Wells' niece. I've been very interested in learning all I can about the business, and this is the part of it right now that fascinates me most."

"Cox, I don't have the slightest bit of interest in fascinating you. My job is to prevent the robbery of this shipment we've been sent to pick up, not educate or entertain you."

The fog caused the man's glasses to bead up with moisture. He took them off and, pulling out a handkerchief, began to wipe them. "I can take care of myself, Mr. Cobb. I was in the Union Army."

"A shipping clerk, no doubt," Zac said, "and lived to tell the tale."

"I was in the quartermaster corps, but in the United States Army every man must be prepared to do his duty."

Jenny interrupted. "Mr. Cox, let me apologize for Zac's rudeness. I'm afraid you caught us at an indelicate moment to make your introductions. Few men care to be interrupted at such a time."

Cox snapped his heels together. "Of course, and I do apologize. Perhaps we can talk again over a meal, and I can tell you what I know. I will work at staying out of your way." He smiled and, turning abruptly, hurried back down the rail and entered the salon.

"Zac, you were being very rude to that man," Jenny said. "Someone you just met."

Zac grunted. "There's two types of people I need to be inhospitable with, those men I'm chasing and tenderfeet trying to do me a favor. Both can get me killed."

"I think he was trying to impress you."

"If he was, then I can understand why he hasn't found those river pirates. He seems to be a failure on both counts." He continued to mutter, almost under his breath. " 'In the United States Army, every man must be prepared to do his duty . . .' Humpff. Yes, I'm sure. Do his duty until he marries into a family with money and a business."

"Now, you don't know that."

"I know the type. Men who can't stand on their own feet seem to make a habit of troddin' on the toes of those who can. They're weak."

Jenny fell silent and began to walk away.

Zac took her by the arm. "Did I say something wrong?"

She looked up at him, a sudden hardness in her face. "Weren't we just talking about our weaknesses? Just what makes you think that ours are any more acceptable than that Mr. Cox's?"

"This is business, my business."

"No, this is life."

"All right." He smiled broadly and rubbed his chin. "One thing I always find appealing about you is that carn sarn way you have of puttin' me in my place. Few people can do that with the knack you seem to have. You're a mystery."

"No, Zachary, I am a woman who thinks."

He held up both hands, as if in a moment of surrender. "All right, then, a *complete* mystery."

Jenny gave him a punch in his stomach, more than a gentle jab.

He began to laugh. "You see, you know where to find my weaknesses, and I know just where to find yours." Reaching around her, he pulled her closer. He took her arm, and they continued on their stroll around the deck.

After stopping to talk several times, they reached the windows that surrounded the salon. Zac looked inside. There, seated at the gambling table with Rance McCauliff, was Cliff Cox with a formidable stack of bills in front of him.

Their attention was suddenly diverted by the sound of scampering feet from the stairway leading up from the engine room. Jack and Skip came running out from the stairway and close on their heels was a Chinaman, covered in soot.

Zac jumped forward and, catching the man by the shirt, spun him around. "Here, here, what's the problem?"

"Two boys. They thieves."

"Thieves?"

"Yes. They come down. They steal. Peng Lee see them. They run away."

"Those boys belong to me. I'll take care of it, and if they took anything, I'll see it returned."

The coal-covered man stood there, shaking with rage, not knowing what to do. "Boys should be beaten." Turning slowly, he went back down the stairs.

"Weak boys do weak things too," Jenny said.

CHAPTER 5

+ + + + + + +

MANNY POLED THE BOAT out into the river. Dr. Page and his niece sat in the stern, huddled together, more for comfort than warmth. With hands bound behind their backs and eyes blindfolded, there was nothing they could do but await their fate.

The fog continued to crawl the length of the river, rolling over the brush and seeping out into the pear orchards that dotted the sides of the river. The Chinese who had built the railroad had settled in this place and had found pears to be the most agreeable fruit they could cultivate. The tree branches had been recently pruned, giving them the appearance of ghostly dwarfs spreading their arms. The fog curled itself around the feet of the trees and snaked its way past the cuts in the sod that carried water for the soil.

There was an eerie stillness to the river. Few people, if any, would be found navigating the stream on such a foggy day. Those who did never came to where they were now. There were too many rumors of bad men along that section of the Delta. The reputation of Princeton and his men kept people away, a reputation based on fear and hearsay. Most of the time, whisperings of pirates had been just that, murmured rumors. But there had been enough disappearances, just enough strange toughs coming in and out of the towns for supplies, that few people wanted to explore the area to find out if the notion had any truth to it, and so they gave in to the stories. They gave in and stayed off the river and surrounding Delta.

"Where are you taking us?" the young woman murmured.

Manny continued to pole the boat without speaking. These were people he didn't want to know. He had killed before, but usually armed men. He knew what Princeton wanted, though, and he had never been one to cross the colonel. The less he talked to them, the better he would be able to sleep. He watched the young woman squirm to free her hands, but he knew it would come to nothing. He was too good at what he did.

The woman wore a gray dress, heavy in its folds and pleated. The top of the dress was covered with an ivory-colored lace. It looked to be well made and no doubt expensive, with carved bone buttons studding the front. It was modest, however. Manny could see the kind of young woman this was from the straight and stiff way she carried herself, proper but with spunk. Her side-buttoned shoes were spattered with mud, the off-white color of the shoes showing through in streaks.

Manny watched. It was easy to imagine her thoughts. At times, he could detect the fear in her quivering mouth, and at other times, a sort of firm determination took over as she held her head high and turned her face into the wind. He had silently refused to answer her question, but with her chin lifted in his direction, he could see a resolve in her that just wouldn't go away. It was the kind of spirit he admired in a woman, but one he had seldom seen.

"I asked," she repeated the question, "where are you taking us?"

"Now see here, young man," the doctor spoke up. "My niece here is only eighteen. We were traveling to the college she was to attend. I was taking her there as a favor to my brother. He is a medical missionary in India. He's there to heal the sick and do the Lord's work. Please take me and do whatever you will, but you must spare Mary."

"Hush!" Manny snapped. "I don't want to know none about you or your family." He continued to silently push the boat down the stream. He wasn't the least bit angry, but he couldn't let on to that. Maybe knowing about them was better than making up stories in his head about them. They were both pretty people, and pretty people were something he didn't like. If he could keep them just that, it would be easier to kill them.

"You can see that my uncle is a good man," Mary said. "He gives himself for others. Please don't hurt us. Let us go. We won't say anything about you or this place."

"Hush up, I said." They seemed determined to creep into his brain with their lives, and he fought it.

The two captives scooted closer to each other. "It's all in the Lord's hands, Mary. There's nothing that ever touches our lives that doesn't have His permission."

Manny listened as the young girl began to cry softly. The sound of her voice twisted him up inside. It was a soft voice, almost musical.

The doctor continued to speak to his niece in low, comforting tones. "You remember the story of Daniel in the lions' den. The Lord himself shut the mouths of the lions. Daniel honored God to the last, and God proved to be his protector. He will be ours as well."

The girl stoically nodded her head and then lifted her chin in Manny's direction. "Why are you doing this to us?" she asked. "We've never harmed you. We wouldn't dream of it, even if we could."

"I'm just followin' orders. I'm a good soldier, and I do just what I'm told."

"I respect that, young man," the doctor said. "You seem like a fine man. You've just fallen on hard times and bad company."

"I do what I need to do."

"You don't need to kill us," Mary said. "You can make us disappear by just taking us to shore and letting us go."

"I can't do that."

"Mary," the doctor said, "the young man is just doing the only thing he knows to do. He is just as frightened by those people as we are."

"I am not," Manny growled. "What makes you say a fool thing like that?"

"Because, young man, you seem like a decent sort. You didn't push us like the other men did, and you helped Mary into the boat. You're doing now not the thing you want to do, but the thing you're frightened not to do."

Manny murmured and continued to pole the boat. A victim making excuses for him was an entirely new experience. It made the two of them even more likable. He wasn't entirely sure he cared for the feeling it gave him, though.

"I think you're doing the only thing you know," the doctor said. "It's a shame, too, a shame for a man to be judged for something so terrible on the last day that he didn't want to do in the first place."

"The only judge I'm worried about is the one that's gonna send me climbin' them steps to the gallows if'n I should let you two go. And I'll tell you another thing. If'n my capt'n ever found out I done somethin' 'gainst his orders, he'd have me on a spit over a fire. No matter what I thinks, I ain't about to take no chance of either of them things befallin' me. You understand that?"

"We wouldn't tell," Mary said. "We'd just go home. We'd disappear from your sight and be gone from your life forever."

"Yeah, you can say that now, but the first man with a star on his chest you come on to is gonna get an earful from the both of you. With what we gone and put you through, you couldn't help yerself."

"We are people who keep our word," Mary said.

"My niece is correct. We would no more think of informing on you after the risk you would be taking to release us than we would think of robbing a bank. For us, both would be equally wrong. I can assure you, both my niece and I are people of utmost reliability. Even if we saw you on the street, we would say nothing. We have nothing but compassion for your situation, sir. You'd always be a welcome guest at our table."

"Boy, you folks beat all. You must take me for a tenderfoot sure 'nuff. I ain't, though. I'm a good soldier and a world-class survivor. I've done gone and lived outside my twenties 'cause I do what I'm told. I don't care what you say. If I let you go I'm a gonna be standin' afore that judge sure as the world turns."

"Young man, there's a far more terrible judge you will have to face someday, and the penalty will not just be a swift execution. It will be the eternal fires of hell. Mary and I will be in heaven with our blessed Lord, but it will grieve us to know where you are and that what you did to us is partially to blame."

"Both of you, shut your faces." Manny drew his knife. He set down the long pole he was using to push the boat and scrambled over to the doctor. Placing the gleaming blade underneath the man's Adam's apple, he said "Hush up now or I'm a gonna cut your throats right here just to get some peace."

+ + + + +

Zac and Jenny walked toward the cabin on the stern of the boat. They thought they'd find the boys there and, sure enough, from behind the door they could hear the boys talking in an animated fashion. Zac stood with his hand on the knob. "You ready to deal with this?" he asked.

Jenny looked sheepish. "It's not my situation to deal with. Like it or not, in the absence of a father, you're it."

"Sometimes I'd just as soon face a bunch of roughnecks than fatherhood. I just feel like a hog on ice skates in that area. Haven't got the first notion of the right thing to do. Got any suggestions?"

Jenny took a deep breath. She placed her hand on his shoulder. "Zac, just try and do what your own father would have done."

"Tarnation," Zac murmured, "I haven't got a razor strap on me." He twisted the knob and pushed open the door.

Skip and Jack sat on the bottom bunk. Skip looked somewhat frightened, and Jack had an air of bravado about him. He'd obviously been in situations like this before. He was an old hand at being on the other side of the bar of justice, even at the tender age of ten. Zac could see that. Beads of sweat were on both of the boys' foreheads. Zac couldn't tell if it was from the heat of the engine room where the boys had just come from or from the tension of the moment.

Jenny closed the door behind them and stood next to Zac. "Okay, boys. Now just what have you been up to?"

"Nothing," Jack spat out. "We ain't done nothin'."

"Then, why was that man chasing you?"

"Don't rightly know," Jack continued. Skip snapped his head around and glared at Jack, a look of disbelief mixed with misery. It was obvious at the moment that Jack felt the situation warranted that he be the spokesman. "Can't never trust them China devils nohow," the boy went on. "They'ze heathens, ya know. They might say anything."

"That's funny. I know a lot of people that would say the same about little boys."

"Well, we ain't done nothin'," Jack protested. "That man is just ornery, working down there in the heat and darkness and all."

Zac stepped over to the bunk and, taking Skip's downcast face by the chin, tipped it up to look him in the eye. "Is that true, Skip? You boys took nothing?"

Skip turned to Jack. The street urchin shot him a stern glance and shook his head very slightly.

Looking back up at Zac, Skip said, "That's not q-q-q-quite true." From behind his back, he produced a wrench and laid it gingerly on the bed. "I took it." He shot a quick look at his young accomplice, then his glance drifted back to Zac. "I just wanted a better look at it up here in the sunlight."

"Is this true?" Zac asked, looking over at the young newcomer.

Jack's eyes popped wide open. He swallowed hard and then regained his composure. "I guess so." His cool, streetwise attitude took over. "I told him not to do it. I guess it was a fool thing to do.

We'll go take the thing back. We can sneak on down there and do it where nobody will be the wiser. It won't happen again." The boy was nervy. It was plain to see he didn't know right from wrong, even when it came to trying to fix things.

"I'm sure it won't happen again." Zac held out his hand. "You better give it to me for the time being. I'll let you return it directly."

Skip handed the wrench to Zac.

Zac loosened his belt and begin to remove it.

"Whatcha doin'?" Jack asked.

"I'm doing just what my own father would have done to me," Zac said. "A boy has to learn that there is pain in doing the wrong thing. There's more pain than a simple apology can deal with. I don't arrest thieves just to have them go before the judge and say, 'I'm sorry.' The law doesn't treat thievery like that and neither will I."

Zac took Skip by the hand and helped him to the floor. "Now, Skip, you just bend over and remember this."

The boy got to the floor. The look in his eyes was one that mixed fear with a deep, unspoken hurt.

"Look, son, I've never been a father before. This is the first time for me, same as you. I wouldn't lay a hand on you in anger, not at any time. But I can't let what you did go unpunished. I got to use my head here and ask myself what your own pa would have done, and from what little you've told me, I think this is about right."

Jenny reached out and took Zac's arm. She held on to it firmly. She didn't say a word, but he could see the look of disapproval in her eyes. He shook his head at her and motioned her back.

With a half swing, Zac brought the thick belt forward. It slapped Skip's backside with a snap. Reaching back again, he sent another slap to the boy's buttocks. Skip's eyes teared up, and Zac continued with several more blows until the boy began to cry.

All the while, Zac observed Jack. The boy winced at each blow as if he were feeling the lashes himself.

Zac sat down and held Skip, who continued to cry, on his lap. He put his arms around him gently. "I love you, Skip. I'm sorry I had to do this. You know I had to, don't you?"

Skip nodded and continued to cry softly. The boy's real pain was inside. He'd never been known to deliberately disobey. Zac knew his parents had raised him better than that. Skip's look, however, melted Zac's heart. He felt unqualified from anybody's point of view at being a father.

"You're ten now, Skipper. You're getting too old to spank, and I don't want to ever have to do this again."

Skip shook his head, agreeing with Zac.

"And I would have never done it in front of other folks, but what you did was in front of people, and what happens to you has to be in front of them too." He held Skip a little longer before lifting him up and placing him back on the bunk. "Now, Miss Jenny and I will wait outside. In a few minutes we can all go below with you to return that tool."

Outside the cabin, Zac could see the distressed expression on Jenny's face. "I did just what you told me to do," he said. "That was just what my father would have done. Like I told you, it's the only thing I got to go by."

"You know Skip didn't take that thing."

"I know he didn't. He was just protecting that street boy. He's got to learn the same as me, though. There's a penalty in trying to protect people that can't take care of themselves, just like that Cox fella. Every time I look after a fool, I'm always the one that comes out lookin' foolish."

"But—"

Zac interrupted her. "I know what you're gonna say. It is unfair. But life's unfair." He pointed back at the wrapped corpse of the small boy on the fantail. "Belts are a whole lot kinder than bullets. I'd a far sight rather he learned his lesson now at my hand than later at the mercy of somebody else."

"I just hate to see the guilty go unpunished and the innocent suffer."

"I do too. In fact that's why my job is so hard. I see just that type of thing day after day. I can tell you one thing, though. Too much kindness today can kill a body tomorrow."

+ + + + +

Silently, Manny continued to pole the boat downstream. He watched the two captives bow their heads and quietly murmur their prayers. He couldn't make out just what they were saying, but he knew they were praying. There was just too much in their faces for it to register as complaining.

The current was moving them now, and he kept the craft pointed in the direction of the stream. Anytime now they would be over the deep part of the river he'd been looking for. He had brought along some extra rope and an anchor taken off a small steamer. It would keep the bodies out of sight long enough for the fish and crawdads to do their work. The catfish would have a field day and he knew it.

"Young man," the doctor said, "we're far enough away now for you to take these blindfolds off. I know we're still in the fog. I can feel it. No matter what you do, it's inhumane to keep us blind like this. I want to see my niece, and I know she would like to see me. Please, at least do that for us."

"All right, but you just hush up about me letting you go. That ain't about to happen."

"We'll cooperate with you, son."

Manny set down the pole and, stooping down, used his knife to cut the blindfolds away. Both the doctor and his niece blinked. There was no bright sunlight, but the suddenness of being able to see made it seem as though there were.

"Thank you," Mary said.

"Yes, thank you, young man. That was most decent of you."

Manny backed away. He picked up his pole and straightened the drift of the boat in the river. The two captives scooted even closer to each other. Manny watched them whisper. "Don't even think about gettin' away. You wouldn't get very far with them hands of yourn tied, and besides, I'd have to shoot you in the water. It sure would make a lot of trouble for me too. I'd have to fish you out before I could weight you down and sink you." He began to shake his head. "You'd be trouble—'course you'd be dead, all the same."

"We won't try to escape," the doctor said. "That would be foolish. Our faith is in the Lord, not in any ability of our own. You must understand us. As Christians our faith goes before us in everything we do. We don't just believe when it suits us. We have faith even when it seems impossible."

"Well, it is. That there faith of yours is plumb busted out here."

"I don't think so. The Lord is with us everywhere. One of the last things He ever said on this earth was, 'I will never leave you or forsake you.' I think when He says something, it can be believed."

"That was a long time ago. This is here and now."

The doctor looked perfectly calm. His thin face and angular nose set off brown eyes that looked straight into Manny's face. The man's gaze was constant. Manny had seen many a man lay down chips with a busted flush in his hand, but this was a man who really seemed sure of himself.

"Our Lord is here with us right now. He has never left us and never will."

"You're wrong about that."

"I am wrong about many things, but that is something that He promised. It's not my idea, and it has nothing to do with our present circumstances, but it's real nonetheless."

Manny hung his head slightly. "My ma down in Louisiana used to tell me such things. She worked at getting me over to Sunday meetin' afore she died too. I never believed it much, though. To me it was just somethin' to make poor folks not feel bad about their being broke and smile in spite of themselves."

"What is offered to you, son, has little to do with what you possess. It's perfectly free, already bought and paid for."

"Don't you be giving me that religion stuff. You don't know how big a sinner I am. I done killed me many a man. Ain't never killed me a woman before today, but I'm a robber and never was much good no how."

"Son, your salvation has little to do with how good you are."

The man's eyes seemed to bore into him. They were all too childlike and simple. There was trust written all over them, trust Manny knew was terribly misplaced.

"It is wholly dependent on how good our Lord is," the doctor went on.

"Please release us," Mary said. "You won't regret it. You don't want this thing on your conscience."

CHAPTER 6

+ + + + + + +

"YOU DIDN'T HAFTA TAKE THAT. He ain't even your pa." Jack paced back and forth around the small cabin, irritated and fidgeting. "I wouldn't a took that from nobody. If'n that man my mom keeps 'round ever laid a hand on me, I'd bash him one with a frying pan whilst he was sleepin'. Now, why'd you let that happen?"

Skip sat back down on the bunk. He was still somewhat dazed by the experience. The blows with the belt had hurt his backside, but not nearly as much as the fact that Zac had done it. He hung his head. "I guess I had it comin'."

Jack bent low, his hands on his knees, to try to look Skip in the eye. "You never had it comin'. I was the one took that wrench, and you was just silly to own up to it yer ownself. What made you do a fool thing like that?"

Skip raised his head and looked the boy in the eye. "I reckon 'cause I was afraid of what might happen to you if you'd been the one that they'd caught. They might just put you off the boat when we stop at Antioch."

"You reckon?"

"Yeah, I reckon."

Jack scratched his curly black hair furiously, as if by doing that he could drive the thoughts away from his mind. "I suppose I didn't think about that."

"There seems to be a buncha stuff you ain't thought about."

"Well, nobody's ever done somethin' like that for me before. You didn't have no stake in keeping me around."

"I guess not. I just didn't want you to go, that's all."

Jack gave Skip a gentle punch on the shoulder and smiled. "Well, I suppose I gots to figure out a way to give you a good time fer that. I'll have to think on it a spell."

"I think we'd both be lots better off if you just stopped thinking, period. It was your thinking that got us into this mess."

Jack stood up straight. "Yeah, I guess you're right there." He scratched his head again. "I sure wouldn't want to get myself kicked off before we even had a chance to eat."

"Now I got to go back down to that engine room and give that thing back, I reckon," Skip moaned.

"Aww, he ain't gonna make you do that. He was just spoutin' off."

"You don't know him. He don't say nothin' he don't mean."

"Really?"

"Yeah, really. He's somebody who keeps his word. When he says he's gonna take me fishing, he does it. When he says he's gonna be back, he comes back. And it's for sure that when he says I got to take that wrench back that he ain't just listenin' to his own gas escape."

Jack looked back at the closed door. It was as if he expected to see Zac standing there. "I guess he appears kinda serious, at that."

"He's gotta be serious. He's somebody that hankers to be believed, and I for one sure do."

"I just think that lady friend of his is gonna talk him outta that. She seemed to be real nervous when he started into whippin' you."

"Don't you just bet on that. Zac'll do just what he says. I'll just have to play this out, I reckon."

"Suppose he's gonna make me go with you? It was me that Chinaman saw take that wrench."

"I think that's a good bet. You just better come when he says and keep your trap shut tight. I feel bad enough as it is without you yammerin' away and getting us both in deeper."

"All right. I suppose it won't be something I'd miss anyway." He shook his head. "You just beat all, by my thinkin'."

"I just can't figure out why you'd want to take that thing in the first place. We ain't got no screws to turn," Skip said.

"'Cause it was there. The thing just sat there all shiny like, practically beggin' to go with me, sayin', 'here, Jack, take me, take me.' I just couldn't pass on by it, now could I?"

"You sure could've. It was a fool thing to do."

"'Sides, if'n I wanted to, I could have sold it back in Oakland fer a pretty penny. I ain't never seen one of them things before."

"It's stealin', all the same."

"Not really. That thing didn't belong to that Chinaman. It belonged to the boat. Now whoever heard of a boat turnin' you in for stealin'. This here thing is like the bay out yonder. Them oysters is just out there. They stay there to be taken by somebody, and it might as well be me that does the taking."

"It's stealin', all the same."

"I guess I don't think of it that way. To me it's just picking something up ain't nobody using."

"Well, you just quit picking things up, at least until you fights shy of us. You got that straight?"

"I won't get caught next time. I'll be more particular."

"You getting caught don't change nothin'. You ought to be sorry you took something, not just sorry you were caught."

"I'm afeared we ain't gonna see eye to eye on that. When I grow up I aim to be a pirate. When that happens, stealin' from other folks is gonna be the way I live." He pushed at the suspenders that held up his borrowed, baggy pants. "I can pick a pocket cleaner than a whistle, but someday I'm gonna sail all over this world takin' stuff. You'll see, I'll be famous."

"And more'n likely, you'll hang."

Jack grinned. "They gots to catch me first."

"They'll catch you; they always do."

The boys sheepishly left the cabin, the wrench firmly in Skip's hand. His face looked ashen as Zac put his hand on his shoulder.

"You boys ready to go below?" Zac asked.

"Yes, sir," Skip replied.

"I guess we is," Jack chimed in.

"All right, Miss Jenny will stay up here on deck, and we'll go do our business."

Moments later, Zac had taken the boys down into the darkness and into the heart of the chugging beast. The doors were open, and men shoveled coal into a red-hot boiler. Overhead, steam pipes hissed as if they were offering their own special judgment of the situation. Zac paused with the two boys before the gang of stokers. "Is Peng Lee here?"

A Chinaman stepped out in front of the gang. His eyes peeped out from the black mask of coal that covered his face. Zac pushed Skip gently forward and the boy held out the wrench.

"Here's your tool back, mister," Skip said. "I'm sorry I took it from you and maybe caused you to miss it for the work you do. I'm real sorry. I already got a lickin', but I'd be sorry all the same."

Peng Lee looked in Zac's direction. There was a look of doubt mixed with protest in the man's eyes. Zac shook his head, cutting off any arguments he might have made. The man took the wrench. He bowed toward Zac.

Moments later, they were back on deck. Skip and Zac were silent. Jack marched over to the rail and looked down at the wake created by the giant turning paddle. "Aren't you going to go off and play?" Zac asked.

"Don't feel much like playing," Skip said.

Jenny caught Zac's eye. She nodded toward Skip, a plaintive plea written all over her face.

He returned her look and nodded.

Zac kept his hand on the boy's shoulder. "I understand, son. That was a mighty hard thing you did, given the fact that you didn't take the thing."

Skip's head jerked up. His eyes brimmed with tears.

"Come over here and sit down on the bench with me."

Skip sauntered over to the bench with Zac. They sat close together. Zac put his arm around him. "I know you didn't take that wrench, son. You were bein' brave and protectin' a boy that just doesn't seem to know any better. I knew that when I gave you that whipping. It would have been hard for me if you had stolen it. It was double hard knowin' that you hadn't."

The look of disbelief on the boy's face hurt Zac. "Skipper, I'd trust you with anything I've got. You're starting to become a man, but on the inside, you've grown up plenty. There's a passage somewheres in the Bible that my daddy used to quote to me. It goes something like this: 'He that walks with wise men will be wise, but a companion of fools will suffer harm.' You think you can remember that?"

"Yes, sir."

"Good." Zac tousled the boy's hair. "You took it upon yourself to suffer for somebody else." Zac looked over at Jack. The boy was continuing to watch the wheel, then moving around to where he could get a better view of the boat's wake. "I'm not too sure that friend of yours even appreciates what you did for him, but I do. Punishment had to be given out for something like that, though."

"I was afraid you'd have him put off the boat."

"I might have at that. Still might before we're through."

Skip grabbed his arm. "Please don't. He ain't really got nowheres to go. He'd just go back to stealin' on the streets."

"But then he'd be somebody else's problem. He wouldn't be mine, and he wouldn't be yours."

"Maybe so, but then I'd feel like I took that whoopin' for nothing."

"All right, but you just keep an eye out for him. One of these days he's gonna take something that's gonna get him in real trouble. I could be chasin' him myself in a few years."

"Okay, I will."

"Then, that's good enough for me. I just didn't want you to go 'round thinking that I thought you were a thief, because I know better than that."

Skip hugged him—a long, strong hug.

The two of them sat and talked while Skip kept glancing at Jack.

Several people who had been gambling came out of the salon's glass doors, among them Rance McCauliff. He was counting a wad of greenbacks. Satisfied at his morning's take, he dropped the bills into his overcoat pocket.

Skip noticed right away that Jack had been eyeing the man. Skip got to his feet at once and raced over to join Jack.

McCauliff walked over to Zac Cobb. "I've seen you before," he said. "Don't I know you?"

"I rather doubt it," Zac replied.

"Name's McCauliff," the man said.

"I know. I saw you when you came on board."

"Of course, you were standing with Captain Van Tuyl. You musta caught yourself an earful with that one."

"What a man does is his own business," Zac replied. "I got nothing against professional gamblers."

"And from the look in your eyes I can see, sir, that you've had your turn with lady luck from time to time yourself."

"I'm not new to the pasteboards."

"I can see that, and from your looks I can tell you to be a fine judge of character as well."

Zac looked up at the man silently. He didn't much like looking up at any man he talked with, but he didn't want to move just yet. Zac could see the gambler searching his brain to try to place him.

"A man that judges people well has to be a fine poker player,"

McCauliff said. "I'd look forward to sitting across the table from you, I surely would."

"I doubt you'll see me there, McCauliff. I'm afraid my time is otherwise occupied."

"Rance. You can call me Rance." A sudden look of awareness came over McCauliff's face. He let out a grin. "You must be this Zac Cobb that Cox has been telling me so much about. If you handle cards like you do firearms, maybe it's a good thing for me you don't have the inclination."

Zac got to his feet. "Cox talks too much."

"He does seem to be mighty impressed with you. Gotta say, however, as a gambler he ain't worth a pitcher of warm spit."

"I wouldn't take him to be. He'll make a nice mark for you in there."

"Already has been. I'd look forward to the competition with you, however."

"Some other time perhaps," Zac replied.

Jenny walked up to the two of them with the boys by her side. Zac watched her, and his tight expression loosened a bit. The bright blue dress she wore, the one that matched her eyes, was enough to capture any man's attention.

As McCauliff turned to greet her, Jack stumbled and fell into him. "Oh," the boy said. "I'm terrible sorry. This here boat's deck is slippery like a fish."

Zac noticed the boy slip and fall, but he was momentarily distracted as Jenny put her hand on his shoulder.

McCauliff straightened himself and shook out his coat. "These folks with you?" he asked Zac.

"Yes, Miss Jenny Hays," Zac said matter-of-factly.

"Pleased to meet you, Miss Hays."

"This here's my boy, Skip. The one with the slippery shoes is just with us till we dock. His name's Jack." Zac motioned to the glass doors. "I think we're gonna find us a table and see about the food on this boat. It's about lunchtime."

"Oh boy!" Jack said. "That'd be real swell. I'm sure hungry."

Skip began to pull on Jack's shirttail, but the boy ignored the gesture.

"I can recommend the oysters, Miss Hays," McCauliff said. "This boat has some of the bay's finest shellfish, fresh caught and on ice. I'd join you myself, but I have more business to do inside. Time and tide wait for no man."

"I'm sure that's true," Jenny said.

"I sold some of them oysters myself," Jack said. "Used 'em to pay up fer part of my passage here. I can guarantee they is fresh."

"You see," McCauliff said. "The testimony of an expert. Now, how can you go wrong?"

+ + + + +

Manny poled the boat toward the shore. In spite of the cool foggy air, sweat beads had formed on his deeply tanned forehead. He pushed the boat into the fog, grunting with each thrust.

"You won't regret this, young man," Dr. Page said.

The two of them now had their hands free, but they were still clinging to each other like insects on a branch.

"I'm regrettin' it already."

"We'll just make our way quickly back to Sacramento. You'll never see us again."

"Humph. More'n likely I'll see you in the witness box at my trial. My pap used to tell me that no good deed would go unpunished; feed a dog and he'll bite your hand every time."

"We would never do that," Mary joined in.

"Far as I know, that boss of mine is followin' us and is gonna be a waiting fer us when we land. You better hope, and do some of that praying that he ain't, elsewise he'll kill all three of us."

"We will be praying for you," Mary said. "I will remember you every night in my prayers."

"Why don't you come with us, young man? This is no life for you. You come with us, and I will see that you are gainfully employed."

"Then, I would be a fool sure 'nuff. Naw, I am what I am. No amount of praying is gonna change that, just the end of a good stiff rope, I reckon."

"There's hope for anyone," Mary said. "None of us can change ourselves, but the Lord can change any man."

"Never mind you me. I made my own bed, and I guess I'll just have to lie in it for a spell yet. When I sets enough aside, I'll light out of here quick enough."

Manny set down the pole as the boat glided up to the shore. He hopped out, squashing the mud beneath his boots and then pulling the boat up with a rope attached to the bow. Holding out his hand, he helped Mary out onto the semidry land. "You folks don't go far tonight. You find yerself a spot and just lay low for a day or two. We got men travelin' these here roads that know you by sight."

Dr. Page gave him a warm embrace. "Thank you, son. Thank you for all that you've done. I know the Lord is working in your life. He's never failed us and He won't fail you either."

"You just do exactly like I say. Stay low. Talk to no one. Trust no one. We have people hereabout that works with us that would send you into a ghost panic if'n you knew."

"All right. We'll do exactly as you say."

The two turned and, keeping low, skirted the tall blackberry growth. The thorns were vicious, tearing at their clothing as they moved into what they hoped would be open space. The foggy river bottom spewed up the airy wetness, forming damp ringlets in their hair. It was some time before they heard the shots, two shots booming from the river.

Mary was startled. "What was that?"

"I don't know, child. Perhaps our friend is just going about his deception."

"You don't think he's been found out, do you?" She clung tightly to her uncle's arm. "Oh, Uncle, I would be horrified to think that man has suffered for showing us mercy."

"Mercy is costly, my child. It cost our Lord everything."

It was over an hour later when they found the road. Mary started back up the seldom used cart path, but Dr. Page stopped her. "We can't go back up that way. If they are looking for us, that will be the direction in which they come."

"But Sacramento is that way."

"Yes, all the more reason to go the other. They wouldn't expect us to go in the opposite direction. We will go south for a day and then turn east. We will need to find a place to do exactly what our friend suggested."

"Find a spot and lie low?"

"Yes."

CHAPTER 7

SKIP HOVERED CLOSE TO JACK throughout the entire lunch, hunched over his beef stew and eyeballing his thieving friend. His silence was noticeable.

"You'd better finish your stew, boy. You'll be meeting your aunt Hattie soon enough, and the first thing that old gal will do is feel your ribs and accuse me of starvin' you," Zac chided.

"That, more than likely, won't be the first thing," Jenny offered.

Zac blushed slightly and broke off a piece of bread. "No, I reckon not."

Skip noticed something pass unspoken between the two of them but said nothing.

"Hattie just can't let up on anything once it commences to crawling up her spine," Zac observed. "And if she discovers a chink in a man's armor, she comes after it for all she's worth."

Jenny looked at Skip. "What Zac is talking about," she said, "is his aunt's insistence that he marry."

Skip cracked a faint smile.

Zac grinned back at him, trying to make some humor out of something that obviously embarrassed him. "Now, why would a perfectly healthy man want to go and do something like that?"

"'Cause he loved her, I reckon," Skip teased.

Jack pushed back his quickly emptied bowl and stuffed a roll into his mouth. Cramming two more of the buns into his pocket, he got up from the table. "Best go to lookin' 'round some more. I ain't seen me the upper decks, nor that there pilothouse either."

Skip suddenly dropped his napkin and sprang to his feet. "I best go with him."

"Yes, I suppose you had," Zac said. "You boys be careful and stay out of trouble."

Skip scampered out the door behind Jack, trying his best to keep the boy in sight. He took the stairway two steps at a time and finally caught Jack on the deck above. Reaching out, he grabbed Jack's shirt and spun him around. "What have you done?"

"Nothin', I ain't done nothin'."

"I saw you bump into that man. Did you take something offa him?"

Jack pulled his shirt free. "What're you, my Sunday school teacher? I ain't got nothin'."

"You are lying sure as you're born."

Jack leaned forward, swelling his chest to full size. "I tell stories, but I ain't lyin'. 'Sides, what if I did? That man takes money that don't rightly belong to him, now don't he?"

"That don't make what you do right."

"Aw shucks, come on. Ain't no need of you spoiling all our fun. Let's us look around some." Straightening his shirt, Jack pranced off down the deck, trying brass doorknobs as he went along.

Skip caught up with him on the bow of the hurricane deck. Jack had positioned himself on the edge of the railing and was peering into the foggy haze. "Ain't that something?" Jack asked.

"What?"

Jack spread his hands outward. "The world out there, all foggy. You'd never know what was sitting out there. It might be a pirate ship or maybe a dragon."

"I don't rightly think so. I think it's just the riverbank."

"Well, now see, that's the difference 'tween you and me. I sees things that could be, and you just sees what is. Sometimes, I ain't even sure you sees what is."

"Oh, I see plenty," Skip shot back.

"You think so, huh? Well, you just look into that fog and tell me you don't see the ghosts of men drowned on this here river."

"I just see the fog."

"Well, it might be ghosts!"

"I don't rightly believe in them things."

"You don't believe in ghosts?"

"No, I believe in angels but not ghosts."

"Ghosts, angels, they is all the same."

"They ain't neither."

"What's the difference?"

"Angels were created by God as His servants. Ghosts are just something storytellers make up to try and tell you where the dead went to."

"And you don't think Robbie's out there in that fog?"

"No, I don't."

Jack clinched his fists and held them to his side. "Well, I does. Sometimes I feel like he's all around me. I spent the whole night with him in the boat with me. He just lay there, not saying nothing, but inside I know'd he was sayin' something all the time."

"Like what?"

"Mostly he was sayin', 'I don't want to be dead.' "

Jack gulped.

Skip's eyes widened. He blinked back the emotion.

"Sometimes," Jack went on, "I was afeared he was telling me that I was gonna be next if'n I didn't watch out for myself. That was when I decided to give up this here oyster pirating. I firmed up in my head that there was a better and less dangerous way fer a body to make a livin' than being chased by old man Riley."

"Well, Robbie was right about that."

"I think that being a pirate, a *real* pirate, is better." His grin broadened. "A grown-up one that takes real money." It was plain that the thought of adventure and money was more than enough to take Jack's mind off the subject.

"You do that and you're gonna be as dead as Robbie." Skip couldn't quit thinking about the dead boy wrapped up on the stern of the boat.

"Come on, let's us go on down to the stern to Robbie and just ask him."

Skip's eyes widened, large brown hollows of fear.

"I heard tell one time that if you asks dead folks stuff," Jack went on, "they'll answer you straight off. I seen plenty of dead folks, but I ain't never tried talking to 'em. C'mon!"

"That's gibberish nonsense." Skip bluffed a bravado, but inside he was terrified.

Jack walked off toward the stairs and motioned toward Skip. "Well, let's us go and see, then."

The boy hurried down the stairs and stood at the bottom, waiting for Skip. He peeked his head back up the staircase. It was plain to see that Skip was in no great hurry to go back and see Robbie's pale white face.

Jack turned around, smiling. Suddenly, from underneath the

staircase, a hand shot out and grabbed Jack's arm, twisting it behind his back. It was Rance McCauliff, and his face was livid with a determined rage. He shoved the small boy forward to the edge of the deck. "I'm gonna break that arm clean off, then throw it and you into that water. You'll never come up."

Jack's face showed how much the man was hurting him. He stumbled forward in the big man's grip. "I ain't done nothing."

"Where's my money?"

"What money?"

"The money you lifted from my pocket, three hundred dollars. I've killed men for a far sight less than that, and I wouldn't hesitate to make you into fish food right now."

Skip cautiously joined the two of them. "Don't hurt him, mister. I'll get your money for you."

McCauliff's eyes snapped around, staring Skip in the face. "See that you do and right now."

Skip edged over to Jack. "You better give that man his money. I saw you take it, and I know you got it on you somewheres."

McCauliff lifted on the boy's arm, and Jack gave out a mournful cry. He twisted in the man's arms. "It's down in my pants for safe keeping."

"Then, you best dig it on out," Skip said.

Slowly, grimacing in pain, Jack plunged his left hand down into his pants. He took hold of the wad of greenbacks and lifted them out.

McCauliff snatched the bills away from the boy and spun him around. Grabbing his shirt, he braced the twisting ten-year-old out over the water.

"Don't drop him," Skip called out.

McCauliff fixed himself on the frightened Jack. "Boy, you ever do any nonsense with me again and I'll cut your throat. I'll come up on you at night when nobody's watching and slice your scrawny little neck clean in two. You hear me?"

Jack nodded furiously. "Yes sir."

Bringing him forward, McCauliff dropped Jack to the deck. The small boy raked the sides of the big man with his hands. He looked like a frightened cat sliding down a pole, trying the best he could to get a claw in somewhere.

Lying in a pile on the deck, Jack huddled himself. McCauliff sent a swift kick into the boy's back. Jack let out a soft scream and then began to shake.

McCauliff bent down over him. "You best do exactly as I say. Next time I won't go so easy on you. I will kill you." With that, the big man spun on his heels and marched toward the glass-doored salon.

Skip stood still until the man had disappeared. Looking down, he could see Jack shaking. The boy's shoulders wobbled, and his face was turned toward the deck. Skip couldn't see him cry, but he reckoned Jack was crying hard. Skip, his ownself, would have been scared out of his skin. He knelt down next to him. "You all right?"

The boy turned over. He wasn't crying at all, he was laughing. He held his ribs as he laughed, the tears coming down his cheeks. "After that kick, it pert near hurts too much to laugh."

Skip backed off, puzzled. "What the blazes is wrong with you? That man coulda killed you."

"Nah, I knew he weren't about to do a fool thing like that. I had me a witness—you! If'n he'd kilt me, he'd a had to kill you too."

"Oh, great!" Skip exclaimed.

Jack sat up and tried to control his chuckles, but somehow he couldn't help himself.

"Well, then, why are you laughing?" Skip asked.

Jack swung his head from side to side. He was obviously looking around to make sure they weren't being watched. A grin was spread wide over his thin face. He opened his clinched fist slowly and held out his hand. In his palm rested a small, pearl-handled, brass-framed pistol.

Skip blinked and backed away farther. "Where'd you get that?" he asked.

"I took it off that gamblin' man when I slid to the floor. It's a derringer—holds two shots, and it's pretty dangerous from up close." He held out the bird's-head-butted pistol for Skip to get a closer look. "It's one of them watch fob .32s made by Frank Wesson. I seen 'em in the store window in Oakland. More powerful than them .22 derringers."

"You are plumb crazy!" Skip exploded. "Didn't you hear what that man said? He said if you messed with him once more he was gonna come by and cut your throat."

"Aww, he ain't gonna do that. He won't even know who took it.

I just looked real scared to him, and I is good. He didn't feel a thing; most folks don't."

"Well, he's got to find out it's gone, and if I was him, my mind would move to you first thing."

"We're docking in Sacramento before dawn. By the time he does find out, you and me's gonna be long gone."

"Maybe, maybe not. There's still gonna be a lot of dark time between supper and the time we leave this boat." Skip looked out at the fog. "'Round here, the daylight looks dark enough for what that man's got in mind."

"You worry like a woman. I swear you do. That man ain't gonna mess with us none, not fer some little old pistol. 'Sides, you was with me. You heard him say what he was gonna do. He kills me, he's got to kill you too."

+ + + + +

Dusk was settling over the Delta. It had been a long day. Dr. Page and Mary had been walking for over an hour when they heard horses on the road. He snatched her by the hand and pulled her toward the thick bushes on the river side of the road. Thrashing their way into places where no opening existed before, they allowed the thorns to tear at their clothes and claw at their exposed hands and arms. The thick branches had little give, but the doctor pushed at them, bending them backward, their thick blood red branches giving way reluctantly. The berries were gone mostly, and what little remained could in no way make up for the pain of their thorny masters, with their thick green leaves and sharp spikes.

They hit a sharp drop in the ground and slid forward, their feet shooting out from underneath them. The ditch below was muddy, the ground seeming to bleed a gooey brown muck that smelled of stagnant water. Dr. Page put his hand over Mary's mouth as she started to cry out. "Sshhh," he said.

The hooves of the horses were louder, pounding on the road and throwing clumps of muddy sod as they passed by. From behind the bushes, Page could hear one of the riders call for a halt. "You see anything?" he yelled.

"Nah, probably just more of them Chinese. There's more of them 'round here than fleas on a dog."

"And they don't much linger long to say howdy," another man shouted.

"No, I suppose not. I would dearly love to say howdy to any of them celestial women they got as daughters. I surely would now."

The riders had stopped only a few yards away from them, and Dr. Page hoped they wouldn't take the time to get down from their horses. He hadn't spent much time worrying about how clear their tracks had been in the muddy ground, but even a blind man could follow them. From the sound of these men, whoever in fact they were, they were up to no good.

"Should we get down and stretch a spell?" one of the men asked.

Page's heart skipped a beat. *Please, Lord, cover these men's eyes so they do not see us,* he prayed silently.

"Nah, let's get on to Walnut Grove. We got ourselves some serious drinking to do before the night's over, don't we?"

The men murmured to each other, and soon Dr. Page and Mary could hear the sound of the horses, once more at a gallop.

Page put his arm around Mary and patted her shoulder. "I know you must be tired and hungry, child."

"I'll be fine. I don't want to be a worry to you any more than I have to be. I can go on."

"I'm afraid we can't take the risk of continuing to walk this road. You heard our friend advise us to lay low for a day or so. Two people on foot, dressed as we are, will inspire grapevine talk all up and down the river. I don't think we can risk that."

"You must be tired too."

"Yes, we both are." He smoothed her hair and plucked out several branches that appeared to have taken root in its raven folds. "Well, we can no longer walk the road, and these brambles along the river will cut us to shreds if we attempt to negotiate them, so we must take to the orchards."

"If someone sees us, there won't be any place to hide."

"We will leave that to Providence, my child. I can see no other alternative for us."

Getting once again to their feet, the two of them pushed back the brambles that surrounded them. Mary picked up the hem of her dress and wrapped it around her hands as she pushed forward. The stiff thorny thongs gradually gave way, leaving their burning scars on her face and ankles.

Stumbling back onto the road, they crossed it and moved into the foggy pear orchard. The ground was soft and matted with grasses. Here and there, branches of long-ago-pruned limbs lay scattered beneath the trees. They snapped beneath their feet, sending a noise that echoed out over the orchard and into the growing dusk. Trails curled between the trees from where growers had led their teams to help in the pruning and picking efforts. The fog lapped at their ankles and coated the surface of the wet ground. It seemed so inviting, like a warm bed of soft cloud to lie down on. Everything inside of the doctor cried out to simply lie down and hope that this situation, like some evil nightmare, would pass by come morning.

Mary shook her head, obviously weak and numb from fatigue. "How could something like this happen?"

"I'm afraid I'm too feebleminded just now to ponder that question, child. 'The rain falls on the just and the unjust.' It's something we just can't know momentarily. I know that Providence is not responsible for our mishaps, but He is still sovereign. We will be stronger in our faith for it."

Mary's weakness was causing her ankles to give way. Each step seemed like torture. The doctor reached out and held her close. He limped slightly. "I have a few dollars in my shoe," he said. "I always carry some there, just in case."

"Perhaps we can find a store to buy some food," Mary said.

"I wouldn't want to stop too close by here," he said. "Remember what our friend said. Those people have spies and operatives all over the Delta."

In the ghostly mist the lights of a farmhouse twinkled. A dark shape began to take form with each plodding step. They moved toward it with deliberation, the doctor holding Mary, her arm over his shoulder. Shingles and a sloping roof hung down over a high porch. A rocky chimney stood at the end of the house, with a thin whisper of smoke blending itself into the fog. Blocks of stone with wooden stairs dotted the front of the shanty, and a light shone from behind the window. Soft white curtains filtered it, the gauzy barrier scantily concealing moving objects inside the house. A wooden-sided well stood in the yard, and a dog barked.

"I'm so thirsty," Mary gasped.

"Let's sit down for a moment," he said.

Making a place on the wet soil, they collapsed to the ground. Nearby Dr. Page spotted a wagon. The sides of the vehicle were high, and empty staves showed it to be in disrepair. "I think we could sleep in that for a while," he said. "As tired as we are, I don't think the discomfort would keep us awake for long. It would be up out of the dew, however, and dry."

"Yes," she rasped.

"I'll put you in the wagon and go to the well over there for water."

"That would be nice."

The doctor helped his niece to her feet, and together they limped toward the derelict vehicle. It was bare, with a tarp folded in the bed and small amounts of straw strewn over the weathered boards. Picking her up, he set her in the wagon. "See if you can make a bed for us, child, out of that straw. We'll use the tarp to cover us. I'll go and get you some water."

He crouched low and, skirting the ground, moved in the direction of the well. Keeping his eyes on the window, he watched for movement. They hadn't come this far to be shot as trespassers. As he reached the well, he felt the wooden sides and moved his hands to the top. A bucket sat on its edge and in it a hollowed gourd. He stood up behind the well and dropped the bucket into it. The noise of the bucket hitting the water below was soon joined by the sound of a barking dog. Turning the crank hurriedly, he saw the dark outline of the big dog, its teeth bared, snarling.

CHAPTER 8

THE GLOOM CAST BY THE FOG at night on the river made headway slow. What was normally a fourteen-hour trip was becoming twenty. The lights on the big boat twinkled in the misty darkness, and the small stringed quartet had quit their playing hours ago. Zac said good night to Jenny and turned the handle on the stateroom he shared with the boys; it was locked. He knocked lightly on the door. "Open up, boys, it's me."

The door swung open. Skip was in his bunk, and Jack's pallet, which took almost all of the available floor space, was scattered about. Jack stood at the door and tried to peek outside as Zac stepped gingerly through it. "We almost there yet?" the boy asked.

Zac closed the door. "No, I reckon we're gonna be a great deal later getting into Sacramento than planned."

"How come?"

Zac could see the nervousness in the boy's face. "This fog is slowing us down a bit, quite a bit, I'd reckon." He grinned. "I'd 'spect you two boys would like that. More of a ride. Why aren't you both up on deck looking around? I expected to see you up there for sure."

"Does anybody else know which cabin ours is?" Skip asked.

Zac pushed up his hat and scratched the back of his head. "The captain does, along with the purser, I suppose. Why would you ask?"

"Oh, no reason," Jack chimed in.

"You boys been up to something you shouldn't have meddled in?"

"No," Jack said. "We've been real good, ain't we, Skip? Real angel like."

Skip was silent.

"Now you have got me worried. Boys and angels don't seem to mix very well."

"We're just in here tending our own business," Jack said. "And tellin' stories."

Zac laughed. "Well, that explains the locked door, then. Little boys, ghostly stories, and a foggy river seem like a combination that calls out for caution. I guess I'm glad I was spending my time with Miss Jenny."

"She's next door?" Skip asked plaintively.

"Yes, right next door. But don't you be keepin' her up by getting yourselves all head up with stories and poundin' on her wall. I think the lady admires her sleep."

"Are you gonna stay and go to bed?" Skip asked.

"No siree. You wouldn't catch me in here till you boys are fast asleep. I wouldn't want your bad dreams, got enough of my own. I think I'll go up top and admire what the captain and that pilot of his are doing to keep us off these sandbars."

"You got a key, don't you?" Skip asked.

"Yes, I do. But there's no sense in you boys locking this door. To the best of my recollection, there ain't no bogeymen on board." Zac opened the cabin door and stared back at the frightened boys. "Now you boys just get your sleep. We got ourselves a big day in Sacramento tomorrow."

When he closed the door, Jack once again twisted the lock. "I guess I'd feel a far sight better if he'd been coming in to sleep."

"Me too," Skip responded. "He said not to lock the door, though."

Jack padded his way back to the blankets on the floor. Sticking his feet in them, he pulled up the covers. "You think I is gonna lay here when that man might just as well come in and slit our throats?"

"No, I reckon not."

"'Sides, Zac's got himself a key, don't he? He'll get in when he has to." The boy took out the small pocket pistol. "If'n that other fella sticks his head through that door or in that porthole window, I'm gonna blow it clean off."

Skip fairly shivered in his covers. He was angry and frightened too. "You brung it on us. You keep taking things that don't rightly belong to you and you'll get everybody that's ever known you killed."

"You sayin' it was my fault Robbie got shot?"

"No I ain't. I'm just saying it'll be your fault if I get my throat cut."

"Well, don't you worry none about that. I just have to pull back these here hammers and let 'er rip."

"You just better make sure at what you're aiming at. You might just as well shoot Zac or Jenny or maybe some drunk that's mistaken our place for his."

"Oh, I'll be sure all right. I won't fire until I sees his face real clear. Then he'll be sorry."

\+ + + + +

Zac climbed the flights of stairs leading to the wheelhouse. A soft breeze blew, not enough to dispel the fog, but just enough to make the wetness gather on a man's face. Zac pushed open the door and saw Captain Van Tuyl smoking a cigar and keeping a watchful eye on how Dennis Grubb was keeping the wheel.

"Well, Cobb, it's good to see you up here with the menfolk," Van Tuyl offered.

"Yes, got my young'uns all in bed now, but I don't reckon they'll be sleepin' for a spell."

"You might be surprised. The noise of the engine and the movement of the boat is a great tonic for fitfulness, even in little boys."

Zac pulled out his briar pipe and stuffed it with his whiskey-soaked tobacco. He scratched a match on the wall and held it over the bowl.

"That smells nice back there," Grubb said.

"Special mixture I get conjured up in San Francisco," Zac said. "It does cost me, but it's mighty smooth."

"Man needs something to keep his senses sharp now and then," Grubb replied. He picked up a glass of water and sipped it.

"That's my general rule," Zac replied. "The only alcohol I take in is the stuff they soak my tobacco in."

"Well now, you could sure 'nuff qualify as a pilot, then," Van Tuyl replied.

"No, I just stick to what I do best. I got no ambitions to plow another man's field."

Zac watched as Grubb suddenly shifted the wheel, spinning it to his left. Moving into the main current, he once again steadied the big, wooden, spar-spoked wheel.

"You look like a man who knows what he's doing," Zac said.

"That I do. I piloted on the Mississippi as a strapling, but the Sacramento is another thing all together, especially in the fog. A man's got to abandon his charts and go by his belly most of the time."

The captain pushed his hat forward and looked at Zac. "I reckon you got to develop a feeling in the innards for what you do too, don't you, Cobb?"

"That I do."

"Well, I don't 'spect we'll have any problems going up river," Van Tuyl said. "'Course, once we pick up that delivery of yours, we'll have to keep a watchful eye. There's been river pirates operating this Delta for over two years now. They've been a pesky sort too, mostly pickin' on small boats and steamers with very few passengers. I 'spect the *Delta King* would be too much for a bunch like that to handle."

"That may be. You haven't had a shipment this size before. All that gold is mighty temptin' for people who want to get rich quick."

"Your people don't advertise what you're guarding, do they?"

"No, but with money like that, it's hard to keep some folks quiet. Wells Fargo has weak sisters working with them, same as the rest."

"I know," Van Tuyl said. "I met up with one this afternoon."

"You'd be speaking of Cox."

"Yes, that was his name. Said he was a special agent for Wells Fargo—said it kinda loud too."

"He's kin by marriage to Henry Wells."

"Well, I guess that explains it. A man can't very well control who his family takes a shine to, although plenty of us would like to. He was gambling aplenty too. I think he had a hankering to make our Rance McCauliff a rich man before we got to the capital."

Zac was silent about that notion. An agent with Cox's job wasn't paid enough to gamble badly. His only compensation above a meager salary was based on what he could return to the company by way of stolen loot and the rewards that went along with the capture of the thieves who had taken it. From his judgment of Cliff Cox, that would have proved to be very meager indeed.

"But we shouldn't have much trouble getting into Sacramento," the captain continued. "Nothing that would disturb your sleep, leastways."

"No, I'm bringing my own trouble with me on this leg, I reckon."

"If you're talking about that boy, yes you are. I've seen his kind many a time, and I wouldn't put anything past him. I don't think we'll be in too much danger coming back, though. The army's got a patrol with that gold, and with them and you on the job here, I 'spect things will pass mighty smooth."

Zac chomped down on the end of his pipe. Most of what he'd ever been told would be smooth had been wrong. He knew one thing. If Henry Wells had expected things to run smoothly, he wouldn't have been sent for.

The captain went on. "Those pirates always seem to know exactly what to hit and what to leave alone. They take the boat and sack it cleaner than a whistle, haul everything away in wagons. They know what to take, I'll say that for them."

"Why is that?" Zac asked.

The short stubby captain flicked the ash off the end of his cigar. Biting down on the end, he smiled. "You won't see them taking a load of cotton. Boats trafficking agricultural products seem to make it through with slack, don't have nary a problem. It's almost as if those rascals know what we're carrying before the captains on the boats have had the time to read their own manifests."

Zac pondered the problem. At the very least, somebody involved at high levels of commerce had to be passing on information.

Van Tuyl went on, "They must have themselves a good means of selling the stuff they steal, too, more'n likely through San Francisco. What they've shanghaied so far would fill plenty of warehouses. My guess is the stuff is heading out of the Golden Gate no more than a week later."

"I don't imagine a shipment of gold would be too difficult to dispose of," Zac observed.

"I should say not. That gold would be in Hong Kong a month later, with every man jack that touched it along the way wealthy beyond his dreams."

+ + + + +

The oil lamp in the boys' cabin burned dim. The wick had been turned down to allow them to sleep, while at the same time allowing Zac to get to bed without tripping over Jack as he slept on the floor. The soft glow through the red globe cast an eerie light on the cabin's walls, making Jack's stories even more frightening to Skip. He sat with his back pressed into the cabin wall, listening to his friend from Oakland replay the fancies of his mind and the tales of horror he had both seen and heard about on the rough-and-tumble docks of the East Bay.

"Someday, if'n I don't get to be a pirate, I'm gonna sail all over the world. I'd sure 'nuff like to spot out the last of it."

"The last of the world?" Skip asked.

"Yep, that would be the most fun, the darkest place where there be no people, none at all."

"That would be Africa, I reckon," Skip said.

"No, I don't think so," Jack replied. "Might just be the land of the northern lights the sailors told me about."

"Northern lights?"

"Yep, they hangs up in the dark sky, real pretty sheets of dancin' colored lights, to hear folks tell of them. The ground is all frozen with white snow as far as the eye can see, and there's bears there, snow white bears."

"You reckon that's true?" Skip asked.

"I reckon so. 'Course a body's got to be some kinda brave to have the stomach fer it. Some men shake fer months after, it be so cold up there."

"Maybe they're just fools goin' way up there."

Jack lay back down underneath his blankets. "I ain't a-thinkin' you'd make it. You be the scary kind. You is even scared of some gambler braggin' 'bout his sharp knife on yer throat."

Jack pushed his hands and arms up over the covers. He spread them. "I seen that man's knife, though—one of them Bowie hog-butcher things. I just bet he keeps it nice and sharp too. Man like that has an appreciation fer fine tools, keeps 'em fresh and clean, I just bet."

Skip lay in silence for a long while, thinking about his feelings on the matter. He was frightened and he knew it. He'd seen danger before. He'd already had men looking to kill him. He never much liked it, but he did what had to be done, all the same. Now, he much preferred the feeling of warmth and safety he'd found sleeping in his own bed on the hacienda in Cambria. He swung his legs out of bed and fished around for his pants.

"Where you think you're goin'?" Jack asked.

"To the privy," Skip said. "Then I thought I just might look around."

"You crazy? We got us a chamber pot in the corner. Ain't no need fer you to go out there where that man might be. Does you know what will happen to you if'n he catches you out there?"

"I reckon I do." Skip stood up and, hitching up his trousers, fixed the suspenders that held them up. He sat back down and began to tug on his boots.

"That man will cut your throat, same as he would me. You heard him, didn't you?"

"Yes, I did." Skip pushed his nightshirt down into his trousers and reached for his jacket and hat.

"Then, why would you go out there?"

"I guess I'm goin' out there 'cause I am scared."

Jack sat up on the floor. "You is crazy, then. If'n you is scared, you just had better sit yerself still till Zac gets back here."

Skip got up and moved to the door. "No, that's just why I need to go." His knees were shaking slightly, a fact that was all too obvious to both boys.

"You do beat all, Skip. I ain't never heard such foolishness."

"I ain't being foolish. I reckon it has something to do with a thing Zac was readin' to me before we came on this here trip. It was from the writings of a very smart man that lived in Greece a long time ago. His name was Aristotle. This Aristotle feller said a man's morals was made up of what he did. He said a body became what he did in spite of how he felt about it. Men come to be builders by building things. Folks get to be violin players by playing the violin."

"Well, what does that have to do with goin' out there in the dark?"

"I guess I'm tryin' to find some balance in my life, that's all."

"Balance?"

Skip put on his jacket and buttoned it up all the way to the top of his neck, turning the collar up. "Yes, balance. I am plum scared to death. If I do something brave, maybe I can move more toward the center and not be trapped by how I feel right now. That's exactly what this old Greek feller said. Said a man has to live in the middle, not too scared and not too foolish."

"Well, you is being real foolish now."

"Guess that's the right thing to do just now, then," Skip replied. "It'll move me to the middle." Skip turned the small brass lock on the door. "You better lock this here thing behind me. Even if that man finds me, it's you he'll be lookin' for."

When Skip closed the door, Jack bounced out of his makeshift bed and hurriedly locked it. He stood at attention, his back against the polished oak door. His mind was alive with jumbled thoughts, not about being a pirate or even about the northern lights over the end of the earth, but about these strange people he had come to know—a boy who would take a beating for him and who was fool enough to pay heed to some long-dead Greek.

He wondered what it took to make someone turn out like that. Was it the love he felt inside these people? Was it the books he had seen on their table? He walked over hurriedly to the nightstand and picked up the leather-bound books one at a time. *The Poetry of Tennyson*, one book proclaimed in gold print. A second book had the title in red letters, *Ivanhoe*.

He began to turn the pages. *There must be somethin' in here that makes people turn out this way*, he thought, *somethin' mighty peculiar*.

+ + + + +

The doctor hunched behind the well as the big dog snarled. The beast rounded the wooden structure, his teeth bared. Dr. Page could almost hear his own heart pounding, even over the vicious growls of the dog.

Sweat beads formed on the doctor's forehead. This was something he had never wanted to face. He had treated many a child and even a few adults who had been attacked by dogs. The wounds could be serious, with gashes that could easily breed infection if untreated. Page knew dogs seldom left a stranger. They would come after a man and continue to protect whatever territory they viewed as their own long after most men would quit. This was the dog's territory, Page knew that much. Anyone or anything coming into it was an intruder, and tonight the doctor was the intruder and the intended victim.

The beast circled him, a large black dog with eyes that seemed to radiate hatred, even in the dark. He could see the animal's muscles ripple beneath the shiny black coat, muscles that were tense, prepared for a sudden strike. The dog crouched low, its spiked teeth bared.

The doctor held up a hand offered in friendship but also to ward off a first strike. He would have to keep the animal away from his throat, a target that was very vulnerable with him on the ground at the dog's level.

Suddenly, the door to the farmhouse flew open and an older, stoop-shouldered man stood on the porch. Light streamed past him to the darkened stairs below the porch. The man held a shotgun in his hand, and Dr. Page scooted behind the well to a place he thought was out of sight.

The dog's attention was suddenly diverted by the man, who spoke in rapid tones in a language Page thought to be Chinese. From behind the man, Page could hear a woman's voice. She barked orders to the man at the door. The doctor could tell by the tone of her voice that she was displeased at the situation, even if he couldn't make out the words.

The dog trotted up the stairs to the porch, and after a few moments, the old man let the dog inside. When the door closed, only the sound of the woman's displeasure came from the house in sharp, overbearing tones.

Once again, the doctor reached up for the rope on the bucket, now deep in the well. He hoisted it hand over hand, the squeaking of the pulley wailing out over the darkness. It sounded very loud to him, but from the sound of the loud female voice in the house, he doubted it could be heard.

Setting the bucket on the edge of the well, he dipped the gourd into the cool, dark water. He held it gingerly with both hands as he made his way back to the old wagon.

"Are you all right?" Mary asked.

"Yes, but for a while I thought I'd met the devil himself."

He held the gourd to the girl's lips. "Here, you drink all of this. If you want more, I think I can get it for you."

She held out her hands under the drinking gourd and sipped at first, then drank it all down.

"I'll take this back to the well and drink some myself," he said. "We can sleep here for a while and try to be gone before the sun comes up. We'll find something to eat in the morning."

CHAPTER 9

+ + + + + + +

SKIP STOOD OUTSIDE THE CABIN for what seemed like the longest time. He pressed his back to the cabin door and peered out toward the fantail of the boat. Robbie was there. Behind the boy's body, the huge red paddles swung up from the river, pouring torrents of freshly gouged water down their blades and onto the white metal flywheel that held the blades in place. The noise of the churning, dripping water seemed in perfect harmony with the chugging of the engine.

Earlier in the day, he had spotted the two smokestacks that rose up from the upper deck on either side of the pilothouse. He'd thought them grand. As he lifted his head, he could see the red glowing cinders drift away over the stern of the big boat. The sparks seemed like a constant barrage of fireworks sent skyward by a red dragon as it crawled on its belly up the river.

The latticed white railing looped itself in a circle around the edge of the deck, and over its side was the darkness of the river. He would stay away from the railing, at least for now. By keeping to the side of the large salon, he might be able to spot someone approaching before whoever it was saw him. He'd have to pass by several large windows, and that was both a problem and a blessing. It allowed people to clearly see him, and that might prove to be a saving grace. At the same time, it might permit a certain someone to see him or, worse still, see him and think it was Jack—and that was the problem. In any event it was a chance he had to take. Bold steps must be taken to move toward the middle to get over the fear he felt.

He edged his way along the wall. The music was over now and that was too bad. He liked music, liked it a lot. It helped to clear his mind, clear away unseemly thoughts and allow it to drift onto more positive things. Now, all he could hear was the tinkling noise of the glasses on the tables and the dull roar of crowded conversation. The aroma of stale cigar smoke drifted out the noisy door. It was a smell that turned his stomach. He didn't mind the smell of Zac's pipe, had come to even like it, but cigars were another matter altogether.

He got to the first of the large glass windows and gingerly stepped across its vantage point. Zac would be topside, like he said. Jenny was in her cabin sleeping. No one who could do him any good would be watching, only someone bent to do him harm. There was no need to linger here.

The door to the privy was just up ahead. He'd have to pass in front of another window. He didn't want to run—that would be foolish. It would attract any amount of attention, even from a casual observer. He didn't want to walk too slow either. No, he'd have to walk the same way he wanted to live, with balance, not too fast and not too slow. Without looking or shying back. He moved deliberately but quickly across the window.

Looking back at the window, he bumped into a man in the shadows. The man spun him around and held him out into the light for a better look. "You, thief boy." It was the Chinese stoker Peng Lee. "You here looking for something else to steal?"

"N-n-no, sir. I was just going to the privy, that's all."

The man released his grip on him. "Boy shouldn't be out so late. You might trip, fall in river. It dark. We not find you again."

Skip was shaking. "I'll be okay."

The Chinaman stooped down slightly to look Skip in the eye. "You not thief boy. You say so, but you not. Why you do that?"

"I don't know. I guess I just figured I could bear up under it, that's all."

"You protect your friend. You silly. Your friend will steal more. You not be there to protect him."

"He'll change."

"He not change. Two things Peng Lee know for sure; I gonna work hard and I gonna die Chinese. That true for your friend. He gonna steal and he gonna die a thief."

"Folks can change."

"No boy. You silly. You live longer and you see." With that the sweaty man turned and headed down the stairs to the engine room.

Skip paused at the stairway. Below he could hear the stokers grunt and swear in Chinese. He heard the door to the boiler open and the sound of the men as they shoveled coal into the flames. The furnace roared, sending sparks up into the dark sky.

People can too change, he thought. *It just takes time and knowing the right things to do.* Still he wondered.

The stairs up ahead that led to the second deck were gloomy. The rails were solid wood, painted white, an easy place to stay concealed and wait for somebody unsuspecting like. He remembered them well. It was the same place that McCauliff fella had caught Jack and tried to tear his arm off. Just the thought of the man made Skip shiver inside. There was something about him, something unnerving. It was as if he could look right through you, straight to the inside. There seemed to be an evil hatred in him, a hatred that stayed hidden behind his knowing smile and smooth face that smelled of lilac water, but a hatred all the same.

Skip stopped and looked at the stairway. If the man was waiting there still, Skip just hoped he'd take the time to see which boy he had before he sliced his neck with that knife and threw him overboard. To be killed was one thing, but to be killed because of mistaken identity was something else indeed.

He ripped the cap off his head and held it in his hands. Jack's hair was black with curls, and his was blond, almost white, and straight as a board. Surely the man could see that, at least see it before he used that knife of his. He hoped so.

He glided toward the stairway. He couldn't feel his feet move, they did it almost on their own, but he knew they were moving, all the same. Approaching the stairway, he took a deep breath and rushed to the other side. He glanced up the stairs as he scooted by them, just in case. They were empty, empty and bare.

Getting to the privy, he cranked open the brass handle and stepped inside. For a long while he stared at his face in the mirror. He pumped on the brass handle and filled the bowl with cold water. Slipping both hands under the drawn water, he splashed it on his face, rubbing it into his stark-white features.

He blinked and leaned into the mirror for a better look. Two large brown eyes the shape of peeled plums stared right back at him. They were his, all right. His father had always said that he got them from his mother. He could only guess the blond hair to be from his father and, of course, from his grandfather on his mother's side.

His face was filled with fright, a fear that just didn't belong inside of anybody, especially someone like him. He wouldn't grow up that way, not if he could help it. He'd fight for the middle, just like Aristotle said. He wasn't bound to be foolish like Jack. Such foolishness could never carry anybody past the age of sixteen, not in this day and time. Of course, he didn't want to live to be an old man cowering in the corner, either. Zac had always said that he had nothing against a man being scared as long as he did what he knew needed to be done when the time came. Skip just had to make sure that when that time came for him, he would still be there, still be there doing what needed to be done.

When he finished his business, he stepped out once again into the foggy air. It was warm, a foggy covering from the cold stars above, the cold stars he couldn't see.

He could barely make out the branches of trees as the steamer chugged by them. They were like ghostly hands reaching out with a warning to him, a warning he would pay no nevermind to. He drew himself up straight to face them, once again turning his collar up. If that man was going to slice on his neck, he'd give him something else to have to cut through.

Maybe he'd already done enough to move to the middle. It didn't much feel like the middle to him, but maybe he had. There was one thing more he should do, something that scared him worse than anything he could think of at the moment. He didn't much know if he was ready for that just yet. Maybe he'd never be ready. He'd shake the feeling and then perhaps forget it. Drawing himself to his full height, he moved off toward the bow of the paddle-wheeler.

The latticework on the front of the boat was a bright red color, blood red. Normally he'd have called it a cherry, but tonight it looked blood red to him. There was nobody on the lower deck tonight. Maybe they were all gambling. 'Course, it might just be late enough that they were asleep. Overhead, he could hear several people talking. It was comforting to hear voices. Maybe they'd hear him scream, if he had the time. He could barely make out what was being said, but it didn't much matter. Just then and there the sound of a voice, any human voice, seemed like music to his ears, sweet music.

He stood on the bow of the boat, watching it cut through the deep, dark water. The sight of the churning was strangely comforting to him. It was as if something new were coming up from below, something fresh and clean. Just watching the water brought a strange and serene sense of peace to him.

Turning around, he looked up. He could see the dark smokestacks, and he knew the pilothouse, the place where Zac said he was going, sat slightly behind and in the middle of both of them, even though it was out of view from here. Out of the dark massive pipes, sparks spewed upward, followed by an occasional breath of flame.

On the top deck, he could see the faint glow of a cigar. Someone stood up there, perhaps watching him even now. It wasn't Zac and his pipe, and he didn't figure it could be McCauliff. That man would still be gambling, gambling or prowling the decks in search of him and Jack. Still, Zac was up there somewhere. That gave him at least a pause of comfort. Zac had always said there were angels looking out over him. He only hoped them angel critters could see through this fog.

He moved casually back in the direction he had come, determined to stroll past the stairway where Jack had met the man. He could do it. It didn't frighten him anymore. Maybe he was in the middle now, after all. Still, he would have felt a right smart better if the Chinaman were still there. Moving with slow deliberation, he walked past the windows, never looking, never bothering to speed up. If he was to be seen, he didn't want to be seen as a frightened little boy.

As he moved closer to the stern, nearer their cabin, he knew there was one more place he had to go. It was the thing he dreaded more than anything else. If he could face that fear, then he'd be in the middle. It was foolish and he knew it. It offered no risk to him, except for what he felt on the inside. He didn't even know the boy. There would be nothing that Robbie could tell him, even if he asked. Maybe it was just the thought of someone his age cold and dead, someone lying by himself so close by. Somehow Robbie made him feel his own sense of mortality for the first time. He could die too. Was he really ready for that?

He wanted to just walk up to the boy and stand there like a man, but his feet wouldn't listen to his wants, not just yet. He stood next to the edge of the row of cabins and looked back at the churning paddle. Looking off to his left, he could see the dim light in his own cabin. Jack would be there waiting for him. He'd done enough already. He was already closer to the middle than he had been in a long while. If he just went back to the cabin and on back to bed, nobody would know the difference.

He bowed his head and gritted his teeth. He'd know. He'd try to close his eyes, but he'd know all the same. Shoot fire! A body just couldn't come so close to the middle and then off and turn around and just run back to the edge. He'd need to go all the way to the middle. He knew that.

He moved each foot in a deliberate manner, one small step at a time. It took him some time, some time of clearheaded thinking, before he stood close to the body. Robbie was there, all right. He knew enough about what his own father had said and about what Zac had told him many a time to know that it wasn't Robbie any longer. It was just a shell that Robbie used to live in. But he was there, all right. Skip could feel it. He dropped to his knees beside the wrapped corpse.

"Robbie, it's me, Skip. You don't know me, but I know you . . ."

Large drivers painted white, driven by the big pistons stroking below, kept the turn of the paddle steady, kicking up the water as the big boat moved up the river. Overhead, orange-glowing cinders floated past him, belched into the darkness and dense fog from the smokestack.

Skip reached ever so carefully for the tarp that covered the boy. Skip's hands shook like leaves on the wispy trees in the fall, shaking and sweating at the same time. Lifting the flap that lay under Robbie's head, he flipped it over, revealing the dead boy's pale, drawn face. His heart raced. He knew there was no cause for that. He didn't believe in ghosts and such, and he sure didn't believe the dead boy could talk as Jack said Robbie had done to him.

He studied the face carefully. There were dreams locked up there, dreams Robbie still seemed to be dreaming. His face had been washed by the men who wrapped him up, but there was still a smudge one of the men had left on his cheek. He had heard before that a body needed to have coins placed on the eyes to keep them shut. It hadn't been done. Maybe Robbie's eyes would open all of a sudden, open and stare right at him. The thought sent his heart beating rapidly.

Fishing around in his pocket, he located two nickels. It was the money Zac had given him for the trip to buy whatever fetched his fancy. He hadn't dared to leave them in the cabin for Jack to find. He looked at the coins thoughtfully, then reached over and laid them on Robbie's eyes. They sparkled, even in the faint light on deck.

"I done all I could for you," Skip said. "I am powerful sorry for what's happened. It don't seem right. I suppose I can only promise you that I'll do my best to see that Jack don't turn up this way."

The only sound that came back to him was the cascading water from the red paddles as they turned in the river. A light spray blew up, sending a mist over both of them. Skip laid the tarp back over Robbie's face. He had done what he'd set out to do, move to the middle. A man had to face what scared him, face it and stand still. Skip got to his feet.

He put his cap back on his head. "We'll see you get yerself buried proper," he said. Shrugging his shoulders, he turned to go to the cabin. He ran right into McCauliff.

The man grabbed him by the shoulders and lifted him up. "Here, here, what are you doing out here with that dead boy? You trying to find something to steal?"

Skip could smell the man, lilac water mixed with stale tobacco smoke and liquor. "N-n-n-no, sir. I w-w-w-was just payin' my respects, is all."

The man held him up, dangling his feet over the deck. "Your respects? That boy is way past you respecting him. I think you're just itching to wind up just like him."

"No, sir, I ain't."

"Well, you is going to do just that. I can see to that my ownself. You'll find yourself floating downstream as fish food, nothing left to bury."

"Please, mister, just let me go." Skip's heart was pounding. "I wasn't doing nothin', just going to the privy and lookin' after Robbie, that's all."

The man lowered him to the deck. Reaching to his belt, he drew out a big knife. The huge blade glinted in the faint light. It shined like nothing Skip had ever seen before. His eyes were fixed on the thing, and his body turned stone still.

"You ever seen what one of these things can do?"

Skip shook his head.

"I've disemboweled a grown man on a gambling table with this in my day, blood and gore flying every which way. A boy wouldn't take no time at all." The man smiled. "No, I'd have you quartered up like a side of beef too quick to talk about."

The man moved toward him, and Skip tripped over Robbie's body, spilling himself near the edge of the big paddle wheel. He could feel the breeze of the churning water below. Looking straight up, he watched the big paddles come down. They seemed to be heading right for him; they were so close. Scrambling to his feet, he weaved on the edge of the fantail.

"Is there a problem here?"

Zac's voice was the sweetest music Skip had ever heard.

McCauliff deftly put the Bowie knife back into his belt. He grinned and turned around. "No problem, Cobb. I just caught this boy here trying to loot the dead. Figured I'd teach him a lesson."

Skip stepped over Robbie and fairly ran to Zac. He stood close to him, his arms around Zac's waist.

"Well, this boy, as you call him, is my son. If there are lessons to be taught, I'll do the teaching."

"I was just payin' my respects, is all," Skip said. "I had to use the privy too."

McCauliff dropped his hands to his side. He smiled. "Well, you know how mischievous boys can be. Some will steal anything that's not tied down."

"Not my son," Zac said.

"Well, you're the best judge of that, I suppose. I just figured to scare the boy."

Zac looked down at Skip. It was a knowing look, the kind that Skip had seen many times before. He put his hand on Skip's head. "We'd best get back to our cabin and get some sleep before morning, don't you think?"

"Yes, sir."

Looking back at McCauliff, Zac spoke in a menacing tone. "I'm afraid my son here doesn't scare so easy. If he did, he wouldn't be out here. I'd suggest, too, that if you really want to practice scaring people, you start with me. It would be interesting to see what you do with people your own size."

CHAPTER 10

+ + + + + + +

IT WAS THE PEEPING OF THE BIRDS that first popped Dr. Page's eyes open. He listened silently for a moment, then made out the sound of whispers and knew they had slept too late. The haze of the fog carried with it the faint glow of the morning light. Nudging Mary awake, he stared into her eyes, trying to communicate his concern without speaking. Mary blinked and then listened.

Outside the wagon, they heard the sound of excited whispers. They couldn't make out any of the words spoken, but it was obvious that the Chinese couple they had heard the night before had found their sleeping arrangements.

Cautiously, the doctor raised his head. The older Chinese man held out the shotgun and shouted. Dr. Page raised his hands and slowly got to his feet. Even in soiled and disheveled clothes, he was a striking figure of respectability. His graying hair, parted down the middle, set off a high forehead. His eyes were clear, brown, and steady. His long gray mustache stood out, giving him a look of passive charm.

The old man with the shotgun waggled the weapon and shouted.

Dr. Page helped Mary to her feet. Bits of straw stuck to her raven locks. She held her hands by her side. Gingerly, they climbed out of the wagon.

"I'm sorry," Dr. Page said. "We stopped here to sleep. We've taken nothing."

"Why you here?"

"We were kidnapped," Mary spat out.

"Kidnapped?"

"Yes, men took us out of our buggy by force," Dr. Page said. "We are trying to return to our home in Sacramento."

The older woman pulled on her husband's shoulder and whispered in his ear.

He looked back at the two travelers and almost apologetically asked, "You got money?"

"I think I have some money in my shoe." Dr. Page pulled off his left shoe and, reaching into it, produced several small bills. "Our money was taken. I had this for an emergency. We were hoping to buy food with it."

The woman once again whispered to her husband. He turned and, continuing to point the shotgun, spoke in halting English. "You pay for sleeping here and we feed you. You pay five dollar."

"Five dollars," Dr. Page gasped. He counted out five one dollar bills. That left him with a five and a ten. He handed the money over to the man. "Can we get down now? We are hungry. We appreciate the offer of food."

Minutes later, the two of them found themselves seated at a rickety dining room table. The older man watched them, the shotgun still on his lap, while his wife fried up a mixture of ham and eggs. She poured the two of them some hot tea.

"Thank you," Mary said. "This is most kind of you."

"God will reward you," Dr. Page joined in. "Can you tell us if there is a town nearby?"

The old man shook his head. "No town close. Walnut Grove north. It long walk for you. Big house near here. It down the road. Rich man live there. He may help you, help you find your people."

"Do you hear that, child? If there is a man of means that lives nearby, I'm certain he will extend us every courtesy. Thank you, sir, I'm sure that will prove to be most helpful."

When the two of them had finished their modest breakfast and received the old man's best directions, they set off across the misty orchards. The arms of the pear trees reached out from the gauzy air, their gnarled branches with knobs of worn wood seeming to stare at the two strangers that didn't belong. They both felt out of place, lost in the maze of the orchards. From the directions the Chinese man had given them, they knew they didn't have far to walk. If they could find shelter, someplace where they could remain out of sight for a little longer, then they could find a way back home.

It was over an hour later when they found the road. The path was well worn, the obvious result of heavy wagon traffic. The two of them walked along the road in the direction the old man had pointed out to them. They took care to listen for the sound of horses, making sure there was a place in the overgrowth along the river where they could quickly hide.

They soon spotted the big house. Palms had been planted along the drive that led up to the house, and on either side of it stood spiraling evergreen trees, their well-manicured tips reaching far above the third story of the structure. The tile roof of the massive house angled down and set off rows of windows on either side of the ornate cannonaded entryway. The windows were surrounded by ornate iron railings, circling balconies that overlooked the river's edge. A long balcony sat inside the first row of columns that dotted the front of the building. Below it, polished stairs rose majestically to a massive set of carved double doors.

Dr. Page and Mary climbed the stairs. The doctor lifted the polished brass door knocker and pounded on the door.

Moments later, the door cracked open and a smallish black man stared up at the two of them.

"Pardon our intrusion," Dr. Page said, "but my niece and I are lost and on foot. I wonder if you might be able to help us."

"Is Mr. Robert Blevins 'spectin' you folks?"

"No, indeed not. But I do believe he'd want to help us."

"Mr. Blevins is gone just now. We're awaitin' his return shortly."

"Fine," Dr. Page said. "Might my niece and I wait for him inside?"

The little man opened the door, and the doctor and Mary both wiped their feet before stepping inside. The butler pointed to a small settee near the window. "Y'all folk set yerselves down there. I'll run down and get Aunt Mamie. She's Mr. Blevins's aunt."

Gratefully, they sat on the red velvet cushions. The foyer of the house was a roomy hall with marble flooring. Intricate Persian rugs, red with blue and gold, covered the floor. The doors and windows were of dark walnut, the perfect contrast to the cream-colored walls with their carved designs. Brass sconces flickered on the walls, each with a setting of numerous candles behind them. There was a stately elegance to the house. Nothing had been overlooked.

From the stairs below, they could hear the approach of a woman as she stomped up each step. "Mercy me, visitors at The Glades." They could hear her clearly. They looked at each other. Obviously, she had no idea that her voice carried so well up the marble stairs. "Visitors at The Glades, now I do declare. I am not prepared. I am not the least prepared."

As the woman climbed up the last flight of stairs, Dr. Page and

Mary got to their feet. The woman had white hair, pulled tightly around the back of her head. Her cheeks were rosy and full, with a double chin beneath them. Her broad shoulders showed her to be a woman of rather ample proportions. She swung her hips and seemed to be breathing heavily as she climbed the last of the stairs . "Mercy me"—she waved a handkerchief at her drooping yet heavily painted mouth—"those stairs are going to be the death of me yet."

Dr. Page stepped forward. "We are so sorry for intruding on your privacy. I am Dr. William Page of Sacramento, and this is my niece, Mary."

The woman held the lace hanky to her mouth and coughed into it. She then held out her hand, obviously expecting the doctor to kiss it. He did. "Charmed," she said. "Did you say you were a doctor, sir?"

"Yes, madam."

"I fear I shall need you and soon if I have to walk up those stairs once more today. And how did you come upon us here at The Glades, if it wasn't for the good Lord's mercy in bringing you to rescue little old me?"

"I'm afraid my niece and I were kidnapped by hooligans yesterday. We escaped them last night."

The woman gasped, feeling for a chair. "Mercy me, kidnappers! Here in California." She plunked herself down in the richly carved but seemingly uncomfortable chair. "Decent people can never feel safe."

The doctor looked down at his clothes and then at Mary. "I am afraid we are somewhat the worse for wear, what with sleeping out last night in a field."

"Mercy me, and with you a man of medicine. Robert shall hear of this." She waved the hanky in Page's direction. "My nephew is a man of some importance and means. When he hears of these ruffians and what they attempted to do to you, he will simply scour the countryside until he brings these rascals to justice."

"That would be wonderful," Mary chimed in.

"I'm afraid what my niece and I need most at the moment are some clean clothes and a little rest," Dr. Page said. "We've had some hard travel. We also need to get back to Sacramento."

"Of course. The servants can see to some new apparel for the two of you and find you beds to sleep on. I should feel perfectly horrid if you didn't enjoy the best hospitality that The Glades has to offer. I'm afraid we don't receive many guests other than Robert's business associates." She waved the handkerchief in her face, once again panting. "I have been used to much more of a social life back in Maryland, you understand."

The doctor nodded.

"Kidnappers! Well I never!"

"They were pirates," Mary added.

The doctor shot her a quick look and shook his head. He had no desire to tip their hand about who had taken them, certainly not with the warning they had received.

"Pirates! Mercy me. I shouldn't think there would be pirates here in California."

"Perhaps my niece misspoke. These ruffians were simply bandits bent on robbing us and holding us for ransom."

"Oh dear!" The woman collapsed back into the hard chair and continued to wave her handkerchief. "How can I ever take to leaving the house with such people in our midst. Robert simply must deal with them. We will report this to the sheriff, but Robert will want to bring these people to justice himself. Mercy me, pirates attacking house guests of The Glades."

Mary stepped forward. "You are so kind to take us into your lovely home. I hope we won't be a bother to you."

"Why no, child." The woman waved her handkerchief at Mary like a flag desperately signaling for a truce. "You just gave Aunt Mamie a start"—she tapped on her chest—"that's all. Mercy me, what will we ever do about pirates in California?"

Several servants materialized out of the dining room.

"Take these nice people who have suffered greatly to the guest rooms. You will need to draw them baths and wash their clothes. You must also find them some nice dinner clothing, something suitable for The Glades." She turned to Mary. "I think I should like for you to have something especially attractive, child. My nephew is a bachelor." She smiled. "We will send for you both at dinnertime. Robert will be home then and will want to know just all about your harrowing experience."

\+ + + + +

The blast of the railroad whistle sounded out the window of the big boat's dining room, where Zac, Jenny, and the boys were having breakfast. "It's exciting here, isn't it, boys?" Jenny asked.

"Sure is," Jack said. "I ain't rightly ever made it out of Oakland." He continued to cram the pancakes into his mouth, wiping the syrup off with the back of his sleeve.

"I should think that we will need to shop for you today, Jack," Jenny said.

"There is something we've got to do first," Zac responded. "We need to find an undertaker for that boy."

"You ain't a gonna bury him?" Jack asked.

"No, just get him ready for it. We're taking him back to Oakland on the return. We'll find his folks and a place over there."

"He ain't got himself much in the way of folks," Jack said. "Just me, I reckon."

"Well, we'll find what he does have."

Jack put down his fork. "I guess I don't rightly understand why you is doing this for somebody you don't even know."

Zac was matter-of-fact. "We're just applying the Golden Rule. We're doing for him what we'd have wanted somebody to do for us."

"Sounds like Bible stuff."

"It is," Jenny replied.

"Guess there's more to that, then, than just stories."

"Yes," Jenny said, "there is, a great deal more. If you read it and try to apply what it says, you can negotiate life in a much more pleasant manner."

"It says not to steal," Skip remarked. He gave out the words in a hard manner, his face looking like chiseled stone.

Zac put his hand on Skip's shoulder. "I guess we all learn lessons about that, don't we?"

Skip dropped his chin and cut another bite of pancake.

"Do you think we'll see Hattie this morning?" Jenny asked.

Zac smiled and nodded in the direction of the window. "I 'spect we will. That's her come lookin' for us now."

They all stared out the window at a gray-haired woman stomping up the gangway. She wore a beaten hat pulled down around her ears and a gingham dress that was much too large, cinched by a leather belt. The belt sported a holster, and a gleaming knife was stuck underneath the buckle. She took big, bold steps up the gangway in a pair of black hobnailed boots. It was plain to see, even from a distance, that she had a large plug of tobacco bulging in her cheek.

Minutes later, she was sashaying through the tables in the dining room, drawing a bead on the four of them with her black, darting eyes.

Zac rose to his feet, pulling Skip up with him.

"Glory be, it's that handsome nephew of mine," she cackled in a raspy voice. "It's a fine day when I gets to come visit y'all folks and goes to the big city, to boot."

"This is Skip," Zac said. "The one I wrote you about."

Hattie reached down and grabbed Skip by the shoulders. She shook him. "Boy, you is a fine sight too, and yer gonna be a handsome devil." She smiled and, pulling up a chair from the table next to theirs, sat down beside Jenny. "Girl, let me just look on you fer a minute. Mmm—mumph. You is just as fine a charge of dynamite as a man ever looked on." She held up Jenny's hands. "Why hasn't that no-count nephew of mine ain't put a ring on one a these here fingers yet?" She shot Zac a look. "Guess he's not only stupefied, he's blind too."

Zac motioned to Jack. "This is Jack, Hattie. We picked him up on the bay, and we're taking him back to Oakland."

Jack had been eyeing the necklace the woman wore. He'd never seen so much gold.

"Pleased to make yer acquaintance, boy. But if yer a hankering to pick up a good time here in Old Sac, you better stick with Aunt Hat. That nephew of mine will have you in the library all day."

She reached out and grabbed a passing waiter by the shirttail, almost spilling the tray the man was carrying. "Listen here, sonny, you bring me some biscuits and a fresh pot a coffee. Make it hot and make it quick."

The man put down his tray and scampered back in the direction of the kitchen. Hattie turned once again to Jenny. "When a body like me gets to be an old gal, she ain't got her looks to make men move anymore." Hattie leaned forward. "So you just gotter be a whole lot tougher." Picking up an empty coffee cup, she spat her chaw into it and wiped her mouth with the back of her hand. When she smiled, her crooked teeth gave off the dull brown luster of the tobacco. "And I ain't found many that I ain't a whole lots tougher than."

When they had finished their breakfast, Zac rose from the table. "I had better be heading on down to the Wells Fargo office to make arrangements for this shipment. We leave tomorrow morning."

"Boy, you don't leave a gal much time to get a good drunk goin'," Hattie said.

"Now, Hat, I thought you had changed your ways. I didn't know you were still hoorawin' towns."

"Well, I don't get blind stupefied drunk like I used to, and I ain't rightly had me a fight in quite some time."

Zac looked down at the chain around the woman's neck. It was gold with several large nuggets dangling from it. "I'd say if you keep wearing that thing, you're bound to get the trouble you want."

"Well, good! I wears it to get good service, and if'n there be anybody foolish enough to try to take it offa me, then there's gonna be plenty a blood on the street, and it ain't gonna be none of mine neither."

Zac smiled at the group. "You greenhorns shouldn't have any trouble today with Hat beside you. I'll plan on meeting you all here on the boat for dinner, if I don't see you before that." He looked at Jenny. "Try to keep her almost sober. She does like the stuff from Kentucky whenever she gets into a town like this."

Skip got to his feet. "Can I go with you?"

"No, son, you've got trouble enough of your own to look after."

Skip shot a glance back at Jack.

Zac put his hand on Skip's shoulder. "I've got business that would just bore you. You just go and see the sights with these folks here. I'm depending on you." He knew the boy just wanted to be with him. He could see it in Skip's eyes. But from what he'd seen of Jack, he knew full well that Jenny and Hat would need his help.

He looked at the confident Hattie, the only one who seemed to know her way around the docks and one few would care to tangle with. "You best watch out for these boys," he said. "They are a handful. Before you know it, they'll turn out to be the toughest litter you ever tangled with."

The old woman spit out a stream of brown spittle into a half-empty coffee cup and wiped her mouth with the back of her gnarled hand. "You watch out fer them roughnecks out there," Hattie said.

Zac reached down and picked up the sawed-off shotgun.

"Why am I tellin' you that fer?" she sputtered. "They'ze the ones that ought to be lookin' out for you."

PART 2

THE HEIST

CHAPTER 11

MANNY ROLLED OUT OF HIS BUNK and rubbed his stubbled face hard. The black beard wasn't anything he'd planned, it just sort of happened. He didn't always take great care with his face, but he loved his clothes. There was something about bright clothing, the way they made him stand out from all the rest, that he admired about himself. He slowly got to his feet and shuffled his brown pants onto his muscular legs. Picking up each brightly polished boot, he stomped them on. He picked the red shirt off his bedpost and, putting it on, walked to the mirror. Blinking at his face, he pumped a basin full of water. He took out his straight razor and opened the gleaming blade. Applying water and soap, he began to rake away the whiskers.

As he pulled the razor over his face, he began to wonder why he'd let the man and his niece go. The thought of disobeying the colonel sent shivers up his spine. He had seen the man take his revenge on men that dared to cross him. It wasn't a pretty sight. Princeton would cross any boundary to maintain trust and discipline. He had watched men being carved up alive, and Manny wanted no part of any punishment Colonel Princeton might be inclined to dish out.

There had been something about those two people that had seemed to compel him; perhaps it was the innocence they possessed. He had killed men before, but seldom the truly innocent. And the woman, what a sight she had been; her jet black hair and dark eyes had taken him by surprise. He'd noticed her right off when the men that brought her to Princeton had pushed her and her uncle forward in the mud. He was only happy that the men had crossed the colonel; otherwise, they might have been given the assignment to kill them and sink the bodies. He knew that if that had happened, he wouldn't have gotten a good night's sleep. As it was, in spite of his disobedience, he'd slept like a baby.

He slid the shiny, black-handled razor upward, along his thick neck, keeping the shave dangerously close. Maybe that was his problem, after all. He liked to live life much too close to the edge. As he wiped what remained of the soap from his face, he smiled at what he saw. Maybe that was the reason for the shave—the memory of the woman. He only wished he had looked better for her yesterday. Pulling the orange silk scarf from his pocket, he looped it over his neck and tied a secure knot.

One of the men burst into the still-buzzing bunkhouse and began to shake the men awake. He was surprised to see Manny already up and looking so clean. "The colonel wants to see you right away."

The tone of the night guard's voice made Manny stand all the more erect. "All right, I'm goin'." He sounded matter-of-fact, but the feelings he carried were anything but that. He picked up his Russian .44 and stuck it in his belt, along with his knife. Picking up the green sash he wanted, he looped it around his waist and straightened it. If he was going to die, he wanted to look his best.

Moments later, he walked into the house. He could smell the colonel's coffee, something he wanted rather badly right now. He'd know the mood of the man if it was offered.

Princeton was at his desk, along with two other men from the pirate cadre. Manny nodded at Hector and Adams. Princeton picked his head up and pointed to the coffee on the potbellied stove. "Help yourself, Manny. I'm going to need you again today." The words made him relax.

"Come over here and look at this map," Princeton said.

Manny edged his way to the colonel's side, coffee cup in hand. "I want you three riding fast for Sacramento today. You will be on the *Delta King* when it leaves in the morning."

He lifted his head and looked at Manny. "You're in charge," he said. "I'll have a diversion planned at Walnut Grove, but with soldiers on board we can't rightly count on them leaving the shipment. That's where you three come in. I want them dead, you follow me?"

Manny nodded his head. "We taking the *King* there?"

"Yes, I'll have enough men waiting there to take the boat, provided we get everyone off, but you leave that to me. We'll take the *King* there and then run it aground on Decker Island. After that, we'll move to our place on Medford Island. It's far enough away to make finding us a matter of weeks at best. By then, we'll be gone.

We can't rightly stay here. It's much too close and uncomfortably near to Blevins's big house to make him sleep well at night."

Manny grinned. Robert Blevins wanted all the rewards of what they did, but he didn't ever want his hands getting dirty.

Princeton got to his feet, a deep smile of satisfaction on his lips. "Gentlemen, this heist will make us all rich men. And we will be striking a blow at the Yankee soldiers right where it hurts them most, in their wallets." He looked Manny in the eye. "I don't want even one of them yellow bellies still breathing when we come aboard, am I understood?"

"Yes, sir."

Princeton put his hand on Manny's shoulder. "Fine. I know I can count on you, Manny. You've never failed me yet."

Russ Korth, a tall, lanky blonde, walked through the front door. The man was poison and Manny knew it.

"I'm here," he said. His blue eyes glinted at Manny like a beacon in the night. "I can see you're wearing your usual plumage and shaved too."

Princeton cast a glance at Manny. He hadn't noticed the close shave, although it was all too obvious.

Korth smirked at Manny from across the desk. "You got yourself a woman somewhere we don't know about, somebody you been giving pillow talk to?"

"You know better than that," Manny shot back. "Just keep that tongue of yours inside your head before I cut it off." Manny had never liked the man. Korth always seemed to have eyes in the back of his head and was quick to make judgments. Korth's sharp mind endeared him to Princeton, but his tongue had always been his undoing. There was one thing, though, that Manny knew Princeton appreciated above all—Korth's aim was without equal, and he was as fast as a rattler. Princeton had spotted him right off.

"Korth will be with me in Walnut Grove. We have to be ready there, just in case that agent Blevins told us about gets off the boat. Although, I have plans that will make it likely he'll never get on the *King* tonight."

"You do?" Manny asked. "How do you propose to do that?"

Princeton looked smug. He was a planner, always thinking ahead. "I have some very good men preparing a special Sacramento welcome for our Mr. Zachary Cobb. If they succeed, you won't have to worry about him being on board the *King*."

Manny knew that whatever Princeton had prepared could be counted on. He had seen the man pore over that ledger of his, separating every item taken in a hijacking. The colonel knew the worth of a thing on the open market too. Blevins would keep him abreast of all the latest sales figures in San Francisco. "Particular." That's what Manny would call the colonel, "particular." He liked no loose ends in anything he did. It was why he had asked Manny to deal with the doctor and his niece—no loose ends, no questions. "And if they don't take care of Cobb?" Manny asked.

Princeton walked over to the coffeepot. He poured himself a cup and held it to his lips. Eyeing the three pirates, he sipped it slowly. "I have a man on board the *King*." He smiled.

Manny had seen the colonel's knowing smile before. All the planning he did made surprises something that happened to the other fella, not to him.

"Well, maybe the use of the word 'man' is too strong," Princeton went on. "He's someone, however, who can get close to Cobb and the guards on board that boat, someone they'd never suspect. He can do what you can only imagine to render those people incapable of responding. If Cobb doesn't make it on the boat, he will have it all the more smooth for himself with just the army guards."

"How will we know him?" Manny asked.

"You won't need to know him. I wouldn't want you boys giving off any kind of signal that could disclose our agent there. You won't know him, but he will know you."

"You only know what you need to know," Korth chimed in.

Manny despised the man's attitude. For all he knew Korth didn't have any more of an idea of the colonel's plans than he did. The man was shot full of bragging. He always was in search of an edge, anything that might unnerve a potential opponent, and right now it was plain to see that he viewed Manny as just that.

"I've heard things about this Cobb fella," Manny said. "He swings a wide noose. From what I've heard, those people in Sacramento and the fella you got on the *King* will have their hands full."

"Then, Korth and I, along with the whole crew, will be waiting in Walnut Grove."

Manny grinned. His eyes blazed into Russ Korth's. "Korth here is plenty good for most, but maybe this time it's not near good enough."

* * * * *

Zac strode boldly down the boardwalk of the dock. He carried the mini-scatter-gun under one arm and marched in the direction of the red-brick building with the green sign that read, "Wells Fargo and Company." So far everything had seemed fairly straightforward, for him, at least. The restlessness he felt had little to do with the assignment at hand. He always liked to work alone, and having Henry's problem relative to assist him, someone he would have to fight hard to ignore, didn't set well with him. It was no mystery why Henry had chosen to leave that part of the job out of the briefing he'd been given. Jenny and Skip, along with Hattie, would only further the complications of anything that might happen.

He stopped for a moment in the crowd and looked into one of the shop windows, admiring a blue bonnet that sat atop a block of wood. Window-shopping was something that was totally foreign to him, a thing he could have never imagined doing. He couldn't help but wonder how Jenny would react to him sizing the thing up for her. The ribbons were bright, just the kind of thing that would show off her eyes. He tucked the thing away in his mind. He would remember it later.

The street was busy, filled with shoppers and locals out to make a living. Sacramento was a different world from San Francisco. The rowdies that hung around the wharf of the port city were missing from the capital. People here seemed more businesslike—fewer of them were loafing about. The shop signs hung low over the walkway, and chairs dotted the front of several stores. Dogs on the street were a rare sight—they tended to bother passing horses—but here two of them were feeding from a dish left out by a shopkeeper.

Two men standing along the boardwalk caught his attention. One of them, a disheveled man in a bowler hat, looked him in the eye. He had noticed the man earlier from the gangway of the *Delta King*, a seedy sort who appeared to be too curious to suit him. The man's cut-away coat revealed a low-slung revolver, with his hand hanging loosely at his side, resting on the butt of the six-shooter.

The man standing beside him was a great deal taller and broad at the shoulders. His sandy hair drooped down beneath a crushed black cap, and he had a blank look on his face that gave the impression that he was unaware of where he was or even who he was.

Zac walked past the men, and they sauntered along behind him, keeping a careful distance. Zac stopped to look in a shop window, and both men abruptly stopped talking in hushed voices. The man in the bowler continued to glance in his direction until Zac stared right at him. Zac's withering gaze brought the man's head down, but the two of them refused to walk away.

Zac turned and continued to make his way down the boardwalk. He turned at the street corner instead of walking on to the office. If he was being followed, he wanted to know it. The security of the shipment had supposedly been a guarded secret, and if it no longer was, it was something he wanted to know. He was not that well known either, at least not to the average passerby. If these men not only knew why he was in town but also how to identify him, it meant they had good inside information. His gray confederate cavalry hat was a dead giveaway, but only if a man knew what to look for. He continued his walk, glancing back occasionally at the men. Coming to the striped pole of a barbershop, he walked through the open door and took off his hat.

The barber, a short, portly man, was bending over to sweep up the remains of a departing customer's hair. Zac hung up his coat, then placing his gray hat on top of it, he took his seat in the brass- and ivory-studded chair. The window had a view of the street that was colored by bottles of colored mixtures, each reflecting its contents onto the aged wooden floor. A polished bar stood along the wall beside several wooden chairs. Gleaming shot glasses and several liquor bottles on the bar showed that along with a shave and haircut, the man dispensed internal painkillers as well.

"Be with you in just a bit," the barber murmured.

"No rush." Zac watched the two men who had been following him pause in front of the window and then move on. It was as if they were unsure of just what to do next.

The barber took the striped apron that he used to cover his customers down from its peg on the door and shook it out. Turning back to Zac, he smiled. "You be needing a cut and shave?" the man asked.

Zac rested the shotgun on his lap. "That's right. Just want my hair lifted off my collar."

The man spread the apron over him. "Well, we can fix you up there, all right. You come in on the *King*?"

"Yes I did. Didn't sleep much either."

"Well, I shouldn't wonder about that. Never did get much shut-eye on something that wasn't standing still."

Minutes later, when the man had finished his cutting, he stirred the mug of soap into a lather. He smoothed the mixture onto Zac's face and took out his razor.

The two men who had been following Zac reappeared. They talked outside the window and then walked into the shop.

The barber waved his soapy razor at them, motioning to the two seats opposite Zac's chair. "You boys just sit yerselves down. I'll be with you directly."

"Oh, we ain't in much hurry," the man with the bowler responded. "Is we, Horace?"

"Nah, we ain't."

The man with the derby stayed on his feet. He walked over to get a closer look at the shave. "Fact is, we'd sure admire to see your work here."

"Why sure," the barber said. "I do 'em all, and I do 'em right fine, too, if I do say so myself. You won't find a cleaner, sharper razor in all of Sacramento."

The man leaned over, closer to Zac. "That thing looks mighty sharp, sure enough." He stood closer and stared.

"Back off," Zac growled.

The man's head jerked back. "I'm just looking, that's all."

"I don't care what you're doing," Zac said. "I don't much like a man comin' too close when somebody's got a razor at my throat."

The man reared back. "Well, that's mighty unfriendly. Wouldn't you call that unfriendly, Horace?"

"I sure would." The second man got to his feet and circled to Zac's left. "Mighty unfriendly." Zac watched the second man circle to his friend's side. The man had a husky build that showed him to be a formidable brawler.

The barber stood erect. "Now, gentlemen, I like to keep my customers happy. Maybe you'd both better just sit down until I finish this stranger here. Then I'd be happy to show you anything you'd like to see. You can pour yourselves a drink."

Zac's eyes narrowed at the two men. Normally, just a look from him was all it took to show a man he meant business, but it was obvious these two had their minds made up.

"We'd kinda like to see how you handle a razor on this here feller, wouldn't we, Horace?"

"Yeah, we'd like to see that mighty fine."

"And besides"—the man with the bowler gave off a toothy grin—"we don't take kindly to folks orderin' us about. When we want to see something, we generally gets our way."

"We sure does"—the man looked Zac in the eye—"lessen you wants them there arms of yours broke."

With that, both men grabbed Zac's arms, pinning him firmly in the chair. The larger man growled. "Maybe I should give this here uppity feller a shave my ownself."

The man with the bowler grabbed the razor from the barber's hand. "Why don't I take the honors on his cheek, Horace, and I'll let you do his neck."

The barber reached out and took the wrist of the man who held the razor. "Looky here, fellers, don't make me go get the marshal."

From under the apron, Zac sent a powerful kick into the groin of the larger man, staggering him and releasing his grip. Zac spun out of the chair and, using the shotgun, cracked the skull of the man with the bowler. Turning back to the stunned big man, who was bowed over in pain, he rammed the barrel of the shotgun into his forehead with a crack, dropping the man senseless to the floor. With a swift kick to the big man's head, he swung back to face the now hatless man on his knees.

Lifting the smaller man up by the lapels of his coat, he stepped over and dropped him on the top of the bar. "You interested in close shaves?" Zac asked.

Reaching back he grabbed the razor the barber had been using. The blade glistened in the sunlight, and the man on the bar fastened his gaze onto it.

"I'll go get the marshal," the bartender called out.

"Yeah, you just do that," Zac barked. He intended to get every bit of information he could out of this man, and being alone to do it suited him fine.

Turning back to the shaking man lying prone on the bar, Zac placed the blade on his stubbled cheek. "You want to see yourself a shave up close? Well, why don't we do just that." He raked the knife over the man's face, removing beard and leaving a crimson burn across his cheek. "You know, these barber razors have been known to give many a man blood poison," he growled.

The man was frozen on the bar, afraid to move an inch. His eyes met Zac's. "I never meant no harm."

"Yeah, I know. You just wanted to see a shave up close like."

Placing the blade back on the man's face, he pulled a steady stroke across his jaw. "We'll just give you a manly shave, one with no soap or water." Zac grinned, and his eyes flashed a menacing look. He wanted to make sure the man knew he wouldn't hesitate to kill him. To make a man who had been obviously sent to get him to feel fear was to make sure he would hesitate to go after Zac again. "We'll just give you a close shave that will last you awhile. Then you can go back to whatever hole it was you crawled out from and show what happens when they send a couple of children to do a man's job."

Reaching under the man's chin, Zac placed the blade on his bobbing Adam's apple. "Now, suppose you just tell me who it is you're working for."

The man stammered. "W-w-w-we ain't working for nobody."

"I'm afraid I don't much like that answer. When there's somethin' I don't care for, my hand gets real shaky like. You can never tell just what it's gonna do. You ever seen a man's throat cut?"

"No," the man moaned.

"It ain't pretty, blood everywhere. They don't die right off either. They kinda wheeze and just have to stand by and feel themselves die. Now myself, I'd never want to go thataway, but it's your call, mister. Now, who are you working for?"

The man blanched. "If I tell you, he'll kill me."

"That's a maybe. This here is a sure thing." Zac placed the blade back on the man's throat and gently pushed it down.

"All right, all right, I'll tell you. We work for the colonel, Colonel Princeton."

The marshal, gun drawn, stomped through the front door, followed by the barber. "All right," he said, "that'll be enough."

Zac relaxed his grip on the prone man on the bar. "Good thing you got here, Marshal," he said. "I was just finishing up a shave."

With that, he picked up one of the liquor bottles and pulled out the stopper. "'Course, I wouldn't want an infection to set in." He poured a stream of the amber liquid over the man's face, producing a series of bloodcurdling screams from the prone would-be assassin.

CHAPTER 12

+ + + + + + +

THE DINING ROOM OF THE MANSION was dimly lit with the faint light that managed to seep its way through the gathering fog. Arched windows laced with a spider web of clear frames gave way to larger windows that ran to the ceiling of the two-story open room. A fire blazed in the marble fireplace. Intricate designs of pale green angels in flight circled the glossy surface of the fireplace. The angelic beings seemed out of place around the lapping flames.

Dr. Page and Mary sat at the end of a long mahogany table, with gleaming white plates filled with wilted spinach and cracked crab. They drank a cranberry punch from ornate crystal goblets and began to probe the glistening red crabs. It was a feast they had hardly expected and one thrown together by their hostess at the last minute. The richness and beauty of the surroundings was also unexpected along the nearly deserted delta of the river.

"The man who owns this place must be a man of some importance," Mary said.

"I should say so," Dr. Page replied. "It takes a great deal of wealth to live this well so far from a large city. Everything must be brought in by boat."

"Did you notice the fixtures in the bath?"

"Yes, gold leaf, to be sure."

Mary laid down her fork. "Oh, Uncle, I just want to go home. No matter what they have in mind to treat us to here, a buggy with a horse pointed north is all I want to see."

"I understand, child."

The stillness of the meal was broken by the sound of the old woman stomping down the hall. Wherever Mamie went, the sound of her shoes and the constant screeching of her voice announced her presence long before she arrived. She had a habit of beginning her conversation as soon as the thought entered her head, regardless of whether or not the intended victim was within her eye contact. "Mercy me, oh mercy me, I do hope you've rested enough to digest your food, simple though it is."

The clatter of the woman's buttoned shoes echoed down the hall, and Dr. Page rose to greet her before she entered the room.

"Oh, mercy me, you poor dears. I shan't rest until those awful pirates are safely locked away. Pirates, here in The Glades, whatever shall we do? Whatever shall we do?"

The woman sashayed into the room, waving her lace handkerchief like a flag of truce before her. She had changed into an emerald green ball gown, with lace embroidery around the collar and at the cuffs. A pearl-colored cameo gleamed on the bodice of the gown, and her face was caked with powder. Her perfume alone would have told them of her presence even if she had been able to remain silent.

Dr. Page dropped his napkin onto the table and bowed slightly at the waist.

"Please, please, please, be seated. I won't have your meal disturbed." Clamping the lace to her mouth, she continued in muffled despair, "This is California. It is supposed to be a civilized place." She shook her head and dabbed the lace doily over her mouth, discoloring it with a mixture of red lip paint and pink powder. "Please sit down, Doctor, and finish your meal. I heard my nephew's carriage just moments ago. He shouldn't be much longer. I know he'll want to hear all about your ordeal. Oh, mercy me, whatever shall we do."

"I am sorry that we are being a bother to you, Miss Mamie," Dr. Page said. "All my niece and I require is some way to get to the railroad or a boat that is traveling to Sacramento."

"This is such awful treatment to show to a man of medicine," she went on. "Refined people should be protected by the law. Crime belongs to the Chinese and the darkies in the streets, not to decent people."

"I'm afraid crime affects us all," Dr. Page inserted.

"And you, dear girl, to subject a lady of obvious refinement to men in the darkness, why I never. I am a lady of Maryland myself. Even when the ruffians in Butternut came marching through on their way to Gettysburg, there were never any violations of the decent folk. They took the chickens, but would never think of taking advantage of a woman."

"Well, I wouldn't know about that," Mary responded. "The leader of this group wore a gray uniform."

Dr. Page slipped his hand onto Mary's and squeezed it.

"A gray uniform? Are you sure about that, my dear?"

"To tell the truth," Dr. Page interjected, "I don't think there's much about those people we could remember. They took us close to twilight. They all appeared to be dirty and with rags for clothing."

"Well, I should think so, merciless thugs, I'm sure." The old woman picked up a small brass bell and rattled it. "I shan't hear of you leaving The Glades, Doctor, not until we have had the opportunity to make amends for the ruffians you encountered and the ordeal they've put you through. You will need to rest for a while, rest and have some food."

She continued to ring the bell and stepped around the table toward Mary. Reaching out she patted Mary's cheek. "Such a sweet thing, too, and so very pretty. My nephew is a bachelor, you realize. I can't have you leave until he has come to see and know how beautiful and refined you truly are."

"I'm afraid right now, I'd feel ever more comfortable in my own home," Mary said.

"Yes, my niece has had quite a fright, I'm afraid."

"I know she has, poor, poor dear."

"Oh, I think I've grown quite a bit tougher in the last day or so. It's amazing what a woman can do when she fights for survival."

The old woman began to pound on her chest with the lace doily. "Why, mercy me, sakes alive, child, I just don't know what I would do with a group of rough men like you encountered. Oh dear, oh dear me, it makes me grow weak and faint at the mere thought of such a thing."

A slow-moving servant appeared at the door, and Mamie screeched orders, "See that you bring some fresh bread for these good people, Soggy. I shan't have them go without anything. I want the finest wine we have for dinner as well. Now, you see to it, do you hear?"

The man bowed. "Yes'm, I will." Turning, he walked back toward the kitchen.

The old woman began to pace nervously back and forth in the large dining room, watching the servant leave and waving her hanky with each word spoken. She slung the doily in the direction of the departing servant. "We call him Soggy. If you should need anything during your stay at The Glades, he can see to it at once."

"We're quite used to doing for ourselves," Mary said.

"I'm sure you are, child, the helpless dependent of a man of medicine. I wouldn't hear of such a thing however, not at The Glades."

Mary muttered to her uncle under her breath. "I'm not helpless, and I'm not a china doll to be dusted and admired."

"We slept in the back of a wagon last night," the doctor spoke up. "Anything you have would be a vast improvement."

"Oh, dear me."

The old woman's show was quite enough to make both Mary and the doctor uncomfortable. This doting dowager of an East Coast family appeared to be helpless beyond belief when it came to the process of complicated thought.

Moments later, the old man came back through the door with a breadboard filled with steaming seeded rolls and a plate of fresh butter, ornately carved into the shape of a swan.

"Please, help yourself," Mamie said. "Soggy, see to it that my nephew comes here to the dining room right away—right away, you understand?"

"Yes ma'am, I surely will."

The two of them continued to eat their crab and listen politely. Listening to Mamie was an exercise in patience. The minutes seemed to crawl by like hours as she discussed the Blevins family heritage and story after story of any slight she or her family may have suffered since the age of ten. It was a welcome relief to hear the boots of what they could only surmise to be the master of the house down the hall.

Mamie shot to her feet and made her way to the door, signaling with the lace hanky in a circular motion. "Robert, come here quickly, dear. We have guests, and they have had a harrowing experience that you must hear about."

The short, rotund man with a close-cropped beard stepped into the room. His dark eyes sparkled, and the wine-colored jacket he wore set off a gleaming white shirt. Tight tan riding pants were tucked snugly into polished black boots. A brace of ivory-butted pistols stood out from ornately carved holsters at his side. Moving immediately to the doctor, who had stood as he entered the room, he extended his hand. "Welcome to The Glades," he said. "I am Robert Blevins."

"Dr. William Page, and this is my niece, Mary."

Blevins moved from the handshake to where Mary sat; taking her hand and bowing slightly, he kissed it gently. "Charmed," he said.

"Robert, these good people have been set upon by pirates—pirates, right here on our river!"

Blevins's eyes narrowed. "Is that so?" he asked.

"Pirates is too strong of a word, I'm afraid," Dr. Page said. "My niece and I were on a journey to San Francisco when ruffians kidnapped us and stole our money. I'm afraid these men were nothing more than common thieves."

Blevins swept his arms toward the chair the doctor had risen from. "Please be seated, sir, I should like to hear all about your experience."

"You have quite a place here, Mr. Blevins," Mary said. "You must run a very successful business."

"Yes, my dear," Mamie joined in. "My nephew here has been a very successful planter. The climate agrees with the fruit."

"I don't think I've ever heard of farming doing quite this well," Mary shot back.

Blevins rounded the table and squinted his eyes in her direction. "I do quite well here, and I also dabble in the shipping business. My aunt keeps the house running very well in my absence."

The old woman sat down across the table and smiled. A cool look took over her face. "Thank you, dear. You see, with Robert's interest in transporting commerce, he has a great deal of concern with your story. You can see that, can't you?"

"I'm afraid our only concern is in returning to Sacramento," Dr. Page said.

"Pirates, kidnappers, ruffians, common thieves, they have no business among decent people," Blevins replied. "You did say these men were pirates?"

"I'm afraid we couldn't swear to that," Mary responded.

"Well, whatever they were, they treated you very poorly."

"Exactly as I was saying, Robert." Mamie got up and moved around the table. Clamping her hands to Mary's shoulders, she continued, "Look at this dear child, Robert, frightened to death at the very least and such a beauty too. Don't you agree?"

"I most certainly do," he smiled.

"I will be just fine," Mary joined in, "just as soon as we get back to Sacramento."

"That's really all we require, Mr. Blevins, some passage to a carrier bound for the capital."

"I told them we couldn't hear of such a thing, Robert, at least not until they've rested and enjoyed our hospitality."

"My aunt is right. We certainly would appreciate your company until we can be sure of your passage."

Dr. Page and Mary exchanged glances. "We are quite anxious to get home, I'm afraid."

"Then, it's all settled," Mamie interrupted. "You will stay right here at The Glades"—the woman shook her handkerchief in Dr. Page's direction, making her point with each wave of lace—"until Robert can arrange your passage and we have the scoundrels who did this in the clutches of the law."

"My aunt is a woman given to hospitality," Blevins went on. "You've given her an excellent opportunity to show off her charm."

Dr. Page smiled. "We've seen a good deal of your dear aunt's charm already. I fear this entire experience has made Mary here far too ready to get back home."

"Poor dear," Mamie patted Mary's shoulders. "I feel positively dreadful about what's happened to this fine flower, don't you, Robert?"

The man smiled and nodded.

"We just can't send her off with so wrong of a notion of life along the river, now, can we?"

"I should say not. I do have some friends here who would be most interested in your story. They are men of action and would like nothing better than to avenge any indignities you may have suffered. No, I think your presence here will be required for a while longer. You may be needed to identify the men who did this to you. Do you think you will be able to recognize them?"

Dr. Page started to shake his head, but Mary spoke up, "I'll never forget those men, not till my dying day."

Dr. Page's expression was pained, but a broad smile crossed Blevins's face. "Well, let's hope, Miss Page, that day will be a long time in coming."

\+ + + + +

Zac walked into the Wells Fargo office more than an hour after his attempted shave. An army sergeant stood casually watching as a tall, dark-coated man rummaged through a massive oak filing cabinet. The large soldier with the gray walrus mustache spotted Zac right off, while the dark-suited man kept his back to the door. In front of them, at the desk, a clerk in green eyeshades reached out and pulled on the coattails of the agent riffling through the file cabinets.

"What is it?" Turning around, the lanky, bespectacled man spotted Zac. The sober look on his face turned into a broad smile. He cleared his throat. "You're Zachary Cobb."

"That I am."

The man shot out his hand. "Pleased to meet you. I'm Keith Webster, the agent in charge. This here is Homer Conway."

The clerk at the desk had gotten to his feet. "Real nice to meet you, Mr. Cobb."

Webster motioned to the barrel-chested sergeant. "And this is Sergeant Adams. He's in command of the detail that will accompany our shipment."

Adams smiled and shook Zac's hand. "Good to meet you, Cobb. We were just talking about you."

Webster pointed to an empty chair beside a half-made cot. "Yes, we were. Please be seated. You seem to have made quite an impression on the capital already."

Zac sat down and, pulling out his pipe, stuck it in his mouth. "I'm sorry about that. It wasn't any of my doing, I can assure you of that."

Webster smiled and looked at the other two men. "Oh, you needn't worry about that. We were just talking about how it will be good for business. People have heard you work for Wells Fargo. We all agree things are safer with you on the job. With folks knowing you're here, we already landed a new contract not more than ten minutes ago."

"Yes, we did." Conway beamed.

"Folks feel a whole lot better when they know we take the trouble to bring you into what we ship."

Zac proceeded to stuff his pipe with tobacco. "Well, I don't want to disappoint either you or your customers, but this isn't a regular thing for me."

"Oh, we know that," Webster said. "But there's just no sense in announcing that to our customers, now, is there? Sergeant Adams here and his men aren't normally assigned to us either, but I suppose Mr. Wells is going all out to make sure this gold gets all the way to the mint in San Francisco."

Zac struck a match and, raking it over the bowl of the pipe, puffed it to life.

"I have a corporal and three good men," Adams said. "Given the shortness of the trip, I shouldn't think we'll have too much to fret about."

"What do you all know of a Colonel Princeton?" Zac asked.

Webster's and Conway's eyes widened. "Where'd you hear of him?" Webster asked.

"The men in the barbershop were working for him." Zac puffed a cloud of aromatic smoke in the air.

"He's a bad one," Webster said, "but we've only heard stories."

Conway pulled off his green eyeshades and ran his fingers through his balding hair. "Been hearing tales with him attached to 'em for over two years now, mostly small boats, though. The man's name has seldom come up, but the description we get about the one in charge fits a military man."

"That's right," Webster joined in. "The man is always prepared. He comes on board with a group of people who know what they're about. They take only the most valuable cargo and leave the rest, mostly whiskey and guns. They usually prey on boats coming in from San Francisco."

"The army's been on the lookout for those people," Adams said. "That delta's full of twists and turns, though. There must be hundreds of channels and islands scattered all the way between here and the bay. They know the territory and we don't. It's as simple as that."

"They ain't never had the wherewithal to tackle something like the *Delta King*, though," Webster said.

"They haven't ever had the promise of a half million in gold before," Zac added.

"You think they aim for this shipment?" Webster asked.

"Why else would they be targeting me? They knew who I was and when I'd be arriving. It's simple to figure out they'd know everything else about our plans along with that."

"I don't think the army can spare any more than the five of us,"

Adams offered. "Henry Wells had to pull more than a few strings to get that."

The darkness across the doorway brought Zac's head around. Cliff Cox, sporting a checkered suit and polished bowler hat, was blocking the light. "Allow me to introduce our other agent," Zac said. "This here is Mr. Clifford Cox. Show the men your badge, boy."

Cox pulled the checked coat aside, showing off a gleaming brass badge that read, "Special Agent—Wells Fargo." He nodded. "Pleased to make your acquaintance, gentlemen."

"Cox here knows all about the men we're up against." Zac gave off a slightly forced smile. "He's been trailing them and working diligently to bring them to justice for two years now. Ain't that right, Cox?"

The young man pulled off his thick glasses and wiped them with a handkerchief. "This is my territory, I suppose," he said.

"You know of this Princeton?" Webster asked.

"Princeton?"

"Yes," Zac said. "I've been in Sacramento for over an hour now, and we're just discussing this Kingfish you've been trying to catch."

"Well, I'm afraid you gentlemen have me at a disadvantage."

"I think we should go over our plans," Webster said. "Adams here will need to position his troopers."

Zac got to his feet. "That can wait. Cox and I have some shopping to do."

"Shopping?" Cox asked.

"Yes, shopping. I spotted me a fancy blue bonnet, and you look like just the man to help me negotiate a fair price."

CHAPTER 13

+ + + + + + +

LATER THAT AFTERNOON, the bullion wagon wound its way through the streets of Sacramento. Zac had been standing beside the marshal's office, listening at a distance to a man playing "Greensleeves" on a violin. The man had a nice touch, one that obviously had taken a great deal of practice time to accomplish. Zac always admired someone who had more than a try to him. If any man was going to show himself in public as something other than what anyone could see outright, Zac always thought it meant to work hard at being the best. To be just a doer wasn't quite good enough for him.

Zac spotted the old man playing at a distance and could tell at a first look that this was a man who cared what music came out of him. He held the instrument lightly under his chin and pulled the bow with feeling.

The clanking of a wagon and the horses and riders that surrounded it made listening difficult. A specially made iron vehicle, it drew more than a few casual glances. People were curious not so much about the wagon itself, because they had seen it many times before, but because the large number of outriders told them the shipment was something unusual. Some forty-odd riders rode with it, each man heavily armed. The mining company was going to make sure their delivery made it to the Wells Fargo office, one way or the other.

The wagon pulled up in front of the red-brick office, and several of the guards jumped down to open the iron doors. One by one, the heavy metal strongboxes were carried into the office. Riders dismounted and held their guns at the ready.

Zac crossed the street with the hat box in one hand. He watched the unloading at a distance. The guards looked grim—of course, they were paid to look deadly serious. No one nor any army would be foolish enough to try to rob that gold from the streets of Sacramento in broad daylight. Because of that, Zac thought the long, somber looks on the guards' faces mildly amusing.

It was obvious the mining company had every intention of the gold reaching Sacramento. They were doing their job, all right. That was plain to see. The weak link in this trip would have been the transport from the gold fields, and the mining company knew that. The only other part of the trip that would require special attention would be the boat ride, and that's where Zac came in. He didn't have forty guards like they were using, only five army personnel and Cliff Cox. That thought alone was frightening.

Zac had managed to send the greenhorn on a wild goose chase back to the boat to get the breakdown of the cruise back to the bay. He wanted a near approximate timing of any stops the *Delta King* was due to make, and he wanted Cox out of the way, to boot. No matter what the man's family connection was to Henry Wells, Zac didn't trust him. He would much rather talk over the plans for the trip without having Cox nearby to hear.

He stopped outside the Longhorn Saloon, where the elderly man sat and played his violin. The man's ragged pants and torn shirt showed him to be less than prosperous. His weathered face was scrubbed, and the scraggly white beard that curled out from the wrinkled face was neatly combed and parted in the middle. It was plain for anyone to see that the man didn't have much, but he did the best he could with what he had. Reaching down into his pocket, Zac produced a silver dollar and dropped it into the open case in front of the man's feet. It was far too much money for a passerby to casually drop for a song, Zac knew that. He also knew he had few extravagances in life and music was one of them.

The old man looked up and, smiling, continued to play. Finishing the song, he perched the violin on his hip. "Thank you, sir."

"No, thank you. I admire a good string player."

"Do you know the violin?"

"From the time I sat on my mother's knee. I suppose I was born to it."

The old man held up the violin. "You'd honor me, then, if'n you was to play."

Zac put down the hatbox and laid his sawed-off shotgun on top of it. He gingerly grasped the instrument and held it out. Somehow, him standing on the boardwalk with a violin alongside a hatbox and a scatter-gun at his feet was a picture few would care to try to put together. He saw the amazement of it at once and smiled. "What would you like to hear?"

The old man leaned back in his chair and beamed. "Just play something that would do honor to your mother."

Zac tucked the violin under his chin and pulled the bow gently across the strings. The sweet music was familiar, but somehow it didn't seem to fit with the boisterous noise pouring out of the saloon. The tune "Blessed Be the Tie that Binds" caught passersby unawares. They drew up to stand and listen to the stranger in his buckskin jacket.

Playing the familiar song caused Zac's mind to wander back in time. His boyhood was a familiar place, a place filled with family and love. Music affected him that way. It was more than just notes being played, it was memories and frames of mind. He had always found it difficult to express how he felt about anything, but somehow his music spoke eloquently about his emotions when nothing else ever could.

He finished the song and handed the violin back to the man.

"That was mighty nice."

"Thank you."

"I can tell the songs speak to you."

"At times music seems to get through to me when nothing else can."

"I know just how you feel."

Zac touched the brim of his hat and turned to leave. The old man called out after him. "You can come on back and play anytime you got a hankerin'. I'll either be here or over yonder by the bandstand."

Zac marched off down the boardwalk toward the Wells Fargo office. From the Acey Ducey Saloon near the office, a drunk staggered out the doors and onto the boardwalk in front of Wells Fargo. The guards ignored him as they continued to cart in the heavy boxes. Zac watched the man carefully. He wore tan coveralls with a bright blue shirt under his suspenders. His black hat was clean, and his boots seemed far too polished for someone who was a common drunk. Often people were not what they appeared to be, and this man sobered up and stiffened his posture when he neared the open office door.

Zac stepped up to his backside and pushed him forward with the barrel of his shotgun. "Move along, you're blocking traffic."

The man stumbled and staggered forward. "Hey, watch it."

Spinning around, Zac could see the man's eyes appeared bright, not the least bit dimmed by alcohol.

"I ain't meanin' no harm."

"Just move along, then, unless you got business with Wells Fargo."

"I just might, at that. Not now, mind you, but someday."

Zac stepped aside and watched the man stagger away as the guards continued to stack the boxes in the office. The quantity of the gold was too much for the safe, and the guards had already begun to make a row of the strongboxes next to the far wall. Zac knew at a glance that the cot he'd seen earlier would have to be the place he tried to sleep tonight.

He followed two of the guards into the office.

\+ + + + +

Down the street at the Blackberry House Cafe, Jenny and Hattie sat with the boys, bowls filled with ice cream in front of each of them. The vanilla cream was covered with blackberries and heavy syrup. Hattie stirred the mixture and grimaced. "This ain't 'zackly what I'm used to." Her eyes darted back and forth between the boys, both of whose heads were bobbing up and down as they gobbled spoonfuls of the rich, sweet ice cream. " 'Course, bein' as I'm with y'all, I s'pose this here is jest about the best an old gal can do."

"I think you'll like it," Jenny said. "Of course, sweets do take getting used to."

"I sure likes it." Jack picked up his chin from the bowl and grinned, a blackberry-smeared smile of enormous proportions. "Where I comes from a body can't rightly even steal somethin' this good."

"I think the best things in life are worth waiting for," Jenny said. "You won't have to steal them, and you shouldn't force them."

Hattie waved her spoon at the boys. "You best listen to what Jenny here says. She ought to know more 'bout that than most. She's been waitin' on that no-count nephew of mine fer more'n a coon's age." She stuck a spoon filled with ice cream cautiously into her mouth and frowned. "This here stuff is cold on an old woman's teef."

Jenny did her best to avoid the subject of Zac. She bowed her head and ate.

"Ain't he never gone and brung up the matter?" Hattie asked.

"What matter?"

" 'Bout you two gettin' hitched. Ain't he never said nothing?"

"He has talked about his feelings for me, but he hasn't proposed, if that is what you mean."

Hattie reached out and gave her a hard slap on the back. "Why then, that's plum good 'nuff. Any time one of them Cobb men talks about his feelings for a gal, that's durn sure a proposal, far as I'ze concerned." She cackled and then shook her head violently, reacting to the temperature of the dessert.

Putting down her spoon, she put her hands together and, stretching, cracked her knuckles. "You best just go and find you a preacher. The boys here and me will stand him up pretty as you please." Leaning over the table, she spoke to the boys. "Now, wouldn't that be a fine thing for this here trip, a weddin'?"

Skip's eyes got large. He looked over at Jenny to see how he should react.

"Now, you'd like yerself a ma, wouldn't you?"

Skip nodded. "Yes, ma'am."

"Hattie, I do appreciate your thoughts. I think I'd just as soon wait, however. When he gets good and ready, he won't need to be forced."

"Girl, time's a wastin'. Why, when I think about all them years I let go by with no man in particular to do for, I reckon I might just go back and do a few of them things over again. A gal's got to take the bull by the horns. Most men ain't got the sense God give a goose when it comes to hankerin' after a full-time woman. They waits and waits, and then afore you know it, they up and picks the wrong woman."

She stabbed at the air with her spoon to make the point. "They has to pick the wrong one by then, 'cause the right one's done gone and got tired a waitin' and married herself off to somebody else."

"Hattie, when a woman loves a man, nothing will ever change that. I guess I'm spoiled. I'm not waiting on the institution of marriage. If I had been doing that I would be disappointed. I'm waiting on Zachary Taylor Cobb."

Jack had long since finished his ice cream. He scrambled to his feet. "I gots to go find the privy."

"Just make sure you come right back," Jenny said. "We need to do some shopping for you in particular."

"You want I should go with the boy?" Hattie asked.

"Gee, I can make out on my own."

"All right," Jenny agreed. "Just hurry back."

Jack wound his way through the glass-top tables to the man at the cash register. After asking for directions, he made his way out the back door. A short time later, he emerged from the small wooden outhouse in the alley several blocks away. He straightened his trousers and tied tight the knotted rope that held them up. He felt a sense of freedom at being in a new city where he wasn't known. He didn't have to worry about people who thought he owed them money, and the police here, while they might eye him carefully, didn't know enough about him to try to arrest him. He liked the feeling.

He pushed his cap forward in a cocky manner. He was gonna be just fine with these here folks. Stepping away from the privy, he felt a jerk on his collar.

"There you are!"

It was the gambler Rance McCauliff. His eyes darted with glee as he wrapped his arm around the boy's neck and drew his sharp knife. "I think I'm gonna start skinning you with your ears."

Jack twisted, but the man held him tight.

"You better hand over what you took from me, boy, and do it right quick. Ain't nobody here to pull your bacon out of the fire now. There's just you and me."

Jack squirmed. "All right, all right. I'll give it back. It's in my shoe, though."

The man loosened his grip on the boy, still holding on to his arm. "Get it then, boy, and maybe we'll talk about lettin' you live."

Jack reached down to his carefully tied brogans. He looked up at the sneer of the gambler and the gleaming blade of the man's knife. Stooping over, he came up suddenly, delivering a swift, hard kick between the man's legs.

McCauliff dropped to the ground in pain, and Jack ripped his arm free and ran.

Turning the corner, he ran up the street and into the first open door he could find. The crowded store was filled with barrels and the musty smell of flour. Racks of merchandise studded the floor, and dresses along with bolts of brightly colored cloth were stacked on tables. He darted under one of the tables that held the material and crouched low. Moments later, he could see the legs of the slightly limping gambler.

"You seen a boy run in here?" McCauliff asked the shopkeeper.

"I thought I saw one a moment ago, but he must have run back out."

"No, he's here all right. He's here and he's hiding from me. The boy's a thief."

Jack watched McCauliff's legs along with the aproned shopkeeper's as the two men wound around the tables. "I know he came in here," McCauliff said.

"We'll find him, then. I won't have a thief in my store."

Jack crouched under the table as the men began their search. "I don't think he came to the back of the store," the shopkeeper offered. "I would have seen him if he had."

Jack waited until the two men rounded his table and began to look under the displays behind him. Quick as a cat, he sprang from under the table and ran for the door. He could hear the men yelling behind him as he weaved his way between strolling people and sprinted for the next street. He'd always prided himself on being faster than any grown-up that might be chasing him, but this was a town he didn't know. In Oakland, he knew every cut in the fences that dotted the city streets, every place a boy his size could safely hide in, but here he was a stranger.

He spotted a sign that read "Attorney at Law" and leapt up several steps to test the door. It was locked. Darting back, he could see the men's heads bobbing in the crowd as they ran up the street. He scampered into the alley. It was blocked. Several brick buildings formed high walls that shaded the cobbled alleyway. Barrels were scattered under the eaves of some of the buildings. He might be able to hide behind one of those. There was no way out. If they came down here they would find him for sure.

He spotted an opening into the basement of the lawyer's office, two wooden doors, knee high, that slanted into the side of the building. He tugged on one door. It was latched from the inside. Yanking with all his might, he popped the latch and opened the door to the dark cellar below.

Stepping into the stairs that led to the darkened basement, he reached for the severed latch. Pushing the screw back into the soft wood, he closed the door behind him and fastened the latch.

Peeking through the weathered door, he watched as the two men rounded the corner. "I think he went this way," McCauliff shouted.

Jack's breathing was heavy as they looked behind the rain barrels that dotted the alley. He was right. If he had hid there, he would've been caught for sure.

The men walked back to the street and stopped by the cellar door. Jack held on to it as McCauliff gave a tug. It held fast.

"I was sure he came down here," McCauliff murmured.

Jack watched as the two men walked back to the street. It wouldn't be safe to go out there, not for a while at least. He sat down on the stairs and caught his breath. The air was musty, but at the top of the stairs he could see the faint light of an office. There might be something of interest in there. A feller could sell pens, paperweights, maybe lots of stuff that might be picked up in a lawyer's office. He moved cautiously toward the faint light.

He could hear the faint murmur of conversation coming from the lit office, something he didn't want to hear at all. Moving cautiously up the stairs, the sound of men talking filtered from the room. He pressed his face to the keyhole and peeked into the office.

The lawyer, a well-dressed man in a suit, sat at his large desk. Jack could make out a man in brightly colored clothing and several others who were crowded around the desk.

"You moved too quick," the man said. "The colonel ain't gonna be happy when he hears about this. I ain't real pleased with having to put up no hundred dollar bail for you neither."

"Now, Manny, you know we're good for it."

"I don't know nothin' of the sort. For all I know you're gonna go out there tonight and get yerself killed. Then where's my hundred dollars gonna be?"

"The colonel promised us five hundred dollars if we blew out the lamp of this Zac Cobb feller. We just didn't figure it was gonna be so hard. I mean, there was two of us, and we had his hands pinned to the chair."

"From what I hear, that man's a piece of work. If you fellers can't kill him when you got him cold, just imagine what he's gonna be like with his gun hand free."

Jack scooted closer and moved around the keyhole to try to get a better look at the men. It was hard. No matter where he turned, there was only so much he could see.

"We'll do better tonight. I got myself a plan. I can tell you one thing, I ain't gonna let that man get close enough to even see us. We'll cut him down on that street late tonight, and he ain't gonna know what hit him. That I can promise you."

"How you gonna see what to shoot at with all this fog?"

"Princeton gave us the name of a man who can give us a signal when he leaves the boat. He says this fella is real reliable, gets information about cargo being shipped all the time."

"And what if Cobb stays on the boat tonight with that woman of his?"

"Oh, he ain't gonna do that. He's got all that gold to guard. You think with all that locked up in that there Wells Fargo office, he's gonna trust it to people he don't know? Not from what we'ze been hearin' about him."

"Yeah, and you were right about trying to take him at the barbershop too, weren't you?"

"We done made a mistake on that, like I told you. We tried to take him up close, and the man's a good close-in fighter."

"He's a good any-kind fighter."

"He can't rightly dodge buckshot, now, can he?"

Jack leaned over to try to see the man who was talking. Suddenly, his foot slipped, sending him down two of the steps.

"What was that?"

Jack scrambled along the floor like a spider across black ice. Reaching the hatch that led to the alley, he pushed it open. Poking his head outside, he swung his head from side to side. Without a second look, he dashed outside and down the street.

CHAPTER 14

+ + + + + + +

EVENING AT THE GLADES glowed with candles and lamps, sending a shimmering dance of flickering light across the drawn curtains and a flush of reddish glow over polished oak walls and ornately designed plaster. There was a richness to the house that was seldom seen beyond the large mansions of Nob Hill in San Francisco. The wealth of the Blevins family was on display and it was a glittering show indeed, a fairyland of twinkling splendor set against the dark river beyond the lawns outside.

Dr. Page and Mary descended the sweeping staircase, and waiting at the foot of the oak steps was Robert Blevins. The short man's eyes fairly gleamed at Mary as she stepped down the Persian-carpeted stairs. She wore a pale dress the color of the inside of a freshly sliced watermelon. It was full with puffed sleeves, and her hair had been put up in a stylish coif, with loose ringlets framing her pretty face. Mamie had chosen well for her, and for the first time in weeks, Mary felt like a lady.

Blevins was dressed in a ruffled white shirt and sparkling white pantaloons. A crimson sash at his waist was knotted, the fringed edge hanging down almost to his knees. In his hand, he held a rapier. The sword's hilt was steel mixed with what appeared to be twisted cords of pure gold. He brushed his hand up the sides of his ravenlike Van Dyke beard.

"You look lovely, my dear. I'm glad to see the clothes Aunt Mamie laid out for you fit you so well."

He looked down at his own clothing. "I'm afraid I shall still have to change before we have our dinner. My fencing exercises required entirely too much time."

"It's rare to find a man who uses a sword in our part of the world," Dr. Page remarked. "More of a European curiosity, I should think."

Blevins extended his hand to Mary, guarding her final step to the floor. "Precisely, Doctor. However, in the course of my business, I do quite a bit of European travel. It pays to be well versed in whatever one may encounter."

Mary diverted her eyes from Blevins's stare. She enjoyed being looked at as a woman, but the way she was being measured by him made her feel uncomfortable.

From the parlor opposite them and down the hall, Mamie began to shriek. "There you are, my dears. Oh, mercy on me." She walked through the French doors with a new yet very noticeable limp, all the while holding on to her hip. "I'm afraid, Doctor, that the pains and miseries are on me once again." She waved her handkerchief back and forth across her face as she tramped toward them. "I just don't know what I shall do."

Blevins spoke under his breath and smiled. "I'm afraid my aunt may have you earn your stay in medical advice."

The old woman stepped forward and latched her arm around the doctor's elbow. "Please come to my room, Doctor, and succor this poor body of mine. I assure you, I can use all of the comfort and remedy that you can possibly muster."

Stopping in her tracks and turning around, she waved the flag of silk at Mary and Blevins. "You two mustn't bore yourselves with an old lady's maladies. Robert, take this delightful young woman out to the gardens. I will have Soggy bring you both some sherry on a tray."

"I don't drink," said Mary. She felt ill at ease at the idea of being alone with this man, especially given the way she was being ogled. The last thing she wanted was a walk in the foggy garden with him.

"Nonsense, child," Mamie said. "It's only sherry. Sophisticated ladies take it before dinner all the time. It will enhance your appetite."

She reached over and gave Mary's thin waist a slight pinch. "And, my dear, you need some fattening up. I only see women this thin in catalogs."

Turning to Blevins, she went on. "Imagine that, Robert. This dear soul never imbibes."

Flinging her hanky in Mary's direction, she said. "You just take a little, child." She smiled. "I wouldn't want you without all of your faculties when accompanied by my nephew here. He's quite the man of the world, you know."

"I can imagine."

Blevins laid his sword down on a polished mahogany table and motioned toward the glass doors at the rear. "Shall we?" He held the door open for her.

Mary reluctantly stepped down the carpeted stairs that led to the gardens out back. She stopped on the landing, looking down the curved stairs that led to the basement of the big house. It was well lit, with lamps that glowed along the iron railings and down into what she could only imagine.

Blevins seemed uncomfortable with her curiosity. "Come here. The gardens are beautiful, even in the fog." Reaching out, he took her arm, moving her out onto the red-brick porch and walkway.

The tall shrubs spiraled upward into the gathering evening fog, and row after row of roses dotted the walkway. The noise of crickets was joined by a chorus of frogs, each signaling the coming nightfall, an event obscured by the fog. Along the path, lamps had been lit, each flickering its own special glow on the roses.

Mary had always been bored with the small talk expected from women, but just now, it seemed like the safest course. "You have a beautiful place here, Mr. Blevins."

"Robert, please call me Robert. I'm not that much older than you." He sniggered. "When someone says Mr. Blevins, I'm afraid I am forced to look around for my father, and he's been dead for years."

"You don't strike me as a man given to informalities."

He patted her hand on his arm. "Don't let these surroundings fool you. With someone as lovely as you, Mary, a man would have to be a fool to remain so stiff and formal." He swept his hand toward the garden. "It is lovely, especially in bold daylight, and it could be made to look even more glorious with the touch of a beautiful woman."

His grin in her direction sent a shiver up her spine. "There must be many women nearby who would swoon at the chance to keep your company."

He turned her around and, taking both of her hands, held her out. "None that match your beauty and charm."

She bowed her head. Taking her hands from his, she picked up her dress and moved down the walk.

He hurried to keep up with her. "No, I mean it. You have a natural beauty that it's best these roses not look upon in the daylight.

I'm afraid to do so, they might just wilt on the spot out of pure envy. There's an innocence about you too, my dear, one I find quite refreshing."

She forced herself to look away from him, stooping over to inspect the roses. "You are being quite bold . . . err, Robert."

Taking her arm, he turned her to face him and brought her closer. "I'm a businessman, Mary, and quite a successful one, at that. I didn't get to where I am by dillydallying over a rare find when it might be better to strike a deal right away."

She pulled away from him and once again began to step down the brick path. The notion of being crowded was something that had never sat well with her. Mary Page had a mind all her own. He quickly caught up to her and once again took her arm.

"Please forgive my impetuousness, Miss Page. It's just that I so seldom have a lady of obvious quality as a guest in my home. I'm afraid my conversation skills with the genteel classification of humanity are somewhat lacking."

She bit her lip slightly. Even though she was growing more irritated by the moment, she didn't want to appear rude, especially to one who seemed so powerful and capable of getting her home. "They appear to be well practiced from my vantage point, sir."

"I can assure you, I mean no disrespect. It's just that time is so short, and it never waits on the coy or backward."

"Of which you are neither, sir." She braced herself.

"No, I suppose you are quite correct. Your beauty and charm could easily make a man of means get carried away. And I do have the means to satisfy a woman's every whim. If it were left up to my fancy, I'm afraid I would sweep you away from here to many glittering months on the European continent—Paris, Berlin, Budapest, the ruins of Italy as well as the glory of ancient Rome. It would all be yours. You'd have only to ask."

"It appears as if I wouldn't even have to do that." A slight frown creased her face. "You appear to be forceful enough for any woman's opinion to count for little."

The doors to the house pushed open, and from the back steps they could see the servant with a silver tray. A cut glass decanter and goblets were being balanced along with a folding table under the man's arm. He gingerly descended the brick staircase and made his way toward them.

"You can place it here, Soggy."

"Yes, sir, I surely will now."

The man set the tray down on the bricks and arranged the teak table. Securing it, he carefully lifted the tray and set it down on the linen-covered table. Reaching into his back pocket, he produced two white napkins and positioned them upright on the table. "I'se sorry if'n I didn't get 'em quite right, masser Robert."

The old man poured two glasses and stood beside the table.

"That will be all, Soggy."

Mary picked up her glass, and as Blevins took several steps away from her to watch the old man retreat, she tossed the contents into the rose bushes. She picked up the napkin and, covering her empty glass, smiled.

Blevins chose his glass and lifted it in her direction. "To you, my dear, a beauty who shames the rose you stand next to." With that, he sipped his drink as Mary lifted the empty glass to her lips.

"I must warn you, my lovely, Robert Blevins generally gets what he bargains for."

"Perhaps we should drink to that, then." She lifted the glass. Her brow wrinkled. Inside she was feeling angry at the leading direction of the conversation, but on the outside, she maintained a ladylike composure. "That you would only generally get what you bargain for."

Putting his glass down, he took hers and set it on the table. Taking both of her hands, he pulled her closer. "You must have been able to tell from the look in my eyes that I was attracted to you at first sight. For years I've been alone, just waiting for the right woman, someone with an innocent beauty mixed with that rare combination of refinement. I believe you to be that woman, Mary Page, and it will do me no good to wait on a similar notion from you. Our time here is much too short for all that formal thinking of the last century."

Mary held herself back. "Don't you have to change before dinner?"

"Oh, I have time," he smirked. "My aunt may be deficient in many areas that constitute good thinking, but she wouldn't dream of having dinner served before I finish with you."

"Finish with me?"

He smiled. "Of course. Now, why do you think she developed that sudden case of the miseries?"

"I think you *have* finished with me."

His eyes narrowed as he stared at her. "You have no idea of how far we yet have to go. Your whole future may depend on pleasing your host."

"Sir, my future has never been based on pleasing a man. I have a higher calling than that."

"There can be no higher calling for a woman than to be at Robert Blevins's side, as you will soon discover."

He hardened his grip on her and, pulling her closer, kissed her.

She arched her back, wrestling her right hand free, and delivered a loud slap to his jaw.

Suddenly releasing her, he stiffened his frame. Rage burned in his face.

"Now, sir, I do think you have quite finished with me."

Spinning around, he kicked violently at the table, sending the decanter and glasses crashing to the red bricks. He strode up the walk, marching like a tin soldier terribly in need of oil in his joints.

Mary watched him stomp back up the stairs. Standing at the top of the landing, with the glow of the house behind him, he spun around. "You will change your mind," he blustered. "Before you leave me, you will beg to have the tenderness of that kiss back."

+ + + + +

Dinner on the *Delta King* was a dressy affair, and Zac had changed from his traveling clothes to a dark suit, white shirt, and tie. Jenny wore a pale blue dress that showed off her eyes, and the boys were both scrubbed and clean.

Hattie wore her usual, but that night she had donned a simple straw bonnet that added a comical touch to her homespun skirt and blouse. Except for the chain of gold nuggets, which she refused to take off, no one would have guessed her wealth.

Jenny watched the boys as they sat quietly at the table. Jack was unusually quiet. Normally the boy babbled at the mouth, and if there was nothing of interest to talk about he made something up. Tonight he sat somberly, stirring the food on his plate, occasionally glancing quickly at Zac and then back down to his plate.

"What's wrong, boy?" Zac asked. "I'd expect you above anybody to have finished your supper by now and be ready for something else."

"He skedaddled fer most of the day," Hattie said, "more'n likely up to no good."

"I think the boy was just exploring," Jenny said. "Being curious is natural for a boy."

"So's mischief," Hattie exclaimed.

Jenny noticed that Zac had brought a hatbox to the table with him, along with his violin. They were well into the veal medallions when he produced the box. Pushing it in Jenny's direction, he wiped his mustache with his napkin. "I did a little bit of shopping myself today."

"I'm surprised you found yourself the time, boy." Hattie had no problem with interjecting herself into any conversation, even if her mouth was full. She continued to spade the meat into her mouth with both knife and fork. "What with giving two fellers a stompin' in that there barbershop, along with a dry shave fer one, I'ze plum surprised you could find yerself a space in that there head of yourn to think about your lady here." She poked at the meat on her plate. "This here stuff is mighty good. T'ain't at all like them steaks I feeds myself."

Jenny began to unwrap the box, smiling at Zac with each pull of the ribbons.

"I think about this lady all of the time," he said. "Few things give my mind more pleasure than thoughts about Jenny Hays."

Hattie grinned with her mouth full and poked her knife in the direction of the two boys. "Now, you two rascals, listen up here. You just might learn yerselves somethin' fer yer future. Womenfolk likes to be thought on." She jabbed the knife at Skip's face to make her point. "They need to be thought on a powerful lot."

"Yes, ma'am." Skip gulped and shot his head backward away from the intrusive tableware.

They all watched Jenny open the box as Hattie continued. "'Course, it's been my experience that a ring comes in a mite smaller box."

Lifting the blue ribbon-bedecked hat from the box, Jenny smiled. "Oh, Zac, it's beautiful, and it's just my color. What made you think to get this?"

He dropped his napkin on the table and picked up his water glass. "I was just passing by a shop, and when I saw this, I suppose I couldn't help but think about your eyes."

Hattie proceeded to squash the peas on her plate with her fork. "Put it on, gal. Let's see you show it off."

Jenny fingered the bonnet and, after placing it on her head, turned to the window to see how it looked. Her face beamed. "Thank you, Zac, it's lovely."

Zac leaned back in his chair. It was plain to see that he was proud of his choice and pleased that Jenny liked it.

She turned to him and put her hands on top of his. "You do surprise me. I would never have thought you capable of something like this. It's so unlike you."

"I sorta like surprising you. You seem to know me so well that catching you off guard might just become a full-time job."

"A full-time job," Hattie roared. "Now, you be careful there, boy. That might be thought on as a proposal from where I come from."

Zac looked flustered at the comment and Jenny blushed. From across the floor, Captain Van Tuyl wound his way through the diners and headed straight for them. The man always maintained a calm exterior, even when something was on his mind. Just looking at him made a passenger feel that all was secure. His coat was open, and he closed his gold watch and dropped it into his jacket pocket.

"You folks enjoying your meal?"

Hattie stirred what little gravy remained on her plate with a biscuit. "It's passable fer travelin' people."

"It's very nice, Captain," Jenny said.

Van Tuyl looked at Zac. "The undertaker brought a box with the dead boy back on board, and we'll finish loading our cargo during the night. You can bring yours on board at first light."

"That's fine," Zac said. "I'll be spending the night at the Wells Fargo office and see that it gets here."

"You're goin' there tonight?" Jack asked, suddenly becoming animated.

Zac's gaze shifted to the boy. "Yes I am, but you boys are to stay in your room." He paused and looked directly at Skip. "All night. Am I making myself understood?"

"Yes, sir," Skip blurted out.

"I won't be around if that gambler friend of yours comes calling, so I don't think prowling around this boat is a very good idea."

"Is McCauliff giving you a problem?" Van Tuyl asked. "Because if he is I can see that he's thrown off my boat."

"That would be great," Jack gulped.

"That's not necessary," Zac said. "It appears the boys here crossed him in some way, and he's just put a scare into them." Zac picked up his fork and stabbed another bite of veal. "If he goes out of his way to frighten them again, I'll throw him off myself."

When they finished dessert and coffee, Zac rose to his feet and turned to Jenny. "Perhaps we can go for a walk on deck before I change and go to the office. It's going to be a long night, and I'll be on a cot, but I do plan on sleeping. Hattie, can you see to the boys for a spell?"

The old woman beamed and, reaching into her bag, pulled out a deck of well-worn cards. "You betcha I can." She skinned a toothy smile at the two boys. "I'm a gonna teach you boys some cards, show you how to cheat where nobody can see."

Zac put his hat on. "That's right, boys. You pay close attention to Hat here, and she'll show you how to hang before you reach manhood."

He started to leave, but Jack reached out and grabbed the tail of his jacket. "I didn't know you'd be going out tonight," he said.

Zac released the boy's grip on his coat. "I'll be back before breakfast. You boys just stay in your room and you'll be fine. Jenny will be right next door to you."

Jack got to his feet and edged closer to him. "That ain't what I'm thinkin' about."

Zac leaned closer to him. "Then, what's the problem? You didn't eat half of your dinner."

"While I wuz gone today, I heard some men talkin' 'bout you."

"After what happened today, you'd be hard-pressed to find anybody on the street that wasn't talking about me."

Jack shook his head. "No, these men was making plans."

"What plans?"

"They'ze planning on killin' you tonight."

"What did these men look like? Have you seen them before?"

"Naw, but I'd recognize 'em if'n I saw them again. Maybe I should go with you."

Zac put his hand on the boy's head. "Son, I've run into men bent on killing me before. Thanks for the warning, but I get paid to take care of myself." He tousled the boy's hair playfully. "And right now, I'm taking care of you for nothing."

Minutes later Zac held Jenny's hand as they walked the deck of the *Delta King*. Below, men were busy storing cargo and running up and down the ramp with boxes on their heads.

"Jack was worried about you."

Zac stopped, and the two of them stared at the lights of Sacramento from the rail. "He wasn't himself, that's for sure. Funny thing, though. I wouldn't take that kid for worryin' about anything but himself."

"Maybe he's changing." She gripped his arm. "There's something about having a man around that you can depend on that does that to a body, you know." She paused. "Now, why did you bring your violin to dinner?"

"I was just reminded of something today." He turned to face her. "I seem to be better at expressing my feelings with music."

Jenny always loved looking into Zac's warm brown eyes, and there was something about the flickering lights on the boat that made them shine. She especially enjoyed the look that came over his face when he played the violin. It was like he was off in another world, a world without shooting and harm. "I think you're doing much better at showing your feelings these days."

"I suppose I haven't had too much to feel strongly about until lately—mostly my thoughts were locked up in the past. Now, I'm giving more thought about the future, the future and the now of what I'm thinking. A man who ties himself to his past might just as well be dead already."

Jenny watched him glance quickly toward the street and the Wells Fargo office. He seemed nervous. It was unlike him."You do have a future, and it's one I look forward to seeing," she said.

Zac looked at her. "I want you to do more than watch it. I want you to share it. I shouldn't go on with this, not here and not now. I've got a full night ahead of me, and I've got to change."

"Fine, whatever you say."

"I best go and change."

"I'll just wait here by the rail and watch the lights, I think."

Zac leaned over and kissed her cheek. "Good. It'll do me good just to picture you here."

A short time later, she saw him stepping around the longshoremen as he headed down the ramp. The gambler McCauliff seemed to be waiting at the bottom of the ramp, and as Zac stopped to look back at her and wave, Jenny noticed the man extract a match and light it.

Jenny's eyes were drawn back to Zac. He was a sight to see, even walking away in the darkened fog. She saw his shape disappear through the trees on his way to the street. A dreaminess swept over her. He had come closer than ever before to asking her to marry him, but there would be a time, she knew that, a better time and a better place.

Looking down, she saw the gambler continue to stare up in her direction. He was lighting a cigar, the glow from his match flaring. She didn't like the looks of the man, especially since he knew Zac was no longer on board the *Delta King*. McCauliff watched Zac walk away.

From below, Cliff Cox ran after Zac. It was as if he had suddenly remembered something that couldn't wait. He began yelling in a loud voice. "Mr. Cobb! Mr. Cobb! Please wait. There's something I need to ask you."

Moments later, apparently concluding his meeting with Zac, Cox walked back up the gangway, passing Rance McCauliff. The gambler relit his cigar as Cox passed by. It was a matter of only minutes when she heard the sound of several booms from the street, the sound of shotgun blasts.

CHAPTER 15

THE BUCKSHOT RIPPED THE POST that held a sign above Zac's head, and one of the pellets tore at his shirt. He dove for the dirt and rolled to a position behind the darkened storefront. Elbowing his way to the opening of the dark alley and pushing the shortened ten-gauge forward, he could see men scrambling for cover. He raised the sawed-off shotgun from his prone position and sent a charge exploding down the alley. The flash of the gun lit up the alley, and he watched a man stagger in the shadows.

Breaking open the smoking weapon, he extracted the spent shells and dropped two more of the wicked loads into the breech. Cocking the hammers, he rolled past the alley opening and slowly got to his knees in front of the darkened window. Pushing the gun forward, he followed its barrels with his eyes, searching through the night air.

A hinge creaked to his left, then a shaft of light darted into the street, followed by the slap of a door. Keeping low, he moved cautiously down the brick-paved alley. Peering through the darkness, he could see no opening between the buildings. Whoever had taken a shot at him was either waiting for him in the darkness or had made his escape through the doorway.

Cautiously moving forward, he tried the succession of doors that dotted the alley. Each one seemed secure until he reached a door with the sound of loud voices behind it. It was a language he'd heard before but didn't understand.

He opened the door slowly, pushing the gun ahead of him. The creaking of the hinge was familiar. In the dimly lit room, scattered tables were surrounded by Chinese men. His appearance in the room brought the pandemonium to a nervous hush. Ivory tiles with writing and dots were scattered on top of the numerous tables.

An older man with a white, wispy beard jumped to his feet and began to point to him and shout. The man's face was livid with anger, and in spite of the loud tone of his voice, there was not one word Zac could understand. He decided to ignore the man and search the room.

As Zac moved through the room, the old man followed him and continued to shout. Staring into the foreign faces, Zac could see fear register in their eyes. Men had different ways of dealing with their fears. Some would run and some would fight. Others became angry, as if by forcing the adrenaline to the surface they could stifle the loss of control that roared inside. It was obvious the old man was one of those. He continued to shout in Chinese and jab his finger in Zac's direction.

Behind the bar, a stairway ascended to a second story. Either the men had left through the front door or they had gone upstairs. It was obvious the gamblers in the room did their coming and going through the alley. Several chairs positioned in front of the door leading into the street made that way unlikely.

Moving around the tables of frightened men, Zac watched their eyes. Other than the angry man who insisted on following him, most of the men's eyes exhibited sheer terror. He noticed several of the men look toward the stairs. Suddenly, one young man's eyes widened as he looked up.

Zac dropped and spun as a shotgun blast erupted from the landing above him. It tore into a table, sending men diving for cover and screaming indiscernible shouts of fear. He saw the shape of a man on the landing at the head of the stairs as he reached over the railing to get a better second shot.

Jerking on both triggers, Zac sent a shower of flaming buckshot in the direction of the darkened figure overhead. The man staggered, then fell though the railing, his body landing with a sickening thud on the floor at Zac's feet. Zac recognized the man right away. It was the larger and less talkative of the two men he had encountered at the barbershop. The man was quite past talking now.

Breaking open the ten-gauge, he dumped the spent shells to the floor and fished in his jacket pocket for two more. Dropping them into place, he moved cautiously to the stairs. The sawed-off stubby weapon was hot to the touch, and smoke continued to pour out the barrels.

Taking one careful look up the stairway, he bounded up the

flight of steps two at a time. At the top, he pushed the gun into the hall ahead of him and then looked around the corner and down the dark corridor.

The faint light showed an open window that looked out on the street below, and Zac moved quickly down the dark passageway. At the open window, he pushed aside fluttering, gauzy, thin curtains and looked out. A walkway connected to stairs that led to the roof of the building. Zac climbed out and moved quickly along the narrow catwalk.

Running up the stairs, he paused at the upper landing. He saw a dark figure moving away from him among the stone-cold chimneys. He was unrecognizable and more than likely a poor target at this distance.

Running along the rooftop, Zac darted in and out of the open doorways that served as fire escapes. As he pushed his head around a chimney, a shotgun blast exploded in the night air and pellets chipped away at the brickwork. The man wouldn't take the time to reload; Zac was counting on that. Rounding the corner of the chimney, he began a dead run in the direction of the blast.

He heard a faint grunt as he approached the edge of the roof and, peering over, saw a figure scrambling up the tin roof of the building on the other side of the alley.

He backed up and carefully set the hammers of the ten-gauge back into place. It wouldn't do to have the thing go off when he hit the surface on the other side. More men had been killed by accident in the West than by any collection of thugs and murderers. He slung the shotgun over his head. He always had a strap on the little cannon, and just now he was thankful for it. Taking a running start, he launched himself over the alley and onto the tin roof opposite him.

He landed with a clatter, his boots banging on the cold metal surface of the sloping roof. Bracing his foot on a vent, he pushed himself forward, inching his way to the top of the roof.

The music from the street rang out in a sharp blare, a mixture of several melodies pouring out of the numerous saloons on the street below. They made a passable sound when heard one at a time, but together they blended to become sheer noise.

The fog made seeing difficult. Certain shapes could be made out, enough to tell the difference between a man and a smokestack, but not enough to be sure of what or who you were looking at. The man he was chasing might have little concern about shooting someone by mistake, and that thought horrified Zac. A drunk trying to sleep off a bender or a child looking to escape the turmoil of a noisy room might easily fall victim to this rooftop gun battle.

He pulled back the hammers on the shotgun and edged discreetly forward, careful not to skyline himself on the top of the roof. Approaching the peak with caution, he sank to his knees and peered over it. Even through the fog he could see no movement, only a railing and a set of stairs that led to the street below. Keeping low, he skirted over the rooftop to the railing.

Peering over the white, weathered boards of the stairway, he could see no sign of life. The street was busy, with several teams of horses bringing supplies into the numerous saloons. A number of men appeared to be parading down the boardwalk, and one man stood leaning against a glowing lamp as he talked to a woman.

Zac got to his feet and walked down the empty stairs. He kept the shotgun cocked. A man who would have shot him in the fog minutes before would think nothing of trying the same thing in a crowd. He could guess at who the man was, more than likely the man he had dry shaved that morning, coming to finish the job this Princeton fellow had sent him to do. What he couldn't understand was how they had known he would be walking past the alley. The street near the river had been seemingly deserted, but from where they had been in the alley they couldn't possibly have recognized him. Someone had to have given them a signal, someone who recognized him and knew where he was going.

A short time later, he walked through the door of the marshal's office. Jenny stood in front of the man's desk, wringing a handkerchief in her hands. She whirled and stepped quickly into his arms. "I heard the shooting and I was scared."

"Well, I'm all right."

"This is something I find hard to get used to."

He put his hand around the back of her neck and squeezed it.

Next to the marshal's desk, several Chinese continued to babble their complaints at the lawman, who was obviously not listening. They spotted Zac and suddenly became animated, pointing at him, their voices spiking to great heights and the pace of their sentences increasing to a speed that would have made their words incomprehensible even if they had been speaking English. He looked at Zac and waved his hand at the men, trying to silence what little broken

English was being spoken. Getting to his feet, he put his hands on his hips.

"I ain't sure how a man can sleep with you in town, Cobb." He leaned forward. "You are leaving tomorrow, aren't you?"

"On the *Delta King* tomorrow."

"Good. We ain't what you might call a sleepy and quiet town, but trouble seems to hunt you down in bunches."

"And it's nothing I'm exactly looking for. I don't think I'd call getting a haircut and walking down one of your streets provocative behavior."

"Well, whatever it is that's bringing the trouble out of the walls 'round here, I can't say as I care for it. I did take the time to wire Jeff Bridger, the sheriff in San Luis Obispo County, inquiring about you this morning, and he said you were okay. He didn't say you were harmless, but he did call you a friend."

Jenny fingered the tear in his shirt. "Are you sure you're all right?"

"I got lucky. It could've been a lot worse."

"I guess Jack was right about what he'd heard. You can never tell about him."

"This wasn't one of his stories. Whoever he heard was making tonight's plan. What I can't figure out was how they knew it would be me walking down that street. They had to have help."

Jenny paused and thought. "Perhaps it's nothing, but I saw that gambler strike a match when you went by, then light a cigar."

"Well, I can't exactly brace a man for smoking."

"No, I suppose not."

"Besides, I know the man that got away and the man who hired him." He looked at the lawman. "The marshal here knows the man too."

"I do?"

"A man named Princeton."

"I know him only by rumor."

"Well, the rumors are true."

The Chinese men began once again to squawk at the lawman and point in the direction of their gambling hall.

He continued to wave them off. "All right, all right. I'll take care of it directly." Turning back to Zac, he leaned over his desk. "Meanwhile, Mr. Cobb, I look forward to waking up tomorrow morning and not finding you in these city limits."

+ + + + +

Jack wore a new tweed jacket, a pair of brown trousers, and shiny new shoes Jenny had purchased for him that morning. He seemed to sit up straighter in his new clothes, and his face looked clean for the first time in quite a spell. He was a handsome boy, that was plain to see. His thick, curly black hair framed a face that promised to one day give birth to a handsome man.

Hattie had noticed his good looks right away. Skip had a plain but very masculine appearance, but this boy was quite comely, and Hattie knew it.

She shuffled the deck of cards and looked up at Jack. "Boy, you is right pretty when you gets yerself all cleaned up. Someday soon you is gonna be breakin' ever' gal's heart in San Francisco, if'n you lives that long."

"What do you mean if I lives that long?"

Hattie continued to shuffle and then turn over the cards. "Well, you had best lay shuck of them thievin' ways of yourn, boy, elsewise yer bound to end up in a small box like that there friend of yourn."

Jack's face fell, and he looked down at the cards.

"My ownself, I'm a changin'," she went on. "I used to be meaner than a teased snake and smelled like a polecat, to boot. People would say they could sniff me fer a full half hour afore they ever saw me. Now I takes me a bath ever' Saturday night, whether I needs one or not."

"Well, I had me a bath tonight," Jack said.

"So did I," Skip joined in.

Hattie reached over and pinched Skip's cheek. "And you do smell purdy, child, mighty purdy indeed."

She could tell he didn't much care for the thought. She turned away from the boy and busied herself with the cards. She talked matter-of-factly, as if she didn't want the boys to know she really cared what they thought about what she was saying. "Naw, I was thinkin' about a different kinda clean that you boys need, a Sunday Good Book cleanin'. You know, a feller can look squeaky new on the outside and be a rare sight fer the beholdin' but on the inside look like the bottom of a spittoon."

Both boys nodded in agreement.

"And I just wouldn't want to see either of you boys turn out bad.

We got too much time and care put into you to watch you run off and go to seed."

Spitting out a stream of brown liquid into the cup, she noticed both boys watching her. She wiped her mouth. "'Course, thing is, fer me I gots to be real careful I don't turn out too perfect. I been so bad that if'n I gets myself changed into some kind a Sunday school teacher, folks is gonna be worried the world's comin' to an end. Might purely petrify them, it might." She shook her head. "No, a few faults here and there is gonna keep me from gettin' all puffed up like and unbearable to get close to."

She leaned forward, looking the boys in the eyes. "I plum hates perfect folks. I feel like they'ze got too much to hide. I wouldn't trust them with my dead horse."

Hattie began showing the boys her so-called card tricks. They were riveted to her every move as her hands flew over the cards.

They had never seen a woman play cards before, let alone so well, and Hattie Woodruff knew she was a novelty to the boys. She chewed vigorously on her plug, pausing occasionally to spit into the once-empty coffee cup.

"I'd sure like to be a gambler when I grow up," Jack said.

Skip cocked his head in Jack's direction. "I thought you said you were gonna be a pirate. You were gonna go up to that cold land of darkness and have treasure."

"Well, bein' a pirate and bein' a gambler is kinda like the same thing. Yer dealing with other folk's money. It ain't none of yours at all, and you never did much to rightly earn it."

"Seems kinda dishonest to me," Skip said.

"Don't you think dishonest money is just as easy to spend as the rest?" Jack asked.

Skip bowed his head, thinking on the matter. "It may be easy to spend, but that don't make it easy to live with, I reckon."

Hattie put down the cards. "That is just what I was talkin' on. You best find yer own way to make money, boy. You start livin' offa the sweat of others and you'll be a lifetime no-count. I seen plenty of them type, run 'em offa my place more'n once. Poker here's a might different, though. This here be a gentleman's game, long as you ain't spectin' to eat offa it. You best learn how to set yerselves down with other men a time or two, though, and hold yer own. Now, you both watch careful like, and I'm a gonna show you how to catch a cheat."

The boys sat up straight and leaned across the table to get a better look.

"Now, boys, tain't many games of chance you'll sit in where some tinhorn won't try one of these here tricks on you." She squinted her eyes at the boys, who sat across from her. "And when y'all see it, you best be ready to get to smoking with yer shooters. Menfolk don't likes to be called a cheat, even though 'most every one of 'em is."

"Zac ain't a cheat," Skip declared.

Hattie spit into her cup and wiped her mouth with the back of her hand. "Ever' man's a cheat in some ways. The Good Book says we is all sinners and violators. He don't cheat none at cards, but given what he does, he rooks death every day." She dropped her tone and murmured, almost talking to herself, "If'n you ask me, he's cheatin' on that Jenny, too." The mumble in her voice mixed with the tobacco juice. "Ought to be an honest man and marry the lady."

Looking up, she noticed the boys staring at her, trying to make out her words. She waved her hand at them. "Never mind what he does. We is talkin' 'bout card cheats here. Now, you just watch my hands real close, 'cause I'm a gonna give Skip here an ace offa the bottom of the deck, and you won't ever know it."

Both boys watched carefully as she shuffled and dealt the cards—so carefully that they didn't notice the gambler who walked up and stood nearby. The man stood behind the boys, close enough to see what was going on but not so close enough as to be a part of it. Hattie's eyes were drawn to him at once. With the salon on board filling up with potential pigeons, she wondered right away why an obvious man of the cards would be standing in an empty dining room watching them.

Putting down her cards, she spit once again into the cup. "You go and lose somethin' 'round here, mister?"

"You might say that."

The boys jerked their heads around, and seeing McCauliff standing behind them, they froze in place. Hattie could see the instant fear register in their faces.

"Well, we'ze been at this here table since suppertime, and we ain't seen nothin'."

McCauliff stepped over behind Jack and patted the boy's shoulder. "I think this youngster here knows what I'm looking for, and if we can just step outside for a minute, we can tend to matters there."

Hattie watched Jack stiffen, his face turning pale.

"We'll be no more than a minute, and then you can get on with this gambling demonstration of yours." He looked down at Jack and smiled. "It was nice to see you on the street today. I tried to find you and give you a treat, but you got lost."

"I don't want to go," Jack said. "I want to stay right here."

"Now, boy, you don't want to embarrass yourself in front of this lady, do you?"

"It don't appear he much wants to go with you, mister," Hattie voiced. "Now, unless yer the one who wants to be embarrassed, I'd say you jest better leave him be."

"Madam, let me suggest that this is just a matter between the boy and myself. I can assure you, it will only take a moment or two. The boy has knowledge of something that I am missing."

"Mister, that young'un there is with Hattie Woodruff. Anything that regards him pertains to me."

"Let me assure you, Miss Woodruff, this is a simple matter that can be cleared up quite quickly."

"I don't know nothin', and I want to stay right here."

Reaching down and putting his hand under Jack's arm, McCauliff started to lift the youngster to his feet. Jack squirmed free.

Reaching into her belt, Hattie extracted the .45 Colt she carried. This was a man's gun, heavy and with impact written all over it. She held it in her hand and pulled back on the hammer. The noise of the readied firing pin froze McCauliff in place.

"Now, you just ease off from the boy." She squinted at him as she spoke. "I may look like just an old lady to you, but there's men pushin' up sod who made that same mistake."

McCauliff raised his hands and stepped back. "You just be real careful with that thing."

"I'm always careful, and I hits what I aim at." She frowned. " 'Course I is so old, and my hand gets mighty shaky like."

McCauliff shivered and backed away. He looked back down at Jack. "We'll tend to this later."

"This is later," Hattie snorted, "and you done gone and tended to all you is gonna tend to. Do I make myself clear, tinhorn?"

CHAPTER 16

EARLY THE NEXT MORNING, Sacramento was still shrouded in heavy fog. Several dogs explored the alleys and streets in the predawn hour, looking for any morsel left from the night before. Zac held the shotgun, and Sergeant Adams clutched his carbine as the army, accompanied by the men from Wells Fargo, unloaded the gold from a wagon and, slinging the boxes between them, walked up the gangway.

Captain Van Tuyl and Dennis Grubb stood on the deck, waiting for them. Van Tuyl motioned the men toward the stern of the boat. "I have a cabin all set aside for your cargo." He looked at Zac. "It's right next to yours."

"Thank you. That will help."

"I figured it would."

The men carted the boxes toward the stern and through the open cabin door, stacking them on the floor.

Adams, looking in, barked orders, "Pile them on the bed first. We'll leave a chair by the door, but I sure don't want anyone lying down on the job."

The string of men laid their cargo down, as ordered, then returned to the waiting guards for more.

Van Tuyl opened his watch. "We'll get up steam right away and be underway inside an hour. With this fog, I'm afraid we won't be breaking any speed records."

"We'll be lucky to hit Walnut Grove before nightfall," Grubb added.

Van Tuyl looked slightly agitated. He stared at the face of the watch and its Roman numerals, even though he knew the time. "We still have some paying passengers who haven't come aboard. I sure hate to leave them, and we may just have to wait a bit till they show up."

Grubb looked off the stern at the fog. The gray murk seemed to be rolling in over the river. He was a tall man and had a steely eyed look about him that smacked of confidence. Pilots were known to be cocky and self-assured, but this one showed no sign of being foolhardy. He stood erect with his jacket buttoned and a cap that had the word "pilot" in brass braced to the front. "One never knows what this river will be like farther downstream," he said, "but chances are it won't get any better. Appears to me the river's dropped a might as well."

"That bad?" Zac asked.

"Just makes my job all the more cumbersome. Some sandbars we could have passed over will have to be avoided, and that will take plenty of care and time. It will make the night something to watch out for too."

Van Tuyl nodded toward Grubb. "Dennis will get us there—that's the important thing. We'll give him a nap this afternoon, and he can take us in after Walnut Grove. With all this fog and the extra time it will require, we'll have to stop there for more fuel."

"You have your watch assigned?" Zac asked.

Adams nodded. "I'll have two men here at all times, one inside the cabin and one outside. If you, me, and this Cox fellow can patrol the deck at intervals, I think we can keep the lid on things."

In the mist below, several new passengers walked up the gangplank, all heavily armed. One man wore a brightly colored shirt and a black slouched hat. The men glanced quickly around the boat as they walked up the gangway.

"Captain," Zac interjected, "I'd like your officers to be carrying sidearms. I've looked over some of the passengers, and if we do have a gang of pirates who try to storm the ship, we're going to need every man jack of you to help."

"I can do that."

"We will be collecting firearms from them," Grubb said. "Normally we don't, but we're making an exception on this trip."

"Good thinking."

Van Tuyl smiled and tapped his cap with his forefinger. "All the time. All the time."

The door to Jenny's cabin cracked open, and she stepped out to watch the loading of the gold. She wore a yellow calico dress that would have seemed dazzling in bright sunlight. In the fog, she still looked radiant.

Van Tuyl and Grubb tipped their caps. "Morning, ma'am," Van Tuyl said. "I'd guess it was difficult to sleep with all this commotion."

"Not at all, Captain. In fact it's far past my normal time to get up."

"She runs a cafe at home," Zac said, "and that has her hopping to get things ready long before folks begin to think about breakfast."

"You see," Jenny beamed, "this has been quite the vacation. I'm afraid getting used to my normal schedule will take some doing."

"One thing I am concerned about, Captain," Zac said, "is how close her cabin is to the action here. Is there another cabin we might put her in?"

Van Tuyl scratched the back of his head. "I suppose we could put her in with your aunt. She's up there on the bow, and that would be plenty safe."

"No thank you, Captain. I think I'd sleep much better here."

Zac smiled. "I suppose you would, at that."

"We could put the boys there," Van Tuyl offered. "That might take a few things off your mind and give you the cabin to yourself."

"That'll be fine," Zac said. "We'll talk about it over breakfast."

"They won't like it," Jenny said.

"Maybe not, but unlike you, they don't have much say-so about it. Besides, Hat can protect them from any bogeyman ever born."

Jenny nodded. "I believe she can, at that."

\+ + + + +

Mary and Dr. Page sat alone at the breakfast table. It didn't surprise her in the least that they were dining on stewed prunes alone. Blevins hadn't joined them for dinner, much to Mamie's embarrassment, and the uneasiness of the evening didn't promise a warm encounter this morning. Even though she hadn't said a word to her uncle nor especially to Mamie about the slap she had given Blevins, anyone could see that something unpleasant had gone on during their evening garden walk.

"You don't seem to have your appetite back," Dr. Page observed.

"I'm not hungry. I feel like a bird in a gilded cage here. We should be going home, yet here we sit—houseguests."

"I'm quite sure Blevins will arrange our passage today."

"Don't be too sure about that."

"And why wouldn't he?"

"Let's just say I suspect the man intends to gain my attention, along with my affection. He has my attention, but my affections he will never have."

The doctor reached over and patted her hand gently. "Perhaps you're reading too much into his hospitality."

Mary grimaced. "Not hardly."

"Common courtesy should dictate that he finds us a way to get back to Sacramento."

"Uncle, I'm not sure our host is familiar with common courtesy. He's polite, but there seems to be an underlying decency that is missing in the man."

"I don't know what he said to you last night in the garden, but perhaps being out here in the delta, away from the social circles that breed civility, has dulled his manners."

"No, I don't think that's it at all. The man is like a king here. Whatever he sees and wants he actually believes he can have. There seems to be no one to question him or his authority, and that's a very dangerous thing in a man."

"Perhaps you're judging him unjustly, Mary."

"I can assure you I'm not. From the way he treats his servants to the way he spoke to me, he expects everyone around him to submit to his every desire."

Dr. Page smiled and stirred his prunes. "Well, I'm quite certain you directed him otherwise."

She dropped her spoon in the bowl. "I most certainly did." She got to her feet. "I think I'll do a little exploring on my own around here."

"Don't do that. I wouldn't want you going outside and by happenstance meeting up with those men."

"No, I don't intend on going outside. I think I'd like to look over the rest of this house, especially the part our host didn't appear to be too comfortable with me seeing last night."

"And where would that be?"

"I'd like to take a closer look at the cellars in this house. They must be quite large—and Blevins tried quite hard to distract me from them last night."

"Yes, I'm sure they are quite extensive and quite dusty, with rats and spiders."

She raised her chin in defiance. "Rats and spiders don't bother me in the least. They couldn't be any more scary than what I've already seen in this place they call The Glades. I won't be long. If they ask about me, you can just tell them I'm still in my room."

"I won't lie for you, Mary."

"Suit yourself, then. Tell them anything you like."

Mary picked up the skirts on her simple calico dress and stepped quietly into the hallway. She paused to listen for servants or for their absent hosts and then made her way down the stairs.

The iron railing that wound along the plastered wall held steady, its joints securely fastened to the oak beams that formed the supports for the big house. Gleaming at each bend was a lamp, showing the way to the levels below the big house. Mary paused at the first level and cracked open the massive oak door.

The iron hinge gave way easily, showing that it had been well used and oiled. Peering into the dark cavern, Mary could see a massive wine cellar. This would explain its frequent use. Mary stepped inside, leaving the door ajar to provide at least some semblance of light on the massive labyrinth. She picked up one of the older bottles, a French wine from the Bordeaux region. *Only the best for Blevins*, she thought.

Replacing the bottle, she quickly surveyed the room. Row after row of bottles lined the room, with labels to announce the occupants of every shelf and a corresponding date. *The man is organized*, she observed. She picked up a sturdy wooden mallet, one used for corking wine kegs. *This might come in handy*.

Backing up to the door, she pushed it open and stepped outside, closing it after her. There had to be levels farther down. The stairs continued to wind their way deep into the bowels of the big house, lights flickering from below.

Mary continued her descent as the stairs quickly ran out of carpet, offering only cold stones for her feet. Each one seemed cleaned and polished, obviously the result of some use. They ended with a landing in front of two formidable oak doors. A brass hasp connected the doors with a shiny lock that held it securely in place.

Mary tried shaking the lock; it held fast. She studied it, and then turning it on its side, she brought the heavy wooden mallet down on it. It sprang open. Taking the sprung lock from the door, she pulled on the iron ring. The door slid open over the rocky floor.

Sticking her head through the doorway, she could see several dark rooms and a corridor that led through them toward the front of the house. There were no lanterns that glowed, only darkness and the shadows that were formed by the meager light from the hall. Inside the door, a stack of torches were kept in a wooden barrel. Drawing out one, she stepped back outside and used the glowing lantern to light it. It flared and gave off a steady flame.

Replacing the lock on the hasp, to at least display a lock that might still appear secure, Mary pulled the oak door closed.

She stepped into the large room and held the torch high. The flood of light showed boxes and barrels, many marked with stenciled lettering. Moving around the room, she could see the letters depicting the contents of the crates and boxes—44.40 ammunition, olive oil, Colt Arms Manufacturing, china, sterling silver, tea, coffee—and something else, something that made the hair on the back of her neck stand on end. There, clearly visible on many of the boxes, were the names of various boats that had been assigned to carry the cargo: *The Spearfish*, *The Maiden Aunt*, *The Belle of Sacramento*, and many other boats, some of which she knew by reading the newspapers had been hijacked by the infamous river pirates. *How did Blevins come by these things?* she wondered.

She inched forward, waving the torch over each box. She knew that if the man wasn't in league with these pirates, there was certainly enough evidence here in this cellar to convince any jury in the land of his guilt. Either he was allied with them, or he made a living buying stolen property.

Moving forward through the boxes of supplies, she turned to a closed door that led into another room. Pushing it open, she shoved the torch inside. There along the walls were rack after rack of rifles. Along one wall, a glittering array of brass-chambered Winchesters gleamed in response to her torch. Boxes of ammunition were stacked at the feet of the weapons. On another wall, multiple shelves of boxes were stacked, each marked Sharps Arms Company, U.S. Army. There was enough weaponry here to start a war, that was plain to see.

She moved to the center of the room, where large, sturdy tables held piles of revolvers. As she waved her torch over the weapons, they winked at her from their heavily blued surfaces. In the wrong hands these guns could be very dangerous. She could only guess at their value.

She retreated out the door and closed it behind her. She'd seen far too much already, she knew that, but somehow she just couldn't resist seeing all there was to see in all the rooms beneath the house.

The next room had yet another lock fastened to the door. Bringing up the hammer, she smashed it several times. The raps of the mallet echoed through the chamber, each one sending a shiver up her spine. With a final blow, the lock sprang open. She lifted it out of place and pulled the door open.

Stepping into the room, she gasped in amazement. There along the walls were beautiful paintings, each surrounded by gold leaf and jeweled frames. Gold and jewels sparkled in the light from the torch. Large boxes were positioned on tables, and silver and gold candelabras studded the mahogany wood. Shelf after shelf of gold statuary and ornaments stared back at her, their brightness almost emanating a light all their own. There was fabulous wealth here, more than she had ever imagined.

She stepped over to the boxes on the tables and opened the first one. Piles of gold double eagles filled the box. She ran her hand over the surface of the coins and then picked one up. It was recently minted. This was no collector's treasure trove; it was the stash of a pirate.

Closing the lid and moving on to another box, she opened it. What she saw amazed her still more. Flashing beneath the glow of her torch were dazzling jewels, some set in gold and others in piles. Rubies burst forth with blazing color, and emeralds glinted a deep green. Diamonds lay in a pile, shining like miniature suns. She stood breathless, taking in the sight.

Fear flooded her soul. If someone found her down here, she could never be viewed as a harmless houseguest. No matter how attracted to her the man was, if Blevins ever discovered she knew about his cellar, she would never be permitted to live. Breathing heavily, she scampered out the door and closed it behind her. Replacing the lock, she hoped it would once again engage. It snapped shut.

The torch in her hand flickered. There must be some opening up ahead, someplace that was a source of the fresh air. She moved past the stacked boxes and in the direction of the faint breeze. Coming to the end of the room, she saw a flight of stairs that led still farther down. Stepping lightly, she descended even deeper into the basement.

The dark walls were wet with dew that beaded up on the hard glistening stone. She felt her way along the cold, icy facade to the dark recesses below. Suddenly, light poured into the hallway, illuminating a large opening that seemed to be an open cavern. Boxes of marked goods littered the room. Pressing ahead, she could see the tall grass outside. The river must be close. She could hear it lapping along the bank. There was another faint sound that caught her attention, the slow dipping of paddles in the river outside the entrance. She heard muffled shouts as men neared the landing.

Waving her torch over the barrels and boxes, she spotted a fresh stack in the corner of the room. Quickly, she dashed for the cover of the stolen goods and crouched behind them. Moments later, she heard the voices of the men, grunting as they carried a load of stolen supplies into the mouth of the cavern. She stifled the torch with the edge of her skirt. It would leave telltale marks on the dress, but right now that was the least of her worries.

"Over here—let's just set the boxes over here for now."

The men moved slowly, swinging the heavy boxes between them.

"Blevins is gonna be runnin' outta room before long," one of the men moaned.

"Well, we got to make us some space in here. When we take down the *Delta King*, there's gonna be plenty still to go in here."

"Don't think so. Most of that shipment is ours as well as whatever we care to take from passengers and the safe on board. All Blevins wants is the gold."

Mary craned her neck to listen closer. The *Delta King* was one of the largest boats on the river. These pirates would never have dreamed of taking something so large unless the booty was considerable.

"That ought to cash him out, I reckon. There'll be enough of that to set him up pretty, from what I hear."

She listened closely. One of the voices belonged to one of the men who had kidnapped her and her uncle. Suddenly, another sound spun her head around. The heavy door that led to the cavern from the house had slammed. There had been no way to lock that door behind her, and whoever was now coming down to the unloading of the new plunder would guess that something was amiss.

Moments later she heard the growl of Blevins's voice. "You men set that over in the corner. I'll catalog it later."

The men swung the heavy box and shuffled in her direction. She slowed her shallow breathing.

"You haven't seen anyone else down here, have you?" Blevins asked.

"Nah, we just got here, and we ain't seen nothing."

"Well, the lock on my hall door was open, and I seem to be missing one of my houseguests."

"Maybe you just left it that way."

"No, I'm a very careful man. Has Princeton arranged everything for the good folks of Walnut Grove tonight?"

"Yep, sure has. Has one of the best sideshows I ever did see. Them folks on the *Delta King* ain't gonna be able to say no to it. Kinda like to be there my ownself, I would."

"You'll have time to get there, all of you. We're going to need every man we've got, especially if that captain insists on keeping his schedule and not letting the people off."

"And what if he does just that?"

"Then you and the rest of the men will board her as passengers. I have two good men traveling with the people there already, and Manny and his men boarded in Sacramento. I'm afraid there will be more in the way of lives lost, and it will bring down the wrath of God on us, but with what there is on board that steamer, it will be well worth it."

Mary held her breath. Scurrying around a box close to her was a rat, a large rat. The creature stopped and stared at her, his bright eyes shining in the semidarkness. Any movement would be heard. She could only hope the creature was as smart as she was and knew the danger they were both in. It moved toward her. She motioned toward it with her head, and it ran back around the box.

"What was that?" Blevins asked.

"Probably a rat."

The man grabbed hold of the crate in front of Mary and, wedging himself between two of the boxes, began to push it aside.

"There it is!" another man shouted.

A pistol shot sounded a deafening roar in the dark cavern. Acrid smoke drifted toward Mary. The smell of gun smoke was all around.

"Nice shooting." The man bent down and, picking the rat up by the tail, carried it to the entrance of the cavern. "That's one less varmint down here."

"I thought it was my houseguest," Blevins exclaimed.

The man laughed. "It *was* one of your houseguests."

"Well, the one I'm talking about is considerably more attractive, and she showed an interest in this lower hall last night that I didn't care for."

"That don't sound good. Maybe she's in one of the other rooms."

The men shuffled off through the cavern and up the stairs to the cellar.

Mary listened carefully to the sound of the departing men. She couldn't stay here and she knew it. Once Blevins began his search of the house, he'd discover where she was or at least be highly suspicious. She got to her feet. The entrance to the cavern would be her only way out. If one of the pirates had remained with the boat, she'd find out soon enough. Skirting around the boxes, she ran for the entrance that led to the river. She would go around the house and make for the rose garden.

CHAPTER 17

+ + + + + + +

COMPARED TO SACRAMENTO, Walnut Grove was no more than a burgh, a small hamlet speckled along the river that catered to the needs of fruit farmers, many of them Chinese, who had come to America to work on the railroad years earlier. The largest store, appropriately named The Big Store, sat on the only high ground that could be found. In it, an older Chinese man hammered away at meat with a large cleaver. He waved the sharp steel baton at customers, shouting out orders as if they were minions in his own private economic army. He seemed panicked as customer after customer left the store to see the new sight that had arrived in town.

Wong Foo was truly the master of all he surveyed—all, that was, except the few white eyes that came into The Big Store from time to time. With them he maintained a safe emotional distance, making his thoughts known only to other Chinese in their Cantonese dialect when the white eyes turned their heads. The man's clean, rotund face betrayed little emotion when speaking with outsiders. He smiled and bowed at appropriate times, wiping his hands on his blood-stained apron.

Today it was just locals in the store, however, and even so, he was having a difficult time keeping them in place. He wiped his hands and slammed the sharp edge of the cleaver into a ready position on the large cutting board. He would go out and see to all the pandemonium, this new thing that was taking his customers away.

The town itself was odd-looking. The majority of its buildings rested on stilts as protection from the occasional flooding during the spring runoff. Wooden shanties looked down from their perches at passersby. Clean and tight, the houses were typically Chinese. Brightly painted shutters and doors with polished exterior trim set off the dull, split-shingle sides of the shanties. In the busy section of town, catwalks snaked from building to building, each with its own set of wooden props, large poles that held the wooden planks airborne. For a large man, to walk through the town of Walnut Grove was to bounce.

But on that day, the strangest sight of all was the large tent that sat along the edge of the river, a carnival tent. Roughnecks were pounding stakes, and men wheeled cages filled with animals into position. This was a first for Walnut Grove. The men and their show had seemed to appear out of nowhere, admitting they had been diverted from their usual tour for this special one-night performance. Groups of bystanders eyed one another in disbelief. The Chinese of the town had never seen a circus act, and the men that ran the Majestic Manage of Madness had seldom seen a Chinaman willing to part with more than a quarter to watch just anything.

Wong Foo stood on the porch of The Big Store and tried to see through the fog. Even in the heavy mist, the brightly colored tent stood out. He listened to the white-eyed strangers yell at one another in their disagreeable tongue, yell and point, shouting orders and giving directions. This would come to no good. There could be nothing here that was worth a man's time and certainly not his money. He watched carefully for a few minutes, and then waving his hand in derision toward the mass of newcomers, he turned and walked back into the store.

+ + + + +

The roughnecks and barkers who were busy setting up the tents and sideshows mumbled to themselves. Wilkes had told them a wealthy benefactor had paid for much of their expenses and that this generosity was the reason for their stop, but no one liked to perform for an empty house, and as they continued to watch the curious but unenthusiastic crowd, that was just what they imagined it would be—empty.

The crowd watched carefully as several handlers managed to move the large elephants into position. These were the things people had come to see, animals they had only heard about. There would be no need to buy a ticket. The roustabouts heard the foreign murmur of the crowd as they wheeled the cages with two tigers into place.

The tattooed lady was wearing a bulky dress, but the most famous ships of the American navy were still clearly visible on her arms. The Chinese who stood by pointed at her and giggled. Large glass cases with snakes curled at the bottom were on carts, and several small but brave boys cautiously approached them, pointing and whispering. The new smell of death, danger, and excitement filled the small riverfront street.

Another man, a stranger, stood and watched the carnival prepare for the evening's performance. Russ Korth had his six-gun tied down to his side, and his black leather vest glistened with a coat of fresh polish. His black hat had been freshly blocked and creased. Korth was always careful to keep himself and the things that belonged to him with great care. Today, his boots had a bright shine from fresh polish. Korth stood in the doorway of The Rusty Scuffer, one of the town's two saloons, and watched the roustabouts do their work. He smiled.

With all the newcomers in Walnut Grove, his presence, along with that of the twenty-some men who accompanied him, would scarcely go noticed. This had been a good plan. He had only six others with him at The Rusty Scuffer, and the others had come trickling in one or two at a time, each making a pretense of turning up to see the big show. He saw several scattered about the crowd that watched the erection of the displays and tents. Looking off to his right, he could see Jamie and two other men watching the same sight from the door of a saloon.

He laced his fingers together and stretched them out. Ever since he had heard about this Zac Cobb fella, he'd been looking forward to this evening. He and Manny sparred constantly for leadership in the group and maybe, just maybe, now it would be his to claim. The man might be tough, but a bullet would stop the toughest man anytime, and Korth knew he was one of the fastest men in all of California. He looked forward to throwing down on this Cobb.

Looking down the foggy street, he caught sight of Princeton as the man ambled with his horse into town. The colonel would be pleased. Everything seemed to be going well, and everyone was in place. Now maybe the elaborate charade would pay off.

If the action they had planned for the evening could be used to entice the men on the *Delta King* to come ashore, then the chances of gunplay would be minimal. They might even succeed in forcing the soldiers off the boat. Manny and his men could take care of those who would be left.

Princeton nodded in Korth's direction, and Korth walked back into the saloon and, taking his seat, poured two glasses of whiskey. Moments later, Princeton pushed the doors open, spied Korth, and walked over to the empty chair.

"Everything ready?" Princeton asked.

"Ticking like a fine watch."

The colonel smiled. "I'm sure these people are gonna put on a fine show."

"Yeah, and we've got something special planned to bring down the curtain."

"We need to get these Chinamen out of their houses and milling about to create as much confusion as possible."

"Been taken care of. Did you see those elephants when you came into town?"

"Yes, they would be hard to miss."

"Well, tonight when the show gets under way, we're gonna send them on a nice run through this town. What with the whole place built up on sticks, it ought to make a fine show, one not to be missed."

+ + + + +

There was no way the boys were going to stay in Hattie's cabin through the whole boat ride home, and they couldn't see Hattie reading to them and keeping an eye on their whereabouts for long. They were antsy to see as much of the *Delta King* as possible, especially the way the big pistons pushed the large wheel through the water. It would be a sight.

"Now, is you boys acquainted with this here Shakespeare feller?"

"Yes, ma'am," Skip shot back. "I study him in school, and Zac makes me read his stuff all the time."

"Fine, fine, then you won't get yerself lost in this here Hamlet, now, will you?"

"That the one about the kid whose mother marries up with his pap's killer?" Jack asked.

"That's it, sure 'nuff."

The two boys exchanged knowing glances. Skip knew they were going to get read to, like it or not. Hattie might be many things, but Skip knew full well she was one who didn't like to change her mind.

"I sure likes books about killers and such," Jack said. " 'Course, I've known plenty of such men in my times."

"Oh, ya have, now, have you? And just what makes you come upon men like that?"

"That's all there is on the docks at Oakland—sailors, killers, and preachers."

"Sorry lot, all of them," Hattie growled. "'Course, I is changing my mind somewhat 'bout preachers—not all of 'em, mind you, just my own."

"You got a preacher?"

"'Course I has. You thinkin' I'm a heathen or somethin'? I wuz raised once upon a time to be a mighty good girl, and now that I'm gettin' on, I guess I'm going more back to them ways." She leaned over and jabbed her finger in the boy's direction. "You young'uns see to it you don't ever leave that there path. There be plenty of hard scrapes if'n you do."

"Yes, ma'am," Skip nodded.

The boys listened dutifully as Hattie read the book, then when they took their turn at the reading, they watched her begin to nod. Within minutes, a buzz rose from the woman's lips. She was fast asleep.

The boys got up slowly and edged their way to the door. Minutes later they were on the deck, watching the hands as the men repositioned the cargo.

"How long you reckon she's gonna sleep?" Jack asked.

"Don't rightly know for sure," Skip said, "but she was up late last night, I hear, gamblin'."

"Well, we better look around. I'd sure like to see that pilothouse up there, wouldn't you?"

"You betcha."

The boys rounded the deck, heading for the stairs. Then they stopped in their tracks. There standing by the rail was Rance McCauliff. The man spotted them right away and dropped his cigarette into the river.

Spinning on their heels, Jack and Skip ran for the other side of the deck. Swinging down the rail on the doorway down to the engine room, they pushed their way into the glowing darkness. Shadows filled the dark corridor, and the roaring glow of the fire ahead of them bathed their faces in a hot light. Jack signaled toward a spot behind the tool cabinet and pulled Skip after him. The boys huddled together in the darkness.

"You reckon he seen us go down here?" Skip whispered.

"Don't know."

Skip peered around the corner of the cabinet. The shadows dancing along the bowels of the boat were frightening. They could hardly differentiate a man walking from the natural glimmer of the fire in the boiler. He leaned back and pressed his spine against the wooden compartment. "I'd sure hate to be down here if he caught up with us."

"Yeah," Jack croaked out a raspy whisper. "That man's liable to do most anything and there wouldn't be anybody to see."

"Maybe this wasn't such a good idea."

"Well, there ain't much we can do 'bout that now. We'd best wait here for a spell."

Skip nodded. "Yeah, we had oughta." In spite of the words of resolve that came out of him, inside Skip was as angry as he was frightened.

"I just hope you're learning something from all this," Skip whispered.

"Like what?"

"Like stealing something that don't belong to you is bad business."

Jack dropped his chin to his chest. "I don't reckon this was such a good idea. I just didn't figure he'd know who took it, that's all."

"Why wouldn't he? You're a thief."

"And I suppose you ain't never wanted something that you couldn't have."

" 'Course I have, plenty of times. But just 'cause you want something don't mean you ought to have it."

"Well, I ain't never had nothin', and when I see somethin' I wants and I can get it, I figure it's mine to have."

"Wants don't mean nothin'. Everybody's got wants. The best thing to do is be thankful for what you got, 'cause no matter how much you got, a feller always wishes on more, and there's more to fancy than a body could ever use anyhow."

"I suppose you're right."

"You bet I am. Stealing is just plain wrong. If I was you, I'd just turn those wants of yours from things to places and people. There's places to get to that you ain't never been before and people to see and meet that you ain't never dreamed on yet."

"Oh, I dream aplenty."

"Fine, then why don't you just set your sights on them things and leave this here pirating be."

"I want to go out on one of them ships in the bay. I'd like to get to them islands, to China, or maybe to that frozen dark land up north that I've heard about."

"Fine, just think on them places and get your mind off of other people's things. If you do that, you just might live long enough to get there."

They listened to the sound of the black gang as it continued to fire the boiler. Steam hissed from several pipes overhead, and the men manning the shovels continued to screech at each other in Chinese. It was like another land, a foreign land below deck.

The boys sank to their knees behind the cabinet and listened. They heard the shouts of the engineer, followed by broken English in response. Listening to the men as they used their shovels and grunted before the roaring fire made Skip understand how hard this work was and that there was nothing of any beauty to recommend it—no windows, few breaks, little fresh air.

Skip watched the outline of a man as he left the boiler and headed their direction. He could see the glow of the fire on the man's bare skin. Quickly darting his head back around the cabinet, he held his finger up to his lips for Jack to see.

To the boys, the dim light of the engine room had seemed like the perfect place to hide, but to a man who worked in the engine room and was accustomed to the dim light it might seem as bright as day. The boys scooted closer together and held their breath.

"What you do here?"

The man's hand shot out and grabbed Skip by the ankle, pulling him out from behind the tool cabinet. Jack rolled over to the other side of the locker and, scrambling to his feet, ran for the stairway.

The man continued to pull Skip into the gangway. "You no belong here, boy. You a thief."

"I ain't stole nothin'," Skip sputtered.

"Passenger not allowed in engine room. You come here to steal."

"No, mister. Let me go. I ain't never stole nothin', . . . honest." Skip could feel his stutter coming back with a vengeance.

The man hoisted him to his feet. It was Peng Lee, and he recognized Skip right away. "Where your thief friend. You steal more from me?"

"No, honest, w-w-we didn't take anything. We were just h-h-h-hiding, that's all."

The man felt Skip's pockets as the boy held his hands high.

"You no belong here, boy. Engine room dangerous."

"Please, mister, let me go. I didn't take anything and I won't come down here again, not ever."

The man pushed Skip toward the stairs. Skip stumbled and fell.

"You go, boy, and not come back."

Skip scrambled to his feet and bolted for the stairway. Finding the rails, he ran up the iron stairs and stumbled once again onto the foggy deck. Swiveling his head around, he peered through the mist, looking for Jack. Despite the fog he could see two figures grappling near the rail. McCauliff must have found Jack.

Skip got to his feet. He had to find Zac and find him quick. Running toward the stern of the boat, he rounded the corner and bumped into a soldier.

"Here, here, boy. You better be careful. These decks can be slippery."

Behind the man, Zac was talking to another soldier.

"Zac, Zac, you better come quick."

Zac stepped in his direction, and Skip grabbed his sleeve. "You better come on and right away. That gambling man has got Jack."

"Where?"

"'Round here." Skip pulled on his arm. "It's bad, real bad."

Zac followed the boy as Skip once again ran past the entrance to the engine room. There in the fog, the two figures continued to wrestle near the railing of the boat. The man had Jack in one hand, lifting his feet off the deck. In his other hand, a knife was perilously close to the boy's neck.

Moving briskly to the two figures, Zac grabbed the man's wrist and jerked him around, spilling his knife to the deck. Jack fell beside it.

"What did I tell you about leaving these boys be?"

"That boy stole from me," McCauliff stammered.

"Well, I hope you can swim, because this is the end of the line for you on this boat."

"What do you mean?"

"I mean this is where you're getting off."

"You can't do that."

"Oh, I can't? Well, you just watch me."

With that, Zac picked the man up by the seat of his pants and the collar of his coat and threw him over the side of the boat.

McCauliff hit the water with a splash and struggled to the surface. His eyes grew wide at the sight of the approaching paddles. He began to violently splash away from the boat.

The boys stood beside Zac at the rail and watched. "Will he be all right?" Skip asked.

"That kind don't die easy. You're better off just cutting a wide swath around them."

Jack held on to the rail, shaking like a stalk of wheat in the wind. "I thought for sure he was gonna kill me."

Zac reached out and grabbed the boy, holding him close. "You all right?"

"Yes, sir."

"Did you take something from that man?"

Skip watched him closely. He knew Jack wanted that derringer bad.

"I did earlier, but I done put the money back, all of it."

"Well, no matter what you did, no man has the right to threaten you with a knife. I hope you've learned your lesson, though."

"Yes, sir, I have."

CHAPTER 18

"MARY, WHY DO WE NEED TO DO THIS?" Dr. Page was reluctant to leave the big house, in spite of the incoherent babblings coming from his niece. "Why don't we just wait and see if someone we can trust comes to the house?"

"Uncle, anyone who would dare to come to this house would be the last person to trust."

She took him by the hand and started down the sweeping stairs to the hallway below.

"Shouldn't we leave these clothes?" he asked. "They don't belong to us."

"We don't have time to change clothes. I don't know how long it will take him to come up here from the cellar and begin to search for us, and I don't want to be here when he does."

"But, Mary, Mr. Blevins has assured us that he will see us safely to some means of conveyance today. I think we should just remain quiet about what you've seen and wait."

She shook her head. "We can't wait, I tell you. He saw the locks open downstairs, and he suspects us already. He'll never let us go, and if he does, the men he entrusts us to will more than likely murder us on the road. The knowledge of what that man has in his basement is dangerous."

As the two of them neared the foot of the stairs, they could hear Blevins's voice on the landing that separated the garden and the passageway to the cellar. The two of them quietly stepped down the last several stairs as they listened to the conversation.

"You sure them locks have been tampered with?"

"I'm sure," Blevins responded, "and there's no one else around here who could have remotely done it but those two. I've left strict orders for all the servants in the most unmistakable terms that they are never to go below the wine cellar."

"What about that aunt of yours?"

"Aunt Mamie? You can forget about her. She's so deathly afraid she might see a spider, much less be confronted in the dark by one, I practically have to use an armed escort to get her into her own closet."

Mary pulled at Dr. Page's sleeve and motioned toward the parlor. They slipped around the corner, continuing to listen.

"Well, what you gonna do about it?"

"The only thing I can do," Blevins answered.

Mary and the doctor were soon out of earshot. The parlor was empty. Apparently, Mamie was taking Dr. Page's advice on getting more sleep.

Moving through the doors in the rear of the parlor, they walked into the game room. This was the place men removed themselves to after dinner in order to smoke their cigars and play billiards while the women sat in the parlor. The billiard table was hand-carved mahogany. Massive, intricately carved birds' claws stood on balls and served as the feet for the legs of the green felt table. Row after row of polished cues stood sentinel along the wall.

"There must be another rear entrance," Mary said.

"And what will we do when we get there? In this fog, I'm not sure we can even tell which direction to go."

"And he'll just have a harder time looking for us. All we have to do is put as much distance between us and this place as possible."

"We could walk around in circles for hours."

"Well then, at least that will be a few more hours for us to live."

A door from the billiard room led down a flight of stairs. The stairs were unlit and below them faint light made their footsteps only dimly visible.

Carefully, they moved down them. The arched door gave way to a room with massive and multiple windowpanes. The floor was covered with brightly colored tiles. A large bar dominated one end of the room. This must have been the place Mamie said served the parties and dances that at one time made The Glades a place of coveted invitation. It was hard to imagine that Blevins had been given to great social occasions at any point in his life. The man lived for one thing now—accumulating the greatest fortune possible, away from the prying eyes of his neighbors.

Heavy green curtains hung beside the windows, and curved

brass handles showed that several of the windowpanes served as doors leading out into the garden.

"This way," Mary said, pulling her uncle behind her. Pushing down on one of the brass handles, she opened the door and stepped out into the foggy garden. "We'd better stay close to the house," she said. "We wouldn't want to be seen."

Running along behind the massive rose bushes, the two of them kept themselves hidden from the windows in the main part of the house. As they darted in between the bushes, several of the thorns snagged Mary's calico dress.

Dr. Page reached down and freed her hem. "Careful, dear. This is all you have to wear until we get home."

She slumped and then turned to hug him. "Oh, Uncle, what a blessed word, 'home.' Right now I can't think of a more beautiful word in the English language. Please tell me we'll see our home again."

"We will, Mary. The Lord will send His angels to watch over us. This fog can never hide us from His eyes."

"I'm just so tired, and I want to be home."

"Mary, we can never make a nest down here. Human beings always try to find roots, something that tells them where they come from and where they're going, but when we do that our trust isn't in the Lord." He placed his arm around her and hugged her gently. "We never know what will come, honey, but we know He will come."

Minutes later, they had passed the rose gardens and found themselves walking between rows of planted vegetables. Beans grew on poles, snaking themselves on carefully laced twine. They stepped through the soft soil, mashing the ground and leaving heavy footprints.

Soon they were once again on the border of the numerous bare and pruned fruit trees. The dark, ghostly shapes of tangled limbs stood mutely in the fog, their bare branches reaching out to them in plaintive summons.

Taking hold of her arm, the doctor pointed. "This way. I think it will take us away from the river."

"Just so it takes us as far away from that house as possible."

Soon, they began to run. The trees came on them with suddenness through the fog, their long gnarled branches giving them one near miss after another. They ducked and kept running. Before long, they were both breathing heavily. Behind them, in the distance, they could hear men shouting.

Turning back to look, Mary could no longer see the big house. The fog was providing a blanket of cover for them now. She was glad for that. Suddenly, the branches of a tree caught her hair, spinning her to the ground. She cried in pain and then quickly covered her mouth.

"Are you all right?"

"Yes," she whimpered, getting back to her feet. "Do you think they heard me?"

"I'm not sure. One thing's for certain, though, we can't stay here."

They continued to run in the same general direction. The fog made any sense of bearings difficult. The sun burned somewhere above them, but it was only a vague light that gave final warning to any obstacle directly in front of them. The fog was a misty curtain, angel hair that hung from the heavens and just this moment a shelter from God. Moments later they heard a new, yet distinct sound—the sound of horses' hooves coming on fast.

The two of them ran side by side. "They're coming for us," Dr. Page panted. "They must have seen our footprints in the garden, and if they did, they know which way we're going."

"How could they? I don't even know what direction we're running in."

The pounding of the hooves grew louder. Some of the men shouted through the mist. Mary could only imagine the obstacles the trees were providing for them in the fog. They were difficult to negotiate on foot in this fog, and on horseback men were bound to run suddenly into the branches.

Up ahead of them, they could see several trees come together, their trunks forming a barrier. "We need to stop so you can catch your breath, Uncle. Let's get behind those." Running toward the trees, they stooped behind them and crouched low.

Dr. Page sat down, panting. He wasn't what could be called an old man; still, no man his age should be kept on a dead run for long. Mary put her hand on his shoulder. "Are you all right?"

He nodded.

Looking around the trees, she watched and waited. It took only a few moments before she saw the dark outlines of the first few horses with their dark-coated riders. They were spread out in a line and came through the fog like the horsemen of the apocalypse. Mary's heart began to pound. They could hear the men shout out directions.

"They had to go this way," one of the men grumbled.

Mary recognized the voice as one of the men she had heard in the cellar.

"We need more men if we're gonna have a search like this, and most of what we've got are in Walnut Grove."

"Just shut up and keep looking." She recognized Blevins's voice. "They couldn't have gotten very far, not in this fog."

One of the men turned his horse around and leaned down, as if to get a closer look at the ground below. "I ain't seen no sign since the garden."

"We know they're heading in this direction," Blevins barked.

The horses came closer. Mary and Dr. Page pressed their backs against the trunks of the trees as they watched the men slowly ride past.

Please, Lord, keep their heads forward. Don't let them look around. Don't let them see us, Mary prayed silently.

The ghostly riders moved on through the fog.

"We have to go in another direction," Dr. Page said. "They're in front of us now."

Getting to their feet, they ambled off in a northerly direction. "Let's walk this way for a while, then we can turn back west," the doctor added.

Over an hour later, they spotted the house. At first glance they could see it was the same house that had offered them protection and fed them. The Chinese man and his wife would be inside. Maybe there they could find direction and some help.

Dr. Page called out, "Hello the house."

\+ + + + +

Zac pushed open the door to the pilothouse. "You mind if I show the boys around?" he asked.

Dennis Grubb was at the wheel, and Captain Van Tuyl stood behind him, eyeballing over the man's shoulder. Wheeling around, the captain put his hands on his hips. "Not at all. Come on in, boys. Have a look-see."

Sheepishly, the boys peered around Zac.

"Step in, boys," Zac said. "This is what you wanted to see, wasn't it?"

"Yes, sir," Skip answered, stepping forward.

"I'm afraid I have a little explaining to do to you, Captain."

"How's that?"

"It seems I've thrown a paying passenger off this boat of yours. More than likely, I should have gone and asked you first, since you're the man in charge."

"Who was it?"

"That gambler fella, McCauliff."

"Well, good riddance." Van Tuyl turned back to Grubb. "I wasn't aware we'd made a stop."

"We haven't," Grubb responded. "We don't stop until we get to Walnut Grove."

Zac took off his hat and scratched the back of his head. "Well, the throwing overboard I did didn't require a stop."

Van Tuyl blinked. "You threw him in the river?"

"That I did."

The captain doubled over with laughter, and Grubb shook so hard, he had to regain his composure and steady the wheel. "Land a Goshen," Van Tuyl roared, "that's a first for the *Delta King*, and it couldn't have happened to a better candidate."

Zac put his hands on Jack's shoulders. "He was threatening the boy here with a knife, and when I called him on it, he gave me a jawing."

"Well, that's a good enough reason in my book. He's lucky we didn't hang him for a thing like that."

"Here," Grubb said, "you boys want a feel of the wheel?"

"Oh boy!" Skip cried out. "Could we?"

"Sure," Grubb said, backing away with one hand on the wheel. "We're in a spot that's nice and deep."

The boys each took a turn at the helm. Behind the polished wheel, each seemed to drift into the notion of being a river pilot one day. On the river, there was no one more respected or admired than a pilot. The man behind the wheel had to have his wits about him at all times. Most were confident and so self-assured that they mixed well only with other pilots. It was a lonely job, and the cocky attitudes that most of them exhibited kept it that way.

Dennis Grubb seemed to be the exception, however. Zac could tell that by the way Grubb took pride in showing the boys the intricacies of steering the large riverboat. He took the wheel back in a matter of minutes and swung it into a deeper part of the channel. The boys backed up and watched him maneuver the boat.

A map lay spread out on the sideboard of the pilothouse, and the boys edged up to it. "Mind if we look this over?" Skip asked.

"No, go right ahead," Grubb answered. "Most of the channels are out of date anyway, especially with this water level so low right now." Turning around, he tapped on the side of his head. "Most of what I need to know is right up here. No pilot worth his salt depends on charts."

"We ain't run aground yet with Dennis here at the wheel."

"Look at all these here islands," Jack said.

"The delta's full of islands. Some disappear during the flooding, only to show up again when the water's down."

"Looks kinda confusing," Jack said.

"That it is," Van Tuyl admitted. "You'd be hard-pressed to find your way around, and oncc you got on one of them islands, you'd never rightly be able to tell which one you was on. Only way to tell would be to ask folks who live there."

"People live there?" Skip asked.

"Ain't so sure someone could call it living. Mostly they stay there when the water's down and try to eke out a living. There's towns along the river. In fact we'll be stopping at one after the sun's down, but there ain't much there, just a bunch of Chinese fruit farmers. You can get some nice pears there, though, when they're in season and plenty of jellies and jams."

"We'll have to try some," Zac offered. "I'm sure Jenny and Hat would like that fine."

The boys both nodded.

Zac looked over the charts. "Captain, you figure those pirates we're watching out for come out of one of these islands?"

"I reckon they do. I don't 'spect we'll have much to worry about till we're past Walnut Grove and Grand Island, though. There's just too many people thereabouts to suit the likes of scoundrels like them. We'll pass a few mighty fine houses thereabouts, too. The large planters keep the Chinese working for them, if they're able. Now, those men seem to make a mighty fine living, even if the rest of the folks hereabouts is starvin' to death."

"That doesn't seem fair," Skip said.

"Fair is what a man's ambition will bring him," Zac said. "Life in general is unfair. It's the man who makes his own way."

Jack nudged Skip and smiled.

"A man's got to make his way honestly, though, doesn't he?" Skip asked.

"Either that or hang," Zac replied. "Those pirates may be enjoying what they see as the good life right now, but it's going to come to a sudden stop at the end of a rope. For a thinking man with ambition, there's too much of a life to be made this side of the law."

"There sure is," Van Tuyl roared. "I seen many a penniless pauper show up here in Californy that lives on Nob Hill today, and they didn't make their money digging for gold, either."

"How'd they do it?" Jack asked.

"Mostly selling things to folks that need them. Some of them did quite well by selling stuff that were nothing more than a waste of a working man's time."

Zac could see that thought intrigued Jack.

"What sort of stuff?" Jack asked.

"Entertainment mostly, that and whiskey."

"Entertainment?"

"Yeah—dancing halls, performers, newspapers and books, that kind a thing."

"You mean folks get rich just writing down the stories from their heads?"

"A few, if they're good enough."

Skip nudged Jack. "You could do that. You got plenty of stories to tell. A few of them even had me going. And you can read and write. That's better than most folks, I reckon. 'Course"—he scratched his chin—"you got to clean up that English of yours first. Ain't nobody wants to read ain'ts. You got to make it come out proper, like that preacher's been teachin' you."

"I reckon."

"Anything beats pirating other folks' oysters," Zac said. "You'll breathe longer."

Jack hung his head.

"We got that friend of yours lashed down to the foredeck," Van Tuyl offered. "The box is small, but it fits him."

"I reckon I should go see to it," Jack added.

"Can we?" Skip asked.

"Sure," Zac said, "but you boys be careful on them stairs. Don't go running up and down them things."

With the boys going below, Zac took out his pipe and lit it. "Thanks for showing the boys what you did."

Van Tuyl laughed. "It's the least we could do for the man who ridded us of a river rat."

CHAPTER 19

THE HOUSE IN THE FOG seemed unusually quiet, then all of a sudden, the large black dog appeared, running from around the barn and barking.

"Whoa!" Dr. Page declared. "Hold on there, boy, it's just us."

The dog snarled, baring his teeth.

"Where are those people?" Mary asked.

"I don't imagine they'd be out in the fields," Page answered. "Not with all this fog."

"Maybe they're used to these conditions."

The doctor lowered himself to the level of the dog and held out his hand in a nonthreatening manner.

"What are you doing?" Mary asked. "Giving him a sample?"

"Just trying to show him he has nothing to fear from us."

"He seems to be the only one who doesn't know that."

Dr. Page stifled his fear and continued to try to coax the big dog to come to him. "I wish I had something to feed him," he said.

"You're offering him the only thing we've got—your flesh."

Moments later, the door to the farmhouse cracked open slightly.

"Someone is there," Mary said.

"I thought I saw some movement in the window," Dr. Page replied. "I wonder why they don't come out." He yelled once more. "Hello the house. It's us again."

The door opened, and the Chinese woman stepped out onto the high porch. She began to yell at the dog in Chinese, sending a series of what could only be commands punctuated by curses. The dog whimpered slightly and backed away, still giving out mixed snarls.

Dr. Page got to his feet and took off his hat. "It's us again, madam, the same ones who were here before."

The woman backed up and looked inside the house, as if receiving instructions. Walking to the edge of the porch, she signaled them to come forward. "You, come then. Come in house."

Mary and Dr. Page stepped forward. The doctor put his arm around Mary, helping her up the stairs. "Thank you, madam. We were hoping someone was here. We thought you might have been working."

The woman was silent. It had been plain to see from their last visit that her knowledge of English was a basic one, one that she was uncomfortable with. She stepped aside, allowing Mary and the doctor to enter.

The woman bowed her head sharply and motioned toward a small, uncomfortable-looking settee. Dr. Page and Mary sat down, hesitantly, on the edge. Mary could see that this woman would not be able to give them the directions they required. She seemed uncomfortable as she backed away from them into the other room.

Mary looked around the room. A bright red oriental rug was spread before the fireplace that smoldered across from them. In the corner of the room a shrine sat under a picture that could only have been someone's parents.

Moments later, the woman's husband shuffled out from the back room.

Dr. Page got to his feet. "Oh, there you are. Thank you for letting us impose on you once again. We are still lost and need directions as to the best way back to Sacramento."

The man spoke to his wife in Cantonese. It was a series of complicated phrases, punctuated by his wife's obvious objections. Though neither Mary nor the doctor could understand a word that was being said, they both knew there was some explaining and disagreement involved.

"Wife get you some tea," the man said. "You sit down and wait."

Dr. Page took his uncomfortable seat once again, and the man pulled up a straight-back chair. "Why you here? I send you to big house."

"We couldn't stay there," Mary blurted out.

The doctor rested his hand on hers and patted it. "What my niece means to say is that we must get back to Sacramento right away. We thought it would be best to find our own way back."

"Why you no stay there? White people come there all time."

"We didn't feel comfortable," Mary said.

"With staying there and imposing on our hosts any longer," Dr.

Page added. "We just felt the need to get home as soon as possible."

The man glanced back at the room from where he'd suddenly appeared as his wife brought a pot of steaming tea. She produced three cups, setting them on a black lacquered table in front of the settee. After pouring the three cups, she retreated back into the kitchen.

"You not comfortable in big house?" The man cast a glance once again in the direction of the back room.

"No, that's not it," Dr. Page responded. "We were just uncomfortable with being away from home, and it looked as though we wouldn't be able to leave for some time. We just couldn't wait any longer."

"You no like big house?"

It was obvious from the way the man continued to probe their feelings about Blevins's home that there was something else he was fishing to find. Dr. Page wondered how much he knew about the man's real identity and profession. If this near neighbor knew nothing, Dr. Page wasn't about to tell him. "No, my niece and I liked it very much. Our host and his aunt were most gracious people." He patted Mary's hand again, not wanting her to say anything they might regret later. "It's just that we were most anxious to be getting back to our own home. Now, can you give us directions on how to find the nearest town?"

"I believe I can help you there, Doctor." Blevins stepped out of the back room from around the curtains.

Mary dropped her tea to the floor.

Dr. Page jumped to his feet. "Mr. Blevins! We weren't expecting you."

"Obviously."

"W-w-we didn't mean to leave so suddenly," Page stammered. "It's just that we couldn't find you, and your aunt was still sleeping."

Blevins paced toward them from across the room. "I am disappointed in you, Doctor, and I can't understand what made you want to bolt our hospitality so quickly."

Mary had busied herself with mopping up the tea. She was shaking. "We just had to get home." She slurred the words out.

"And to risk your lovely niece on the roads, where you might once again run into those pirates of yours."

Dr. Page dropped his gaze to the floor.

"You do have an obligation to make a police report before you leave, you know. It's your civic duty. As far as I know, the sheriff has already arrived at The Glades to hear your story. I asked him to come by this morning, and now what will we do?"

"Mary and I can find him."

"No, I'm afraid that won't do. You see, he's a very busy man. He may not be in his office—"

"We can wait," Mary interrupted hurriedly.

"For several days," Blevins finished his sentence and smiled.

Mary flushed. "And why were you just standing back there, listening to us?" she asked.

Blevins stepped over to her and gently lifted her chin. "Poor creature. You really think people are out to do you harm. I just walked in the back door, hoping to inquire about your whereabouts and if these good people had seen you. I was worried, you see."

Mary pulled her chin away. "I'm sure you were."

"And I found it hard to believe you would leave without saying good-bye or thank you . . . and with our clothes."

Dr. Page stepped in front of him, distracting him from Mary. "And I apologize for that. It was all my doing, I'm afraid. We were just over anxious about getting back to Sacramento. We were going to clean and send the clothes back to you, you have my assurance of that."

"Oh, I'm sure of that, Doctor. It's just that I much prefer my thank-yous in person."

Mary got to her feet. "Then, why don't we just say thank you and good-bye right now."

"You and your aunt have been most kind," Dr. Page added.

"I'm afraid it won't be possible to say our adieus just yet. Mamie has been preparing quite a feast for you tonight, and the sheriff might just be present as a guest. You see, we can kill two birds with one stone"—he smiled—"so to speak. Besides, the day is far spent. You won't get far before darkness overtakes you, and my conscience couldn't bear the thought of you walking in this strange and dangerous country alone and at night."

+ + + + +

The darkness crept along the river's surface like the soft underbelly of a cat, curling around the senses and purring a warm foggy breath into the ears of the people on board the *Delta King*. Given the heavy fog that day, the end of the day was barely noticed. Zac dined on fresh-water mussels, prying each one open while trying to avoid any embarrassing eruptions of the mussels' wanton airborne juice. He grimaced as a solid squirt of juice flew across the table, landing on Hattie's blouse. "Sorry about that," he said.

The woman put down her knife and fork and attempted to wipe the juice from one of the few passable articles of clothing she owned. She squinted her eye at him. "Boy, you do that once more and I'm gonna load up with my chaw and fight fire with fire."

Jenny laughed. "Now, that would be quite the sight to behold, wouldn't it, boys?"

"Yes, ma'am," Skip agreed.

"Sure would be fun to watch, though," Jack added.

Captain Van Tuyl stepped into the glass-walled dining room from the deck outside and walked toward their table. "I hate to disturb your dinner, but you folks should come up to the pilothouse and see the sight. Ain't likely you'll see the equal in a long time. We're pulling into Walnut Grove a ways up ahead, but there's a mighty unusual sight out there."

"Can we?" Skip asked.

"'Course we can," Zac said.

As the party rose from the table, the captain turned to the packed dining room and announced, "Folks, can I have your attention? We're coming into Walnut Grove. We don't normally stop here, and when we do it isn't for long, but tonight seems to be different." The crowd's noise died down at once, each wondering about the importance of the upcoming announcement. "There seems to be a carnival or circus in town, and since we're going to be late into San Francisco anyway and would like to see the fog clear, we will stop here for three hours. You can go ashore and enjoy yourselves, but be back on board by ten-thirty."

The crowd was abuzz as the captain led Zac and his party outside on deck. "You'll get a better view of the lights from the pilothouse."

After climbing the four flights of stairs, the group stood behind the glass windows of the pilothouse. There through the fog, a ghostly glare and the brightly colored tents glowed in the misty darkness like a string of Japanese lanterns mushrooming along the river's edge.

"I ain't seen me a circus since I was a boy, and since the fog's thick and the going will be slow, maybe all the way into San Francisco, I figured Grubb here could use himself a nap while we go ashore for a look around."

"I ain't never seen one of them circus things," Hattie said.

"I think that will be fun," Jenny said, looping her arm through Zac's.

Van Tuyl stared off at the lights. "Well, I figure I can leave Grubb sleeping here with that Sergeant Adams, and maybe I can see the sights for an hour or two. Then I'll come back to get up steam."

"I think I should stay on board with the shipment," Zac said.

Jenny was disappointed, but she wasn't going to question Zac's judgment. This was his job, and he knew best how to do it without her coaching. This assignment had turned out to be more formidable than he first thought it was going to be, or she was sure Zac would never have considered taking her and Skip with him.

Moments later, Cliff Cox joined them in the glass-walled cabin. He tipped his hat to the ladies and turned to get Zac's attention. "I saw you leaving with the captain," he said. "I thought I'd just come up and volunteer to stay on board and let you go to the carnival with your family."

"Oh, that would be wonderful," Jenny exclaimed. She clung close to Zac. "Isn't it nice of Mr. Cox here to let you go?" She knew once she said the words that her excitement over the possibility was something that would have been better to have kept hidden. When it came to work, Zac kept his own counsel. He certainly didn't need her enthusiasm to pressure him in front of the boys and the men in the pilothouse. She was sorry she said it.

"Well, I'm not so sure about that. I think I should stay with the shipment."

"I think the possibility of trouble here is highly unlikely," Van Tuyl volunteered. "There's just too many folks milling around to worry about pirates."

"And we could leave the entire group of army personnel on board to watch it," Cox added.

Jenny watched Zac without saying a word. She'd already said enough. She patted his arm. "You do what you think best," she said. "We'll be fine either way." Zac looked down at her and then at Skip. It was plain to see the boy wanted them to be a family at the carnival. There would be something missing without Zac, and all of them knew it. "All right, but just for a short while. I don't feel right about straying too far."

"You can't get very far in Walnut Grove," Van Tuyl added. "There ain't much to it."

"Will there be bears there?" Hattie asked. "I skinned me plenty a bear in my day. Probably them poor little critters in their cages couldn't stand knee high to the ones I done in."

"You mean it?" Jack asked. "You really killed bears?"

"A passel of 'em, and mountain lions, to boot."

"Wowsers! I'd sure like to hear stories about them."

Hattie grinned. "Well, I'll just have to tell you boys all about them wild things in the woods when we get back from seein' these here puny ones." She straightened her shoulders and threw her head back. "I don't go to brayin' like some fool donkey of a normal like, but I don't mind jawin' 'bout the ones I brung down."

Zac smiled. "You boys should hear those stories too. Hat here would go grizzly hunting with a switch if we didn't make her carry a gun."

A short time later, Zac and the group followed most of the travelers off the boat. The vast majority of the passengers were looking forward to seeing the entertainment. It was the gamblers in the salon who couldn't pull themselves away from their cards, them and a Mrs. Elkins, who said she had a bellyache.

Zac took one last look at Sergeant Adams as he stood beside the rail on the boat. Adams had assured him that two men inside the room and two guarding the outside would be more than adequate to handle any difficulties that might arise, at least until help could arrive. Zac, however, seldom felt comfortable letting another man do his job.

Jenny noticed his discomfort. She knew full well that no matter what pleasant distractions there were in the glittering carnival, he wouldn't feel at ease until the gold shipment was secure inside Wells Fargo's safe in San Francisco.

The sound of the calliope filled the street in the town, its brass whistles belching out one shrill note after the other of "The Farmer in the Dell." Just as predicted, most of the townspeople were still on the front porches of their shanties. They had seen all many cared to see when the big show had pulled into town, and now with the whistle of the music below, they were getting more than an earful. The catwalks were full of Chinese, many with their hands to their ears.

Several whites stood at the edge of the small crowd. They didn't appear to be going in, but seemed to be watching the passersby. Jenny saw Zac looking intently at the group. Following his gaze, she noticed that some of the men were armed. Even to her, sidearms seemed out of place in this town full of Chinese farmers.

The boys walked slowly, carefully surveying the sights and smells of the midway. Each tent held the promise of a new and illustrious delight for a young boy's eyes. They both stopped at the tent marked "Hilda, The Amazing Tattooed Woman" and stared as much as they dared at the painting depicting only part of what was being shown on the inside.

The barker ignored the youngsters and continued to cry out, "Come inside, gentlemen, for a feast to the masculine eyes. Only here can you see all there is to see of the beauty of the female anatomy, carefully colored with a rainbow of pictures only the great Michelangelo himself could duplicate." The man hardly paused or took a breath. "You'll see the mystery of the East marked by the pen of thc Wcst on a glorious body from the North. From the four corners of the world, all there is to see of the Hedonistic Helen of Hamurabbi, the wonderful to look upon, Hilda."

The boys stood listening to every word. Hattie gave Jack a sudden slap on the back of the head. "You forget that," she screeched. "Show-off hussies ain't never done no boy no good. You boys just back on off and behave yerself, ya hear?"

The boys ducked their heads and ran to catch up with Zac and Jenny. "What you reckon there is to see in there?" Jack asked.

"I don't rightly know," Skip said, "but I think we had better steer away."

Jack crammed his hands in his pockets and stuck out his lip. "I think it'd be fun to see. Don't nobody need to know."

Skip stopped and stared at him, blinking his eyes in disbelief.

Zac signaled them from up ahead. "Come on up here, boys. This man tells me this is the tiger tent."

They ran to see.

The man held the curtain back as Zac placed several coins in his hand. There in two cages paced two very large Bengal tigers. The beasts' green eyes seemed to glare at the people who neared the cages. One of the tigers bared his teeth and snarled.

"Do they bark or growl or what?" Skip asked the attendant nearby.

"They growl"—the man leaned close to Skip and, placing his

hands on his knees, grinned—"something fierce."

With that, he picked up a long shaft and shoved it at the beast. The tiger swatted at the wooden intruder and gave out a deafening roar. The small crowd jumped back.

Zac steadied Skip and Jack. "I don't reckon it pays to get one of these things too upset."

Jack beamed and leaned closer to the cage. "Boy, they is a wonder, sure 'nuff."

Skip frowned. "You gonna write them stories of yours, you better speak it right. They *are* a wonder. I reckon that's how they say it."

Hattie signaled them from one of the glass cases that stood nearby. "Looky here. Sign here says these things is the deadliest snakes in all the world. Now whatcha think about that?"

She began to point them out one at a time. "This here's a cobra." The snake lifted its head and spread its hood as Hattie put her hand on the glass, then quickly pulled it away.

An attendant stepped forward. "Ma'am, there hasn't been many folks who would do even that, not with these things."

Zac, Jenny, and the boys stepped closer.

The man went on, "In spite of the fact that this glass offers perfect protection, a body's natural instinct is to pull away. Fear is an amazing thing. It tells us what to do without our even thinking about it." He motioned Hattie forward. "Go ahead, give it a try. I ain't seen nobody who didn't pull away at a strike. One thing though, you got to watch the snake all the time. You can't turn your eyes away so you don't see."

Hattie dropped her hands to her side. "I kill critters like that. I don't tempt 'em."

The man's smile gave way to a smirk. "People are controlled by their fears. It's the most powerful instinctive motivation on the earth." He looked at Zac. "You try your hand on the glass, mister, you look the steely eyed sort."

"Go ahead," Jack insisted. "I'd like to see if it could be done."

"It can't be done," the man joined in. "Fear is much too powerful."

Zac rolled up his sleeve and placed his right hand next to the glass. He looked the hooded cobra in the eye as the beast raised his head and drew a bead.

With the sudden quickness of a lightning strike, the black snake hurled himself against the thick glass. Its fangs hit the shiny surface next to Zac's hand, but Zac's hand stayed still, unmoved by the strike.

The group gathered around gave out a collective gasp, and the attendant's mouth fell open. He swallowed hard. "Mister, if I didn't know better, I'd say you was blind."

Zac buttoned his sleeve back up and turned to the group. "We best be going. There's still lots to see, and we don't want the time to run out on us."

Jenny watched him back away from the attention. "Zac's right, boys, we should go."

When they left the tent she held his arm and squeezed it. "Now, tell me, why did you do that back there? It was so unlike you!"

"Pigheadedness, I suppose. I hate to see any man as sure of himself as that fella seemed to be. In the long run, it ain't healthy."

She looked up at him and smiled. "Well, you seem mighty sure of yourself."

"I am when it comes to my feelings about you."

CHAPTER 20

+ + + + + + +

MANNY DEALT THE CARDS. Right now, winning or losing was the furthest thing from his mind. Watching carefully as the people left the boat, he passed an occasional glance at the three other men who were with him. Brian was seated across from him. Brian was a lummox, clumsy and dull-witted, but when it came to using his hands to kill someone, there was none better, and Manny was glad to have him.

Doyle and Opie were seated at the other table. They were capable men, and Doyle had once served aboard a steamer. They relied on him to make sure any boat that was taken could be negotiated in the river. To depend on a member of the crew to help with the hijacking of their own boat was much too risky a proposition.

Manny slumped over his cards and withdrew a cigar from his vest pocket. He nodded at Brian, only hoping against hope that the man would recognize that this was their time to move. "I fold," he said. "Gotta go outside for a smoke."

"What's wrong with right here?" another man piped in.

"I just need some fresh air. Maybe that will change my luck."

The man grinned. "Suit yerself, but from the way you been playing, that ain't about to happen."

Manny got up from his chair. He knew the man was right. His head hadn't been in the game. Since he started to play midafternoon, he'd already dropped more than three hundred dollars. "You're more'n likely right," he said. Turning to the door, he brushed aside a waiter and stepped outside. Lighting the cigar, he calmly waited for Brian to catch on to the timing of the matter. The man was undependable when it came to thinking, Manny knew that. If he had a good string of cards in his hand, Brian might just as likely play them out. He lit his cigar.

It was several minutes more before Brian stumbled out of the door. "What kept you?" Manny asked.

The man blinked at him. "Uh, I had me a right fine set a cards. If'n I'd just thrown 'em in, I was afeared somebody mighta picked 'em up and looked to see."

Manny stared at him. It was surprisingly good thinking for Brian, although he didn't want to admit it to the man's face. "Did you bring your hide-out pistol?"

"I sure 'nuff did." Brian reached into his shirt and withdrew the Sharps and Hawkins four-shot pepperbox he carried for emergencies.

"Good, then put it away. Don't touch it till I give you the go-ahead. I don't want any shootin', you understand?"

The big man nodded and replaced the pistol in his shirt. Soon, Doyle and Opie had joined the two of them on the deck. Manny had both of them check their weapons. "All right, here's the plan. Doyle, I want you to go up to the pilothouse and brace those folks up there. I don't want shootin', but if you have to, you have to. Opie, you go to the engine room and make sure the orders that come from the pilothouse are carried out. Brian and me are gonna take the cabin with the gold." He narrowed his eyes, looking at Doyle. "We make steam when the ruckus on shore starts. They'll be too distracted to notice. If anything does go wrong, then I want you to leave right off. We're running this thing aground on Decker Island. You all get that?"

The men all nodded, and Doyle and Opie moved off to their respective assignments.

Once again alone with Brian, Manny made sure he had his complete attention. "I'm gonna pay the room those soldiers are staying in a visit first before we go 'round to the cabin they're guardin'. Need to see how many men's on the job. You wait for me to come out."

The two of them ambled down the deck and, producing a bottle, Manny knocked on the door.

"Who is it?" the man inside asked.

Manny deliberately slurred his speech. "It's me un I gots me a bottle of mighty fine stuff here. I talked to you'ze earlier today, m-m-m-member me?"

The soldier cracked open the doors, and Manny grinned, holding up the bottle and sloshing it around.

"I ain't never talked to you."

Manny slumped against the door. "Well, maybe it was one of them other soldier boys, I can't quite recollect, but I gots me some fine stuff anyhow."

The man opened the door. "I hadn't oughta. I'm supposed to be on duty."

"Then, why is you here?"

"Well, it ain't my time yet, so maybe I could."

He opened the door, and Manny went inside. Minutes later Manny stepped back outside, wiping his blade with a handkerchief. Planting the now clean knife back into its sheath, he motioned Brian forward. "The sergeant's up in the pilothouse, and they've got two men inside the cabin and another two outside. I'm gonna distract the men outside and have you come up behind them. Whatever you do, I want it done quiet like, you understand?"

"Yep."

"Fine, then just wait till you hear me talkin' to them, and then come up behind them real cat like."

Manny threw his cigar overboard and produced another unlit one. Holding the bottle in one hand and the cigar in the other, he walked toward the stern of the boat, followed at a distance by Brian. Smiling, he rounded the stern.

"Howdy, boys. How y'all doin' back here?"

The men snapped to full height and turned to face him.

Moving around them to put their backs to where he'd just come from, he continued his friendly banter. "I just come outside for a smoke and a drink, and now I see I ain't got no matches. Got a proposition for you boys. You produce me a match and I think I can find another one of these here see-gars for y'all."

The soldiers looked at each other, and one shrugged and began to fish in his pocket, producing several matches.

Manny took out two fresh cigars and handed them over as Brian moved up slowly behind the men.

"Here, let me light those for you fellas first."

Taking a match, he watched the two men as they took the cigars and, placing them in their mouths, leaned into the match. Brian was on them in an instant, wrapping his arms around both of their necks and pulling them off of their feet. Manny watched their feet dangle as they struggled against the choke hold. It was only a matter of moments before both men hung in Brian's arms, limp as two rag dolls. The whole thing had been quick and silent. Brian gently lowered the men's bodies to the deck.

Manny signaled toward the door of the waiting cabin, and Brian followed him. Knocking lightly on the door, he tried his best to mimic the voice of the man he had killed earlier. "Time for a duty change, boys."

A muffled voice came from inside. "That you, Corporal Stevens?"

"The same. The sergeant wants me to change with you."

"He ain't said nothing 'bout no change. I can't open this here door, till I hears from him directly."

Manny looked perplexed, but only momentarily. His quick thinking was one of the many things the colonel admired about him. "I have some written orders. Come on over here, and I'll slide them under the door." Backing up slightly, he motioned for Brian to break the door in.

The big man backed up slightly. He was a hulk of a man and the flimsy door would present little problem for someone his size. Manny drew his knife as the big man ran for the door. It seemed to explode on impact, crushing the soldier behind it. Manny rushed in, and he and Brian quickly secured the cabin.

Wiping his knife on the bedspread and listening to Brian finish the man underneath the door, Manny mused, "It wasn't the easiest job we've ever done, but it's over."

Turning his head, he surveyed the stacks of boxes that lined the walls. "This is some haul. It's gonna make you and me mighty rich men."

"Uh-hunh," Brian nodded.

"'Course it's gonna make Blevins and the colonel *filthy* rich. They'll never know want for anything ever again."

\+ + + + +

Russ Korth was a patient man, but a man of action when it was timc, and it was time. He had been watching this Zac Cobb since the man got off the boat. Even though he'd never seen him before, Cobb had been described to him, and indeed the man was hard to miss.

Zac Cobb was formidable looking, to be certain, but not for just his stature, although he was long and lanky and broad at the shoulder. It was the look in Cobb's eyes that Korth noticed first—a sharp, penetrating expression from large, dark eyes that seemed to take in at a glance all that he surveyed. He carried himself in a way that stood out to Korth as well. He could move through a crowd like a lion among house cats, confident and self-assured. But there was no lack of wariness to the man. Even though Cobb was with his family, Korth could see that the man's mind was still on his job.

Korth signaled three of his men to take their positions just as Zac walked by. The men were to stand alongside the gangplank leading up to the boat and stop anyone who might want to reboard before their plan snapped into action. The men nonchalantly sauntered toward the river, moving into place. They would put their plan into action just as soon as he saw Zac and his party enter the big tent for the evening's performance.

+ + + + +

There was a restlessness in Zac's mind that was hard to explain, a vague uneasiness about the evening that was making it hard for him to relax and enjoy himself. He had the distinct feeling of being watched. It was something he'd felt before, but something he wouldn't have expected in this sleepy little river town where he knew nobody.

The boys had run off to who knows where, and Hattie stomped off to retrieve them before the big show. Jenny walked beside him with her hand in his. In spite of the fog, or perhaps because of it, the night air was cool. They could see members of the township still filling the catwalks between the houses like a flock of birds on a fence. The irritating music continued, playing the same sing-songy tune over and over.

"What did you mean back there when you said your feelings about me were the one thing you were sure about?"

Zac walked on with her, thinking about how to explain himself. He stopped to survey the scene. "I wouldn't exactly call this the most romantic spot on earth, would you?"

Jenny smiled, chuckling slightly. "No, I wouldn't, at that."

Facing her, he held both of her hands. "You know me well enough to know that I don't soon change my mind about anything. I'm muley like in all there is to be stubborn on."

"Yes, you are and so am I."

"I know you are, in some ways more than me. You're patient with me to a fault, though."

"See, you're confusing patience with my stubbornness."

He laughed.

"I'm glad I amuse you. Stirring you up is a goal of mine, even if it is at my expense."

"I'm sorry, it's just the thought of you being so calm on the outside, but inside you're set in something you want and refusing to give up on it."

"I'm stubborn about loving you, Zac Cobb. I gave up being just patient over a year ago."

He looked around at the surrounding glare of the torches that stood near the tents, the music blaring in his ears. "I have so much I want to say to you, but I can't, not here, not now. I do want you to know, though, that I love you. I love you, and that's not going to stop."

Before Jenny could respond, the sight of Hattie towing the two boys by their ears caught their attention. The boys were tiptoeing, for Hattie had them lifted off the ground with a firm grip on each of their ears. Stomping up to Zac and Jenny, she continued to lift the boys with her firm grip. "I looked for them and found 'em all right. At first I just seen their legs and feet. They was hunkered down under that tattooed hussy's tent, spying on the show inside."

Jenny laughed.

Zac looked somber. "You boys are just robbing yourself. Now I'm going to have to take you back on the boat."

"I'm sorry," Skip said.

"We never did see nothing," Jack wailed.

"Well, it wasn't for lack of trying," Zac responded. "All right, Hat. I'll take the boys with me."

"Nah, I'll take 'em back my ownself. I seen enough of all this here nonsense, and 'sides, you got that lady there to mind. They'll just be with me in my cabin."

Zac studied the boys. Both appeared to be in the midst of great torture. "All right, maybe that'll be punishment enough."

Hattie spun the boys around and marched them toward the boat. They squalled as she continued to lift them on their toes. As she approached the gangplank, three men stepped into her path. She dropped the boys' ears and pushed the first man aside. "Get outta my way, you galoot. I got myself some discipline to do here, and I ain't rightly got the spare time to trim yer face too."

The man stumbled and stuttered, a lit cigarette dropping from his mouth. There was something about the old woman that made the men step aside. She meant business and they knew it. They gawked at one another, each seeming to lack the courage or the inclination to move.

Picking up the boys' red, sore ears once more, Hattie stepped them in tow up the long gangplank.

Zac watched from a distance. Where Hattie was concerned, ruffians and town hooligans didn't cause him concern in the least—she could handle herself. He was more disturbed by the notion of having to explain the old woman if he had to bail her out of jail. "She's something else," he said.

"She certainly is. I'm just glad she's on our side."

"Hattie Woodruff is on her own side, and woe be to the man who discovers that too late."

Jenny laughed.

"We better go in and see the show. I do need to get back on board before long and, if nothing else, ease my mind."

They followed the small crowd into the oversized tent just as the circus master was describing the juggling feats of the men in pink tights in the center of the ring. Both Zac and Jenny gawked, not so much at the bowling pins flying through the air as at the sight of grown men in tight pink tights. Taking their seats on the wooden planks stretched out between barrels, they continued to gape at the spectacle.

Zac bought a bag of peanuts, and they settled down to watch the tumblers prance into the arena. He held the bag out for her. "I can never get used to these things. Coming from Georgia, where they grow these things, I'm used to eating them boiled, not all dried out and tasteless."

"Goobers."

"Yes, goobers. My mother would put a big black kettle on a fire outside, and we'd salt and stir the things all day long. They were mighty good eating, oft times for days on end."

"I guess it's all in what you're used to."

"Yes"—he handed her the bag—"and I'll never get used to these."

The group of tumblers took turns throwing each other in the air and catching the airborne member, seemingly at the last second possible. One wiry, short man began first to prance for the crowd, then tumble head over heels in a series of backward somersaults.

"There's liable to be a broken neck before they're through to-night," Zac mumbled.

"It's very exciting, isn't it?"

"Yes, I guess it feels kinda different to watch other people risk their necks for a change."

It was a short time later when Jenny smelled the first whiff of smoke. "Do you smell that?" she asked.

"Yes, and it ain't cigar smoke."

Moments later, the crowd watched in horror as a sheet of flames erupted over the far side of the tent. Women screamed, and the crowd stormed for the exit. Grabbing Jenny, he swung his head from side to side. "Let's go under the tent," he yelled. "There's too many people there. We'd never make it."

Holding on to her around the waist, he pulled her out of the bleachers and pushed her in the direction of the tent's wall behind them. Forcing her to the sawdust-covered floor, he wedged first his foot and then his knee under the material. She shimmied forward under the tent. Zac followed quickly behind her.

The scene outside the big top was one of total pandemonium. They could hear the terrified sounds of the tigers and assorted animals, and the two elephants were stampeding free, swinging their heads from side to side and charging behind the fleeing crowd.

"This is awful," Jenny screamed.

Pulling her around, he hurried for the rear of the tent. "I got to get you out of this crowd," he shouted. "Some will be heading back to the boat, and they won't be taking their time about it. I'll steer you that way, but don't try to get on, not yet. I won't have you attempting to go up that gangplank with a hundred other panicked people on your heels. You'd all go into the river, if you were lucky. When I get you safely out of the way of these flames, I'll see what I can do to help. "

The screams of the people were ear shattering, but above it all, the calliope player continued to give out his wails of the now too familiar children's tune.

When Zac and Jenny got safely around the side of the tent to a spot close to the river, they stopped to watch the tent burn. Showers of sparks flew into the foggy sky, and large patches of flaming material floated on uprising currents of air in the direction of the row of houses on their stilts.

"This is dangerous," Zac said. "They may just lose the whole town before this night is over."

"You go ahead and help where you can. I'll be all right," Jenny said. "I'll just stay right here for a bit and then walk back and see to the boys."

Zac nodded. Leaving her in the secure spot they had found beside the river, he ran back to the sounds of screams.

As he turned the corner on the glaring glow of the midway, he spotted a man running with a torch. The man ducked into the still-standing tent that held the tigers and snakes they had seen earlier. Zac ran after him.

CHAPTER 21

+ + + + + + +

THE LAMPS GLOWED SOFTLY at The Glades, sending flickering shadows up the heavy curtains. Mary sat at the table in a deep cherry color dress that Mamie had laid out for her. It showed off her black hair and sparkling eyes. The doctor sat quietly in a dark gray suit. It was slightly oversized for his wiry frame, but perfectly presentable. Blevins had assured them that the sheriff would drop by sometime during the evening. His promises were lost on Mary, but Dr. Page still held out hope that someone from the outside would learn of their fate and offer them assistance in returning to Sacramento safely.

"Why, Mary, dear," Mamie said, "you've hardly touched your salad."

"I'm sorry, I think I've lost my appetite."

"Probably all that exercise you had today," Blevins interjected.

"Well, I should think that would *improve* one's appetite," Mamie countered. "Isn't that right, Doctor?"

"Normally that would be right," Dr. Page responded. "I think Mary's just feeling very homesick."

Reaching out, Mamie patted Mary's hand. "Poor child, poor, poor, child."

"Where do you get this salad dressing?" Dr. Page asked. "It's wonderful."

"It's my aunt's recipe," Blevins interjected.

"It's extraordinary," the doctor offered.

Mamie patted her chest and blushed. "Why, Doctor, you do me proud. Goodness knows I try to keep a fine table. It's so seldom we have company these days, however, and for a lady like me, used to doing for men, you can't imagine how delightful it is to be complimented." She smiled at the doctor and batted her eyes. "You know I am a widow woman?"

Dr. Page smiled and nodded his head.

"And are you a widower, Doctor?" Mamie asked.

"Why no, madam. Medicine has been my bride for over thirty years now. Of course, I'm not without family. Since my brother and his wife got the missionary call to India, I've had the privilege of caring for Mary."

"And a delightful child she is, too, isn't she, Robert?"

"Very much so."

"I just think it's quite providential that the two of you should be cast on our doorstep in your hour of need," Mamie gushed. "Mercy me, how ever did we deserve to be able to provide for you in such a way?" She waved her hand at the luxuriously appointed dining room. "To think that we have all of this and now are allowed to share in our bounty with our equals who fell upon robbers—it makes me think of our Lord's parable of the good Samaritan. Doesn't it make you think of that, Robert?"

Blevins nodded slightly. He had been unusually quiet during the beginning of their meal, almost brooding. It was obvious that this meal had been planned by Mamie, and Mary got the distinct impression that his plans for them had been placed on hold until he had his chance to act. They were no longer innocent guests to Blevins, but meddlesome intruders who knew far too much. Mary was sure they would never be allowed to make a report to authorities that Blevins had no influence over.

"I'll just be glad to get home," Mary said, "and put this entire episode behind me."

"And you shall," Mamie responded. She sat between Mary and Dr. Page, with Blevins on the other side of the table. Reaching over to the doctor and placing her hand on his, she smiled sweetly. "But, Doctor, you won't forget poor Mamie, will you?"

"Why no, madam, how could I? Your charm has brightened this event considerably."

"You see, Robert, we have made quite the impression on these two people."

"I'm sure we have."

The meal was nearing an end when the knocker on the door sounded. Blevins's eyes brightened, and he got up to see to the door that Soggy was opening. From where they sat, the front door in the hall was hidden from view, but they could hear voices in the foyer, and the new one that mixed with Blevins's voice was not totally unfamiliar to them. It sent ripples of fear up their spines.

"Would that be your sheriff?" Dr. Page asked.

"Why, yes, Doctor, and a fine man he is. I think you'll enjoy his company very much. He's a man of the South, a veteran of The War between the States, Colonel Princeton."

Mary gasped.

"He received his colonelcy from the Confederacy, but we still call him that out of respect. I'm sure he'll be quite interested in your story."

+ + + + +

Zac had been carrying the Shopkeeper Colt .45 under his arm in a shoulder holster, and he drew it as he followed the man inside the tent. The man in a black hat and black leather vest was hammering on the lock to the tigers' cage with the butt of his pistol. Zac stood beside the glass snake enclosure. He leveled the .45 and shouted, "Stop that! Put that thing down."

Swinging around, the man opened the door to the cage, pointing the revolver in Zac's direction. He fired several shots wildly, shattering the glass of the snakes' cage. Zac dove for the ground as the tigers bounded out of their cage. Roaring with the smell of newfound freedom, they raced around and over the top of Zac's prone body, knocking the .45 from his hand.

Zac got to his knees and began a slow crawl to the revolver. The man raced over and, placing his boot on Zac's hand, grinned.

"Who are you?" Zac asked.

"Name's Korth, and I'm your worst nightmare. I been looking forward to this for days."

Zac relaxed his body, looking up at the man. "Why are you doing this? Those tigers are gonna kill innocent people."

"Let's just say it'll keep them busy for quite a spell."

The smoke from the midway drifted across the opening of the tent. Outside, Zac could hear the renewed screams caused by the two Bengal tigers running loose in the panicked crowd.

"It's almost a shame to kill you this way." Korth pushed the barrel of the revolver closer to Zac's face. "I been watching you all night. I figured you to be lots tougher to kill."

"Oh, I am." With that, Zac grabbed the revolver with the hand that had been holding him up, freezing the cylinder in his grip.

Taken by surprise, Korth pressed the trigger hard, trying to discharge the weapon.

With all the strength he could muster, Zac pried his other hand free from Korth's foot and latched on to the top of the man's boot, twisting it.

Spinning his arms and trying to keep his balance, Korth fell to the ground. Zac was on top of him in the blink of an eye, the two of them rolling toward the shattered case. They both rolled repeatedly over the glass, like barrels down a hill. Several snakes already freed from the case slid to one side, hissing.

Korth fought back viciously. He pounded Zac's face with several swift jabs as they rolled in the sawdust. The fact that he didn't have the space to give his swings much impact made Zac hang on and continue to hold him close.

Behind the man, Zac could see the large black cobra rise up from the ground. The serpent spread its hood and stared at the two men wrestling close to him. The beast began to swing its head from side to side, seeming to take stock of the two men.

Korth continued his short punches, trying for all his worth to free himself from the viselike grip, but Zac held him fast. The two of them held each other solid, each refusing to give up his grip.

Zac reared his head back and with a sudden impact, rammed his forehead into Korth's face with a crack. The shock of the blow stunned the man, and he loosened his grip. Getting to his feet, Zac pulled Korth up and planted a hard blow into the man's stomach, doubling him over.

Gasping for air, Korth maintained a grip around Zac's body. With unexpected energy, he swung a leg, knocking Zac's legs out from under him and putting him on the ground. Stepping forward, Korth delivered a quick kick to Zac's head. Looking for his revolver, he spotted it and reached around to pick it up.

The blow from the cobra took Korth completely by surprise. He yelled and withdrew his hand.

Zac was on his feet in an instant. Finding his short-barreled Colt, Zac took aim and fired, jerking the snake into the air. He stepped toward the prone gunman and stooped down beside him.

"That thing bit me. You got to find me a doctor."

Looking outside the tent and listening to the continued screams from the crowd in the night air, Zac shook his head. "I have a feeling if there was one to be found, he'd be plenty busy undoing the damage you've done tonight." Reaching behind him, Zac picked up the man's pistol and stuck it in his belt. "Here," Zac said. "Take off your belt and give it to me."

Korth used his uninjured left hand to remove his belt, then handed it to Zac.

Taking the man's right arm, Zac cinched the belt tight. He handed the end of the tightened belt to Korth. "You better keep this thing tight. Clamp on to it with your teeth and pull hard."

"Am I gonna make it?"

"If you do, you'll never use that right hand again. But from what I've heard about that thing that bit you, I wouldn't give you long." Zac got to his feet. "Of course, all things considered, it's a better way to go than the end of a rope."

Zac walked toward the door of the tent. Turning around, he took one last look at Russ Korth.

The midway was in a shambles; strewn debris littered the ground. The flames in the big tent had done their job. It lay in a still-flaming heap, the blaze lighting up the foggy night. He could hear gunfire. The people who once were on the catwalks had formed a line to the river—a living chain of swinging buckets.

One of the elephants had run into a row of stilted houses, sending the inhabitants screaming into the street. The second elephant seemed to be in the control of one of the handlers. Zac could only wonder where the tigers were.

He moved along the midway, occasionally passing someone who sat with head in hand. Some were crying. Others simply stared, their eyes searching into the misty night air for something, any thought or vision that might deaden the pain of the evening. Walking toward the dock, he reflected on his feelings. His instincts had been right. They usually were. Often a man's thinking became clouded by unexpected opportunities, and tonight's promised entertainment had been just that. He remembered the words his father used to tell him. "Son, nothing can get you further afield in life than an opportunity you just can't pass up on. If you didn't plan on it, you best think twice about doing it." His father had been right. The man had never been a rich man and would never have taken a step out of his way to get something that wasn't his. A promise of something that wasn't planned was just empty smoke.

Rounding the flaming tent, he saw at once that the *Delta King* was gone. A number of the passengers and crew stood beside the dock—among them, Jenny and Captain Van Tuyl. The captain shook his head slowly as Zac approached.

Zac took Jenny by both of her arms. "You all right?"

"Yes," she said. Worry registered all over her face. "The boys and your aunt are still on the boat."

Van Tuyl muttered, first looking down the river at the lights of the departing *Delta King* and then to Zac. "You were right. Those pirates slipped up on our stern and gave us cause to look elsewhere."

Zac looked back at the town of Walnut Grove. Fires continued to blossom; isolated screams and cries rose at various locations; and men and women were working the line of buckets between the river and the fires that were still burning. "They had this pretty well planned," Zac observed. "Even if we could have found a posse to give chase in a town full of Chinese, we couldn't hope to do that now."

Van Tuyl bowed his head and shook it. "They had it figured pretty good. These here folks ain't exactly no amateurs."

"Well, it's us, then. We just need to find out how to give chase."

Van Tuyl looked back at the burning stables. "Don't think I'd count on renting no horses."

A sudden shrill whistle erupted into the night air. It brought every head around. Heading right for the dock through the fog was a small cutter under steam. At the controls, his hair matted from dampness, was Dennis Grubb. "Grubb!" Van Tuyl shouted. "It's my pilot!"

Zac turned to Jenny. "You better stay here. I can come back for you."

"I'll do no such thing. You're leaving me in a town on fire with elephants and tigers running loose while you go off on a boat ride?"

Zac held up both hands. "All right. It's best for a man to bow to his betters."

"You think I'm going to stay here and do nothing with those boys under the care of a group of pirates?"

He put his hands on her shoulders. He'd been used to dealing with crisis, and while Jenny was plenty tough, he'd seen that many a time, it was obvious that she was in no mood to be crossed. "I said you can come. All I ask is that you take cover and stay there when I tell you to. You promise me that?"

She blinked at him and bit her lower lip.

"Do you promise?"

She nodded her head. "I promise."

Grubb swung the small open steamer into the docking area, pulling it close and then finally touching the dock. He threw out a line, and Van Tuyl took a turn around a piling. "After you," he said.

Chugging away from the dock, Van Tuyl began to toss some of the stacked cord wood into the steamer's boiler. "How'd you get this thing, and how'd you get here?"

"The boat belongs to Gantry up at the firewood yard. He's gone, probably fighting that fire, but I didn't think he'd begrudge us this boat of his. I jumped off the *King* when the fella that had the gun shot the sergeant."

"That was quite a way to jump."

"Well, I can swim, and with him gunning down Adams like he did, I figured my chances were just as good in the river. They must have the boiler room too. I listened as the man called down the tube to get up steam."

Van Tuyl threw another piece of wood into the boiler and peered through the fog at what looked like the faint lights of the *Delta King* up ahead. "Unless the man down there understands Peng Lee's gibberish, he won't know what they're really doing or thinking, for that matter."

Standing erect, he looked up river once again. "Whoever's on that thing can handle a steamer, that's for sure, but I wonder how well he knows the channels."

"Not well enough," Grubb offered. "It would take a good pilot to make time on this river in the fog, and I know them all. Not one of them would lift a finger to help pirates." He looked back at Zac and Jenny, sitting on the wood pile. "I brought Gantry's rifle from his office. I figured we could use it."

Zac spotted the rifle and, picking it up, slid back the bolt. "It's one of the new Hotchkiss models," he said. "Holds five in the magazine and one in the chamber."

Reaching into his wet coat pocket, Grubb tossed Zac a box of shells. "Took this too."

Zac looked at him with surprise, then turning to Van Tuyl, commented, "This man of yours, Captain, is quite the enterprising sort."

Van Tuyl lifted his chin. "That's why he's working for me. I only pick the best for the *Delta King*."

Fishing in his pocket, the captain pulled out a short, stubby pistol. "I got me one of them side-hammer Root-brand pistols."

"Well," Zac said, "I'd say we don't make too formidable a boarding party with two pocket guns and an army rifle, but we'll do. What we lack in the way of firepower, we make up for with fire."

"That we do," Van Tuyl roared.

\+ + + + +

Blevins and Princeton continued their conversation in the foyer as Mary and Dr. Page exchanged glances. In spite of Mamie's presence, the doctor spoke plainly. "You were right, dear. I should have listened to you."

Moments later Blevins walked Princeton into the dining room. With clean appearance and new clothes, Mary could only hope the man would not recognize them, although few men who had ever seen her soon forgot her. That simple fact had always given her great confidence, but now it struck terror in her heart.

"Colonel, allow me to present Dr. Page and his niece, Mary."

Princeton paused and blinked, taking the two of them in.

Mamie rose from her place, ever the hostess. "Colonel, how good of you to drop in on us. Please be seated, and I'll have Soggy bring you a place setting."

As Mamie hurried to the kitchen, Princeton took a seat beside Blevins's chair. He couldn't take his eyes off the two people in front of him.

Blevins noticed the cool stares between Princeton and his two houseguests at once. His explanation broke what was a moment of icy silence. "The colonel here serves as our sheriff. I'm sure if you can tell him of your troubles, he'd be the man to help."

Princeton stopped him. "That won't be necessary." Turning back to face Dr. Page and Mary, he continued, "Will it?"

"No," the doctor said. "I think not."

Princeton leaned forward, his knuckles white as he gripped the side of the table. "And did you enjoy your little boat ride the other day?"

Mary's and the doctor's faces turned white.

"I can see that my man Manuel has some explaining to do when he comes back. Perhaps the three of you can renew your obvious friendship."

PART 3

THE CHASE

CHAPTER 22

+ + + + + + +

HATTIE WATCHED AS THE FIRES blazed on shore. The shouts of the men as they stormed up the gangplank and the sudden departure of the boat from its moorings told her something was dreadfully wrong.

"You young'uns keep back," she shouted.

Closing the door, she reached for her carpetbag and rummaged into the bottom of the well-worn valise. Finding the old Colt, she pulled it out.

"What you gonna do with that thing?" Jack asked.

"Somethin's amiss out there," she sputtered. "We'll know afore long, I reckon. I jest wants to be ready when we does find out."

"Did Zac make it back on board?" Skip asked.

"I don't 'spect so, otherwise we'd be bound to hear plenty of shootin'."

"Do you think it be pirates?" Jack asked.

"You lookin' to join up?" Skip queried. The boy narrowed his eyes at Jack, working to understand the rascal's excited motives.

"Nah, I learned my lesson 'bout that. I wuz jest tryin' to figure on what to look out for."

"It jest might be them pirates Zac and the captain was so afeared of," Hattie responded. "If'n it be them, they'ze gonna be comin' 'round to try and gets what's left of us passengers."

"What are we gonna do?" Jack asked.

"We're gonna fight 'em," Skip shot back.

"One thing is for sure," Hattie said, "they'ze gonna lay a hand on you two boys over this woman's dead and stiff carcass."

Skip reached out and held her hand. "I don't want anything to happen to you. If you wasn't around, this would only be a whole lot worse."

Hattie looked down at the boy. It was seldom that anybody, other than Zac, cared one way or the other what happened to her, and she suspected much of Zac's concern was because she was his mother's sister. She put her hand on Skip's head. "You forget, I'm the grown-up 'round here, though most of the time it don't quite seem thataway. If anybody's to look out for a body, it's got to be old Hat that looks after you two."

Cracking open the cabin door, she pressed her face to the narrow gap she'd created. The boys heard her mumble, and then backing away, she closed the door.

"What's happenin'?" Jack inquired.

Hattie chewed on her tobacco, the plug swelling her cheek. "They'ze makin' whoever's left on board jump over the side and swim fer it. Can you boys swim?"

They both nodded their heads.

"Well, old Hat here never could swim a lick. 'Sides, what with them paddles a churnin' back there, a body might just get pulled into that thing." Leaning over and squinting at the boys to make her point, she chomped down hard on the tobacco. "And them paddle blades would just chew you up and spit what was left of you back into that river fer the fish to chaw on."

"What are we gonna do?" Skip asked.

"I figure we best stay put for a while. I ain't sure they'ze gonna be checkin' all these here rooms, and if'n we can just keep to ourselves, we might as well just ride this here thing out till Zac catches up with us."

"You figure he's gonna do that?" Jack asked.

She waved her hand at the boy in a nonchalant manner, trying to assure herself as much as him. "Pshaw, that nephew of mine is gonna be comin' on strong. I ain't never heard tell of nobody getting far from him fer very long. He'll be on them pirates like a duck on a June bug. I don't mind tellin' you either that what's gonna be left of these here rascals when he gets through with them ain't gonna be fit to bury. Meanwhile, we just better set ourselves down and keep back from this here door—and I 'spect you two boys to be quieter than a couple of church mice."

The boys nodded nervously.

Some time later, Hattie and the boys heard the men moving from cabin to cabin. The doors that were locked were being kicked in. All three of them looked at one another. Hattie could see the fear that registered in both Jack's and Skip's faces. She'd faced many a dangerous man before, along with bears and mountain lions. The rush she felt that accompanied fear was something that was neither new nor unusual for her. There was something about the feeling that made her come to life inside. She was an overcomer and she knew it.

She held out her hand to the boys, then holding up her fingers to her lips, whispered, "Don't say nary a peep." Pointing to the corner of the small cabin, she murmured, "Now both y'all young'uns get yerselves over there. If them fellers decide to break in here, they'ze gonna get the warmest welcome they done ever got. If and when that do happen, you young'uns dash on outta here. They ain't a gonna be countin' on that. You two try to make it on 'round to that kitchen the cap'n done showed us the other day. You get yerselves in there and wait on old Hat. Y'all hear me?"

"Yes'm," Skip mumbled, "we will."

Hattie tied the strap that held her straw hat in place tight. "Now, mind you, don't you go to stoppin' to see to old Hat here. This girl's been takin' care of herself fer many a moon."

She spit a stream of brown tobacco juice into the brass spittoon. It landed with a ringing splat. "See, I don't miss much. If yer gonna feel sorry fer somebody, y'all better feel fer the galoot that decides to come a bustin' in here, 'cause he's gonna meet his maker right off, and he's gonna have some tall 'splainin' to do."

Hearing the approaching sound of the search, she waved her hand at the boys, sending them into the corner. Cocking the pistol, she moved to the bed in front of the door.

The banging at the door was loud. The man was using his clinched fist. "Anybody there, you better come out and right now. All the passengers are to be on deck."

Hattie chewed her plug furiously.

The man put his shoulder to the door, ripping it from its hinges. Stepping into the cabin, his eyes widened at the sight of the business end of Hattie's revolver. He gulped and raised his hands. "Hey now! There ain't no call for that thing."

"Step away from that door!" Hattie screeched.

The man moved aside, his hands still in the air.

"Light on outta here, boys. You get yerselves hid like I done told you."

The boys stepped carefully around the man and ran for the far side of the deck.

"Now s'pose you just tell me what y'all wants with an old woman and two children."

The man dropped his hands to his side and stepped closer to her. "You just put that thing away. You know you don't want to get anybody hurt."

"I don't want nobody hurt, but you take yerself one more step and I'm a gonna want you kilt."

"You don't mean that."

"You don't think so, you jest keep comin' on and test old Hattie Woodruff."

The man drew out a knife from his waistband and moved forward.

Hattie pulled the trigger, filling the small room with a concussion of smoke and noise. The slug jarred the man. He staggered backward, grabbing hold of the doorway. Reaching down, he pulled his hand back, red with blood. He seemed stunned, blinking his eyes and mouthing words that were indiscernible. He sank to his knees.

Hattie stepped forward and, placing her foot on his chest, pushed him out onto the deck. "You lay out there and die. Like I done told you, I don't want y'all in my room."

Stepping out onto the deck, she felt a sudden blow to the back of her head, then all was black.

\+ + + + +

Skip and Jack darted through the door to the dining room. It was a large room, and the tables had been set for the breakfast meal, a meal that now would not be served. Large windows extended from several feet off the floor to the ceiling, providing an excellent view of the river from almost any seat in the house. Glass wrapped around both sides of the room.

Jack's gaze darted around the room like a bird unable to settle on any one branch. Jack was in his element on the run. Far from being frightened, he loved the excitement of the chase. Deep down, it may have been the reason for his taking McCauliff's derringer after his theft of the money had been discovered. Having the man know it just added to the thrill.

He'd been told before that he was like any other boy, full of vinegar and mischief, but he knew that wasn't quite true. He didn't steal just to get the thing he was after—there was something in the thrill of taking it, the danger, that made him want to go back for more. His heart would pound like a hammer in a blacksmith's hand, rapping against his chest. He would breathe hard, and his mind would race. He was fully alive when he was doing something wrong.

Living on the streets of Oakland, he had been able to tell himself that he was no different than any other boy. Skip had showed him different, though. On the inside, Skip was one of those good boys who always wanted to do the right thing. Jack got the sense that more than anything else in the world, Skip was afraid of disappointing Zac. It wasn't like he toed the mark just because of that, though. Deep down, Skip really did want to do the right thing. It was the big difference between the two of them. Jack knew he had such confidence in himself that no matter what jam he got into, he could always wiggle out of it. Skip was the type who didn't want to get into the jam in the first place.

Skip's kind of life had always seemed boring to Jack. If a fella couldn't get into trouble, how would he ever know how good it felt? Jack knew he could always skip back to the other side when the time was right, just dance back across the line and smile at people. When the preacher he read books with asked him questions, he always knew just what to say, but what would be the fun of really believing the words?

Listening to the preacher and people like Zac, Jenny, and Skip, a fella could get the idea that there were two different worlds, a good one and a bad one. They seemed bent on just living in the good one. Jack's world, though, was a bigger place. He loved the good things in it, the nice things. He also loved the bad part of the world he knew, the dangerous, the wrong, the sinful things. He never wanted to see himself trapped in one world over the other, although to hear his friends talk, they seemed to believe a feller had to stay on one side of the line and pay the piper wherever he decided to light.

There had to be something special about him, though—maybe it was his black hair and sweet face. There was something that made the good people he ran across think they could rescue him, change him, make him a better person for good. Maybe they felt they themselves would feel better about who they were if they managed to get him changed.

He'd seen it so many times before, even from a woman on the

street whose purse he'd snatched. It was one of the few times the cops had put the pinch on him. The woman, however, just took one look at his sweet face and dropped all charges on the spot. He could still remember her voice. "Poor dear. He just needs the tender love of a mother to change him. He's not responsible." To that sentiment, he'd just pouted and stared intently at the woman. Many was the time he thought if he didn't make it as a thief, he might just become a politician. It was close enough to being a respectable pirate, and some said it paid a whole lot better.

As the boys wound through the tables, they spotted a pirate running on deck in the direction of Hattie's shot. Jack pulled Skip's arm, and both of them sank to the floor, out of the man's view. "We had better crawl on our bellies to the kitchen," Jack said.

The two boys crawled toward the kitchen door on hands and knees. *The one thing about hiding in the kitchen*, Jack thought, *is we won't have to go hungry.*

Scooting quickly on all fours, they got to the swinging doors. Jack slowly pushed them open. Sticking his head in, he looked around. "It's okay," he said. "We can get up."

The kitchen was large, clean, and white. Steel pots were set on the stove to boil water in the morning, and crates of eggs sat on one of the large pine tables in the middle of the room. It was all too obvious that whoever the cook was in this kitchen had made sure someone could see a spot on the floor or anything that was out of place. It spoke of an orderly man, the kind of man Jack had seldom known.

Jack reached out and took a big, shiny orange from a large basket. Someone had been squeezing them for juice. "You seen one of these things before?" Jack asked.

"No," Skip answered.

"They be oranges, just like the color, and sweet like any sugar you done stuck in yer mouth. Taste mighty fine. Here, take a couple and stick 'em down in your shirt."

Skip backed away and held up his hand. "They don't belong to us."

"Oh, come on. We is s'posed to eat here, ain't we? You think that cook would leave us to starve just 'cause we ain't sittin' on our behinds in the dining room?"

Skip blinked, then stared at the fruit. Jack watched his reaction. Skip's straight blond hair tumbled down thickly beside his head.

His blue eyes were wide like two pieces of clean ice floating in a mountain stream. It was just this kind of thinking Jack couldn't understand. There were times when these good people's consciences got in the way of their better sense.

Jack stuffed his shirt with the oranges. He would take some for Skip. When the boy got hungry enough, he'd set aside these scruples of his. Jack knew that much. There was something about hunger that did that to the best of people.

He looked around the kitchen for someplace to hide. The trouble with orderly people was that they seldom left anything out of place, and this cook appeared to be just such a man. Boxes were neatly packed into the corners of the room. They could be moved to make a spot for two boys, but from the looks of things that would be a lot of work.

Kitchen utensils and knives were hung close to the cooking and cutting areas. They gleamed, sparks of light dancing off them. Stacks of white dishes towered from the cabinets behind latched windows.

He hadn't noticed much about the kitchen when they had toured the place with Zac, except the knives. Jack had thought them to be fine knives when he saw them the first time. Now, they might just come in handy. He picked two long, sharp ones from the rack and handed one to Skip.

"Here," he said, "stick this in your belt. We may just need it before we're through. I ain't gonna let them pirates kill me without no fight."

Skip took the knife and slid it into place behind his belt.

The two of them heard a noise in the dining room. Quickly glancing around the room, Jack spotted a white metal door. He pulled Skip's sleeve. "Let's get in there."

Hauling back on the handle, the two boys stepped into what felt like an icehouse. Sides of beef hung on large hooks, and steam from blocks of ice rose in the semidarkness.

Jack closed the door behind them. "Let's get our behinds to the back of this here place," he said.

The two boys felt their way through the darkness. They inched their way around the sides of cold beef.

"What if it's Hat we heard?" Skip asked.

"You wanna go out there and see?"

"No, I don't reckon so."

"If it is her, I reckon she'll find us. She sent us in here, didn't she?"

The cooler was pitch black, and the boys slid their feet along the planks that covered the floor, carefully moving around and past the hanging beef. "You know, if those men do catch us," Jack said, "we're gonna hang here alongside these cows."

"I know," Skip whispered.

Finding the very back of the cooler, Jack felt a large block of ice. "I s'pose we could set ourselves down here and just wait it out."

The two boys inched their behinds onto the cold block of ice. Skip shivered.

"This is plenty strange," Jack said.

"How so?"

"Well, you know that preacher I told you about, the one that reads with me?"

"Yeah."

"He was some kind of missionary one time up in Alaska. This place kinda reminds me of what he used to tell me about what it was like up there."

"It don't sound like no place to be."

"I s'pose not, but to hear him tell about it, you'd think it was like being next to heaven."

"Don't sound like it to me."

Jack went on. "He said in the dark wintertime a body could step out onto the roof of the world and just be with God. There was nobody else around, none at all. You could yell as loud as you had a hankering to and just hear the sound of your own voice bouncing off the ice and coming right back at you. And the winter was long, too. He said sometimes a body would spend months at a time in this here kind of darkness."

"I wouldn't like that."

"Well, to hear him tell it, he felt kinda special, being alone with just God like that. A body could catch his own thoughts without none of the noise to go up against. You could just sit and think about what was next in your life and what ya had better do about it when it came about. A body needs to know the vitals of just livin', I guess."

"I'd think it might be better for a fella to know that ahead of time."

"Nobody knows that ahead of time. Time just kinda comes on

you and makes you do things, and if you ain't thought it through, no telling what you might do."

"I'm cold," Skip said.

"Maybe we should just sit real still and think about what to do, just like that preacher did."

"Maybe we should pray and ask God what to do."

"And how we gonna know what He says? God ain't never been in no meat locker before hidin' from pirates, now, has He?"

"No, but I was always told that He knows exactly what a body should do, and if you ask, He lets you know somehow."

"Well, pirates or no pirates, if I hear God answer us in this here icehouse, I'm hightailin' it outta here so fast it would make your head swim."

The boys heard movement in the kitchen. They pressed their backs to the wall and shivered.

Moments later, they saw the door to the cooler crack open.

"Whatcha lookin' in there fer?" a man shouted.

The light from the kitchen stabbed into the darkness of the locker. It bathed the sides of beef, painting them pink with orange stripes. "I thought somebody might be hiding in here," the man said.

"Now, would you go and hide yerself in that there place, even if you had a mind to?"

"No, I reckon not. Still, maybe we should take a look-see anyhow."

CHAPTER 23

+ + + + + + +

HATTIE WAS STUNNED WHEN she hit the river. The cool water jerked her eyes open. She thrashed and began to kick, her heavy boots weighing her down. She could hear the paddles coming closer, and she struggled to clear herself from the big boat. Hand over hand and with all of her strength, she pushed the water from her face, thrashing wildly in the murky river.

Suddenly, in the dark fog, her hand brushed a floating log. She grabbed it and hung on as the steamer's wake moved her and her waterlogged raft toward the shore.

The milky mist hung low over the water, creeping on padded claws of silence. It hugged the shoreline, and faintly through it, she could make out the brambles that clawed their way to the water's edge—dark clouds of brush with soft, fuzzy edges, their black fingers scratching at the face of the fog.

Holding on to the log, Hattie kicked her heavily booted feet, pushing both herself and the log toward the uncertain shoreline. Moments later, she could feel the first of the grassy arm of land that pointed out from the riverbank. She stumbled to her feet and then fell headfirst into the black, grassy water. Getting to her knees, she carefully rose to her feet. Putting one soggy foot in front of the other, she made her way to the riverbank.

The undergrowth of blackberry bushes clawed at her wet dress, grabbing on to her waterlogged skirt and tugging at her with each step she took. Moments later, she found herself on the road that ran beside the river. She began to trudge down the river in the direction the steamer was taking, water squashing between her toes with each footfall. If that boat put ashore any time soon, she wanted to be there. The boys were waiting for her, and she was responsible. Nothing short of a mortal wound was going to keep her from finding that steamer and the men who had thrown her overboard.

She marched straight and tall. She'd always been a proud woman and her looks—the wet dress she wore and the knot on the back of her head from those ruffians—wouldn't change that a bit.

Just now, as she marched down the dark road, she remembered her father. The people who lived around them had always called him "Old Eddie," but out of respect. He'd fought in nearly every war the country had been in, starting with the Revolution. A fire-eater, his gray beard had covered his gaunt belly, and he had stood ramrod straight as he took his place at the front of every fourth of July parade she could remember. He had been quite the distinguished picture in his worn war tunic, his musket shouldered and his chin jutting in the direction of the march. Just now, she assumed the same posture, throwing her shoulders back and tramping along the road. She was proud of who she was and always would be.

This newfound faith of hers had softened her a mite. It had also made her feel clean and free. It was something the pastor had reminded her of over and over again. But it wouldn't make her no coward, of that she was determined. If anything, it made sure that whenever she went to battle, like her daddy, she'd march into it for all the right reasons. There wouldn't be any thought of saving her own skin, and she wouldn't spend more than a second of worry as to the consequences.

She hated the thought of the boys who were depending on her, alone on that boat with those pirates. The men who had done this would pay, she'd see to that. Men like that deserved to hang. There had been a time in her life when that thought wouldn't have satisfied her in the least. Revenge was something that used to belong to her and her alone. The courts had no business butting in to her affairs and interfering with what she had in mind. Now, though, she'd have to satisfy herself with just helping to bring these men to justice. It didn't seem nearly as satisfying to her way of thinking, but she'd have to do it all the same.

With each footfall in the misty darkness, she thought about the boys and wondered about Zac. Now there was a man who got to do his job with a gun, meting out justice whenever he could. She envied him that. The thought gave her mixed feelings. She shouldn't be that way anymore. Right now, though, more than anything, that was just what she wanted to do. If she ever got them in her sights again, she'd make those pirates pay.

Had she been in the water just minutes more, she would have seen the chase boat coming, or they would have seen her. She heard the engine of the small boat as it chugged by her. Hurrying toward the bank of the river, she pushed the briared bushes aside and watched it go by. "Hey!" she screamed. "Over here!"

* * * * *

Zac tossed cord wood into the boiler of the little steamer. They had seen a number of survivors on the riverbank and assumed them to be what they were, gamblers who had refused the offer of going on shore at Walnut Grove. The four of them had already reluctantly decided that unless they saw someone floundering in the water in front of them, they'd not stop to offer either assistance or explanation. There was no time, not if they were going to stay close to the *Delta King*.

"I feel bad that we're not stopping for these people," Jenny said.

"You feel bad!" Van Tuyl exclaimed. "They're my passengers."

"We're losing time anyway," Grubb stressed. "We go to stopping now and we can't hope to catch those pirates. That steamer's the fastest boat on the river, and since those people don't own it and aren't worried about any damage, I don't expect them to be slowing down for this fog."

"I don't reckon so," Van Tuyl shrugged.

"What about one of these big houses you were talking about?" Jenny asked. "Would there be someone there who could help us?"

"There might be," Van Tuyl offered, "but by the time we stop to ask, we might as well just give up the chase."

"Let's just keep making the best time we can," Zac added. He tossed another piece of wood into the fire and slammed the boiler door closed. "They won't be taking that *Delta King* all the way to San Francisco, and I doubt they'll care much for passing another town, either. I suspect they'll put in somewhere up ahead to unload. That'll be our best chance to catch up to them."

"They more'n likely have already got wagons alongside the road," Van Tuyl muttered, "all hitched up and ready to go."

"It'll be the heaviest one we need to follow," Zac said.

"Now how we gonna keep up with them on foot?" Van Tuyl asked.

Zac thought about the question. Chasing criminals had been his specialty, and when other people saw him at work, they often assumed that he relied solely on his reactions at the spur of the moment. He knew that was only a part of it, a small part. Usually he had a plan based on what he knew about the people he was chasing. He also prided himself on being better armed. Nearly always, he was outnumbered, and when that was true he couldn't afford to be outgunned and outthought. But here, these men had already shown the best of thinking and preparation. They also had Hattie and the boys, and that might just cloud his thinking unless he was very careful. And he only had his close-in short gun. Any way he cut it, he wasn't off to the best of starts.

"That's why we need to keep as close to them as we can," Zac answered.

Van Tuyl scratched the back of his head. "Whoever it was that figured this out had some planning to do. This Princeton fella must be quite the thinker. They say he was a colonel in the Confederacy—you know anybody by that name, Cobb? You served in that war, didn't you? I can see your hat says you did."

"Yes, I rode with Moseby in Virginia. I was kinda young, though, mostly held the horses."

"Them folks gave off quite a chase."

"We did do a lot of riding and quite a bit of quiet walking, too, as I recollect."

"I spent the war in the Union blockade," Van Tuyl said, "mostly sufferin' in the sun and heat and waiting to hear tell about the war. I can tell you, though, I rightly admire the fightin' you boys did. You did yerself proud, though it don't please me none. We left three hundred thousand men stiff in the Southern dust."

"A man will do more than he's called on when he's defending his home."

"I reckon so. You ever come across this Princeton?"

"I know one man it might be, but I wouldn't want to say."

"Heroes with no war to fight," Grubb murmured over his shoulder.

Van Tuyl smiled. "Dennis here was a bit too young for that hoedown, I reckon. You didn't miss much," he snapped back at the pilot.

"If it's who I think it might be," Zac offered, "the man was no hero. He was clever, all right, but he never stuck his neck out to get it shot at."

"Smart man," Grubb added.

"Well," said Van Tuyl, "whoever the scoundrel is, he sure is leading us on a merry chase."

"That's why we can't be stopping for folks," Zac said, "unless we have to. I'm hoping to catch them before they have that boat unloaded."

"Well then, you better pray that something happens to slow them down," Grubb offered. "They're making much better time than we are, and nothing on this river can catch the *Delta King*."

+ + + + +

Manny paced back and forth in the pilothouse behind Doyle. The river was dark and the fog hid even the largest of the obstacles they might encounter.

"We're making ourselves good time," Doyle said.

"You just go to making certain we don't run aground before our time," Manny responded. "The wagons are waitin' for us on Decker Island, and if we plow into that riverbank before we get there, we'll be trapped like a bug on sticky paper. I don't want that."

"All right. I'll have to slow it down a mite."

"Then, you best do that. I don't rightly think we have too much to worry about. Those people back in that town will be chasin' critters and puttin' out fires all night. I don't expect they'll have much time to organize no posse till morning, if that."

Doyle grinned. "This has got to be about the slickest operation we ever pulled off."

"I'd say so. The colonel planned it pretty good, if I do say so myself."

They heard the heavy footfalls on the stairs, and Manny knew at once who it was without even looking. Only Brian made that much noise. The man hoisted himself up the last flight of stairs and stepped into the pilothouse, followed by Cliff Cox.

"We got the boat!" Cox blurted out. "I knew it would work and all with a minimum of gunplay."

"Figured that might appeal to you, Cox," Manny added.

"Why do it when there's no reason?"

"Templeton's dead," Brian droned. "Done been shot."

"That must have been what that shot was," Doyle observed from the wheel.

"How'd it happen?" Manny asked.

"Some old lady with a horse pistol didn't take too kindly to having her cabin broken into. Shot him right in the gut."

"It was Zac Cobb's aunt," Cox added. "We threw her overboard."

"Where is Templeton?" Manny asked.

"He's on the deck."

"What did you do to the old lady?" Even though Cox had already acknowledged the fate of the woman, Manny ignored him. He'd much prefer to hear a report from one of his own.

"Knocked her senseless and threw her overboard."

"Just like I said," Cox added. "Your men didn't kill her, but I wouldn't expect her to survive in the river."

Manny shook his head, muttering to himself. "Shoot, I didn't want anybody getting himself up and killed on this thing. The colonel ain't gonna like that, not one bit."

Brian shrugged his shoulders. "That old biddy like to have kilt more of us than she did. She come outta that cabin swingin' that there Colt 'round like she was aimin' to take more with her. Had to admire her sand."

"Like I said," Cox added, "it was Cobb's aunt. I got to meet her, and I'd never be the one to describe her as the matronly sort of aunt that one might expect."

Manny looked past him at Brian. "You just make sure you make a careful search of this boat," Manny said. "I don't want to be carryin' any passengers to where we're going, and I don't want any witnesses."

"Cobb's boy and one other youngster might still be on board," Cox offered. "They came back on board with the old woman, and I didn't see them leave. Of course with little boys and that carnival on shore, you can never tell."

For the first time, Cox had his attention. Manny thought on it. "You make sure we find those boys if they're here. I don't want no kids with us when we unload. Find them and throw them in the river."

"We're doing that right now, searchin' high and low," Brian said.

"Good. And I don't want them boys killed outright. We'll have plenty of folks stirred up along this river without that. We go to killin' passengers and kids and they'll have out the army, the navy, and every man and boy old enough to carry a gun."

Manny paced back and forth in the small cabin. "I just hope Korth did what he was supposed to do and took care of that Wells Fargo agent."

"I'd have to see that for myself," Cox sniggered.

Manny looked at him. His eyes narrowed. Most of the men Manny was used to dealing with had little in the way of pretense. They were the roughest sort of men—thieves and murderers. This man was a total pretender. Supposedly, he worked for Wells Fargo, but that had just been an act, an act for the money. Now he was playacting at being a pirate. Manny spoke to him with deliberateness. "You go back down to the salon and wait for the landing. This here pilothouse is crowded enough as it is."

Cox's eyes blinked behind his spectacles. He obviously didn't like the idea of being left out of the thinking and it was plain to see he was. Nodding, he turned and made his way back down the stairs.

"Like I said, I hope Korth delivered on all those promises of his. With all the bragging he did about what he was going to do to that Cobb fella, he just better have delivered."

"What we gonna do about Cox?" Brian asked. "I don't trust him a smidgen. He's got too much book learnin' for my likes. Should I just throw him over like the rest?"

"Nah, we'll have to keep him 'round for a while. I ain't sure if we'll need him or just what the colonel has in mind for him, but he has given us plenty of information, and he just might know what they'll do now to try to find us."

"He don't seem worth much, if you ask me," Brian offered. "If we get ourselves caught he's gonna just pretend he's one of them."

"That's the problem with traitors. Most of 'em don't even know their own minds. He ain't worth much more than a pitcher of warm spit where I'm concerned either, but the colonel places some stock in him. Same social standing, I reckon."

+ + + + +

Dr. Page stumbled down the stairs. The sudden push from Princeton caught him off guard. He grabbed for the iron rail. "Here, here, there's no need for that."

"Move along like I tell you."

Dr. Page raised himself to his full height and straightened the borrowed coat he wore. He held his chin high. "I am perfectly willing to go along without duress, if you will be somewhat more patient."

"You just move along like I ask. I wouldn't care to shoot you right here. Then I'd have to drag your body."

The doctor turned around and looked Princeton in the eye. His steel gray eyes blazed at Princeton, ignoring the revolver in his hand. William Page was educated far beyond the practice of medicine. His was a classical education, spiced with a great deal of Chautauqua revivalism. He could quote Tennyson as well as lengthy passages of the Bible, and both had served him well for years. His withering glance at the man was dignified and showed not the least in the way of panic. "Then, sir, I would suggest that you allow me to walk like a human being rather than be herded like a beast of burden. It seems to be in your own best interest to do so."

Princeton waggled the gun in his direction. "Just turn around and walk, Doctor."

Dr. Page wasn't moving. "And what have you done with my niece?"

"Blevins has taken care of her. He didn't want to see her locked up in the dark with you. It seems he has plans for her."

"Plans?"

Princeton stifled a smile. "Why, yes, Doctor. A young woman with her good looks . . . there's always a man who has plans for her."

William turned and continued to walk down the stairs. He wanted to hide any expression that might give away his feelings to the man.

Princeton continued, "When I first saw the two of you, neither of you had gotten cleaned up. Even then I could see that the young lady was nice to look on, and now I can see why Robert is so taken with her."

"My niece has absolutely no desire for any relationship with Mr. Blevins, of that I can assure you."

"She may not have much choice, Doctor."

Dr. Page reached the bottom of the stairs and turned around at the locked door. "And what are your intentions, sir?"

"That depends on the young lady."

Page's eyebrows dropped, a question mark written clearly on his face.

Princeton pushed him away from the door and, reaching into his pocket, extracted a key. He inserted it and turned the lock. Opening the door, he motioned with the revolver into the darkness.

William stood fast. "I'm afraid I don't understand how our fate depends upon Mary. Just as I told you, she has no intention of assisting you in any fashion."

"Robert seems to think she would do most anything to protect you. We discussed this when I came to the door tonight. Of course, I had no idea that the two people he spoke of were you and your niece."

"She would never agree to a relationship with Mr. Blevins, not for me nor the archangel Gabriel."

Princeton pushed him into the darkened cellar. Taking a torch from the barrel beside the door, he reached back and ignited it on the flaming sconce hanging in the stairway hall. He swung the flame back into the darkness. "Well, Doctor, let's hope that for your sake Blevins knows your niece better than you do. Now, move along. We're going to find you a place to stay at least for part of the night."

Marching into the darkness, they passed stacks of contraband before they came to a locked door. The lock hung loosely on the hasp. Princeton took it off and opened the door.

Dr. Page stepped into the room. Silver and gold candelabras glittered among the expensive furniture. "Might I have a light in here with me?" he asked. Reaching into his jacket pocket, he pulled out a small, leather-bound book. "You have the appearance of a gentleman, sir, in spite of your circumstances. I have my Bible with me, and if this is to be my last night on this Earth, I would very much like to read."

Princeton glanced first at Dr. Page and then down at the Bible. "I don't see why not." Moving to the candles, Princeton swung the flame over several of them, coaxing them to life. "How will that work?"

"That will be satisfactory. You have my gratitude."

He watched Princeton eye him as he settled into a chair. The broad-shouldered man was obviously a soldier, with a businesslike demeanor and a piercing gaze, yet his lips quivered slightly as he spoke. "Will you be comfortable?"

"What's the matter, Colonel? I should think that you've killed many a religious man before."

"Not one that I've spoken to beforehand."

"Believe me, Colonel, we die just like the rest. The only difference is we know where we're going and who will be there to greet us. I can assure you, I've been with many a person in death, and their faith seems to make all the difference."

"There's nothing personal about what I may have to do, Doctor."

William smiled. "I'm sure of that, Colonel Princeton. What you do has little to do with your feelings, only your greed."

CHAPTER 24

+ + + + + + +

MARY BACKED UP TO THE WALL of her room as Blevins closed the door behind him. He turned and locked the door, then dropped the key into his vest pocket.

"What will your aunt say?" Mary asked.

"She's still preparing supper for the colonel. I'll have to make excuses for you and the doctor, but don't you worry about that. My aunt and I have an understanding—she never asks me questions, and I allow her to stay and resist throwing her on the streets of San Francisco—a perfectly amicable arrangement."

Mary's face was drawn and pale. Blevins held himself erect and determined, and the look in his dark eyes frightened her. They were like pieces of smoked glass—he could see out but other people couldn't see in. The twisted soul inside him was totally without scruples. Mary knew enough to know that. He pulled on the lace cuffs that blossomed from the bottom of his sleeves. Running his stubby fingers along the sides of his coat, he straightened his lapels.

"You know," he continued, "you are quite fortunate that I've stepped in and intervened. Princeton would have killed you. He never likes to make the same mistake twice."

"Where is my uncle?"

"You needn't worry about the good doctor. He will be quite safe. Of course his continued good health all depends on you." He gave off a knowing smile, the grin of a man who gets his way without worry, without struggle. Everything about Robert Blevins indicated that work and hardship were foreign concepts to his mind. There was a smugness to him, and Mary hated that in anybody. It was obvious that all he saw in her was a pretty face. But she knew she could use her quick mind to her advantage; she would find a way to outsmart the vile serpent.

"He will be safe for the time being. He's in a place where no one can hear him and where he could never hear you. Princeton took him to the cellar. You remember that place, don't you?"

She shook her head.

He walked toward her. "You need not deny it. I know you've been there. You were curious, and a woman's curiosity is a terrible thing to arouse. As you saw, I have a great deal to lose here and now so do you."

"I just want to go home."

"In any event, with what I stand to gain tonight, I plan on leaving The Glades. I plan to travel comfortably for quite some time. The only question before us tonight is will you go with me or will you stay here on a permanent basis?"

"What do you mean?"

He moved closer, putting his hands on her arms and holding her tightly. Moving his hands up and down her arms, he looked into her eyes. "I mean, my dear, there are two ways to keep you from testifying against me. One would be very pleasant for the both of us and the other, unfortunately, would be most unpleasant for you."

Leaning back, away from him, she shivered. "I just want to go home."

"You see, dear Mary, only two people cannot testify against a man in a court of law in California—a corpse or a wife. Those are the choices before you tonight. You can come with me to tour the Continent as my wife or remain here and allow the colonel to finish the job his man failed to do."

She strained back against his arms, stiffening her spine.

"You have attracted me since I first set my eyes upon you." He gently fingered her hair. "You are a beautiful woman and so very young."

She shivered.

"I know you have little feeling for me now, but in time that will change. You'll see. You're a lady of refinement and good upbringing, just the kind of woman I've always envisioned for myself."

Once again stroking her hair, he lowered his voice. "The mind is so very strange. In time you will forget how this happened. You will only be thankful that it did."

"I would never do that. You must think me some pliable cow, some mindless debutante."

Reaching behind her, he pulled her closer. "I should much prefer you as a wife to a corpse, but those are your only choices, my dear." Leaning down, he kissed her cheek.

The man's trimmed beard scratched her cheek, and the forced kiss made her sick inside. She pushed him away. "You are wrong about me in one thing, however. I have a great deal of feeling about you."

He cocked his head, registering disbelief.

"I have deep feelings for you."

With the back of his hand, he brushed her ravenlike hair. "There, you see? This won't be so bad."

Her lips curled down. "I loath you. In all my years, I've never met a man I despise as much as I do you. As for the matter of becoming your wife, I would rather die than do that."

His eyes smoldered, refusing to blink or look away. Slowly he released his grip on her and stepped back.

"You see, death has no dread for me," Mary continued. "The thing I detest the most would be dishonor, and to be married to a man I disrespect would be a life of pain, something I couldn't possibly endure."

He turned and, taking the key from his pocket, walked to the door. Unlocking it, he looked back at her. "Perhaps for you, dishonor might be just what Princeton chooses before he resolves your situation. You may have sealed your own fate, my dear." He opened the door. "I will leave you to think it over. The men in the colonel's crew might prove to be brutal, but I'm sure they would find you quite entertaining."

Mary watched the door close. She placed her hand to her mouth, suddenly feeling very sick. Hurrying to the ceramic commode that sat on the dresser, she held on to its sides and looked up at her face in the mirror. Shaking with horror and disgust, she struggled to regain control over her overwhelming emotions.

Sponging water in a cloth, she wiped her face. The cool touch of the water settled her stomach. Moving slowly to the window, she parted the shades. "Lord, send someone to help us," she prayed.

Sliding the brass bar that blocked the pane, she unlocked the window and lifted it open. She stuck her head outside the window.

The fog hid the river. Occasionally she saw a glimpse of the water. Large oaks dotted the grounds, their black branches tantalizingly out of reach. Her room was on the third floor, and the smooth stones that formed the exterior of the house offered little or no foothold. It would be a straight drop to the ground, a drop she couldn't risk.

* * * * *

Hattie trudged down the road. The pruned fruit trees dotting the fields in the gathering fog seemed to be watching her, observing her every step. The road itself was isolated and lonely, although it had been recently well traveled—she could see that from the ruts worn deep into the soft ground by wagons that obviously were heavy. Her boots pressed the soft ruts flat as she sloshed over them, the water from the river still seeping between her toes. More than anything else, she wanted to take those big boots off. Having her feet drying in front of a fire was a luxury that seemed to be out of reach, but one she wanted badly.

Rounding a bend in the river road, she spotted the big house. It was impressive, larger than many of the buildings she had seen in Sacramento. *Whoever it is who lives here must be a body to be reckoned with,* she reasoned as she stomped up the grassy slope that led to the hill. Candles flickered through gauzy curtains, muted lights that showed signs of life. Large pillars supported iron balconies that hung over the entrance. Carefully trimmed trees lined the entry drive. Hattie walked between them, surveying the stately manor as she approached a high and lofty front porch. She walked carefully up the massive stairs, holding on to the railing as she climbed.

Approaching the two massive doors, she spotted the large, ornately designed brass knocker. Lifting it, she banged twice on the door. She waited in silence and then once again lifted the knocker and banged on the door. Moments later, it opened.

A gauntly built Negro man with a bald black head shining above a circle of salt and pepper hair blinked out at her. "Can I hep you?" he asked.

Hattie straightened her wet dress. "I done come off the steamer. It's been took over by pirates. I got two young'uns still on the thing, and I shore could use a pistol and a horse."

The man surveyed her up and down. She had obviously been soaked to the skin. "You just wait yerself right here, please, ma'am."

With that, the man closed the door, leaving Hattie to shiver outside and wait. Moments later the door opened once again. Behind the servant stood a woman in a full dress, twisting a handkerchief in her hands. "Mercy me," she said. "Can we help you?"

Hattie raised herself to full height and cleared her throat. "Ah..mmm . . . like I done told yer man here, I come off a steamboat. It's been took over by pirates. I got myself two young'uns still on the thing, and I could use a pistol and a horse, if y'all got 'em to spare."

"Please, Soggy," the woman said, "let the poor woman in."

Hattie raked her feet on the mat and stepped inside.

The older woman's face twisted at the sight of Hattie in her wet dress. "My stars," she said, "you'll catch your death if we don't find you something else to wear. Please, Soggy, see if you can find this lady something presentable."

Hattie waved her hand. "Don't bother none 'bout that. I shore could use some dry socks, though, and a stove or fire to dry off my feet some." Untying the scarf that held her hat in place, she set the water-logged bonnet on a table beside the door and tossed her gray hair.

The matron dabbed the silk hanky to her mouth and then beat on her chest with it. "Goodness sakes, yes. You must feel a fright. We have a fire in the parlor. You're welcome to sit and rest for a while, if you like. Soggy, get this lady some dry clothes."

After exchanging introductions, Hattie followed Mamie down the decorated hall, eyeballing the fixtures and the soft glow of the lamps. "I can't be stayin' long. I gots to be after them yahoos before they gets too far with them boys."

The woman in front of her continued to beat on her chest with the silk and murmur. "Mercy, what is California coming to. I simply can't believe my ears. Pirates! Pirates on the Sacramento River and right in front of The Glades."

Entering the stylishly decorated parlor, Hattie spotted the blazing fire at once. She picked up a chair and, pulling it to a position in front of the flames, sat down and began to unlace her boots.

Mamie hovered over her like a bird trapped suddenly in a small cage. Waving the silk hanky in front of her face, she went on. "Oh dear, this is most distressing. We've had houseguests just leave The Glades tonight who were set up by pirates. The sheriff took them to town, and my nephew is organizing a band of pursuers even while we speak."

"I ain't got time to wait on no posse. Never set much store on them disorganized bands of farmers, no how. I gots to get back on the road, and a horse under me would help me some."

"I should have Soggy bring you some food."

Hattie grimaced. "Ain't got no time fer no sit-down eatin'. I could use some whiskey and a cigar to warm my innards, though."

The woman's face froze, her handkerchief stopping in mid motion. "Whiskey and a cigar, for a lady?"

"I ain't been a lady fer some time. Right now I is just an old wet gal that needs some warmin' inside me."

Mamie walked to the butler's table beside the fire and shakily poured amber liquid into a cut glass.

"Pour it tall," Hattie squeaked in a high-pitched, raspy voice. "It's got a ways to go to reach into these old bones."

Blinking at Hattie, Mamie's face registering her surprise, she continued to pour. Opening the polished humidor, she pulled out a black cigar.

Hattie extracted her white, wrinkled feet from her boots and socks, first pouring and then wringing out her socks into a puddle on the Persian rug in front of the fire. She held her feet up to the fire. "Tarnation, that feels mighty good."

Mamie handed the full glass and the cigar to Hattie, followed by a match. "I don't know many women who drink powerful spirits and smoke cigars," she said.

Hattie slurped down the whiskey. "Ahh . . ." she exclaimed. "This here is mighty fine stuff." She grinned at her hostess. "Then you ain't never know'd Hattie Woodruff afore. I takes my liquor heavy and my tobacco strong."

Reaching into her dress, she pulled out a wad of wax paper. Opening it, she scooted the black mass toward the fire. "I gots my plug of chewin' tobacco all water-soaked."

"My goodness."

"Betcha ain't never met many women that carried a plug, neither."

"No, I can't say that I have."

Lifting the glass, Hattie drained it. She held the empty glass up to Mamie. "That there is mighty fine corn. I could use another, if'n you could spare it."

Moments later, Soggy walked slowly into the room, carrying a dress draped over one arm and holding a pair of socks in his hand.

Snatching the socks from his hand, Hattie waved off the frilly dress. "I wouldn't know what to do with one of them things. Ain't no good fer ridin' or walkin', just for prancing about in front of menfolks."

The sound of boots on the polished floor snapped Hattie's head around.

Mamie burst into explanation. "Oh, Robert, this poor woman has just had an encounter with those same pirates the Pages spoke of."

"Is that right?" The man's eyes blazed at the sight of Hattie, her feet propped up in front of the fire.

Hattie spat out the words. "I was on the *Delta King*. It's been took over by pirates. I got two young'uns still on the thing, and I could use me a pistol and a horse."

"I'm afraid that will not be possible. The sheriff is organizing a posse to chase down those men. I'm sure that if you wait here with us, we can see that they are brought to justice."

Hattie lit her cigar. Shaking the flame out, she wagged her head. "I ain't a body given to waitin' on justice from other folks. Hattie Woodruff makes her own justice. I generally do it, though, with a pistol, and if'n you got yerself one, then I'll just use it and get on my way."

"I'm afraid that will not be possible."

"Robert, if the lady insists, we have a trunk of revolvers."

"One would be a plenty," Hattie added.

Blevins placed his hands on the lapels of his jacket and, leaning his head back, glared at Mamie. "Like I said, that will not be possible."

Pulling the fresh socks onto her feet, Hattie announced, "Then I won't be a wastin' no more of yer time. I gots me some skallywags to chase after, and that'll be something I'm a doing with or without yer help." She mashed her feet once again into the damp boots and pulled the laces tight.

Blevins stepped forward. "I can assure you the men you are chasing are too far ahead of you to catch. You'd be well advised to let the sheriff do his work while you rest."

Cocking her head at him, she tied the laces. "Now just how can you assure me of that? Fer all you know them critters is pulled that boat to shore nearby, and that's where I intend to be. If'n you won't give me use of a horse, then I'll jest haf to hoof it on outta here."

"But you have no weapon," Blevins said.

Hattie got to her feet and twisted her dress straight. "Let me tell you somethin', mister. When folks get Hattie Woodruff all riled up, I becomes a weapon my ownself. I'm a bag full a bobcats when I needs to be." She held up her hands. "I'll use a stick, a rock, or these here hands of mine to scratch those men's eyes out."

"That's foolish," Blevins said.

"I just hope them pirates feel the same way you does." Her eyes gleamed. "I glom on to one of them folks and he'll feel plenty sorry he was ever born."

Blevins walked her to the door, accompanied by Mamie. "You're making a big mistake, madam."

"Nah, I ain't. It's them folks that made the mistake. I latch on to them and there won't even be a holler left."

Mamie waved her handkerchief and sputtered. "You worry me so. This is work for men. It's dangerous, and it's so late and dark outside."

Hattie held on to the door. "Don't you worry none about me. This here is work fer somebody that cares." She shot Blevins a wicked glance. "It ain't no casual gentleman's business, none a-tall."

They held the door open and watched her briefly as she walked down the stairs. She heard the door close behind her and stood still as the fog swirled. She wiggled her toes. They were dry now and that was at least something.

Looking back at the big house, there was something that troubled her. The man had seemed especially cold and unhelpful. It was plain to see he had the means to give her what she wanted, and Lord knows she had the need. Anyone in the same position who stopped by her house would have had what they wanted and more. Perhaps she should just be grateful for the whiskey, the cigar, and the socks. Yet it still troubled her.

She didn't have much time to lose, especially since she was on foot. She'd never been known to be a horse thief, though at times people had called her that behind her back, never to her face. Perhaps if she circled the house, she just might find the stables. With a bridle, she could ride bareback and plenty fast, at that. She'd return the animal later, after she had the boys. She'd take one for her and one for them too.

Turning, she began to circle the house, making sure she avoided the windows. The house was huge, its stone walls climbing above the trees. Above the first floor, most of the windows were black. High up above, though, she could see another window on the third floor with a light in it, and it was open. She could see someone inside pacing back and forth. She stopped to watch.

The person inside came to the window. Hattie could see that it was a woman, a young woman with dark hair. The woman stuck her head out the window, and Hattie hurried to a spot behind the nearest tree.

"Hello there." The woman spoke the words out the window in a hushed tone. "Is there anyone there? Please, help me."

The words and the tone in which they were voiced startled Hattie. She didn't want her presence known to any member of the household before she had the horses, yet there was something in the way the words were spoken that told her the woman didn't belong in that house. She crouched behind the tree, curious.

"Please help me," the plaintive voice said. "I am being held here against my will."

There would be no avoiding it now. Hattie had her own troubles and two boys that needed her, but she couldn't leave this woman at the mercy of the man she had seen minutes before. Cautiously, she stepped out from behind the tree. She spoke to the woman in a low tone. "I'm just a passin' through," she said, "on my way to get hold of some pirates."

"Oh, please then, you've got to help me. The man who owns this place is the ring leader of those pirates. He has me and my uncle as his prisoners. Please don't leave us here. He intends to kill us."

CHAPTER 25

+ + + + + + +

"DON'T BE MESSIN' 'ROUND in that there icehouse. There ain't nothing in there that be near ready to eat."

The man stood with the door open and the boys worked at keeping the sides of hanging beef between them and the door.

"Hadn't we oughta look in here real good?"

"Naw! Who'd go and hide himself on a block of ice? Look here at these oranges!" the man in the kitchen exclaimed.

Jack peered around the beef and watched as the man at the door turned around to see the fruit. The boy held his hand back toward Skip, trying to keep him still.

Leaving the door open, the man shuffled back to the table where the oranges were piled in the basket. The first man had ripped one open and was devouring it, smacking his lips. "I do declare, this here is plenty worth the wild goose trip to look for them kids."

The second man pulled open one of the pieces of fruit. He bit into it cautiously. "I ain't never had one of these before."

"You ain't never had an orange?"

"Nope, had me plenty of apples but nary a one of these things." He squeezed it in his hand and watched the juice blossom. "It sure be a might peculiar thing."

"Maybe so, but it's sweet like honey."

"You reckon this kitchen's got some honey?"

"I reckon so."

Jack and Skip listened to the men fumble through the kitchen cabinets. They could hear cans and silverware hitting the floor. Leaning over to Skip, Jack whispered, "They ain't gonna be here long, I'm a bettin'. Before long they'll figure on movin' on."

"What we gonna do then?" Skip asked.

"What we gonna do? We be best to just sit here real tight."

"I don't much think Hat's gonna come for us."

"No, I don't 'spect so."

"Then what are we gonna do?" Skip asked again.

Jack sat back in the dark on the block of ice, mulling over the question. "I ain't rightly figured on that."

"Well, we have to do something. I don't cater to just letting these people steal this here boat while you and me sit on a block of ice."

Jack looked puzzled.

"I mean, Zac's gotta be chasin' us down right about now. We got to ponder a way to stop this boat, somehow."

The boys both heard the movement of the swinging doors, and then they could hear neither rummaging in the kitchen nor the men as they mumbled.

"I think they left," Jack said. Getting to his feet, the boy edged his way around the hanging beef. He approached the opening of the cooler, and then satisfying himself as to their departure, he hurried back to Skip, who was shivering. "They're gone," he said.

Skip got to his feet. "I think we better figure out some way to get this thing stopped. Meanwhile, I gotta get myself warmed up." Skip walked out of the cooler and took one of the leftover oranges and broke it open. He peeled it and dropped several sections into his mouth.

"See," Jack said smiling, "stuff that's stolen tastes a whole lots better."

"Don't neither. I figure, though, with what we got to do, it'll be payback."

Jack took off his cap and scratched his black hair. "There ain't no way two kids can stop this here thing." He walked toward Skip and began gesturing to make his point. "They gots men up in that pilothouse, and I can guarantee you, they gots somebody down in that there engine room, to boot."

Jack stopped suddenly. He reached down and, taking the derringer out of his sock, held it up. "We could use this thing, I reckon."

Skip shook his head. "I done a lot of things before, but I ain't about to go shootin' somebody. I can tell you one thing too, if they see two boys and that little stubby pistol of McCauliff's, they're gonna rush us for sure."

Jack turned the little gun over in his hand. "I suppose you're right."

"Put that thing away before it goes off accidental like."

Jack stuffed the little weapon back in his sock. "Then, what you reckon we should do?" he asked.

"You 'member that locker down in the engine room?"

Jack nodded his head.

"Well, I saw a long steel bar down there. If we could get that thing and crawl out onto the catwalk around them paddles, I think we could wedge it in them things. That oughta stop this here boat sure enough."

"It might work."

Skip slammed his fist into the palm of his hand. "It's gotta work. It's the only chance we got."

"What we gonna do if we do get them paddles stopped?"

"We'll duck into Jenny's cabin. They more'n likely already searched that place; it's right next to the gold."

"Won't they have men guarding that place?" Jack asked. "I mean, we'd have to walk past it to get to the paddles."

"Why should they guard it? It's them that's the thieves, ain't it?"

"I reckon you is right there." Jack shrugged. "Well, it's worth a try, I suppose."

"All right, let's look out and make sure the coast is clear, then we'll go down to the engine room. We got to watch that bar, though. It's long, and we don't want to go bangin' around down there. We got to slide it out and get up them stairs so we don't make no noise."

Jack moved cautiously toward the door. "Okay, I 'spect we best get at it, then. The quicker we stop this here thing, the quicker Zac can catch up to us."

The boys moved out to the empty dining room. The foggy darkness outside was of little comfort to them in the well-lit banquet hall. They sank to their hands and knees and began a fast crawl toward the door. Skip pushed it open slightly and stuck his head outside. Turning back around, he whispered to Jack, "That stairway to the engine room is a few yards off. We won't run, but we'll stick close to the windows here and make mighty quick about it."

Jack nodded his head vigorously.

Getting to their feet, the boys scampered out the door and onto the deck of the boat. The fog hung low. It would conceal anyone's movement on deck, unless that person happened to be close by—and that was something both boys wanted to avoid at all cost.

They quickly found the familiar stairway and descended into the darkness. Their strides on the iron stairway were cautious and deliberate. Reaching the bottom, they could see men outlined by the fire from the boiler. The men were feeding the flames, grunting and swearing in Chinese. Finding the locker, the boys skirted around it.

Skip felt for the long metal bar, hoping in the interval somebody hadn't moved it. Finding the cold steel, he grabbed Jack's hand and positioned it on top of the icy metal. Jack nodded. They began to slowly wrestle the metal bar from its resting place.

Suddenly, Jack froze. Grabbing Skip's shirt, he pulled on it and pointed down the gangway to the boiler. There, a shirtless man was walking toward them, the blaze gleaming off his bare skin. Both boys sat still, suspended by fear. To move now might mean they would be heard. They could only hope that whoever was walking in their direction would stop before he got to them.

The man continued to walk. Both boys looked at each other, and Skip silently prayed, hoping at just this moment in time to be invisible in the near blackness of the engine room. The man opened the locker and abruptly stopped. His eyes fell on the two boys. It was Peng Lee.

The man's eyes narrowed, and he nodded slightly.

A voice boomed out from the area next to the boiler. "Hey, what you doin' down thataway?"

The sudden intruder came stomping down the metal walkway, his voice growing louder with each step. "Who told you to move from where I put you?"

Peng Lee took the wrench he had come to find and, turning quickly, walked toward the man who continued to shout in his direction. "Got wrench," Peng Lee said.

The man wheeled a revolver he carried into the neck of the Chinaman, sending him sprawling to the floor and the wrench rattling over the metal walkway. The intruder continued with a string of curses. Turning back to the boiler, he shouted, "Don't none of you move. I'm gonna shoot the next man who so much as burps when I don't tell him to."

Picking up Peng Lee by his britches, the man shoved him toward the flaming boiler. The noise and confusion made Skip pull on Jack's sleeve. Picking up the iron bar, they lifted it and moved carefully out from behind the metal locker.

The bar was heavier than they thought it would be. On the engine room's catwalk they could see that it was nearly ten feet long. It had to be one of the largest pry bars they had ever seen.

The man's continued cursing behind them would help if they did manage to bang the bar on the stairs. There was a great deal of commotion, and the noise made them move faster. Reaching the stairway, they lifted the bar and negotiated each stair carefully.

Jack was the first to reach the deck. He stopped and peered out into the foggy darkness. Pulling the bar slightly, he motioned Skip forward.

The stern of the boat was now in Skip's direction. The boys moved cautiously. They would have to go past the well-lit salon, and experience told them the place would be filled with bragging men.

Skip stopped and, turning back to Jack, spoke in a low tone. "This fog will help us a mite, but we can't get ourselves too close to the windows. Let's move over to the side of the rail over yonder."

"Won't they be able to see us there?"

"Maybe, but I'm a prayin' we'll be invisible."

Moving over next to the rail, the boys skirted past the gleaming lights of the salon. It was just as Jack had thought. The place was filled with men who were drinking. Skip could see Cliff Cox talking to a group of the men as they passed by. He seemed to have their full attention. Passing the windows, Skip stopped near the rounded corner of the deck that led to the stern of the boat. Peeking around the corner, he glanced back in panic and motioned Jack to step back.

"What is it?" Jack whispered.

"I was wrong. There's a man in front of the room with all that gold. I can see a cigarette glowing in the fog."

"Do ya think he'd be able to see us if we moved real still and quiet like?"

"I dunno. I can't rightly see him none, just that cigarette."

"Well, we ain't smokin', so I reckon we might be able to get out there."

"Maybe so, but we sure can't make no noise."

Jack tucked the iron bar under his arm, reached down into the depths of his pocket, and drew out its contents.

"What ya got?" Skip asked.

"Just a few things from Robbie that he give me. I reckon it's the only stuff I got that weren't stolen. Robbie said it might bring me luck."

"What is it?"

"Just a piece of antler and an opal. He used to say a feller's got to be like this here stuff to make it in this world—hard, sharp, and pretty."

Skip swallowed hard. "Well, I guess 'tween my prayin' and them charms of yours, we got ourselves a chance."

Sticking the charms back in his pocket, Jack nodded. "We best get at it, I reckon."

Skip nodded.

The boys gripped the pry bar and, hugging the rail, moved out onto the foggy aft deck. The fog swirled around them as they took deliberate steps, glancing occasionally toward the end of the still-burning cigarette. It glowed with each puff the man took, shining in the darkness like the eye of the devil himself.

The large red paddle churned the water, the white flywheel spinning its continual revolutions and the white steel pistons driving the wheel with their continual pulsating, backward and forward motion. The water seethed with a boiling rage, vibrating the entire stern of the boat. They were far enough into it now that the slightest noise might go unheard.

The narrow catwalk that stretched from the stern of the boat to the sides of the enormous wheel would be a dangerous place in the daylight and with the boat safely docked. With the movement of the water under them and in the fog, it would be perilous. The fact that they had their hands full of steel didn't help them feel any more secure. One slip and they would either fall to certain death into the paddles or lose the bar and their chance to stop the boat. Either option seemed to be a poor choice.

Jack whispered, his voice barely audible over the splashing of the foaming water. "Well, if'n we don't make it, I shore take a peck of pride in knowin' you as a friend."

"Me likewise," Skip countered.

The boys slid their feet along the narrow walk, too afraid to lift them from the wet metal surface, moving inches at a time and watching the big paddle spin. Overhead, sparks from the smokestacks flew off into the foggy night air. Like fireflies caught in a maze of mist and refusing to stay, they swiftly flew away.

Jack's foot slipped slightly. Skip could feel a sudden jerk from the end of the bar. He froze in terror as Jack swayed back and forth over the edge that dropped to the paddles below. He braced his end of the pole, trying his best to give Jack some leverage to hang on to.

Jack fought to keep on his feet, watching the paddles spin and the river churn. He steadied himself. He was shaking now. Swallowing hard, he croaked out the words, "I reckon I'm all right now."

"You better be," Skip said. "We're almost there. It's the spot just over the flywheel, if I remember right."

Jack nodded. "Okay, I'll be careful now. You go 'head on, and I'll foller real slow."

Moving once again, the boys were soon standing in the spot on the catwalk just over the spinning flywheel. Below them they could see the long drum turn, its connections leading to the paddle. The flywheel spun from the power of the pulsating pistons, and with several large steel inner wheels they joined the paddles to produce the power to turn them through the water.

The catwalk they precariously balanced themselves on formed the superstructure that covered the pistons and held the flywheel and all its connections in place. Steel arms reached out toward the paddle and held the spinning drum secure. Several gaps in the edge of the catwalk, three small holes, could possibly provide a spot to hold the end of the pry bar. They'd have to leave enough of the bar to catch itself in the hole while the other end of the bar fouled the paddles.

Neither one of them knew what would happen when they forced the bar through the hole and into the paddles. It might just shear off with the force of the big blades, or it might spin out of control and fall into the river below. No matter what happened, that's all there was to it. At least they would feel better for having tried.

"You'll have to swing your end out over the river a ways," Skip said, "till I can stick my end in this here hole."

Jack tipped his head over the side of the catwalk, eyeballing the river below. "There ain't much room over there," he commented. "And this here bar is mighty heavy."

"You wanna trade places with me?" Skip asked.

"Naw, go 'head on."

"Why don't we get down on our behinds," Skip said. "Then you can swing yer leg 'round and lock it under this here walk."

Jack nodded. Both boys sat on the walk, and Jack looped one leg underneath the structure. Pushing the end of the bar close to the hole, Skip waited as Jack held his heavy end out, extending it over the river. Skip guided the bar into the hole. There was plenty of room, but not so much that it would pull out when the steel rammed into the wooden paddles.

Skip looked back at Jack. "Scrunch up close to me while we push this here thing into them paddles. We got to hang on to this bar till the thing catches."

"Okay."

Skip guided the end of the bar into the hole, and together they pushed it forward. When it was almost to the paddles, Jack scooted up, saddling Skip between his legs as both boys held on.

"You ready?" Skip asked.

"Ready as I'll ever be, I reckon."

Together they held on tight to the bar and shoved it forward. Aiming it at one of the spinning gaps in the swirling paddle, they plunged it into space.

The bar jerked in their arms, sprawling both boys flat onto the surface of the catwalk. The bar was wrestling with the biggest machine either of them had ever seen. It jerked into the sides of the steel hole, and they could hear the paddles as they shuddered and then began to splinter. Suddenly, the bar held fast, and the big paddles hung in the water like the arms of a slain giant.

"We better get," Jack said.

"Yeah, them folks is gonna be all over here pretty quick."

Jack looked at the dead paddle wheel and then grinned at Skip. "Maybe so, but I don't rightly think there's anything they can do about it now. We done whupped 'em."

Skip smiled back at him. "Yeah, I guess we did that, all right."

Moments later the two boys were skirting the surface of the suddenly drifting boat's stern. When they hit the deck, Skip looked in the direction of the cabin of gold. The burning cigarette was out. Only the dark fog remained.

"They're gonna be here pretty quick," Skip said.

"Yeah, where you reckon that feller's gone to?"

"I dunno, but we best hightail to Miss Jenny's cabin and lay low for a spell."

"I'm fer that," Jack said. "Then maybe we can eat some of these here oranges."

"Sounds good," Skip replied. "I figure we done earned 'em."

CHAPTER 26

+ + + + + + +

THE SUDDEN STOP OF THE PADDLES brought Doyle's head around from the wheel. He locked his eyes on Manny. They could hear the splinter and tear in the wooden paddles at the stern of the boat. "What's that?" he shouted. "We didn't run over nothin', no growlers that I could see."

Manny looked panicked. Grabbing the voice pipe, he blew down it. "What's going on down there?"

Moments later they heard the voice from the engine room. "I dunno. The steam's up but the pistons are froze."

"The boat's drifting," Doyle said. "If we don't get some power under us soon, we're going to be stuck on the riverbank."

"I'm going to find out what's going on down there!" Manny shouted. With his hands on the rail, he headed down the winding stairway, two steps at a time. Moving down two more flights of stairs, he reached the main deck. He joined several other men as they ran toward the stern of the boat. "What's going on?" he roared.

Brian was leaning over the stern of the boat, staring intently at the suddenly still paddles. "Somethin's hung up in that thing. It ain't movin' a smidgen."

"Well, go see what it is!" Manny shouted.

"I ain't gonna go out on that there thing."

"Well, somebody's got to." With that he spotted the narrow catwalk that led out over the pistons. Moving carefully and balancing himself, he walked out onto the narrow, metal catwalk. In the foggy silence, the boat continued to drift toward the riverbank. Through the mist, Manny could see the approaching branches of trees along the shoreline. Glancing down, he saw the twisted bar wedged in an opening of the catwalk. He followed the bar with his eyes down to the paddles. Scurrying over to where it was wedged, he tried to wrestle it free. It held fast. Turning back to Brian, he shouted, "I've found the problem. Get me a sledge hammer, and quick."

It took Brian several minutes to return to the stern of the boat with a large sledge hammer. Carefully inching his way onto the catwalk, he handed the steel mallet to Manny. Manny stood up on the catwalk and began to swing at the iron bar. The sound of the sharp metal on metal rang out over the boat. He continued to swing, banging on the bar as it bounced in the paddles. Moments later the metal pry bar loosened its grip on the catwalk and dropped.

The big, red paddle wheel lurched forward, loose and broken ends continuing to buckle and splinter. Manny watched the approaching fog-shrouded shoreline. There wasn't a moment to lose. If they didn't get power up on the wounded vessel, and quickly, they would be aground. Turning around, he looked up at the pilothouse. "He better swing that wheel around and quick," he growled at Brian.

The noisy clatter of the wounded wheel emitted a groaning sound filled with sharp splintered snaps. It lurched, stopped, and then lurched once again.

The trees along the shoreline were on them before they could feel the mud underneath, but Manny knew it was coming. Hurrying back to the stern, he grabbed for the railing and hung on. The boat struck the mud at the riverbank hard, sending Brian sprawling to the deck. Manny hung on. They were aground now, stuck in the mud.

Cupping his hands to his mouth, he yelled up at Doyle. "Doyle! Doyle!"

Moments later, the man stood at the doorway of the pilothouse, looking down at the deck below.

Manny spotted him. "Can you back this thing up?"

Doyle's voice echoed back. "I ain't sure we could do it even *without* the damage, but we'll give it a try."

Manny glanced back at Brian as the big man got to his feet. "How'd this thing happen?"

"I think it was them kids we been chasin'."

"Kids?"

"Yeah, you know, the kids that Cox fella said come back on the boat."

"You mean you ain't found them yet?"

"Naw, we'ze been lookin', though."

Manny leaned forward, his hands on his hips. "You get every man on board this boat lookin' for them kids. I want them found. I want them found now! Am I makin' myself understood?"

"Well, we done searched all the cabins, the dining room, and the kitchen. Opie's down in the engine room. I ain't rightly sure where else to look."

"Then search the cargo, and when you finish with that, start your search all over again. I want them kids found. Children are little, so they just might hide anywhere." Turning back, he looked at the broken paddles. "But they've been here, that's for certain."

The men scampered over the deck. Pointing to several of them, Manny shouted, "You men go up on top. I want all those cabins searched again, starting from the top down. Look under every bed. Those boys are small." He walked toward the bow of the boat. Trees and brambles covered the railings, pushing themselves out onto the deck.

Several of the men were rummaging through the cargo. One of them looked up. "We got us a coffin here, Manny, a little one, at that. Should we throw it overboard?"

"No, just make sure there ain't no live boy in there. I want them kids found." Walking back toward the stern of the boat, he ran into Cliff Cox as the man stumbled out of the salon.

"Why are we stopped?" Cox asked.

Manny grabbed him by the lapels. Even though Cox towered a good six inches above him, Manny pulled him down, stooping the man's shoulders, until he had him face-to-face. "It's those kids, those kids you were supposed to watch. That old lady killed one of my best men, and those kids who were with her wrecked the paddles on this boat. Now if you can't keep an eye on those people like you were supposed to do, you can at least look for those young'uns."

Cox swallowed. "What am I supposed to do? It was my job to pass on the information about the shipment. You're in charge of security."

"Talkin' seems to be all that you're good at," Manny snapped. "I expect you to pull your weight, not just take our money."

Releasing his grip on Cox, Manny stormed toward the stern of the boat. Doyle had managed to reverse the engines, and the pistons were churning, sending the big paddle wheel in reverse. The broken blades continued to snap and splinter, but water surged from underneath the *Delta King*. Whether it would be enough, nobody knew. All Manny knew was that this wasn't Decker Island. There were no wagons waiting for the gold. And for all he knew, Zac Cobb and a posse were just up the river.

+ + + + +

Zac had pulled the knife out from its special sheath that hung down behind the back of his neck. Taking a sharpening stone from his pocket, he began to rake the long blade over it.

"That looks to be plenty sharp as it is," Van Tuyl exclaimed.

"That's the way I like to keep it."

"Won't do much good against a firearm, however."

"Don't be too sure of that. It throws real nice and comes up on a man unexpected like."

The captain gulped. "I can see how that might work, at that."

The small boat continued to chug through the fog. It seemed like hours had slowly snaked by since they had left the panic of Walnut Grove. Grubb swung the wheel on the small paddle boat, avoiding a floating log. They had long since lost sight of the *Delta King*, and almost everyone on board had given up hope of ever seeing it again, everyone except Jenny.

"It should be just up ahead," Jenny said. "I just know it."

"Girl, that *Delta King* is long gone," Van Tuyl mused. "That thing had plenty of steam under it, and I can't see it slowing down until those folks are good and ready to."

"Whoever is behind that wheel isn't much worried about the fog, either," Grubb added.

"Well, I can't explain it," Jenny said. "I just feel it. I don't think the Lord is going to allow those boys to stay out of our reach for very long. I can't see that happening; I just can't. We're responsible for those boys. Somehow, I wish Hattie hadn't found them. I wish they'd seen the entire performance of that tattooed woman."

"You don't mean that," Zac said.

"I most certainly do. They wouldn't have seen much. Those carnival people only tantalize. And somehow boys and men"—she looked over at Zac—"are compelled to see the counterfeit before they can appreciate the genuine article."

Zac looked at her and smiled. "But once we see the real thing, we don't want to let it out of our sight."

"Just see that you don't, Zachary Taylor Cobb."

Zac blinked, then smiled.

"That's what I like to see," Van Tuyl added. "An optimist."

"Not at all," Jenny responded. "I've seen plenty of hard things in my life. I'm no empty-headed lady of leisure. I'm just a firm believer in the providence of God, although not in the way the term is usually used."

"And what way would that be?" the captain asked.

"I believe that most people only see the sovereignty of God in His provision for the pleasant things of life. They blame their hardships on the devil."

"Right now, I'm blaming a bunch of thievin' pirates," Van Tuyl exclaimed.

Jenny watched the foggy river ahead. Dark and deep, it wound its way through the thick bramble-covered ground. She spoke in almost inaudible tones. "Pirates or not, God is still God. Not everything that happens tonight will depend upon us."

"Maybe not," Van Tuyl said, "but we'd better just make sure that we think it does. Prayer is one thing, but preparation does the job. Don't you agree, Cobb?"

Zac got up from his spot on the cord wood and, from behind her, slipped his arms around Jenny. "Captain, I make it a point never to argue with a lady, especially this one."

Van Tuyl chuckled. "I can see your point there. I guess if I were in your position, I wouldn't either."

Zac held her close. "Captain, this lady here has seen plenty of adversity in her short years. She's been through a lot and had more than a little bit to worry about when it comes to me. When it comes time for us to prove our mettle, my money will be on her."

"Well, that time may come sooner than we think," Grubb exclaimed. He pointed up ahead at the foggy bend in the dark river. Above the trees they could see the faint glow of sparks as they poured out of the smokestacks of the big steamer. "I'd say the spot they've decided to land is just up ahead. You'd all better check your weapons and get yourselves ready."

Sweeping his cap off his head, the captain turned to Jenny and bowed at the waist. "Ma'am, I do defer to your feminine instincts. Far be it from me to ever question the workings of a woman's mind again."

\+ + + + +

Hattie listened to the woman at the window, glancing occasionally at what she knew to be the parlor windows on the first floor.

"You have to come quick," the young woman said. "I'm not sure how much time we have."

Hattie was concerned about raising her voice so close to the house. She stepped closer, directly under the girl's window. "Maybe I should go and get some help—find the law or somethin'."

"Oh no, don't do that. The sheriff is one of the pirate leaders."

"Girl, I don't rightly know how to help you."

"Come in through the back door. It's around the house through the garden. Come up the stairs and unlock my door. I think he left the key in the lock."

Hattie swung her head and looked around. The fog made seeing anyone who might be listening difficult. This might be her one chance at finding a horse and rescuing the boys, and now this woman wanted to take her time, time that she didn't have. But getting to the boys now was a maybe, and this woman needed help right now—and she sounded desperate.

"All right," she said. "Keep yer drawers on. I ain't got long, but I'll find you."

The young woman clutched her hands underneath her chin. "Thank you. Please hurry."

Hattie hurried past the side of the house. Circling it, she could see the stables. Several horses poked their heads out of the stalls. She stopped and looked at them. There wouldn't be any second thoughts, though. She'd given the woman her word on the matter, and that was that. She'd remember where they were, though, and just as soon as she had this woman out of the house, she'd be on her way quicker than a squirrel with his tail on fire.

Rounding the building, she could see the rose garden. The roses were tall and seemed to be well cared for, laid out in row upon row. She skirted through the flowering plants, and stepping onto the brick walkway, she could see the lights of the house through the French doors that led inside.

She didn't know what she would say if the people inside caught up with her. She didn't want to say anything that might mean harm to the girl upstairs. Then, putting her hand on her head, she remembered that she had forgotten her hat. She smiled. *I'm comin' back fer my bonnet,* she thought.

Walking over the bricks that led to the back door, she caught the toe of one boot on a brick protruding up from the path and stumbled forward. She lay on the walk and muttered, stopping herself before any words she might have to apologize to the Lord for came out. She got to her feet, rubbing her skinned hands on her damp dress. "Okay, Lord, I didn't go and violate your ears. Now you just make sure you get me in there and back out again with that there woman."

Stepping gingerly over the bricks, she climbed the back stairs to the porch. Pressing her face to the glass, she watched and listened for any sound that might mean the man or one of his servants was close by.

Slowly, she pressed down on the brass handle and opened the glass door. She stepped inside, closing the door behind her. Stairs fell away below her to what she could only imagine to be the basement. The carpeted landing she stood on led to stairs that opened up to the hallway she had seen earlier. She started up them.

"Mercy sakes, Robert, I don't know why you couldn't have helped that poor old woman."

Hattie heard the voices and, quickly scampering back down the stairs, ducked behind them on the lower flight, the stairs leading to the level below.

"Just as I told you," the man replied, "it's precisely because she was poor and old that I had no desire to help her. She looked to be the type that if she didn't fall off the horse and kill herself, she would never return it, and the thought of her loose with a loaded pistol is one I wouldn't want to contemplate."

The man's words made Hattie's blood boil.

"Now, auntie dear, I think you should follow the good doctor's advice and get some rest. I'm going for a short ride and will return directly. I have business to do tonight with Sheriff Princeton."

The two of them walked past the stairs that led to the upper wing, but it was obvious to Hattie that before long, he would come past her on his way to the stables. She listened to their muffled voices as they walked down the first-floor hallway. Hurrying back up the landing stairs, she rounded them quickly and bounded up the flight of stairs that led to the floor above. Coming to an upstairs hallway, she turned and raced up another flight of stairs.

The hall was dim, with lamps flickering in sconces set into the wall. Walking down the length of the hall, she stopped at a door with a key protruding from the lock. Slowly, she turned it and stepped inside.

"Oh, God be praised, there you are." The young woman quickly walked toward her, wringing her hands. "My name is Mary Page, and my uncle's being held prisoner in the cellar."

"Name's Hattie Woodruff, but folks just calls me Hat. We best get, girl. I gots more miles to go than I can rightly count afore light."

Closing the door behind them, the two women hurried down the hall. They made their way quickly down the first flight of stairs.

"Your pirate man said he wuz about to go fer a ride tonight with the sheriff," Hattie murmured.

"Probably to steal from that boat you came from," Mary whispered.

"There's some horses out back. Can you and that uncle of yours ride?"

"Yes, not well, but we can ride."

Hattie pulled her aside. She had to make sure the girl knew their plan before they went much farther. "All righty, then here's what we're to do. We get yer uncle outta here, then we'll hide out by the stables till this man starts off. Then I'm gonna jest foller him, and you two can make off on yer own. That be okay?"

Mary nodded her head, and the two of them started down the flight of stairs leading to the main floor.

Rounding the last of the upper stairs, Hattie paused and held Mary back. They listened carefully. Hearing only silence from the hallway below, they walked quickly down the last flight of thickly carpeted stairs. Moving to the landing that led to the gardens, Mary led the way to the cellar. Reaching the bottom of the stairs, Mary shook the lock. It sprung open.

"I broke it yesterday," Mary said.

The girl pulled back on the massive door, and it opened into the dark cellar. Picking up one of the torches in the barrel just inside the door, she reached back and ignited it with the lamp that burned in the hall.

Hattie's mouth fell open as the girl pushed the blazing torch into the dark room. "Land a Goshen," she exclaimed.

"Like I said, the man's the ringleader. There are things here that I've never seen the equal to."

Mary spotted the light from under the door and moved toward it as Hattie walked, slowly taking in the enormous nature of the booty that lay around her.

Reaching the door, Mary paused and knocked lightly. "Uncle

William, it's me, and I've brought help."

Moments later, they could hear Dr. Page's voice. "Are you all right, Mary? He hasn't harmed you, has he?"

"No, I'm fine, Uncle. I don't have a key, however."

Hattie had spotted a crow bar that sat on top of one of the large boxes. "We won't be needin' no key, lamb. Just step aside."

Placing the bar under the hasp that held the lock in place, Hattie pushed down hard. The nails squeaked as they pulled themselves free from the doorway. Moments later, the lock and hasp fell to the floor. Mary threw the door open. She and the doctor fell into each other's arms.

"I thought I might never see you again, Mary," Page said.

She hugged him. "And I prayed to see you." Suddenly realizing that Hattie was standing behind her, Mary stepped back. "And this lady was the answer to my prayers, Uncle."

Hattie stepped forward. "Name's Hattie Woodruff."

"Pleased to meet you, madam. I'm William Page."

"Well, much as I'd like to keep our howdys goin', we best scat."

"Yes," William said, "you are quite right."

"Follow me," Mary said.

Turning back into the oversized room, the three of them made their way toward the riverside escape that Mary had found earlier. They wound their way around the massive stacks of booty. Finding the stairs that led to the lower level, Mary stuck the torch into the narrow passage, illuminating the stone steps. "There's a passage here that leads out to the river. It's not much farther."

Descending the narrow stairs, they could feel the wetness of the stones that made up the river entrance. The steps spiraled down, making sharp turns. Coming to the bottom of the steps, Mary bent down and, stepping into the room, froze.

There in front of them were the three pirates she had seen earlier. They were hunched around a blazing grate, chewing on their supper. Seeing the would-be escapees, one of them got to his feet. "Now, looky. What have we got ourselves here?"

CHAPTER 27

+ + + + + + +

PRINCETON WAS WAITING in the shadow of the stables when Blevins arrived from the house. He stepped out from the shadows. The colonel had always cut an erect and dashing figure, his square shoulders never giving any hint that he was anything other than pure military. His cutaway coat and the hat he wore, slightly cocked over the right brow, spoke of cavalry. Tonight he was wearing two pistols, their ivory handles facing forward, butt first. His boots were the cavalry variety, up to the knee with a bright shine on them, and his spurs winked their silver in the dim light.

The horses stamped the loam, and the fog swirled over the wet ground, curling under the fences and melting into the gray barn wood. Blevins had said his good-byes to Mamie, making sure she got to bed. The last thing he wanted was for her to prowl the house and discover that what he'd told her about the sheriff taking the Pages to town was untrue. The doctor would be safe enough in the cellar, but he was concerned that Mamie might visit the girl's room upstairs.

Lifting his head back toward the house, he pondered what he might do later on that night. The girl and her uncle would have to wait, but the thought of her up in that room excited him more than a little. This young woman wasn't one of the easy women he'd been used to; she had fire in her soul. He liked that. The challenge of a thing always made the taking of it sweeter. She surely wasn't after his money. No matter what the enticement his wealth might be to other women, she had seemed to find it repulsive. If she did come with him, though, she'd soon learn to respect his strength. "You put the old man away?" Blevins asked the colonel.

"Some time ago. What kept you?"

"We had a visitor."

"A visitor?"

"Yes, an old woman. She came off the *Delta King*. She was dripping wet, it seems, from being thrown overboard. She wanted to borrow a horse and a pistol, and from the looks of the old lady, I'd say we were very fortunate she left my house still unarmed."

Princeton threw his shoulders back proudly. Blevins could see a slight glint in his eyes. "It was a good plan. They ought to be nearing Decker Island shortly."

"Yes, it's far enough away from The Glades to allow us to keep the gold here until the furor dies down and I can take it to Europe. A month from now, I'll have it in a Swiss bank."

"I have wagons waiting on Decker," Princeton said. "We ought to have it in your cellar before dawn."

Blevins rubbed his chin. "That will be just about the time anyone will even begin to look for the *King*. By the time they find it beached on Decker, we'll be taking lunch."

"The men have other wagons there for the rest of the goods on board. They see you giving them the cargo as an added bonus."

"Yes, I know they do," he chuckled. "It's also a very smart thing to do. By the time that posse arrives there tomorrow, there will be so many wagon tracks going in so many directions, no one will be able to make heads or tails of it. It will be like ants from a hundred ant hills picking one carcass clean to the bone."

Blevins opened one of the stalls, took out his best gelding along with a halter, and slipped a bridle around the animal's muzzle. "So you didn't just kill the good doctor, then?"

"No, I put him in the room with all the tables and chairs. Figured we might as well make his last night as comfortable as possible."

"That's very Southern of you, Colonel. You're turning into quite the gentleman on me."

"The man's harmless."

Blevins studied the colonel. For all the man was doing in the way of thievery, Princeton had always feigned a sense of morality. At times the outward show of honor grated on Blevins. They both knew they were in this for the money, but somehow the man continued to hang on to the illusion of being in one of the last great battles of the war, leading the charge. The thought made Robert smile, but only on the inside. Princeton was better known for running away from shot and shell than for facing it. Maybe that was why the bravado appealed to him, a last chance to redeem his soul from the stigma of cowardice.

He wondered, though, if Princeton's chivalrous nature might someday be his undoing. "You'd see how harmless he is if you were to face him on the witness stand," Blevins offered. "He'd put you on the gallows too quick to talk about."

"There's no call to be ungallant, Robert. Victors can afford to be chivalrous."

"We haven't the gold just yet, Colonel. I wouldn't be too hasty in declaring victory if I were you. I know, what with your war record, that victory is something you hunger for, but it's not ours yet."

"You can leave my war record out of this."

Blevins could see how touchy Princeton was about his reputation, but still he enjoyed bringing it up. There was something about knowing the chink in another man's armor that gave him a sense of power. Knowledge was power, and knowledge about another man was the ultimate in control. "I'm sorry to offend you, Princeton, but at times you do seem more interested in proving yourself than you do in the money."

"It's who we're taking the gold from that settles the matter most in my mind. Wells Fargo money is blood money, and I don't mind taking it from them."

It was plain to see that Princeton's grudge against the Union carried over to Wells Fargo. He'd always seen them as a mere extension of the Black Republicans in Washington. It was a motive that crawled constantly in Princeton's mind and one that served Blevins well. He had no intention of leaving it far behind in their discussions, at least until he had his fortune made.

The colonel went on, seemingly anxious to change the subject. "As to the old man, I did the same thing any civilized man would do. I just made him comfortable and gave him enough light to read by."

Blevins saddled his gelding and tightened his cinch. "Why, Colonel, if I didn't know better I'd say that old doctor provoked some sympathy in you. I find that strange given the fact that you ordered his murder."

Princeton, placing his feet in his stirrups, swung onto his saddle. "Yes, and I'll do it again, only this time I'll make sure of it myself."

Blevins ignored the inconsistency. He got into his saddle. The colonel had always seemed to have the complete loyalty of his men.

It was something Blevins envied. Perhaps if they knew all that he knew about the colonel they might not be so quick to obey without question. This slight gap in duty was something to be explored. It apparently made Princeton uncomfortable, and that was just how Blevins liked him best. He would dig at the wound a little deeper. "Well, it's obvious that whatever effect that old man had on you, he used those same skills with your man."

"Manny is an individual given to emotion. I would suspect his Portuguese ancestry. I'll see to him, you can be sure of that. I expect a man to follow orders no matter what his feelings may be on the matter. Those two people should be feeding turtles and fish right now, not locked up in that house of yours."

Blevins laughed. "Perhaps I should thank Manny, then, for that oversight of his. I find the Page girl very attractive, and before long she'll come to see the error of fending me off. I'm quite certain the knowledge that I have her uncle, as well, will serve my interests."

"You won't have long to extend those thank-yous to Manny, I'm afraid. I can't afford a man who won't obey orders as one of my lieutenants. I'm afraid once his work is done tonight, he'll have to share the same fate as those other two."

The two men stepped their horses out of the stables, closing the gate behind them. "You may do as you please with the old man, Colonel, but we shall have to wait and see as to the fate of the young woman. She may yet come around." With that, Blevins slapped his spurs to the sides of the gelding, and the two of them bolted down the foggy road.

+ + + + +

Manny stood beside the rail on the stern of the boat, watching what was left of the paddles churn away at the muddy water. Several of the men had joined him, each hoping that somehow the wounded leviathan would pull itself from the mud and back out into the river.

He snapped his head around and, spotting a slightly built man, Johnny Pogue, motioned him forward.

"Looky here, Johnny, we might just not get offa here. We ain't very far from Blevins's house. I want you to pick a man to go with you and run—run, mind you, not walk—to that place. If Blevins is there, you tell him what's happened and get two wagons from that place. If he ain't there, bring them wagons anyway. We're gonna have to let go of these plans of ours. I want this gold offa this here boat tonight."

Johnny nodded and, picking another man standing nearby, started off. Doyle craned his neck from outside the pilothouse, high above. "We ain't budgin' offa here."

"You got all the steam we can get from the engine?" Manny yelled out the question.

"I think so," Doyle shouted down. "I'll go make sure they got it fired up all they can." He pointed down. "The problem is them paddles. They ain't pushin' enough water to make much headway."

Manny turned to the spinning sternwheel. Several of the blades had broken off, and a number of the support girders and spokes that held them together had snapped. They hung in splinters, spinning freely as the big red wheel turned in the water. His eyes narrowed as he continued to survey the damage. It was hard to believe that two small boys had done all of this, but there it was, an entire operation endangered by children.

Cox joined the men on the stern as they anxiously watched the paddle spin. Turning back to face the group, Manny glared at Cox. There was something deep inside the man that Manny found hard to like. He seemed too anxious to please everybody. Always seeming to know when to smile and when to feint a frown, this Wells Fargo man had a face that couldn't be trusted to tell the truth. His boyishness and the height he used to look down at others had probably always served him in good stead, but Manny knew different. Everything was just too easy for men like Cliff Cox, and he was all too ready to sacrifice anything and anybody to make his life a little easier. The man stood for nothing. "You found those kids yet?" Manny asked.

Cox backed away from the tone he heard in Manny's voice. "No, and we've searched both the top decks all over again."

"Then, they must be somewhere down here."

One of the other men interjected, "We done gone through all the cargo."

Cox put on a concerned look. "Perhaps they jumped overboard. I mean, they had already done the damage they set out to do. There would be no reason to stay on board and be discovered, now, would there?"

Manny was taking in all of Cox's words. Each one seemed to be designed to minimize his concerns and make his instructions about the continued search seem foolish.

Cox continued, "I know if I was one of those boys, the first thing I would have done would be to get in that river and get as far away as I could."

Manny slurred out the words. "I'm sure that's true. 'Course these here kids got *guts*." The words stung Cox—that was plain to see. Manny went on, "They might have figured on staying around to see the fun of us stuck in this here mud or maybe to find you and take you on man to man."

"Now there's no call for that."

Manny stepped forward and, grabbing Cox's white shirt, hauled him down to eye level. "I'd say there was. You were supposed to keep your eye on those people. It was the only thing you were hired to do—get that Cobb fella off this here boat with his family and see that they stayed off. Only thing is"—Manny dragged him closer—"they didn't stay off, now, did they?"

"That wasn't my fault. I got them to leave."

"Cox, tonight everything's your fault. You better hope you find those boys, 'cause if you don't, I'd just as soon put a bullet right between your eyes. I don't care if the colonel does like you." Manny smiled. "I'd just say you were a casualty, an unfortunate casualty, but dead all the same."

Cox pulled himself up and straightened his tie. "I am sorry about those people getting back on board, but like I said, I had little to do with that. If they are still here on the *Delta King*, then you can be assured that I will find them. They won't escape."

"Take these men with you," Manny said, "and make a careful look-see. I want them kids found. You bring 'em to me, and I'm gonna skin 'em myself."

The men on the stern scrambled and returned to their search. Manny was usually the easygoing type, always free with his bottle and a story to liven up the campfire, but it was obvious that the grounding of the *Delta King* had changed all that. No one was going to question him at this point, even though most of the men now believed the boys had long since slipped overboard. Only Cox remained on the stern.

Manny turned around and continued to survey the boat's futile attempt to extract itself from the muddy riverbank. Cox cleared his throat behind him and Manny turned back around.

"Now, see here," Cox said. "I can't say as I appreciate your attitude tonight. You seem to forget, I'm the one that supplied you with the information necessary to conduct this enterprise. If I'd had my way, I'd have been the only agent on board."

"Plain to see that company of yours had better sense than that," Manny snapped.

"I take it you don't like me very much."

"You can take what you like, mister businessman, but no, I don't reckon I do."

"May I ask why?"

"Never cared much for turncoats, even when they was on my side. Always figured if the folks on the other side made it slicker for 'em to stay, they'd just as soon turn on me." Manny leaned toward him. "I may be nothin' more than a Louisiana thief and pirate, but I still got some druthers 'bout who I ship with."

\+ \+ \+ \+ \+

Skip was in Jenny's cabin, hunkered down in the corner, but Jack refused to hide just yet. He stood by the small window where even in the dark cabin and through the fog he could see some of the goings-on at the boat's fantail. "They're sure fit to be tied out there," he said. "Crawlin' all around, but stuck like flies in a spider's web."

Skip looked nervous.

Jack turned his head and continued to sound chipper. "I'd say we done them folks in real good, I would. Ya wanna come and have a look?"

"No."

"Well, what's wrong with you?"

"This was a bad idea."

"T'weren't neither. We killed 'em dead. This here old boat ain't movin' nary an inch."

"No, I mean comin' back to this cabin. We should've just gone over the side and into the water. We'd be wet, but we'd be safe."

"You sure are the worry wart, ain't you?"

Skip shook his head. "No, I ain't of a natural way. You saw how I went out over them blades out there. I only go to thinkin' on things when I figure I did something wrong."

"Well, they already searched this here room, didn't they?"

"Yeah, but it seems like they're in for another go-around."

Getting back on his toes, Jack took another look out the round window. He then sank back to his feet and turned around. "You might just be right about that."

Skip hugged his knees and continued his silent debate.

"Maybe we could go on out there and slip over the side now. They might not see us with all that there fog."

"What if that man who was in front of the door with the gold is back now? You couldn't see him from where you stand. He'd be right next door."

"Well, maybe they'll figure he's been there all along. If they do, then they won't bother to look over none of this stretch of rooms."

Skip cocked his head and looked directly into Jack's eyes. "You'd believe anything if it made you feel better, wouldn't you?"

Jack wagged his head back and forth and began to pace the room. "Way I figures it, there ain't much we can do 'bout our situation anyhow, so why not get yer head turned in the right way. Won't do a body no good to be miserable, even if it be his last day on this here earth."

"I just wish Zac would get here," Skip said.

"Well, we done 'bout all that we could, didn't we? He can't be 'spectin' much more than that."

"I reckon he might."

"How's that?"

"I'm just thinkin'. If'n I was him, I'd been thinkin' about getting to them pirates, and I wouldn't want to worry my head none 'bout two little boys stuck on this here boat. He is gonna have his hands plenty full as it is."

Jack reached down into his sock and pulled out the derringer.

"Put that blame thing away," Skip snapped.

"Well, it might just be our only way out. You wouldn't have to use it."

"You ever killed a man before?" Skip asked.

"No, but that don't mean I never wanted to. There be plenty of men that I knows that needs killin' real bad."

"Maybe so, but it's one thing to dislike a man, and it's another thing to take everything away he ever was and ever will be."

"Everybody dies. It's just that some folks deserves to go before the rest."

"Like Robbie?"

The words hit Jack like a hammer. He dropped the gun to his side and shook his head slowly. "No, not like Robbie." Raising his head, he frowned. "But Robbie weren't like them men out there."

"I 'spect every one of them fellers out there was a whole lot like you and Robbie when they was ten. Only thing was, they was allowed to get away with stealin' stuff in the first place. Then they just got themselves meaner and meaner till they didn't much care who they hurt when they was takin' stuff that didn't belong to them."

Jack bounced the little gun in the palm of his hand. "I suppose you is right about that, only I never much thought 'bout it in that way. Maybe thievin' jest ain't the thing to do 'cause of where it might go to."

"It's just wrong. Don't much matter where it's going."

Turning back to the small window, Jack got on his toes once again. He craned his neck in all directions. Suddenly, he got down and scurried toward the corner with Skip. "We best get under that there bed. There's somebody that's comin' up them stairs."

Both boys scooted as far under the bed as they could. They heard the cabin door next to them opening. Moments later, their own cabin door swung open. They could see the man's legs as he walked around the room. The next thing they saw was the man getting to his knees. He looked straight at them. It was Cliff Cox.

"Come out from there, right now."

Jack put his finger to his lips. "Shhh. . . . Mr. Cox, them fellers is lookin' fer us," Jack said.

"I said, get out from under that bed!"

Both boys reluctantly slid out from under the bed.

Cox grabbed them by the arms and pulled them to their feet. "We've got somebody to go and see. You boys have caused a lot of trouble here tonight."

"Is you with them?" Jack asked.

"Never mind that now. I'm with me."

CHAPTER 28

+ + + + + + +

JACK WIGGLED IN THE CLUTCHES of Cox's grip. The man was tall and lanky, much taller than most men Jack had ever seen. Cox's dark suit and white shirt, coupled with his spectacles, would have given anyone the impression that the man was most comfortable sitting behind a desk, but his powerful grip showed otherwise.

"Let go of me," Jack squalled.

"In a pig's eye."

Skip was more subdued. He found it hard to imagine that this was the same man introduced to him as an agent for Wells Fargo. His mind flashed back to the way Zac had spoken to him, and he could tell there wasn't a great deal of appreciation on Zac's part for the man, but he had just assumed that it was because Zac was much more comfortable working all by himself. "I thought you worked for Wells Fargo?" Skip asked.

"I work for myself," Cox replied. Wadding a portion of the boys' shirts in each hand, he pushed them out onto the deck, then held them upright. He lifted his head up and shouted at Manny and two other men at the stern of the boat. "I got them! I found those boys."

Jack turned, twisting his body in Cox's viselike grip, and sent a hard kick with his brogans, directly into the man's shins.

"Owww!" Cox doubled over in pain.

Reaching down into his sock, Jack pulled up the derringer and cocked it. Turning in the big man's direction, he struggled to point the gun.

Cox grappled with the boy. The pain was racing through his leg, but he dropped his hand to Skip's wrist. The loud pop of the palm gun dropped Cox to the deck. He grabbed for his leg as it spurted blood.

Moments later, several men grabbed the boys, lifting them into the air as their legs churned and kicked at the air. One of the men tended to the downed agent as the other two hauled the boys toward Manny. In the confusion, Jack crammed the derringer concealed in his hand deep into his pocket.

The men held out the two boys to face Manny while they both continued to kick and scream. "Hush up, you two," Manny growled. "Cryin' and bawlin' ain't gonna help you much now." He leaned forward into their faces. "You caused me more than enough trouble for one night, and now you're mine to deal with."

He looked back at the still furiously churning but wounded paddle wheel. The water sent up a brown murky spray, sprinkling the boys' faces. "Did you two boys do this?"

Skip had stopped his kicking, but Jack continued to swing his legs. The fight was not near out of him yet. He smirked. "You betcha we did. Fouled you up somethin' plenty too, we did."

A third pirate joined them on the stern. "One of them boys done gone and shot that Cox feller."

Manny blinked at the news, then his face softened. "You boys shot Cox?"

"I shot him," Jack bragged. "He was a traitor and I shot him."

Manny looked back at the pirate who had given the news. "How is he?"

"The boy shot him in the leg. He's losin' lots of blood."

"Will he make it?"

"I'm not 'zackly sure. Couple of the men are workin' on him up there. I can tell you one thing, he's plenty angry—all horns and rattles."

"Did you find the gun?"

"We ain't looked fer it just yet. Too busy with Cox."

"Well, you find that gun."

The man hurried back in the direction of the stern cabins.

Manny looked down at the two boys. "Now, what am I gonna do with you two?" He snickered slightly. "I gotta say you did spare me some trouble. If you hadn't shot that son of a gun, I was gonna."

The two men who held the boys were growing weary. One of the men drawled. "What is we gonna do with these here two boys?"

"Drop 'em, but hang on to 'em. They look like more than a handful."

Once back onto the deck, Skip looked up at the man. "You ain't gonna get away with this. My father's going to find you."

"Oh, he is, now? And just who might that be?"

"Zac Cobb."

"His daddy works fer Wells Fargo," Jack interjected. "He ain't exactly his real pap, but the man cares fer him."

Manny bent down, putting his face close to Skip's. "Well now, little Mr. Cobb, I reckon that daddy of yours never made it outta Walnut Grove back yonder ways. So I wouldn't 'spect to find him comin' up on to us any time soon, if at all." Standing back up to full attention he smirked. "Besides, if he did find us, he couldn't rightly pin the death of you two boys on us, 'cause you ain't gonna be 'round to say nothin' to nobody."

"We gonna kill 'em, then?" one of the pirates asked.

"Well, let's just see if our Mr. Cox is able to. It's about time he got his hands dirty with this enterprise."

Manny looked back at the men near the cabins and, cupping his hands to his mouth, yelled, "Get that man over here if he's able to move."

Minutes later the group watched as two men held Cox between them and helped him hobble forward. They held him steady with his arms draped over each of their shoulders, carefully allowing him to drag his wounded leg while hopping forward on his good one. A tourniquet was wound around the leg, tied off at the thigh. His face was white as the flour in the bottom of a pie pan, and he grimaced with obvious pain at each bounce. The men stood him up in front of Manny and the boys.

"These the men who attacked you, Cox?" Manny asked the question with subdued sarcasm.

One of the men holding him up spoke softly, as if to inform Manny of the seriousness of the man's wound. "He's hurt pretty bad. We tried to close the bleedin' off, but I think he's still losin' some blood."

"I'm going to kill those two," Cox growled. He then proceeded to let out a string of curses.

There was something about the foul language coming from a man in a suit and tie that seemed entirely out of place to Skip. It was one thing for a dock hand to talk that way, but something different to have curses spat out by a man who looked like a Sunday school teacher.

"That's why I brung you over here," Manny said. "Figured you wouldn't want these here youngsters showin' you up."

Cox looked past the boys to the sight of the tumbling wheel. The large, red, wooden blades continued to spin through the water. The engines had been thrown into reverse, and the paddles rose from the stern of the boat, sending water pouring onto the stern. The fresh breaks in a number of the blades displayed sharp spikes of broken wood, each flying through the air as they made their circuit, then going into the river below only to once again thrash about as they came to the surface and began their circular motion all over again.

Manny took the revolver from his belt and shoved it in Cox's direction, butt first. "All right, mister businessman, let's see what you're made of."

Anger flashed in Cox's face. This man held him in contempt, that was plain to see. Exploding with rage, he pushed the revolver aside and held out his large hands. "Here, give them to me. I can settle this right now."

The men holding on to Jack and Skip spun them around and pushed them next to the wounded man. Cox lashed his grip to the boys and shoved them toward the fantail of the boat, in the direction of the spinning, broken paddle. He gnashed his teeth as he spoke to them, agonizing pain registering in his voice. "I'm going to make both of you pay for this. I'm feeling pain and so will you. I want to hear the sound of your screams."

He wobbled as he pushed the boys closer to the edge of the stern, hopping on his wounded leg. It was obvious the man had great strength. The blood loss was beginning to take its toll, however.

Closer to the edge of the fantail, both boys began to struggle. Manny smiled as two men stepped over to help Cox. Turning his head, first to one, then the other, Cox roared out his protests, "I don't need your help. Just step back and let me do this." It was obvious that the challenge to his manhood had reached a boiling point.

The men looked at Manny and reluctantly complied, holding up their hands as they backed away.

Cox held on to the boys by the collars of their shirts, pushing them near the edge of the stern. The river water roared from the upward sweep of the wheel, sending a heavy rain of muddy water on top of the three of them. Looking back, both Jack and Skip could see the rising paddles. To fall in here would mean to not come back, and they both knew it.

Jack looked over at Skip and yelled at the top of his lungs, "Grab on to him and pull him down."

Both boys took handfuls of Cox's coat and pulled down. Jack kicked hard at the man's good leg, sending a leather-covered missilelike blow to Cox's ankle.

Cox howled in pain. He wobbled, weak from the loss of blood, and his knees buckled. He fell into a heap, and the force of the boys' grip on his jacket spun him to the edge of the boat.

Manny held the others back. Cox blinked at the boys, then struggled to get to his feet. Suddenly, a look of panic shot through his face. He swung his arms wildly and opened his mouth as if to yell. No words came, only a muffled scream as he fell back into the paddles and the foaming water.

Jack grabbed Skip's arm and pointed to the side of the boat. Over the noise of the water he yelled, "Let's jump."

They raced for the side of the boat and without hesitation scrambled over the rail. Without looking back at the men who were racing toward them, they let go and fell into the dark water below. They hit the water and plunged deep, the darkness of the river enveloping them.

Breaking the surface, they could hear the men shouting. Suddenly, shots were fired. Around them the water erupted with the splashes of bullets as they hit the water. Small sounds of deadly pebbles, they struck terror into both boys.

"Let's go under," Skip yelled. "Swim for the shore."

Both boys upended themselves, plunging down into the murky darkness. Skip had gone with Zac to the beach many times in the last two years. There he'd had to fight the tides and the currents. He'd learned that diving under the incoming waves was often the best way to make distance.

Swimming for all he was worth under the dark river water, he could hear the shots overhead as they ripped through the surface of the water. He continued to swim, pulling himself forward with each stroke and kicking his legs furiously. Pushing the water out in front of him with evenhanded strokes, he pulled himself through the darkness. He would go as far as the air inside of his bursting lungs would take him.

Exploding to the surface, Skip sucked the foggy air deep into his chest. He swung his head around, trying to spot Jack. The boy was behind him. It was obvious Jack had spent time under the surface of water before. He splashed toward Skip, breathing hard with raspy noises.

They were out of sight of the men on the stern of the boat, and if they could keep the turning paddles between themselves and the shooters, they'd be plenty safe enough. He grabbed for Jack's shirt. "Let's head to the shore and hide in them bushes. They're gonna come for us sure 'nuff."

Jack nodded and both boys began to paddle for the shore. They weren't too far away from it, since the boat had beached on a sandbar close to shore. With the men's panicked voices behind them and the sound of several more wild shots, they were relieved as they reached the weeds and brambles of the river's edge.

They pushed themselves onto the mud, scooting their backsides into the soft silt. Jack flopped back into the muck, panting. "Man, I never thought we'd get outta that."

Skip turned over on his belly, raising himself onto his elbows. "Me neither."

"I just saw them paddles, and I knew we wuz gonna be dead," Jack croaked. He sputtered and coughed. "I had me one other time, that time with Robbie, where I just knew I was gonna be kilt. I couldn't do much about that, though. This time I could."

"And I'm glad you did."

Jack sat up, his face suddenly animated. "I played possum a mite, relaxed myself a little before I told you to pull. That feller was weak as a kitten—only thing was, he didn't know it."

Skip reached over and tugged on Jack's shirt. "We better get ourselves on outta here. Those men might start lookin' for us, and they're gonna come right down this here riverbank."

Jack nodded. "I s'pose you is right about that. We had better move on." He shook his head. "I gotta catch my breath, though. Man, I sure am glad I had all that time diggin' 'round fer them oysters. Maybe I didn't make much money, but tonight it paid off."

Slowly, they got to their feet. The brush along the river was thick. Any movement at all would be accompanied by a great deal of noise. They had to get clear of this and quick. If the pirates decided to try to find them, all it would take would be a listening ear.

They began to break the branches as they moved through them. "Ouch!" Jack recoiled. "There's stickers aplenty in these things."

"We're in a mess of blackberry bushes," Skip replied. Reaching out, he began to pluck handfuls of the full berries, stuffing them into his mouth. "They're good, too."

Jack stopped and started to pick the berries.

Suddenly, two hands shot out from the bushes, grabbing both boys by the collars of their shirts and pulling them headlong into the bushes. The boys screamed and began to kick as they were raked through the brambles and thorns. But this man wasn't a weak and wounded one like the last man that had his hands on them had been. He drug them under and over first one set of bushes, then another. Reaching a clearing, he laid them down and, releasing the two boys, stepped over them. "You boys all right?" he asked. It was Zac!

\+ \+ \+ \+ \+

Manny was on the river side of the boat, continuing to look out at the foggy water for the boys, when two men ran up to him with guns drawn. "There's horses on the road, and they're comin' on fast," the man yelled.

Manny ran behind the two men and signaled several more to follow. The search for the boys would have to wait. He couldn't look for them no matter how much trouble they had caused. There just wasn't time. Right now he had to worry about a posse that might be on the road coming up to the boat. He had enough men to give the law a good fight, but he wasn't near ready for that.

Reaching the shore side of the boat, he signaled several men to fan out. "Get behind whatever cover you can find," he shouted. "Don't shoot until I tell you to."

The horses stopped on the road, and Manny could see at a glance that it wasn't a large group as he had feared. Through the fog, he saw two men tying their horses to a branch. They stepped toward the riverbank.

"Manny!" one of the men yelled. It was Princeton.

Manny got to his feet. "Come ahead on, Colonel. We've got the boat. It's safe."

He watched as both men waded through the mud. One of the other pirates ran the gangplank out toward the surface of the mud. Princeton and Blevins reached the walkway and climbed toward the deck. This was something Manny had been dreading. The beaching of the boat would make their plans hard to pull off, and how it had happened was something he didn't want to begin to explain, although he knew he'd have to.

"I'm sorry about this, Colonel. We had some unexpected problems."

"I know," Princeton said. "Your men on the road told us all about it. Did you find the boys?"

"Yes, sir, we did, but they both jumped overboard. I was just 'bout to organize a search."

"Don't bother," Princeton shot back. "We've got ourselves bigger fish to fry."

The colonel seemed unusually calm, but there was a distant air about his demeanor that sent a chill down Manny's back. He seemed like a tightly wound snake, ready to strike, calm on the outside but death written all over him. Nervous that something he might say would set off the colonel's wrath, Manny forged ahead. "I sent those two men to get wagons so we could get the gold off while it was still dark."

Princeton made no response.

"I know we're in trouble timing wise," Manny went on, "but nothing we can't handle."

Princeton's gaze at him was a calm look right into his soul. "There's nothing I've sent you to do that you've handled so far. Why should I trust you to undo the mess you've gotten us into?"

Manny's head dropped. "I'm sorry, Colonel."

Princeton walked away from him, his hands cupped behind him. "Sorry just isn't going to get it done."

Blevins smirked. It was a sly smile, one that said the man knew all the answers, a smile cloaked in smugness. "It seems we have some old friends of yours at my place, Manny. I just know they'll be happy to see you."

Manny shuddered at the words. No matter how pleasant Blevins was trying to make his voice sound, there was a definite threat to it. Instantly, he knew what had prompted the man's snide expression. Those people he'd shown mercy to had made their way to Blevins's doorstep. He'd told them not to stop, but if that had happened—and the colonel's posture coupled with the cool greeting he'd gotten told him that it had—then he was a dead man. He'd have to look for a chance to get away. Meanwhile, he'd play dumb. Both these men thought he was anyway, so that might not be too difficult.

Manny faked a chuckle. "Sounds right fine to me. Just so they ain't relatives of folks I kilt down in Louisiana."

"No," Blevins said, "I can assure you they are not."

Manny had to find a way to make his escape. The colonel had gone to the stern of the boat to survey the damage. Manny hurried to catch up.

"You let two little boys do all of this?" Princeton asked.

"They slipped by a guard in the fog and rammed a pry bar into the paddles. I was up in the pilothouse with Doyle. I reckon I can't be everywhere."

Princeton spun around. "But can you be anywhere, anywhere that I can trust you?"

"Cox is dead too."

"Cox? How did that happen?"

Manny could see the news had shocked Princeton. Maybe it would take the man's mind off of him, if only for a little bit. "He was trying to push the boys into the paddles when he slipped and fell in himself."

"Clumsy oaf. How could a man that size be overpowered by two youngsters?"

"One of them kids had shot him in the leg. He was gamed up on it some."

Princeton shook his head. "Those two little boys sound like quite the enterprising pair." He looked up at Manny. "What I wouldn't give for a few men like them."

Manny changed the subject quickly. "Colonel, we need to ride up to Decker Island and get those wagons here before morning. I know the roads well. I could take either yours or Mr. Blevins's horse and have them back here and unloading this cargo before dawn. You could go back to Blevins's place with the wagon."

"No, I want you with me tonight," Princeton replied. "I want you with me when we get back to The Glades."

Manny's heart sank. This wouldn't be easy, not as easy as he had hoped.

Princeton motioned toward the group of men who were gathering. "You'll have to send one of them. Given the time we have left, I'm not even sure that will work."

"Yes, sir, Colonel. It will work, all right." His mind raced. "I know it's gettin' late, but if they get here by dawn and there is a posse on our tails by then, we'll need more guns to handle them. The wagon tracks goin' all over will help you stay under cover too. I don't think anybody in his right mind would suspect Mr. Blevins."

He paused. He had to make his case well, and he had to throw off any notion that he had any idea of their discovery. "Who we send is important, though. These here roads are mighty tricky, 'specially in the dark and fog. We'll need somebody who knows the roads and the crossings real well, and I'm the best there is. You and me can talk when I get back."

Princeton's eyes narrowed. He looked right into Manny's eyes. He was thinking the matter over carefully. Manny knew it was only a matter of what the man wanted most right now, the possibility of a clean getaway or the surety of revenge and Manny's death.

"No," Princeton said, "I want you with me tonight."

CHAPTER 29

+ + + + + + +

THE BOYS BLINKED THEIR EYES, too stunned to move. There was something about seeing something that you'd hoped for but never expected that took a body's breath away. All at once Skip jumped to his feet and wrapped his arms around Zac's neck. He said nothing, just squeezed.

"Here, here, pardner, I'm mighty glad to see you too." Zac looked at the boy on the ground. "Both of you boys."

Skip began to sniffle. His raspy voice breathed out the words, "I was so scared."

Zac pushed him back, holding on to him and looking him in the eye. "Do you know what? I was scared too, plenty scared." Zac could see the stunned look in the boy's eyes. Skip looked like a deer that had suddenly heard a twig snap in the woods. "My heart was pounding when I had to fight a feller with a gun back there in that town, but the biggest scare of all was havin' you gone."

"It was?" It was still hard for Skip to adjust to the notion that a man, any man, would care for somebody who wasn't his own flesh and blood. Skip cared about Zac, but after all, he had to. Zac was all he had. But Zac had a life of his own and had one long before Skip ever came on the scene. There was just no reason for him to feel that way about one little boy who wasn't even his.

"Yes, Skipper, it was. You're a part of me, son, a big part. If I was to lose you it would be worse than having my right arm cut off." Zac's eyes bore down into Skip's soul. "I just use my arm, but I love you."

The sound of the word "love" ripped through Skip. It made him feel uncomfortable and yet warm all at the same time. A year or so ago it had been a word that Zac never used. He'd say things like care, concern, admire, respect, but never love. Something was happening inside of Zac. Skip could see that. What he couldn't do was understand it. Skip blinked his eyes back at Zac. What couldn't be understood might be best to avoid.

"Hattie's not on the boat," Skip said.

"Yeah." Jack got to his feet. "We 'spect she got throwed off after she kilt a man."

Zac's face turned down, his mustache arching below his lips.

"How'd that happen?" Zac asked.

"They was searchin' all the cabins fer folks," Jack said, "and Hattie braced up the man with her pistol after he broke into ours."

"Bad mistake for a man to underestimate any woman with a gun, but especially that one," Zac mused. "She hates most men anyway."

"We don't know what happened for sure after that," Skip went on. "We was hiding out in the kitchen at the time, but they threw the other people over the side, and we thought they just mighta done the same thing to her."

Zac looked up the river. "She's the last of my mother's brothers and sisters. Most of the time I'd say old Hat was just too mean to kill, but the woman swims like a potbellied stove."

"Old Skip here had the idea on how to stop that boat. We both done it, though."

The boys took a few minutes to explain about how they had damaged the paddles. Jack told the tale in his usual animated way, swinging his arms around to punctuate the story of the running aground of the *Delta King*.

Skip listened in silence, then dropped his glance. "We killed somebody too, that Mr. Cox."

"Cliff Cox."

"Yes, sir."

"The man was a traitor," Jack blurted out. "He was tryin' to kill us, but we done him instead."

"He fell into the paddle blades," Skip inserted. He didn't want Jack to exaggerate and make it sound like the two of them were cold-blooded killers.

"But we helped him along a mite."

Skip looked somber as Jack told about Cox; he knew there was nothing at all exciting about a man dying. It seemed like just so much waste to him, a sad waste, at that.

"I'll have some explaining to do to Wells," Zac said, "but the man was no good."

Suddenly, he walked away from them. Stepping into the shadows, Zac drew the little revolver out from his shoulder holster. The boys watched him. His movements always fascinated them. Every fiber in his being seemed to be alert. He stooped slightly, swinging his body in the direction of the boat, and listened carefully. They were away from the river now and well into the brush that was often underwater during flood season. The ground was spongy, but the twigs and brush that quickly grew up during the dry season and thrived during the rainy one would sound an alarm if anyone was walking in their direction. Zac was careful in making sure no one was coming, though, like a coon raiding a favorite stash.

Skip figured they'd made far too much noise as Zac was dragging them through the brush, and they'd probably been sitting here in one place, close to the *Delta King*, for much too long. Zac would be wary, and he'd want them to be moving on and quick.

Zac turned back to the boys, pulling his coat back and stuffing the short gun into its leather rigging. "We'd better get on back to the others," he said. "Jenny's upriver a short piece along with Captain Van Tuyl and the pilot. She's frettin' something fierce over you two. We have a small steamer, but if it hadn't been for what you boys did on the *Delta King*, we never would've caught up to you."

Zac pushed aside several of the larger bushes and stood back for the boys to pass. They moved as quietly as possible, taking the time to unhook their clothing from the briars as they passed. It was as if the river itself was reluctant to lose them to solid ground. It fought to keep them beside it, one thorn, one sticker at a time.

Some time passed before Zac once again turned them in the direction of the river. They rounded a bend, and moving through an opening in the brush, the boys spotted the boat.

"I'll have to tell them it's us," Zac said. "I left by myself, and they won't be expecting three men to walk back."

The idea that Zac had lumped the two of them in with him, calling them men, made Skip swell with pride. He'd never thought of himself as a man before. He was a boy. For him that only meant that the possibility of being a man was somewhere off in the distance. He'd often wondered how he'd know when he got to be one. Now to be called a man by someone he knew was one was all he needed to know.

The little white steamboat had a canvas awning that stretched over the area next to the boiler and engine. There was no cabin. The boat was more than a rowboat, but not much more.

Zac raised his voice slightly as they approached. "Yo, the boat! It's us."

Jenny stepped out of the boat and ran to meet them. She dropped down and hugged the boys one by one. Skip could see that female affection was something brand-new to Jack. Jack's eyes widened as Jenny hugged him.

"I've been so worried about you two," she said.

"I guess you needn't have been," Zac said. He raised his eyes to Grubb and the captain. "It was these boys here that put the *Delta King* aground."

Van Tuyl and Grubb exchanged glances as Zac related the story. When he finished, Van Tuyl shook his head. "I ain't sure I've ever heard of such a thing. You boys were very resourceful. How you came up with that idea I'll never know."

"But it worked, didn't it?" Jack crowed.

"It worked, all right." Van Tuyl added, "It ought to be easy to repair the *Old King*, but it will take fresh parts from either San Francisco or Sacramento."

"And that's something these pirates don't have the time to be waitin' on," Zac offered. "They'll be anxious to be cleared out of here come morning."

"Then what are we going to do?" Van Tuyl asked. He climbed out of the small boat and, standing beside it, crossed his arms.

Grubb held up a rifle. "We could make it plenty hot for them, especially in the dark. Keep them pinned down until help arrives in the morning."

"Yeah, that's a good idea," Jack blurted out. The boy seemed to be feeling his oats, and it was plain to see that his taste for action had been aroused.

"We could keep them plenty busy for a while," Van Tuyl chimed in.

"No, I don't think so," Zac said. "There's only a few of us, in spite of our hankerin' for a fight. To hear the boys tell it, there could be twenty or more of them on that boat, and they still have the black gang and that engineer below to hold as hostages. When the shooting starts, they have enough men to circle around, but we have the boys and Jenny here to concern ourselves with."

"We can fight too," Jack said.

"You already have," Zac said. "You done run that big coon up the tree." He shook his head. "No, I think we should follow the rascals when they move the shipment. They won't be takin' those hostages along with the gold, and we just might be able to separate them."

Van Tuyl marched forward. He trod the marshy ground as if it were the deck of his boat. "Well, Cobb, as far as I'm concerned, this is your show from here on out. You know best how to handle these people. I ain't never heard tell of somebody hiring a man to do a job and then standing over his shoulder to tell him just how to do it."

Grubb sputtered and grinned. "Is that so?"

The irony of the statement was not lost on anyone standing there. It was obvious that that was just what Van Tuyl did on a more than regular basis. He straightened his coat and lifted his chin defiantly. "Well, leastways something the man knew nothing about."

Grubb chuckled.

"I'll watch the road for a while," Zac said. "If I see the shipment being moved, I'll follow it the best I can. They can't make much speed with that heavy a load."

He paused and looked at Jenny, then the boys. "I want you to take Jenny and the boys to the far side of the river, then come right back here. Be available close by, in case I need you."

"Why do we have to go over there?" Jack asked. "The fightin's gonna be here, leastways, near as I can figure."

"Exactly." The deep tone of his voice made it clear that that was all that needed to be said on the matter.

"Zac's got enough on his mind without worrying about his backside," Skip interjected. He'd begun to see himself clearly as the arbiter of the other boy's better judgment. Common sense was something he took a great deal of pride in; it was his best weapon. "And with two kids and a woman not far behind him, that would be just what he would do."

Zac tousled Skip's hair. "That's good thinking, son."

The words made Skip's chest swell.

\+ + + + +

It was several hours later when the wagons from Blevins's house rolled up the road.

Manny had separated himself from the others, under the pretense of waiting for the wagons on the road, but try as he might, he couldn't lose the ever-present colonel.

"I think I hear them now," Manny said.

Princeton waited by his side in total silence. It was the hardness of the man that, before this, Manny had most admired, but now it was unnerving him. He walked up the foggy road to get a better look at the oncoming wagons. Princeton still insisted on silently keeping pace, moving slowly behind him, keeping up with him step by step.

Moments later the wagons and the teams of mules that strained against the soft ground rolled out of the fog. The wagons looked like ghosts reappearing from a long sleep. The fog swirled around them and steam poured out from the nostrils of the animals.

"What kept you?" Manny growled.

"Weren't nobody 'round much to help," Johnny replied. "Just that old black butler of Blevins's. Guess most of the help went off to see the big show in town."

"Well, they saw one, then," Manny replied. "Ain't that right, Colonel?" Manny forced a toothy grin.

Princeton remained silent, his face craggy and unmoved.

"Howdy do, Colonel?" Johnny greeted Princeton.

The colonel mumbled a greeting.

Manny directed the two drivers, "Pull them things alongside the river, but stay on the road. That gold's heavy; I ain't gonna want to see these here things stuck in the mud. It'd be easier to have the boys carry them boxes a little bit farther than to have you up to yer hubs in mud."

He shot Princeton a glance, hoping somehow that the fact that he was thinking about the welfare of the shipment might soften him just a little. It didn't. Princeton's face remained rock hard, a solid stone of grim determination.

As the wagons pulled off, he began to regret what he'd done. Mercy was something that he was not accustomed to exhibiting. He'd gotten to this point in life by obeying orders and shooting before he'd had the time to think the matter over. On very few occasions, the men in his sights or on the end of his knife had voiced an appeal for leniency. Always before, he'd ended the clemency plea before the words had a chance to find his conscience. The one time he'd been asked to kill the truly innocent just happened to be a time when he was forced to listen to them, to have some company with people who didn't deserve to die by his hand or any other.

To those two people, Manny had been their only hope, Manny and the God they both prayed to. Perhaps now was the time for Manny to pray too. It was unfamiliar ground. As a boy, his mother had taken him to one of the revival meetings in the woods near their farm. He'd gone not so much for the preaching as he did for the sport of watching the other people do and say things that would only embarrass them the next day.

He followed the wagons closely on foot, determined not to say anything to the colonel that might provoke him until the man had a time to think the matter through. There might be a time in unloading the shipment when Princeton's back was turned and he could slip away. If he could get one of the horses and just a few minutes unobserved, he'd be gone quicker than a jackrabbit.

His mind raced. He could turn suddenly on the man and try to kill him, but that was something he didn't want to do unless it was absolutely necessary. Knowing just when that might be, however, was the trick. If he moved too quickly, he'd be forced to kill a man he'd always respected. If he hesitated just a minute longer than he should, he'd be dead himself.

Manny barked out orders to the men on deck. "Get them boxes outta that cabin, and let's start the loadin'. We ain't got us much time."

He turned back to Princeton. "If them folks from Decker Island don't make it here before the sun comes up, there'll only be one set of tracks. You figured out yet what yer gonna do about that?"

He could see the idea was a new one to the colonel, which was unusual in itself. This man generally thought way down the line. He may have emotions, but Manny had never before seen him act in an emotional way. He'd always acted according to plan, and he had always laid out a very good plan. Quick, on-the-spot thinking had never been the colonel's strong suit, however. That very fact must be the reason Princeton hadn't confronted him thus far with what he knew about the doctor and his niece. *He must have somethin' in mind,* Manny thought. *More'n likely, he plans on shooting the people right in front of me just before he does me in.*

"What would you suggest?" Princeton asked.

Well, at least that's something, Manny thought. *He wants to know what I think.* "I wuz just rememberin', Colonel. Blevins over there's got that steam launch down by the riverside of that grotto, under his house. I could get the thing fired up and have the boys load the gold onto it. I could take you all the way to San Francisco and the warehouse. You'd give 'em the slip if we could get that far. Don't seem to me that it would be the smartest thing to keep that stuff in his cellar. There's gonna be law aplenty runnin' 'round these parts in a day or two and, like I say, if them boys from Decker don't get here, the tracks will only run in one direction."

"Do you think that boat can hold all that gold?"

Just the fact that Princeton was responding to his ideas pleased Manny, and if he bought the notion that Manny would be the best man to guide and power the launch, then it might mean Princeton would delay his plans to kill him. It might even mean that he could slip overboard when they got out onto the river.

"We might not be able to get all the gold in. We'd have to watch we don't get too low in the water. The swells on the bay would do us in. But I've navigated them waters before. None of these other men know much about how to do it, but I reckon I could."

The final thought was the best hold card Manny had, and he knew it. He could see Princeton turning the notion over in his mind. *Come on*, Manny thought. He watched Princeton mull the matter over. *Surely you can wait one more day to kill old Manny here. You could change your plans just this once.*

"The idea has merit," Princeton responded. "I'll talk it over with Blevins directly and let you know."

Manny and the colonel walked up the gangplank, passing several of the men on their way down with boxes of gold between them. Manny stood at the top of the gangway and supervised the carrying of the gold. He watched Princeton carefully as the man took Blevins aside to talk. They seemed animated in their discussion. It was plain to see the timing on the matter didn't suit Blevins one bit. Perhaps he didn't think it would give him enough time to do what other clearing of his booty he had in mind to do, but the idea was a sound one, and Manny and Princeton knew it.

Minutes later, Princeton and Blevins walked over to where Manny continued to direct the men. "I understand you're to be our launch captain," Blevins said.

"Be glad to do it, Governor," Manny replied. "I could get that heavy-loaded boat across that bay and you and the gold tucked away tomorrow night. I wouldn't think anybody else here could."

"Colonel Princeton and I have just been discussing that very fact, and it seems you have us at a disadvantage."

"Naw, sir," Manny grinned. "You got me and what I can do to your advantage, and I don't mind doin' it at all."

Princeton spoke up. "Those boxes are heavy. How will we unload them when we get to San Francisco?"

Manny smiled. His thinking had worked. Now Princeton wasn't just listening, he was asking for his advice. Maybe he could live another day, gain their confidence, and make his escape.

"That would be easy, Colonel. I could have the men paint over the boxes tonight when they load them. When we get to San Francisco, I could go out on the street and hire men straight off to unload them boxes. There's more than a few in the saloons. I could find them."

"I'd have to go with you," Princeton snapped.

" 'Course, Colonel, I wouldn't think of going anywheres without you," Manny lied.

CHAPTER 30

HATTIE STEPPED IN FRONT of the others. "Howdy, fellers, we'ze jest about to go on out fer a stroll. Understand there be a way outta here."

The men got to their feet. "Who the blazes are you?"

Hattie put one hand under her belt and pushed out on it, bending her knees up and down. "Name's Hattie Woodruff. You boys live here?"

The men seemed to be at a loss as to what to do with her. They looked at one another in wonderment.

Hattie saw the expressions on the Pages' faces. They seemed to know these men, and both of them were frozen with fear and disappointment. They'd been so close to getting away from this glittering prison, and now this. Hattie could see something else in the girl, however, a brewing rage. Mary's hands were clenched by her side as if it was all she could do to say and do nothing. Hattie could see the desire building inside the girl to act, but a rash action could prove to be fatal. She'd have to do something to calm things down. Even if they were stopped now, as long as they were alive there would be another day.

Reaching into her blouse, Hattie pulled out the waxed paper that contained her chewing tobacco. Opening it up, she bit off a corner and began to chew. She held it out to the men and mumbled through the chaw, "You boys like some? It got soaked a might, but it's still plenty good."

"What we gonna do with her?" one of the men asked.

"Don't rightly know"—the man looked at Hattie—"who she is or even what she is."

The men all looked to be the scruffy sort, the kind of riffraff Hattie had known all of her life. Their boots were scuffed and beaten;

their hats hung down without any smoothness or pressed nature to any of the brims.

One of the men wore bright red suspenders, a trapping he seemed unusually proud of. He pushed them out as he spoke. "We gotta lock 'em up in that chair room. Blevins would have rabid fever if he knew they was out."

"Looky here, boys," Hattie said. "You all appear to be thieves and such. Now that be all right with me. I done some thievin' in my day too, but you go to lockin' folks up and seein' 'em killed and that be a hangin' offense. Now, why don't you all just go on 'bout yer business, and we'll just go fer our little stroll out yonder way. You didn't see nothin'. You'll get yer share of whatever it is yer dibbyin' up, and you won't go to gettin' yerself hanged on our account."

The men once again exchanged glances. Turning to the three would-be escapees, they looked them over carefully.

The man in the red suspenders spoke to the other two. "Blevins said the colonel's savin' them two to show to Manny when he brings him here. We best not be lettin' 'em get loose; he'd plum skin us alive."

He motioned to one of the other men. "You take that gal back up to her room, and we'll take the old folks here back to the chair room and lock 'em up tight."

"Who you callin' old?" Hattie growled. "Why, young feller, I'd jest as soon fight you with skinnin' knives or jest bare knuckles, if'n ya weren't so feared of embarrassin' yerself."

The man drew his revolver. "I don't fight with old-timers, especially women."

Hattie spit a stream of tobacco juice onto the top of the man's boot. "Little boy, you lock horns with old Hat and I'll knock yer ears down. What they don't bury they'll be puttin' in pickle juice."

Mary reached over to Hattie. The sight of the older woman so ready to fight had surprisingly calmed her down. She put her arm on Hattie's. "Please don't. I'm sorry I got you into this. Our problems are our problems, and if the Lord can shut the mouths of lions, He can deliver us from these men. I wouldn't want anybody else hurt."

"Mary's right," the doctor added. "The Lord will send someone else to save us here."

Hattie looked at the young woman. "Girl, you don't know what yer sayin'. I'd say we just sashshay ourselves right on outta here.

These men are cowards. I doubt they be men at all." She swept her arm at the man with the suspenders, shoving him aside. "Don't crowd me."

The other two men pointed their revolvers at her. Lifting his gun in her direction, the man with the red suspenders spoke in low, menacing tones, "You may not think we're real men, but these here shooters of ours has got themselves real bullets. Now, you just do like we say or we'll shoot you down right here and throw you right back in the river you come from."

✦ ✦ ✦ ✦ ✦

Zac looked on as the last of the boxes were loaded onto the wagons. He watched the brightly clothed pirate climb into the driver's seat of the lead wagon, followed by Princeton. Zac recognized the colonel right away. It had been many years since he'd seen him, but he'd never forgotten his first look at the man, even though he'd been only seventeen at the time. The soldiers he'd been with had carefully pointed the colonel out, and given the story they were telling, Zac had made a careful study of the officer's features. It was a face he wouldn't soon forget.

The wagons rolled down the road into the fog, and Zac waited a few moments to make sure they weren't being followed by a rear guard. They weren't. The distinguished-looking, well-dressed man that mounted his purebred horse rode on ahead of them. There would be no reason to suspect the gold was being followed, and whatever was left of the men on board the *Delta King* would remain there to confront anyone who might find the boat come morning. Zac followed on foot.

The sound of the creaking, heavily loaded wagons echoed in the night air. For the most part the men on board were not talkative. Zac padded his way up the road, pausing occasionally to listen and then moving on.

He squinted through the fog. There, moving back in his direction, the horseman was making a check of the wagon's back trail. Zac drove for some brush nearby.

"Who goes there?" the man yelled out. He stepped his horse in Zac's direction, carefully padding the big horse back down the road.

Reaching his hand under his coat, Zac rested it on the butt of his Shopkeeper Special. If he needed to, he could pull it and unhorse the man right where he sat. He'd prefer to take him off the horse without a shot being fired, though. Not that it would make much difference. In all likelihood, the riderless horse would storm past the wagons on the road ahead, alerting the men to his presence. He'd be far better off to just stay quietly out of sight.

The man stepped his horse closer. "Who goes there?"

Zac wasn't sure if the man had seen his outline through the fog or if perhaps some sixth sense had warned him that they were in fact being followed.

The man drew one of the ivory-handled six-shooters he had been carrying at his waist and dropped his hand to his side, still holding the weapon.

Zac watched as the man looked first in his direction and then back down the fog-shrouded road. The horse stamped, moving from side to side. It was obvious the animal had spirit. Standing in one place was something he seemed unaccustomed to, or perhaps like most horses, it was the fact that he was heading back to his own stables and fresh oats that the animal had in mind. Horses returning to the barn seemed to have a mind of their own, and it always involved getting there with the minimum of interruption.

The horse's ears shot forward, as if he had picked up Zac's scent. A man's smell would be difficult to conceal, even in the fog, and Zac could only hope the man wasn't a good student of his own horse. The animal snorted, then suddenly froze.

The man swung the revolver toward the road. Suddenly tugging on the reins, he backed the horse up the road, continuing to survey the foggy road in silence. Moments later, he pulled on the reins, swung the animal around, and galloped off toward the retreating wagons.

Zac would be more careful now. He'd follow the caravan at more of a distance. He might not be able to keep them in sight, but with the weight of the wagons, he'd have no trouble following their tracks.

It was more than an hour later when Zac saw the big house. The tracks of the wagons led to the river, below the house. It was obvious that whoever was behind this robbery lived in the big house on the hill. Straddling the heavy ruts in the soft ground, he stepped softly toward the river.

Crouching behind the bushes that formed a well-concealed cover for the riverside entrance, he watched the four men as they loaded the gold. One of the men had driven the trailing wagon he had followed, and the other three he hadn't seen before. The lead pirate in the brightly colored clothing was missing from the group, as was the colonel and the man who had been riding the spirited horse. The men were hurriedly slapping paint on top of the Wells Fargo insignias and then lifting the boxes into the boat.

The small boat was larger than the one Grubb had managed to find, but it was obvious it wouldn't be able to handle all of the gold and still stay afloat. The boiler on the boat was being fired up, and occasionally one of the men climbed aboard and threw several more pieces of wood into it, then backed up, slammed the door shut, and took his place with the others. It would be some time before they had the boat filled to capacity, time Zac would need to find the missing men.

Walking back to the main road, Zac climbed the hill up to the big house. The lights on the main floor were ablaze, and on the third floor, several lights glimmered through gauzy curtains. Moving to the windows in front of the house, he peered through them.

The hall was enormous. Between the curtains he could see tall candles burning, casting flickering shadows onto the expensive carpet. The walls were dark and ornately carved with large sections of lightly trimmed plaster between them. Rugs and paintings hung on them, giving off the appearance of great wealth.

He paused at the window. Whoever was responsible was in that house along with Princeton. He looked back down the hill at the place where the men were loading the gold. There would be no time to wait for help. Whatever was to be done, he had to do and right now. He'd always worked that way before, and tonight would be no exception.

He drew out the small revolver and moved carefully back down the hill. He'd dispose of the men he could reach first and tend to the men in the house later. The bluff the house sat on hid the opening below, and with the brush that surrounded it, a man would have to know just what he was looking for to find it. Following the fresh, deep wagon ruts had been easy. He knew who they belonged to and knew enough not to be distracted by the house that sat above the bluff. He spun the cylinder on the stubby .45. Four men and six rounds; it would be plenty.

Moving down the hill, he rounded the bend of the concealed roadway and crouched in the bushes. The men were still hard at work. He watched carefully. When the four of them had boxes suspended between them, he stepped out from the bushes.

"That's far enough, boys," he said, pulling the hammer back on the .45 and waggling it in their direction. "Just stand still, right where you are."

The sound of the clear cock of the hammer froze the men in place. "Who the blazes are you?" the man in the red suspenders asked.

"Never mind who I am. I just want you to stand real still like, and with your left hands pull out those revolvers you're packing. Pull 'em out real careful like, with two fingers," he instructed as he walked closer, "and drop them right into that river."

Frozen on the gangplank that led up to the boat, the men were silhouetted against the water, and even in the fog, each of them knew they'd be prime targets. They exchanged glances as Zac stepped ever closer. Reaching down with their left hands, the men moved to comply with the stranger's directions.

Zac pointed the gun at the man with the red suspenders and spoke in a forceful baritone voice that carried a clear but menacing tone to it. "Just get that thought clean out of your head right now. That isn't your gold, but it is your life we're talking about here. You're gonna drop dead in that water, and I won't even have to clean you up."

Zac could see the menacing look in the man's face suddenly change. The stubby revolver wasn't pointed at the group, but right at him. No matter what happened, the man could see that he'd be the first to go.

"We better do as he says," the man mumbled. "He ain't gonna get very far all by himself anyways."

"Who said I'm alone?" Zac asked. "We got the whole place surrounded. The rest figured I could handle you boys by my lonesome, and I can. You'd be bettin' your life if you figured otherwise. It'll go a whole lot lighter on you boys, though, if you do just what I tell you to do."

One by one the men complied, dropping their revolvers carefully into the river.

"Fine, boys, now just set that shipment down in that boat like you were told to do, and back on out here next to me."

Two by two, the men set the cargo down in the boat and walked carefully back down the gangplank.

Zac motioned with the revolver toward the grotto's opening.

"Now all you boys go right over there and kneel down, hands behind your back. I'll do my best to get you through this here roundup without you getting yourselves killed."

Meekly, the men walked toward the grotto's entrance and knelt down, cupping their hands behind their backs.

Zac walked around them, looking for anything with which to tie the men up. Spotting a spool of heavy line, he reached into his shirt for the sharp blade he carried between his shoulder blades. He cut sections of the line into a number of manageable pieces. Forming locking loops out of four of the pieces, he walked back to the men on their knees.

"Now, boys, get flat on your faces with them hands held up behind you."

The pirates reluctantly submitted as Zac stepped around them. "Who are you?" the man in the red suspenders asked.

"Name's Zac Cobb, and I work for Wells Fargo."

One of the pirates mumbled to the suspendered man, "Ain't he the one Korth was supposed to take care of?"

"You bet I am, but as you can see, this Korth feller of yours didn't do much better than you did."

Zac pushed the man's face into the ground with his boot and looped the line around his hands, pulling them tight. "Just lie there and relax. Your night is over."

In a matter of minutes, he had all four of the men's hands tied behind their backs. He hauled them one by one to their feet. "All right, boys, we're gonna take a little walk and find us a tree."

"A tree!" one of the men gasped.

"Several trees," Zac shot back. "I ain't about to hang you, though. I'm just gonna keep you safe for a jury to decide your fate. I can tell you one thing, though, the quieter you are, the better it'll go for you come time for trial."

The men marched up the road some distance. Zac walked behind them until they were safely out of earshot and away from the sight of the big house. He spotted several oaks that grew along the edge of the river. "All right, boys, this is plenty far enough."

He sat the men each beside their own tree and, sticking the gun into his belt, tied them up tight, hand and foot. Removing the scarves from around the men's necks and one from his own pocket, he gagged them firmly.

He planted the revolver back into his underarm holster and, facing the men, tipped his hat. "I'll be seeing you boys in a bit. Now, you just set yourselves here and relax a mite. They say this night air ain't good for a man, so you better hope I have as easy a time with them bosses of yours as I had with you. I wouldn't want you still here when the army gets here in the morning. You just might catch cold. Hangin's mighty uncomfortable for a man with a cold."

Moving back down the road, he jogged up the hill to the house. He'd take a walk around the place. He never liked to go anywhere totally blind. Making a careful loop around the massive house, he discovered the stables. He checked the stalls. The man had left the horse he'd been riding still saddled and ungroomed. Zac loosened the cinch on the animal. The man who had been riding the horse was obviously unused to caring for it. Zac had seen this kind of behavior before. The rich always had someone to do their dirty work or finish what they started. Zac thought to himself that tonight was going to be different for the man, whoever he was—tonight he'd have to finish what he started.

Walking back to the house, he moved from window to window, taking in all of the structure he could. Rounding the corner of the building, he looked at the window above him. It was out of direct sight, but he could see movement inside. He crouched below and watched it carefully. Getting inside might be a problem. Perhaps the best way would be to just knock on the door.

+ + + + +

Blevins sat beside the fire, sipping a snifter of brandy, as Princeton paced back and forth. "Sit down, Colonel. There'll be plenty of time to get nervous once we get underway. I think it will still be dark by the time we pass the *Delta King*, and if Manny here has sent the right man to the wagons on Decker Island, you may even get to see them unloading the rest of the cargo when we pass."

"That can't be soon enough for me."

Blevins flipped open the lid on the humidor. "Here, Colonel, have yourself a cigar. It might settle you down."

Manny held up his lit cigar. "These Cuban smokes are mighty fine," he said.

"You see, Colonel, you have men with good taste."

Princeton paced to the parlor door that led to the hallway. He found it hard to take his eyes off of Manny. There was something about the man seeming to be so comfortable when there was work still to be done that didn't set well with him, and every glare he sent in the pirate's direction said as much.

Blevins had noticed the looks that passed between the two of them. He was going to take the woman with them, but with the way she looked tonight, so radiant and so beautiful, perhaps Manny wouldn't even recognize her. He knew Princeton still had settling the score with his lieutenant in mind, but that could wait until they were in San Francisco. They'd need the man until then, and the pirate didn't seem to catch on to the fact that they knew of his betrayal. The longer he stayed in the dark, the better.

"Relax, Colonel," Blevins said. "When I spoke to them, your men reported that our guests were quite comfortable and that my own special guest"—his eyes twinkled—"is back in her room, waiting for me. You have nothing to worry about, you'll get your share of the take when we get to San Francisco. It ought to be more than enough to keep you quite comfortable for a very long time."

Taking out a pen and paper he started to write. "I'll have to leave a note for my aunt. I'll tell her I'm going to Sacramento on business. She'll be confused enough with all the visitors we're likely to have in the morning."

"I don't know what's taking them such a long time." Princeton spat out the words, continuing to pace the floor.

Manny got to his feet. "Colonel, if it'll make you feel any better, I can go down through the cellar and check on them," he said.

"Fine idea," Blevins chuckled. "Right now, I'd support anything that would get this commander of yours off my rug. He's wearing a path in it."

"I'll go with you," Princeton said.

Blevins got to his feet and set down the pen. "All right, why don't the two of you go and check on their progress. I'll go up and see that our special guest has her traveling clothes on."

The three of them moved into the hallway. He watched as the two men started down the stairs. Turning around the room, he surveyed the glimmering candle-lit paintings. It would possibly be the last time he saw The Glades in a very long time.

As he turned to go up the stairs, he heard a loud knock at the door.

CHAPTER 31

+ + + + + + +

HATTIE BEAT HER FIST on the big door. "Hey! Open this here thing up."

"I'm afraid no one can hear you," William Page said. "We're quite alone down here."

Hattie swung around and glared at the man. "Well, you don't seem to get yerself one bit riled 'bout this, now, do you?"

"After a while, a person learns to accept what he can't change."

"Well, I sure ain't 'ceptin' this." She turned around and continued to pound on the door.

"Madam, that type of behavior will only serve to bruise your hand."

Heaving a big sigh, she swung around and leaned back against the door. "I can't be gettin' myself stuck here. I got two young'uns I was s'posed to watch on that there boat. No tellin' what's befallen 'em by now."

"I can sympathize with you completely, but I'm afraid little will be served by bruising your hand in the process." He scratched his chin. "And if the pirates have discovered the children, then it stands to reason that you may see them here shortly."

He waved his hand at the rich furnishings around the room. "You see, our host seems to be the leader of this band of brigands. If they've been captured as you suspect, his men may bring them here."

Hattie cocked her head, thinking the matter over. "You jest might be swerving into some truth there, mister. 'Course, fussin' jest makes me feel a mite better on the inside. Ain't got much in the way of calmness about me, I reckon. Somebody that's a sufferin' and just sets herself down and frets like one of them society womenfolk deserves everythin' that comes down the pipe in her direction."

She began to pace the room, walking with a sustained limp.

"Have you been injured?" Dr. Page asked.

Hattie stopped and hitched up her shabby dress. "Mister, I been bit by a grizzly. A Paiute took to give me a musket ball in the thigh. Then a drunk figured he could carve up on me with a knife. Been in many a cat fight with low-down women. Got myself stomped on, sawed on, shot at, hammer-locked, and trifled with a time or two in my younger days. Fact is, though, I'm here and them folks ain't. I reckon I can take care of my ownself till somebody flops my carcass into the ground."

"You do seem to be favoring that hip of yours. I'd be glad to look at it for you."

"You what?"

"I said, I'd be happy to give you an examination."

Hattie put both hands on her hips and glared at him, sticking out her lower lip. Crossing her arms, she walked toward him. "Mister, I don't know what kinda foolin' 'round you got in that head of yourn. You look to be a favorable sort, and any other time I jest might take you up on that. My mind may look like it's goin' but I got myself some serious memories."

She raised her chin, putting on her most dignified look. "I'ze a Christian woman these here days, though, and I ain't about to go a liftin' my dress without a ring on my finger."

Dr. Page sputtered, his face turning a pale red. He raised both hands. "Madam, I can assure you I had nothing indecent in mind. I'm a medical doctor."

Hattie thought the matter over. "Well, yer a man, ain't ye?"

William Page nodded. "Yes, I am."

"You a single sort?"

"Yes, ma'am, I am a bachelor."

Hattie walked away, mumbling over her shoulder. "Doctor or no, you being a man's 'nuff fer me." She stopped in her tracks and swung around with a slight grin on her face. "'Course, at my age, indecent or not, it's a fine thing fer a gal to get herself any proposal at all. It's been a lot a years since I had one, and the feller was drunk, too drunk to do anythin' about his words."

She looked the doctor over. "I reckon I'll make out jest fine. Ain't nothin' to go getting yerself all fumbly about."

Dr. Page cleared his throat firmly. "Well, I'm afraid, madam, that we seem to be thrown in here together." It was clear he wanted to change the subject, change it to anything. "We are at the mercy of these men until they decide just what to do about us."

"Don't go to settin' that medical mind of yourn in that dee-rection, Doctor. We best go to figurin' jest what we is about to do the next time one of them low-down, good-fer-nothin's opens this here door. Them candlesticks over yonder looks like a likely basher to me, and if'n I was you, I'd go to pityin' the noggin of the next feller that opens this here door."

+ + + + +

The door to the big house opened slowly. Zac straightened his suit coat, partially to conceal the holster and the gun he had tucked under his arm. He tipped his hat to the man he had seen on horseback on the road. "Pardon me," he said. "The name's Taylor. I'm looking for anyone you may have seen that come off of that steamer tonight."

"Boat tonight?"

"Yes, it seems that the *Delta King* has been hijacked."

"Hijacked, you say. That would be impossible."

"No. I can assure you it isn't, and people have been thrown overboard. I thought you might have gotten one or two that swam in this direction. It happened not far from here."

Zac watched the man ponder the situation over. To turn him away would be to allow him to be on the river as he passed by in his boat, and that might not be something the man would want to do. In Zac's mind, he wanted all of the men in the house together when he drew his revolver. It would be best to bag all the birds at one time.

The man opened the door wider. "Why don't you step in, sir. I can ask the servants if they've offered assistance to anyone who might have passed by tonight."

Zac stepped into the hallway. He carefully surveyed the room. It was larger on the inside than it had appeared to be from the outside looking in. On the table beside the door, he spotted Hattie's straw bonnet. It was most definitely out of place in a house like this, and it presented a new dilemma to Zac. If his aunt was here, she was either dead or offering them more trouble than they could have realized.

Blevins spotted his gaze at the overlooked hat. "And what is your business with this thing, Mr. Taylor? Are you connected with the law?"

Zac grinned and shook his head. "No, I'm afraid not. I was just riding the road when the commotion started." He rubbed his backside. "With all the shooting, my horse spooked and ran away. I was looking for him too."

"I see. Well, I may be able to help you there."

"I'm afraid I haven't got the means with me to buy a horse tonight," Zac countered, "and I wouldn't expect you to loan one to a perfect stranger."

The candles flickered softly in front of the curtains, casting a soft, rich glow onto the woodwork. On the walls, crossed swords of every description studded the plaster and dark wood.

These people were from the East, Zac decided. He'd seen many large houses in the East decorated with symbols of the owner's power. Weapons on the wall served as more than decorations—they were supposed to intimidate visitors as to the power of their host and place a hint of fear into anyone coming to conduct business. He'd seen one house in Virginia with a circle of muskets attached to the ceiling and stacks of the arms surrounding the walls of the massive entryway. Being asked to wait in the hall usually had the desired effect.

"Are you a swordsman, Mr. Taylor?"

"Not lately. I swung one a time or two in the war."

"A saber, no doubt," Blevins snapped. "I can see by your hat that you served with the Confederacy."

"That I did, though I wasn't a mite much more than a boy."

"Cavalry?"

"Yes, with Moseby."

"Moseby? Colonel John Singleton Moseby, the gray fox?"

"That's right."

"Odd."

"How's that?"

"Well, I should think a man who rode with Moseby wouldn't allow himself to be thrown by a horse."

Zac could see the man was probing. Maybe his ruse wasn't working. He smiled and bowed his head. "And I must say, that is plum embarrassin' too. 'Course, being familiar with them like I am, I tend to get the most spirited animal I can drop a halter on."

"Perhaps you overmatched yourself tonight, Mr. Taylor. I

wouldn't let that become a habit, if I were you."

He stepped back and motioned toward the parlor. "Why don't you make yourself comfortable while I consult with my servants? I might see if I have a horse as well, perhaps an animal you can control." He smiled. "After you, sir."

Zac had taken a couple of steps when Blevins drew one of his ivory-handled revolvers. He cocked the hammer back, and Zac froze in his tracks.

"Just a moment, Mr. Taylor, if that is your name. Turn around."

Zac turned slowly, his hands at his side.

"Now, why don't you just lift that coat of yours, and let's see just what you're carrying."

Very deliberately, Zac lifted his coat, showing he wasn't wearing a holster around his waist."

"Lift it higher, Mr. Taylor. Let's see it all."

Zac lifted the coat, exposing his underarm holster.

"I thought as much," Blevins said. Carefully reaching over, he removed the .45 and tucked it behind his waistband. "Now, why don't we discuss your real identity. You followed us tonight, didn't you?"

"Yes, I followed you, and before long you'll find that the army is right behind me. I think you'll soon discover that you've bit off a little more"—Zac eyeballed the rich decorations—"than even you can chew."

Blevins walked casually to the wall and removed a saber. He swung it back and forth, sending the ripping sound of the cold steel through the air. "Normally, I prefer the foil, Mr. Taylor, but since you have some experience with this weapon, albeit a dated one, I'd like to allow this duel to take on the air of fairness."

Zac watched the man stretch and continue to swing the saber. It was obvious that this was a weapon of comfort for the man, and there was an arrogance in the way he smiled when he swung the sword back and forth that made the hackles on the back of Zac's neck stand at attention. "I wouldn't want to give you the satisfaction," Zac said. "If you intend to kill me, why don't you just be a man and do it?"

"I'm more of a sportsman," Blevins replied.

"I think you're more of a coward."

The word "coward" brought Blevins's display of bravado to an abrupt halt. He glared at Zac. "That's a word that has never been used concerning me."

"Consider it used. I see you as a coward hiding behind some sort of display of sportsmanship. You pretend to be a successful businessman when all you are is a thief, preying on other folks' success. Now you're masquerading as a sportsman, but inside you're just a cold-blooded killer. Why don't you quit playactin' and just shoot me down?"

The words stung deeply, Zac could see that. It was just what he wanted to do, get the man angry, good and angry. Angry men tended to be rash, and right now that was just what Zac needed—a man who made mistakes, a man who reacted when he should have been thinking.

Quickly taking another saber from the wall, Blevins tossed it to him. "Now you've made this even more pleasurable." He started his practice swings once again. "The sidearm is much too quick for what I have in mind for you." Holding the saber up to his face, Blevins grinned over the gleaming blade. "With this I can kill you one small piece at a time."

Blevins slashed down at Zac with the saber, and Zac parried it, dancing backward.

"You see," Blevins said, "you can defend yourself." Blevins playfully spun his blade in the air. "Ever seen a man die by the sword, Mr. Taylor? It's a beautiful death, slow and with the crimson flow of blood. I've seen it many times."

Swinging the sword once more, he sent a sharp thrust in Zac's direction. Zac jumped back, once again brushing the saber aside with his own.

Blevins continued to talk his way through the duel. Zac could tell the man took great delight in the process of his kills. "I especially enjoy the part when a man first realizes he is going to die. The look of panic in the man's face when he realizes he's facing a better opponent and will soon meet his fate is most satisfying." Pausing dramatically, Blevins spread the fingers of his free hand in front of his own face and peered hypnotically at Zac as he lowered his hand. "A slow but sure coming to terms with death."

"You won't get that pleasure from me." Zac spat out the words and began a series of wild slashes in Blevins's direction, from which the man danced backward, parrying each blow with an ease that produced a continued smile.

"You see," Blevins smirked, "you aren't helpless. At least in your own mind you aren't. Let's just see when the notion presents itself to you."

With that, the man initiated a series of maneuvers with the saber, forcing Zac to first block a high blow and then moving onto a series of thrusts to the midsection, ending with a flick of the sword that caught Zac's leg. The sharp edge of the saber cut through his trousers, releasing a trickle of blood.

"Ah, first blood." Blevins grinned. "I always find it better to incapacitate a man first, take away any notion of victory. Hope is always the first casualty of a duel, Mr. Taylor. Death comes later."

A slight breeze blew in from the river, billowing out the gauzy curtains. The flickering candles cast dancing shadows over the warm walls.

"You don't scare me in the least," Zac said. He moved forward, sending a series of brutal blows in the direction of Blevins's face.

Blevins tore into each blow with a stiff parry, sending Zac's sword away with the banging of steel on steel. He laughed with each counter blow delivered, finally pausing when Zac stopped and began to circle.

"I like that in a man," Blevins said. "Someone who refuses to die easily. A little bit of fire always warms the battle."

The breeze rippled the flames on the candles. The massive brass stands stood around the hall with stout wax bases under the flames that lifted the light overhead. The rippling effect of the light threw shadows over the ceiling, quivering shades of darkness and flame.

Lifting his eyes to the stands, Zac noticed the curtains continue to billow themselves around the base of the brass candelabras. "Why don't we just warm this battle up a little more," Zac snapped.

With that, he kicked over one of the stands in the direction of the billowing curtain material. It landed with a crash, spilling the candles and lapping their flames into the flimsy material of the inner drapes.

Blevins watched the flames rise up the curtains. His face paled and then turned a bright crimson. Swinging his saber with increased fury, he mounted a hurried attack.

Zac two-stepped backward, parrying the furious blows. "What's the matter? I interrupt that timetable of yours?"

"This won't take more than a minute or two," Blevins shouted as he continued his furious slashing.

Zac backed up to the stairs that led to the lower landing.

Blevins continued his hard blows, driving Zac down the stairs one at a time.

The flames in the hall now leaped from the curtain to the carpeting. They began to run along the fabric, leaving a trail of blazing light. Overhead, the light flickered across the plastered ceiling.

Blevins delivered a smashing overhand blow. Zac met it, holding his saber up against the man's blade. The two men pushed and wrestled behind their respective blades, Blevins groaning with the effort. Being above Zac gave him an advantage, but the look on the man's face showed his astonishment at the strength behind Zac's blade. He groaned and, with one big push, sent Zac tumbling to the landing below.

Zac was on his feet rapidly. He met the man's blows as he backed down the stairs, crashing his saber into the man's overhead slashes.

Once again, they found themselves locked saber to saber, Zac wrestling for the man's wrist. Twisting in an overhead viselike grip, Zac held firm.

Suddenly, from behind, a crashing blow fell on top of Zac's head, sending him to the landing. Lights buzzed inside of his head, sparkles of faint consciousness.

Princeton stood on the landing, revolver in his hand. "What are you doing?" he asked.

Blevins swung the sword furiously by his side, livid with rage. "What did you do that for?"

"The men are gone!"

"Gone?"

"Yes, they've disappeared."

Blevins turned Zac over with the toe of his boot. "Perhaps this man had something to do with that."

Manny had been watching silently from behind the colonel. "That's Zac Cobb," he said. "I caught a look at him in Sacramento."

The fire crackled in the hallway above them. The three men turned to look as the flames grew higher. "He started the fire," Blevins said.

The three of them bounded up the flight of stairs. The flames had crawled up the curtains to the ceiling and were continuing to spread over the carpet. They licked at the woodwork, spreading black smoke into the hallway and down to the dining room, toward

Mamie's apartment. The fire blazed on the furniture, blossoming new and more deadly smoke.

"We best get," Manny yelled. "The boat's still there."

Blevins stood frozen by the sight of the fire, mesmerized by the racing flames.

"The boat is there," Princeton said, "and the gold is on it."

Blevins reluctantly nodded. "I'll go get the woman," he said.

"Then you'd better hurry. This fire's out of control."

Blevins bounded up the stairs, racing toward the upper floor. Finding Mary's room, he fumbled with the key. As he opened the door he saw her, cowering in the corner.

She shook her head at him. "I'm not going anywhere with you."

The smoke was filtering down the upstairs hallway. "You will." Reaching out, he grabbed her hand, jerking her to her feet. "The Glades is on fire. You stay here and you'll die."

He dropped the sword and pulled her from the room. Running down the hall, Mary covered her face. Both of them took the stairs, fighting back the rising smoke. Reaching the bottom of the hall, they stepped over the flames on the carpet.

A subtle sleeve of flame touched the bottom of Mary's dress, and as she scurried down to the landing, it erupted. She screamed.

As they ran down the steps toward the cellar, Blevins saw the flames trailing from Mary's dress. He threw her to the landing in front of the door and, taking off his jacket, smothered the flames.

She was crying as Blevins jerked her back to her feet. "Where is my uncle?" she cried out.

He pulled her, dragging her through the big door. "This house is burning down around us." He pulled harder. "Come with me. Come with me now."

She pulled back. "My Uncle William, where is he?"

"He's safe." Picking up a torch, he reached back and shoved it into the flaming sconce. Holding her tightly, he wrestled her into the dark, cavernous room. "You come with me and he will stay safe."

CHAPTER 32

+ + + + + + +

ZAC MOANED, REACHING FOR the back of his head. He had felt the people step over him and make their way down the stairs. The smoke from the hallway above had begun to tumble down the stairs to the landing below. It made his already buzzing head seem light and cottonlike, floating and swirling. The floor seemed to twirl beneath him as he worked to gather his senses, getting to his knees.

Hattie was in this big house somewhere, and it was burning down all around him. He wobbled to his feet.

Taking off his coat, he covered his head and started up the stairs. Rounding the first flight, he stared down the hallway erupting with flame. Fire was crawling up the walls of the big house, and the furniture was engulfed with the blaze. "Hattie!" he yelled out.

Running up the first flight of stairs, he moved from room to room, yelling out her name as he went. Each room was dark as he entered it. He paused at the stairs. The flames below would only become more advanced, and he knew it, but there was one more floor to go. He ran up the stairs.

The first door was locked. He kicked it in. "Hattie! Hat! You here, Hat?"

Running down the hall, he continued to call out her name as he raced from room to room. There was no one there. *She must be in the basement,* he thought.

Once again covering his head with his suit coat, he ran down the stairs.

The flames were making their way up the staircase. A ribbon of fire had traced itself over the banister on the last flight of stairs. It wouldn't be much longer before the big house was nothing more than a heap of ash. Princeton and the man he had fought would be below. He didn't think they'd bother to look for the men he'd tied up and left on the road. They would be in a hurry now. They might even have left already.

He wound his way down the semidarkness. The stairs underneath the house had very little smoke in them. They were even cool, unaffected by the inferno that raged above them. Pausing at the door, he peered into the dark room. He noticed the barrel that contained the torches and, reaching in, drew one out. Lighting it on the flame burning in the lantern that hung outside the door, he stepped into the room.

As he moved deeper into the massive room, he heard a pounding on a door. "Hat! Is that you?" He shouted the words into the darkness, and from across the room heard a muffled response.

"Zac."

Running across the room, he came to the locked door. "Stand back," he yelled. Rearing back with his foot, he kicked at the door with all his might. It shuttered, the frame of the door giving slightly. Once again, he sent a powerful kick into the bulky door. The frame splintered, pushing the door ajar a fraction.

He felt a sense of panic. The men would be leaving, and the house was becoming engulfed in flames. It had to be now if he was to catch up to them. Rearing back, he put his shoulder into it, sending it crashing to the floor.

"Well, it's about time, boy," Hattie croaked. "This here's Dr. Page. At least he says he's a sawbones."

"We don't have any time," Zac said. "This house is burning down."

The doctor started to run past him. "My niece is upstairs," he said.

"Nobody's up there," Zac replied. "I just came from there, and you don't want to go up there. Those men must have taken her with them."

"What about the woman of the house?" the doctor asked. "Mamie?"

"I ain't seen another woman."

"She has an apartment near the kitchen."

"I didn't go down that way. She'll still be there, if she didn't find a way out."

"I have to go find her," Dr. Page sputtered.

Zac held on to his arm. "You really don't want to go up there."

William pulled himself free. "Sir, I am a physician. It's my sworn duty to save lives. I must go."

"All right. I'll see my aunt outside and join you."

"I simply can't wait, sir." Pulling himself away, the doctor ran for the lighted door at the end of the darkened room.

They watched him run through the darkness. "They got themselves a way out over yonder," Hattie screeched, pointing off into the darkness.

Soon, they had found the stairs that led through the rocklike wall and down to the grotto.

"They be pirates down there," Hattie said.

"I took care of them."

Moments later, they were in the grotto. The fire the men had hovered around, cooking their supper, was dimly glowing. They both ran through the room toward the landing with the boat. Outside, they could see Princeton and Manny as they worked to wrestle still one more box of the gold into the boat.

Blevins spotted the two of them. "Colonel," he shouted, "go kill them. Kill them and hurry back."

Zac forcibly pushed Hattie behind him as the man drew his revolver and stepped off the gangplank.

"Just leave her be," Zac said. "She's an old woman, and she can't harm you."

"I can too," Hattie sputtered.

Zac pushed her back, hard.

The man seemed determined as he marched closer to them. He held the revolver to his side.

Zac straightened the gray hat on his head. "Whatever happened to that company of yours, Colonel?"

The notion of the sudden remembrance drew Princeton up sharply. "What company?"

"I was in the war. I saw you once that I can remember. You know the one I mean—the company of cowards. You commanded them, as I remember, if you can call that a command."

The man was in a hurry. The boiler on the small boat was putting out steam. Zac knew the ploy might not work. He and Hattie had walked right into this. Being without a gun, he had to use the most powerful weapon he had, his mind. If he could get the man upset, it might throw his aim off, might just make him too hasty to take deliberate aim. One thing was certain, though. From the way the man was coming on, he had no intention of missing. That was fine with Zac. If he could get him even closer and just a mite hesitant, then he could shuck the one real weapon he had left, the knife between his shoulders. He'd have one chance and one chance only.

Princeton's eyes narrowed. "Do I know you, sir?"

"Don't think so. I was just a sixteen-year-old corporal when somebody pointed you out to me, the colonel who was a coward and commanded a company of cowards. As I remember it, even though we needed men badly, those men and you just commanded prisoners being taken to Andersonville. They said they couldn't trust you to do any real fighting. Somebody might just need you, and then they'd turn around and you'd be gone."

Blevins shouted from the boat. "Kill them, Princeton, and be done with it."

Zac looked over the colonel's shoulder and saw the men in the boat with the girl. "I see that you're still being told what to do with unarmed people. Guess the man figures with all that experience, you're just the right man for the job."

The words stung Princeton. He swung the gun up just as Zac dropped to a crouching position, drawing the knife out as he sunk to his right knee and shot his left foot out. The boom of the revolver sounded simultaneously with the throw of the knife.

The shot was wild, but the flight of the polished dagger spun straight and true. It flashed through the foggy night air, a deadly jewel of death, landing in the man's midsection and dropping him to his knees.

Zac diverted his eyes to where he had pushed Hattie. She lay prone, face down on the ground. "Hat, you all right, Hat?"

She lifted her head from the ground. "No thanks to you, I is."

They heard the boat get up steam, the clatter of the engine and the sound of the propeller rattling as it pulled away from the dock. Hattie scrambled to her feet and ran to where the fallen man lay. "Them scalawags is getting away."

She picked up the gun, and Zac grabbed her arm. "Don't shoot! There's a woman on that thing, and in this fog, you just might hit her."

Reluctantly, she lowered the revolver.

Zac scooted over to the fallen man and turned him over. He groaned. Zac wrapped his hand around the knife, gently removing it from the bleeding wound.

"Ohh..unn." The man gave out a mournful groan.

Hattie stood over them. "He ain't gonna live long 'nuff to hang."

The man blinked his eyes. "I never saw it coming," he whispered.

"Colonel, I think you saw it coming a long time ago. I'm afraid the whole army saw it coming where you were concerned back during the war."

The man closed his eyes. Zac got to his feet.

Turning back toward the house, they watched the dancing flames. "I gotta get that doctor out of there," Zac said.

"I'm afeared it's sorta late fer that."

"I sure can't go back in the way we came out," Zac said. "You go 'round to the barn and saddle us some horses. I'll circle 'round the house and see if there's another way in."

\+ + + + +

William made it to the top of the landing. The house was fully ablaze. Flames licked the walls, and the drapes were falling to the floor, heaps of blazing rich material. Looking through the flames to the dining room in the distance, he could see the flicker of the fire shining off the glass windows.

Taking a deep breath, he ran for the dining room. The flames stabbed at his clothing, the smell of smoke seeping into every pore in his body. He felt his face blossom with scorched skin. Scooting up the lapels of his jacket over his mouth, he continued to run.

As he entered the dining room, he blew the breath from his mouth. The smoke hung low in the room, thick and black, a cloud of superheated death. The tables and chairs were pockmarked with fire.

He'd been to Mamie's room only once, when she'd taken him there to see to her many ailments and get his advice. Now he'd have to find it again and in the darkness of the black and billowing smoke. He ran for the door at the far end of the room.

Groping forward, he found the brass handle of the woman's room and opened the door, shutting it behind him. Through the thin smoke and glimmering night stand candlelight, he could see her still in bed. He moved briskly to her bed and shook her.

"Miss Mamie, madam!"

Her eyes blinked open. "Doctor! What are you doing here? I thought you had gone."

"No. Please don't panic, but there's a fire."

"A fire! Mercy no."

"Yes, madam, I'm afraid so."

He looked back at her door. The smoke was pouring into the room from underneath the door, a rising flat cloud of black smoke that squeezed itself under the door and, finding space in the room, mushroomed up to the ceiling.

Seeing the menacing smoke, she screamed.

"Do you have towels?"

She pointed in the direction of the bureau and continued to shriek.

"Put a robe on, madam. We must go now."

The doctor tore though the drawers before finally retrieving several soft towels. Plunging them into the ceramic basin on the nearby stand, he withdrew them from the water and moved quickly to the door. Laying them down into the path of the incoming smoke, he stifled the flow of the black cloud.

Mamie had donned her robe and bedside slippers. She ran toward him, hanging on to his arm. "Doctor, Doctor! Oh, dear Jesus!"

He patted her hand. "Don't fret, Miss Mamie. We'll find a way out of here."

She clutched his arm tighter, starting to cry.

"Don't cry. I fear you'll have much more to cry over before this night is complete."

Tearing her hand from his arm, he moved to her bed and ripped the top sheet from the large feather mattress. He pointed toward a door on the backside of the room. "Where does that lead?"

"To the kitchen. Oh, Doctor, I fear I shall faint."

"Is there an exit from the kitchen area? It looks as if our way out the front door is now impassable."

"Y-y-y-yes," the word jerked out of her throat.

"Then, we'll have to go out there. There will be fire there too, but I do believe it's far worse in the hall."

"Oh dear, whatever shall we do?" She waved her hands. "Our beautiful house, our very beautiful house. What will Robert say? Oh dear, dear me."

"Never mind that now."

She waved her hand at him. "I do feel faint, Doctor." She began to sob and shake uncontrollably, collapsing in a heap on the floor and continuing to cry.

He pushed the sheet into the basin and, taking a nearby pitcher, poured water on top of it, soaking the flimsy cotton.

"Oh dear Jesus, have mercy on us, Jesus." She cried out the words at the top of her voice, her throat cracking with tense emotion. Shaking her head, she started crying again.

"Get on your feet."

"Oh, I can't." She continued to cry.

Dropping the wet sheet on the floor, he put his arms under hers and pulled her off the floor.

She fought him, her panic growing with each sob. Pushing him back, she screamed, pounding on his chest. "How could this happen here at The Glades?" There was anger in her face now, anger at the loss of her home. "This is too beautiful to leave," she sobbed. "I can't. I just can't."

"Here, wrap yourself in this wet sheet. It will protect your clothing from catching fire."

Once again, she pushed him away. "No! No, no, no! This can't be happening."

Pulling back his hand, he gave her a hard slap on the face.

She was stunned. She stood motionless, unable to scream or cry. Placing her hand to her face, she spoke softly, "You slapped me."

He wrapped her in the wet sheet. "And I will be more than happy to apologize for it when I get you safely outside."

With that, he scooped her up in his arms. The woman was heavier than he had first thought, and he'd never imagined himself capable at this age of doing anything that vaguely resembled what he was about to do, but his heart was pumping wildly, the blood coursing through his veins.

Placing her arms around his neck, she hung limply in his arms. He moved around the bed and pushed the door open with his foot.

Flames had erupted into the kitchen, the roar of the fire in the dining room pouring smoke into the spacious room. The walls closest to them were a sheet of flame. They scorched his face as he hurried beside them to the tiled walkway that wound around the tables and counters.

He held his breath and walked hurriedly, as much for the weight he was carrying as the flame itself. Reaching the French door, he kicked at the glass panes.

"Oh my dear," Mamie shouted. "Robert brought that door back from Paris, France."

Dr. Page coughed. "That can't be helped," he spat out the words between hacking coughs.

Raising his foot, he continued kicking, shattering the glass and splintering the frame of the door.

The flames behind them were growing. He heard the blast of the fire as it fully erupted into the kitchen. He looked behind them and saw the wall of flame as it raced into the room. There was no time left.

"Cover your eyes," he yelled.

Backing up slightly, he ran for the door. It exploded with the mass of their two bodies, and he spilled the woman onto the grass outside, collapsing beside her. Getting to his knees, he helped her to sit up.

"Move!" he yelled. "We've got to move away from this house and right now!"

He held her tightly around the waist, pulling her toward him in a semiembrace. The two of them stumbled away from the house and into the vegetable garden. The soil was cool, mashing itself under their feet as they plodded on. Behind them, the glow of the blazing house painted their backsides and coated them with hot air, rushing out after them.

Moving into the fruit trees, the two of them fell into a heap together, Dr. Page gasping and coughing. He began to wretch, crawling away on all fours.

Mamie, on her hands and knees, was soon beside him. "Are you all right?"

He sputtered out the words. "I'm alive, barely."

She put her arm around him. "And you saved my life, Doctor." She turned and looked back at the blazing house. "If you hadn't been so brave, I'd be in there right this moment."

She placed her other arm around him, pulling him tightly toward her. "I knew from the moment I set my eyes on you, Doctor, that you were that kind of man, the kind of man women only seem to dream of."

William pulled back suddenly. "Madam, I'm not that kind of man." He shook his head. "I'm quite ordinary, I can assure you."

She ran her fingers over his face and gray mustache. "You are a wonderful man, Doctor."

"Men are prone to be disappointments, I'm afraid, madam."

"Oh no," she shook her head "they are wonderful."

William turned and sat upright. "Miss Mamie, I fear I have some bad news for you, shocking news."

CHAPTER 33

MANNY SPUN THE WHEEL, sending the boat through the fog and into the deeper part of the channel. The fog hung low, caressing the black water. Tonight Manny was grateful for the fog. They would be able to pass the wounded steamer and not be seen. The small, clattering engine would be heard, but they'd be able to slip by the *Delta King* like a ghost in the night. He preferred it that way. The men still on board the steamer would be convenient targets, just waiting for the army to arrive in the morning. The wagons would never arrive in time, and he knew it. Those men had been loyal to him, and now he was passing them by with the bulk of the gold, and since Princeton was now gone, there would be no one left to call him to task.

He watched Blevins and the woman. He smiled as he saw her pull away from him. Something in him took great satisfaction in anyone that wouldn't be swayed by the man's wealth and power. Very few men had ever crossed him and lived, and now this woman was doing just that. And from what he already knew of her, it was a frame of mind that she was bound to continue.

Blevins took the woman's rebuff with stoic silence. He stood erect, staring straight ahead into the dark fog. Finding that his hands around the woman's waist was an unwelcome overture, he clasped them firmly behind his back.

Manny cleared his throat. "Mr. Blevins, we sure could use you to throw some of that cordwood into the boiler. I'd let you steer while I did it, but this here channel can be plenty tricky, and we're pretty low at the waterline."

It gave Manny great delight to force the man to face the prospect of honest work. He could see right away by the way Blevins turned and stared at him that it was a disagreeable prospect. He could see the sense of it, though, and Manny knew he wouldn't make the lady work.

Blevins tugged slightly at the sleeves of his tailored jacket and moved quietly to the face of the flaming boiler. He opened the door to the fire.

"We just have to keep the steam up," Manny said, trying to break the tension in the man's eyes.

"This is something I have never gotten used to," Blevins growled.

"What's that, Mr. Blevins?" Manny lied to try to cover the man's obvious embarrassment.

"Being outnumbered and chased. A man gets himself quite accustomed to having the upper hand."

Manny could see that he'd underestimated the depth of Blevins's discouragement. The man's plans had been sabotaged by two little boys. His house had been burned to the ground. His men were staked out like sacrificial goats and would no doubt give out his identity upon capture. His chief henchman had been killed before his eyes, and right now he had to suffer a woman's disinterest and the prospect of labor. For the first time in quite some time Manny found that he was quite indispensable.

"Well, you just leave everything to me," Manny crowed. "I'll see you get this here stuff safe on some outbound ship. I know a few of the captains, and if'n we can get ourselves into that mess that's tied up at the docks, you can make it more than worth their while to take you any such place you want to go."

Blevins tossed a piece of wood into the fire. "Perhaps I've underestimated you, Manny. You may prove yourself very valuable."

Manny beamed, a big grin crossing his face. "How's that?"

"I don't think I'd look forward to sailing with all this gold on board a ship where I knew no one. This gold would tempt St. Peter himself, and I'm going to need a man with me I can trust."

"I think Colonel Princeton lost some of that faith in old Manny here."

Blevins threw another piece of wood into the flames. "Maybe so." He looked back at Mary. "But I can see where you'd view killing Mary here and her uncle as a terrible waste. Under the circumstances, had I been you, I might have done the same thing."

Manny swung the wheel. "Somehow, Mr. Blevins, you don't strike me as the sentimental sort."

"Normally I'm not, but where beauty is concerned"—he looked back at Mary—"I can become quite poignant."

Manny snickered. "I can see what yer sayin', whatever it is that means."

"I would make it quite worth your time and trouble, Manny, make you richer than you've ever dreamed."

"Oh, I dream about quite a bit."

"You'd receive the colonel's share. You'd have it coming."

"And just what would that be?"

"I was going to pay him thirty percent, and of that figure, he was to divide the spoils with you men. If you can assist me to some neutral country where I can deposit this in a bank, I'll see that you get twenty-five percent, free and clear."

Manny surveyed the boxes of gold. He'd have been quite happy with just one of them, but the prospects of ten boxes filled with gold ingots sent his blood racing. "You got yerself a man," he said. "What I couldn't do with all that, I wouldn't know. I'm a man of pretty puny tastes."

"Then, your share of the take will keep you very happy for a very long time."

Mary had overheard the conversation between the two men. She turned and glared at them. "You men sicken me. Even if you managed to get away with all this, it would be dry to the taste. Ill-gotten gain brings nothing but hollowness to the soul."

"My dear," Blevins replied, "all that money will provide a lifetime of easy forgetfulness. When a man rises to a great posture of wealth in this world, he soon lays aside any thought concerning the means that placed him in that position."

She shook her head. "That's where you're wrong. This short lifespan of ours is followed by a long eternity. In the final accounting, a man is measured by what he's given away, never by how much he's managed to acquire."

"You're a foolish child," Blevins said. "A foolish but beautiful child. You just keep that Sunday school teacher mentality to your own head and allow the men in your life to consider how to keep you comfortably accommodated. This innocence of yours makes you all the more attractive."

"I can assure you, being attractive to you is the last notion I have in my mind." Then she looked at Manny. "And I would have expected more of you. You displayed your humanity when you showed mercy to my uncle and me. I thought it fit you well."

Manny scratched his chin. "Yep, and I reckon I'm showing my humanity too by wantin' what all that money can give." He laughed. "I s'pose when all is said and done, I is just a pirate at heart."

"Good man!" Blevins roared.

Manny pointed toward the far side of the river. He lowered his voice. "There's a strange launch yonder. Might be the same one that carted our Mr. Cobb close to your place."

"We don't want any shooting," Blevins said. "Not now."

Manny edged the small craft nearer the shore. The small white boat on the opposite side of the river was quiet. He could barely make out the outline of two men on board. Manny knew that with the heavy load on their boat, it wouldn't take the other small craft long to catch up to them if they wanted to.

Moments after they rounded the bend, the small craft had the *Delta King* in sight. The paddles had stopped their fruitless churning, and now the only sound on the river was the sputtering noise of their own launch.

"You folks, keep yer heads down. It'd be a plum shame to get shot by them fellers of ours on the *King*."

\+ \+ \+ \+ \+

Zac and the doctor had managed to mount the horses Hattie had gotten from the stables, but Mamie refused to ride. She sat with her head in her hands beside the landing in front of the grotto. "I can't go," she said. "I can't leave The Glades now."

"My dear, there's nothing left for you here," William responded.

"It's all I have left on this earth." She continued to cry.

William knelt beside her and placed his arm around her. "My dear, you must understand, I have no desire to leave you here alone, certainly not in your upset condition. But my niece has been kidnapped. I simply cannot allow other men to take my responsibility while I remain here with you."

Zac and Hattie mounted their horses. It was plain to see that they were both anxious to take up the chase. Hattie spun her hand forward in Zac's direction, circling it around and around, as if to say, "Let's get on with it."

Zac spoke up. "The army will more than likely be here come morning. I'm not sure how much more you can do here, and I ain't rightly sure how much help you'd be to us, apart from treatin' wounds. You'll have to make up your own mind, but be mighty quick about it. Every minute we spend here puts those folks farther downriver."

"You're right, of course," Dr. Page said, looking up at Zac.

Hattie shook her head. It had always been hard for her to contain a single thought in her head, unless she had her fingers wrapped around a hand of poker. Then she could be as quiet as a crypt. She just had to have the right incentive. "Carn sarn it, men all the time fuss over womenfolk like they'ze gonna break with the slightest breeze. Jest leave her be. Come mornin' she'll figure out things by her ownself."

"I feel terrible about doing this," Dr. Page said, "but with the prospects of gunfire, these people may need my services."

Mamie cleared her mind momentarily. "Go ahead, Doctor." She reached out and took his hand. Her lips trembled. "Just don't forget me here."

Dr. Page patted her hand and, taking it from his arm, dropped it in her lap. He then mounted his horse. "I won't, madam, and I can promise you that as a doctor it's my duty to treat him like he were my own."

They tugged on their reins and in moments were bounding down the foggy road. A short while later they passed the bound pirates. The men seemed to wiggle helplessly as the horses raced by them, their gagged faces contorted in muffled protest.

Inside of an hour, Zac raised his hand to slow the other two down. "We're gettin' close," he said. "I can see the lights of the steamer up ahead. We better not let the sound of these horses spook what's left of them pirates."

They had just begun to walk the horses when Zac spotted the launch. He signaled the other two, and they got down.

They slapped the rumps of the three horses, and the animals bounded back in the direction of the stables. The three of them pushed their way through the brush, and Zac identified them before walking up on the boat. "Yo!" he said. "It's us. Don't shoot."

Pushing past the last of the brambles, he saw Grubb and Van Tuyl lower their weapons. "We heard the horses," Grubb said. "We figured you for more of them thieves."

"No, but look who I found."

Hattie stepped out and wiped her pricker-infested hands over her dress. "You boys pick about the worst place to hold up in. 'Course a month from now, you'd get to fight off skeeters."

Zac motioned toward William. "This here is Dr. Page. He and his niece were being held prisoner."

"Pleasure to meet you, Doctor," Van Tuyl said.

"Likewise," Grubb added.

"Did you boys see a launch go by in the last few minutes?" Zac asked.

"Just a few minutes ago," Grubb responded. "Frankly, we weren't quite sure whose side they were on. There were a few shots, though, when it went past the *Delta King* up there."

"It would be something if those boys up there shot their own boss. That boat has the bulk of the gold shipment and the man that planned and financed this operation."

"Well, I'll be," Van Tuyl added. "Why you figure they didn't identify themselves?"

Zac looked up the foggy river. "I'd say they were making a run for it. Their plans have already gone to blazes, and they'd just as soon leave those men there to keep the army busy and off their trail for a day or two."

"Guess it's up to us, then," Grubb said.

"Guess so," Zac added.

Hattie rubbed her hands together. "That be just the way I like it. I sure wouldn't have no bunch of Yankee soldiers doin' my shootin' fer me."

Zac gave her a long, fixed stare. "I think it might be best if we pole our way across the river first to tell Jenny and the boys what we're up to," Zac said, "and then pole our way past the steamer. In the fog they might not see us, and that's just the way I'd like to keep it until we get past them people."

"We best get on with it, then," Hattie croaked.

"I think you should stay with Jenny and the boys when we do get over there," Zac said. "It wouldn't do to have my mother's sister catch a slug trying to help me do my job. Besides, we have enough guns to get the job done, and we'll make better time with less weight."

Hattie drew herself up to her full five-foot height. She scowled and pointed her bony finger directly at Zac. "Boy, I washed that bottom of yours when you was a baby, and I can paddle it just as well now. I go my own way, same as always, and no man ever thought to say otherwise. Now you 'spect to be in any shape to face them people you best not cross old Hat."

Zac smiled. "All right. I don't fight with womenfolk, least of all you, Hat."

"The boat that passed us wasn't making very good time," Van Tuyl said.

"They've got a heavy load," Zac responded. "We've got time to do what we've got to do and still catch them by the time they get to the bay."

"This fog's gonna make it tough," Grubb offered. "We best try to overtake them while they're still on the river."

A short time later, they pushed the launch quietly toward the opposite bank of the river. Jenny stood on the riverbank with the two boys. Zac stepped off the boat and dragged it close to the shore, grounding it in the mud. Turning around, he took Jenny in his arms. "I'm afraid our work isn't quite done with." Zac informed her of the situation and introduced her to the doctor. "This fog is going to make our job a little iffy."

"Why don't you take me with you," Jack said. "I knows them waters real well."

"That's why we have the pilot here, son. I think I'd feel a whole lot better with you three back here, waiting on the army. Then I wouldn't have to worry about you getting shot."

"You'd do better with me there," Jack said. He looked sheepishly at Jenny and Skip. "I'ze kinda bored here, just feel like I ain't in the action. I s'pose I don't do too well a waitin' 'round fer nothin'."

Zac put his hand on the boy's head. "You do seem to be a man of action, at that."

The boy beamed while Skip frowned.

"And I'm sure you'd handle yourself pretty well, but you'd best stay here. It'll give me one less thing to worry on."

Zac pointed over to Grubb. "You best put that damper down. I wouldn't want any sparks when we pass the *King*. They might see us, as it is, the boat being white, but it wouldn't pay to tip our hand if we don't have to."

Jenny walked with him to the launch, gripping his arm tightly.

"Don't go to worrying about me," he said. "I think you've got your hands full with these boys. We'll get a boat with replacement parts and be back here in a day or so. I left you a tarp to set up a tent with and some supplies from the launch."

"We'll be fine. I just want you to keep your head down."

He kissed her gently.

Moments later the men were poling the boat on the far side of the river, away from the *Delta King*. The big boat's lights shone brightly through the fog, twinkling eyes of hundreds of lamps glimmering through the mist. They could see the outline of several men as they moved on the aft deck of the boat, shifting cargo to make it easier to unload.

The current of the river moved slowly, ebbing against the deck of the small boat and lapping against its sides. Zac and Van Tuyl pushed the poles steadily, digging into the mud in the shallow side of the river and walking with great effort toward its stern. Zac had chosen the side closest to the *Delta King* on purpose. He watched the men moving cargo very carefully as he pushed on his pole.

Zac had hoped the thing would still be trying to pull itself off the muddy riverbank. The splashing of the paddles made an awful noise, one that could have gone a long way to concealing any sound they might make. The fact that it was now silent and had given up the effort made him wary. Any sound they might make would carry well over the water.

A crane flapped its wings, moving slowly through the fog and along the top of the water. The big bird was bound to attract the attention of any man who happened to be watching even casually, and its sudden appearance sent a shock wave up Zac's spine. He pushed harder on the pole. They were directly abreast of the *Delta King* now. A few more minutes and they would be past the thing.

Suddenly, Hattie struggled and growled at the rear of the boat. Zac set down his pole and, looking off at the silent steamer, made his way toward her. From the water at the stern of the small boat she was wrestling something onto the deck. It was Jack. The small boy struggled, kicking his feet as the old woman hauled him aboard.

Zac looked off at the steamer. The men on the deck were shouting and scrambling now. More than likely they were dropping their cargo and hunting for their rifles. He barked softly at Van Tuyl and Grubb. "You better get that thing fired up now. We gotta get on outta here and real quick like."

CHAPTER 34

+ + + + + + +

WITHOUT THE MEN PUSHING on the poles, the boat began to drift in the current. Van Tuyl threw open the door to the boiler and stirred the coals with his knife. He tossed in several small pieces of kindling, igniting a small blaze. "It's going to take a bit of coaxing here," he snapped.

Zac pushed Hattie and the boy into the bottom of the boat. He grabbed the military-style rifle and slid the bolt into place.

From the deck of the *Delta King*, several men spread themselves out and began to fire. The flashes of the guns were followed by splashes near the small boat as the bullets corkscrewed their way into the murky water.

"They'll get out of range before long," Grubb shouted.

The next shot landed on the side of the boiler with a clanging sound that carried out over the water.

Zac sighted down the barrel of the long rifle. It was a cumbersome thing, more suited for an infantryman, but Zac was used to it, and the weapon would shoot straight and true, of that Zac was sure. It also had better range than the firearms being fired from the deck of the *Delta King*. He watched the flashes of the guns on deck. A well-placed shot would do a lot to keep the heads of the shooters down. He carefully squeezed the trigger, and the big gun exploded and bucked in his hands. He saw a man pitch forward and several men nearby scramble for cover.

Zac shouted in Van Tuyl's direction. "Better build up that steam. When I shoot, you can jump up there and toss some more of that wood in."

Several more shots were fired from the deck of the big steamer, and Zac followed them with two well-placed shots. The captain jumped for the door to the boiler and, throwing several pieces of the clean-burning wood into the blaze, slammed the door shut, hunkering down behind it.

Grubb did his best to steer from his knees. His head was still above the side of the boat and any hit would be deadly, but he was a small target indeed. That fact was of little comfort. Stray shots found their mark all the time.

The groups continued to exchange shots as those on the small boat watched the little boiler build up steam. Van Tuyl slowly turned the screws on the thing, and they listened to the sputtering cough of the small engine as it began to slowly sputter to life. They were making a little headway now, too slow for any sense of relief, but the little boat was coming to life once again. The current of the river moved it slowly downstream, and the weak but new life in the engine kept it in the shallows of the far riverbank.

The sputter of gunfire kept on coming from the *Delta King*, sending several shots glancing off the engine and dispatching sickening thuds into the wooden hull of the small boat. The thick fog continued to roll in between the combatants. Shots that landed at this distance would be a matter of sheer luck, but Zac dispatched several more rounds into the deck of the steamer.

After several minutes, the small boat had drifted out of range. Zac stood up to inspect the damage.

"We'll have to wrap one of these pipes," Van Tuyl shouted. "It'll slow us down a mite, I'm afraid. We won't be able to keep a full head of steam."

"Did we all come out of it okay?" Zac asked.

The doctor tore a leg on his trousers. "I'm afraid I didn't. One of the rounds seems to have penetrated my calf, and I don't have my instruments with me."

Zac made his way over to the shaking man. "Here, Doc, you just lie down. The more moving around you do, the more you're gonna bleed."

The doctor nodded and stretched himself out on the bottom of the boat.

Zac inspected the wound. He lifted the man's leg and turned it slightly. "I think you're lucky, Doc. Seems the bullet passed through."

Dr. Page unbuckled his belt. "Wrap this tight," he said. "I'm afraid I don't have that much blood to lose."

He gulped as Zac wrapped the belt around his leg tightly.

"I guess I won't be as much help to you men as I had planned," Page said. "You'll be spending your time keeping me alive."

He was beginning to shiver as Zac took off his coat and, kneeling beside him, laid it on top of the man. "You just rest easy, Doctor. We'll all make it through this."

Zac got to his feet. He looked at Grubb. "We best find us a house somewhere that we can get some bandages for the doctor here. I think I'd feel better if there was something warm in him too."

"Might be easier said than done, and we'll lose some time, to boot."

"Better to lose time than him."

Zac looked back to the stern of the boat where Jack continued to shiver in fear in Hattie's arms. Zac didn't have to say a word. The damage had been done, and Jack knew it full well.

"I'm sorry," the boy said. "I just thought maybe I might be able to help."

"Boy, obeying what you're told to do is the best help you can give any man."

"I'd say we'd be best served by throwing him overboard right here and now," Van Tuyl said. "The kid's been a Jonah ever since he came aboard the *Delta King*."

"No." Zac shook his head. "We'll leave him be." He stepped over to where he towered over the boy. "You just better make sure you make less noise than the sound of the water. Am I making myself understood?"

"Yes, sir," Jack said.

+ + + + +

The launch with the gold chugged down the dark river with Manny steering it past several large snags. The rattle of the little engine brought scant comfort. They had managed to make it into the main part of the river that flowed into the bay without being overtaken or shot. Still, the engine was small and the boat had never been designed to carry the load it was bearing up under.

Hours passed, and the silence of the foggy river was beginning to get on all of their nerves. The dull gray of the new day brought no brightness and even less visibility than the night had, with the billowing fog rolling in from the bay.

They were in the main channel now, and the fog shrouded much of the houses high on the banks of the river. The river had widened considerably, and had Manny not chosen to keep the launch close to the south bank, they wouldn't have been able to see either shoreline.

Several gulls took their turns along the surface of the water, moving their wings ever so slowly and scanning the surface of the water with lifeless, black eyes. The birds sailed out of the fog, as surprised to see the little boat as anyone. Rippling their wings, they curved off into the fog in the direction of the riverbank that no one could see.

The smell of the bay's salty brine was stronger now, a heavy thick scent that smelled of faraway places and pounding surf.

Manny watched carefully as Blevins continued to cast his eyes toward Mary. The man had been watching her for quite some time, yet she remained as mindless to him as a stone statue in the park. It had been plain to Manny that there would never be a return of romantic interest on her part for the man. Some women might respond to power and great wealth, but Manny knew enough about this woman to know that she was not one of them.

It worried him, though. Blevins was not a man to be easily crossed. No wasn't a word he settled easily to. In some ways he was like a child who had been doted on by his mother, too little of brain to understand there were other things to ask for and too proud to quit crying for the thing it was he wanted.

What worried Manny most was what the man would do once he found out the girl couldn't be bullied and wouldn't be bought. It might be days before they could sail, and Blevins would never let her walk free.

Blevins moved closer to her. Seeing him, the girl stepped quickly around the man. Without saying a word, she moved back toward Manny, who was steering the boat from the small stern wheel.

"You gettin' chilled?" Manny asked.

She shook her head, refusing to speak.

She had a cold resolve in her gaze that would have sent shivers up the spine of a man who crossed her. It was not a blank stare, however. He wished it had been. The look was one that was filled with thoughts, silent and unspoken emotions, feelings of cold rage that came from deep within and bubbled beneath the surface like a queer combination of molten lava lapping itself around blocks of solid ice.

Her lips were screwed shut, and her beautiful cheeks were hardened. Manny could have sworn that a man could have struck a match on one of her cheeks, if he had a mind to. She faced toward the rear of the boat, staring right past Manny and into the silver fog.

There was nothing there. Still, it seemed to be just what she wanted to see at the moment, nothing.

"We'll be in San Francisco tonight, ma'am," Manny said. "We got the rest of the day on this here big part of the river, then we ought to get onto the bay after dark."

She said nothing. Her eyes didn't even blink in response to the hearing of the words.

"Whatcha thinkin' on, missy?"

"I'm not thinking about a thing. I'm just praying."

It comforted him a mite that words had crossed her lips, even though he didn't much like or understand what he heard. "I wouldn't worry much, if'n I was you."

"I'm not the least worried. I'm very prepared."

Manny knew she had to guess as much about Blevins's character as he knew. She had to be thinking that this was to be her last day, and she was slipping into some unknown quiet resolve over the matter. The notion saddened him.

"You don't need to be prepared for anything, missy."

She turned her eyes and looked directly at him. "You know better than that. I'm not going with that man."

Manny lowered his voice. "I know. Still, you don't have to worry."

"I told you, I'm not worried. Some see misfortune as something that falls upon them unawares, an unwelcome surprise. My life has always been in God's hands, however. He's been shaping and preparing me throughout my entire existence. If this is what I've been fashioned for, I will accept it just as I've taken everything else from His hand, like a gift."

Manny squinted. This was a woman of fight, not someone who would fall down and take what came her way without a struggle. It was a mystery.

"You ain't tellin' me there's a quit in you, are you?" He lowered his voice and spoke softly. Blevins could tell they were talking, but Manny didn't think he could hear their words.

"There is no quit in me." She said the words slowly and with a crisp, sharp twang to the word "quit." "I am prepared to do what I must. But there will never be a disappointment either, no matter what may happen."

Manny breathed out a sigh. He admired this young woman's spirit. There was something about her, her and her uncle, that carried a strange view of life to everything they thought. Neither one of them wanted to die, that much had been clear. It was just as apparent, however, that neither of them was willing to compromise one iota of their values in order to take one more breath on this earth. Whatever it was that these people carried on the inside was something that was far more valuable than life itself.

Mary took a seat beside Manny as Blevins opened the door to the boiler and continued to feed the blaze. It would be a long and silent trip to San Francisco. Unheard words would be spoken, words that Manny didn't begin to understand.

The hours crawled by, and darkness began to descend behind the fog. The sky would be black shortly. Whatever was going to happen to the men on the *Delta King* had no doubt already occurred. It made Manny's mind reach out to the men he had known for years, the men he and Blevins had passed by in order to find their own personal safety. He didn't like the feeling it gave him. He could just as well have been one of them. If Princeton had been able to work his plan, he'd already be dead. This day had been just like the woman had said, a gift.

As they rounded the eddy into the bay, the wind picked up. This was the spot known to sailors as the golden triangle, the place between the islands on the bay where the wind blew out and the tides rolled in. It was a tricky spot, even for a large boat with a light load.

He hollered at Blevins, "Give me lots of fire. We're gonna skirt 'round close to Oakland and Alameda afore we head across. We'll be away from them incomin' tides thataway."

Blevins threw open the door and tossed in piece after piece of the dwindling wood supply. He groaned with each new piece of the wood and swore.

The blackness of the bay and the sudden swells of the seas rocked the little boat back and forth. Manny zigzagged through the rolling tides, first heading into them and breaking the low waves over the bow, then swinging the boat around and surfing on them as the seas pushed the stern of the small craft. Getting across the bay would be tricky at best.

+ + + + +

On the chase boat, Jack edged his way up to Grubb. "You figure them to head straight for 'Frisco?"

"Not unless they're crazy," Grubb murmured.

"Then they'll swing round to Alameda and go 'cross thataway."

"If they've got half a brain they will."

The kid's eyes brightened. He rubbed his hands together from the cold wind on the bay. "Then that be the place I know best. I know all them bars out there and which way these here waves breaks over 'em."

He listened to the waves break on the island in front of them. "You best swing off northwest, then. This here tide'll be pushin' us along."

Grubb stared down at the boy. It would be hard to catch these people in the fog, but he knew the boy was right. He swung the wheel over without explanation.

"Where are we going now?" Zac asked.

"The kid here's right," Grubb responded. "They won't try to take that thing straight across. They'll go on to Alameda and make their way across that way. They try to buck this tide and they'll be on the bottom pretty quick like."

Jack tried hard not to smile, maintaining a sober face and looking off at the twinkling lights of Oakland that glimmered through the fog. "I know this here place," he said.

Zac opened the door to the boiler and threw more wood inside.

It was some time later when they heard the sound of the little boat's engine ahead of them. It was a gentle chug, but unmistakable.

"You hear that?" Van Tuyl asked.

Zac nodded and picked up the rifle. He pulled the bolt back, then slid a round into place.

They continued to shadow the distant sound of the little engine, Zac and the captain straining to peer through the dark fog in order to pick up even the faintest outline of the craft. They knew they were on the bay side of the sound now, and they wanted to keep it just that way. Whoever was guiding the little boat they were trailing was working hard to keep to the shallow side of the bar away from the incoming swells.

The waves broke gently at first on the side of their boat, but as they cleared the small island, the swells grew larger, rocking them back and forth.

Van Tuyl held on to the wrapped pipe, fighting the motion. "Being as top heavy as they are, they couldn't fight this here stuff," he said.

"I don't reckon so," Grubb responded as he fought to keep the wheel steady.

"Let's swing in a mite closer," Jack said. "Them waves are gonna give us a little push and afore long that there tide's gonna be comin' right out at us. Be best to pick up some distance on 'em whilst it be behind us."

Grubb froze at the wheel and then looked back, first at Zac, then at Van Tuyl.

Zac was silent, but Van Tuyl grumbled and hung on to the wrapped pipe. "Kid's right, much as I hate to own up to it," Zac murmured. "I sure hate being beat on by these here waves, to boot. If I had my druthers, I'd sure like them at my backside."

Without further discussion, Grubb swung the wheel and headed the craft toward the lights of Oakland. The seas lifted the stern of the boat like an unseen hand, pushing it toward the glowing fog that was the Oakland harbor. They were heading straight into the offshore breeze, and it slapped their faces with spray.

Zac hunkered down and scooted toward the doctor. He loosened the tourniquet slightly and felt the man's cold cheeks. The quick stop they had made at a house near Antioch for bandages, ointment, and some hot soup had done them all some good, especially Dr. Page. He handed a flask of brandy they had purchased to the man. "You'd best take a little of this."

The old man's hand shook as he took hold of the metal container. He held it to his lips. "I felt a lot better after that soup this afternoon. I think I'll be all right."

"You better be. Having you alive and kicking will go a long way to cheering up that niece of yours once we get her back."

The old man smiled and nodded. That thought alone seemed to bolster his spirits.

"I see 'em," Jack said. He pointed off toward the bow.

Through the fog they could see the faint outline of the small boat. One of the men inside had opened the boiler, and the glow of the light twinkled through the fog.

"I'll fire a shot across their bow," Zac said. "It might drive them in."

"This is gettin' pretty close," Jack said.

"Close to what?" Van Tuyl asked.

"Close to them oyster beds I know about." He grinned. "I know these here waters like I was born in 'em. You just listen for the sound of the bell. Riley's got a bell buoy that marks the start of his beds. You shoot and make 'em turn in, and we'll be on it in no time."

Zac took careful aim. He didn't want to take any chance of hitting someone, for fear of hitting the girl by mistake. He just wanted to make sure they knew he had a long gun. If he was right, they had only pistols, including his.

The sound of the shot echoed across the waters.

Once again, the boiler in the distance opened. It was all too obvious that the men on the little boat wanted as much steam as they could make. They listened to the small craft as it chugged.

Minutes later, they heard the sharp ring of the bell.

Jack pointed off the bow, excitedly. "See, like I told you, that's Riley's beds over yonder."

Soon, they saw the faint light of an approaching boat. The phantomlike skiff was a great distance off, but they could see a lantern on it as it swung in the wind and soon after heard the shouts of men on board.

Jack clapped his hands. "This is the first time I ever been glad to see that old buzzard. Them folks tangle with Riley and they'ze gonna be dead sure 'nuff. He got hisself a four-gauge shotgun mounted on that boat of his."

"He can't outrun them," Grubb said, "not with oars and a skiff."

Jack shook his head and smiled. "Nah, but that's why he'll shoot quick. He figures this here part of the ocean belongs to him and he ain't gonna take no time to argue over the matter."

Moments later, they heard the distinctive boom of the shotgun. The noise rattled out over the surface of the water. In rapid succession it was followed by several shots from small arms, most likely from Blevins's launch, and then just as quickly by several more eruptions from the massive mini-cannon. The final blast sent a shower of sparks from the boiler of the launch. They could see the fireworks fly and the blaze glow from new holes in the steam engine up ahead.

They watched the boat begin to silently spin around in the fog as the skiff with the lantern drew closer to it.

Zac cupped his hands to his mouth. "Hello the boat! This is Zac Cobb with Wells Fargo. Those men are fugitives from justice."

A few moments of muffled talk passed before they heard a response. "Them folks is on our beds."

Grubb continued propelling the boat in the direction of the two other craft. Zac raised his hands once again to yell. "They have a stolen Wells Fargo shipment on board that boat."

Drawing closer, they could see several men climbing aboard the suddenly powerless steamer. Steam was hissing from the small engine and the men were stooping into the bottom of the boat, making a close inspection of the cargo.

"Ask if Mary's all right," Dr. Page croaked.

Zac held his hands to his mouth. "Is the woman all right?"

A moment or two passed before the words rang out. "We got one dead, one badly shot up, but the woman's okay."

"Thank you, Lord," Dr. Page sighed.

CHAPTER 35

+ + + + + + +

MOMENTS LATER, ZAC'S small boat pulled up alongside the other two. Zac could see the man who was obviously in charge, a stout man with flaming red hair and beard.

Jack pulled on his sleeve. "That's Riley. He's got wool in his teeth that won't quit. He's the one that kilt Robbie."

Thc large man with the flaming beard wore a checkered coat, the black collar turned up against his stubby neck.

Zac lowered the rifle. Digging into his pocket, he produced a gleaming brass badge that read "Wells Fargo—Special Agent." He held it up. "I work for Wells Fargo," he said.

"Hmph," the man grunted in obvious disapproval. "I ain't be a carin' who you says you is. These here are my oyster beds," he roared. "Anyone or anything that floats on it belongs to me, and I'm claiming the rights of salvage."

Zac looked aside at Van Tuyl and Grubb. "You better be ready. We may have traded one batch of pirates for another." Zac set down the rifle and held up the badge. "I'm coming aboard." With that, he stepped onto the gold-laden launch.

Blevins lay on the bottom of the boat, his eyes open in death like a fish just pulled up from the sea. Manny lay doubled up beside him, groaning and clutching his belly.

Mary knelt beside Manny and spoke softly into his ear. "I'm praying for you. You may have been a thief, but you always treated me with respect." She stroked his hair as he groaned.

Zac touched her on the shoulder. "I have your uncle on board. He's hurt, but he'll be mighty glad to see you."

She jumped to her feet, but Zac held her back. He looked at Riley. "Seems to me you're gonna be hard-pressed with a claim on this vessel."

"How so?"

"Well, there's people you've shot and killed aboard this boat, along with this woman. There's no way it's abandoned. You try to make a claim on it and you'll be guilty of piracy. That seems to be a hanging offense from where I see it."

The two men on board the boat with the big man began to murmur, but Riley's flashing green eyes quieted them down.

Zac stepped toward the redhead, still showing the badge. "And besides that, I've already identified myself as an agent for Wells Fargo, and this is Wells Fargo property." He clamped the badge case shut and dropped it back into his pocket.

Riley glared at him. "And these here are my waters." He pointed in Zac's direction, motioning with the pistol he brandished. "And from where I stand, you don't look armed enough to back up them words of yours."

"I'm armed with the law, and that's aplenty." Zac stepped closer to the man.

"Not on my water, it ain't. Out here I'm the law. If I was to tell these here men of mine to shoot you all down, nobody would even find yer bodies. The crabs would be feedin' on you same as this man here."

Zac casually looked at the men with the Irish redhead. They were smiling. Obviously they had seen the big man operate before, and their confidence was unmistakable. Zac liked that. Overconfident men were the best kind to face.

Zac shrugged his shoulders and reached up behind his head. Without warning, he sprung into action. Taking a quick step toward the big man, he pulled the sharp knife out from the sheath between his shoulder blades. His arm shot out, wrapping itself around Riley's neck, and as he spun him around he placed the sharp blade under the Irishman's Adam's apple. "You were saying about crabs?"

Riley grew stiff, too afraid to move.

"Now, why don't you just toss that shooter of yours into that water, since this ocean belongs to you anyway."

The big man slowly complied.

"Good. Maybe you are smart, after all. Perhaps you should tell your men to do the same. We wouldn't want an accident, now, would we?"

The big Irishman trembled. Zac pushed the keen edge of the

blade into his pudgy flesh, ever so softly. "You best do as he says, boys."

One by one, the men tossed their pistols into the brine.

"Fine," Zac said. "Now that deck gun of yours. Break it down, and throw it overboard."

The man who had remained on the skiff did exactly as he was told. The big gun hit the water with a splash.

"All right," Zac said, "do you see any of your oysters on this boat?"

"No." Riley croaked out the word in a barely audible tone.

"I didn't hear you."

"I said no. There ain't none of my oysters here."

"Fine." Zac eased up on the knife slightly. "Then, I'd say you best get back to where you come from, them men of yours first."

Riley motioned to the men, who climbed back onto their boat.

Zac spun the big man around, facing him to the water and, with a boot to his backside, pushed him into the bay.

They all watched as Riley struggled in the cold brine.

Zac put the knife back into its place, leaned over the side of the boat, and spoke slow and deliberately. "This is your ocean. You enjoy it."

\+ \+ \+ \+ \+

Zac made sure that what had been taken from the shipment was safely stored in the vault at the San Francisco Wells Fargo office before he set about to return to the *Delta King* with the repair boat. Dennis Grubb and the captain had made all the necessary arrangements, and Zac stopped by to say his good-byes to both the doctor and his niece at the man's hospital bedside before he started the boat ride back up the river.

Arriving back at Walnut Grove, Zac learned that the army had indeed made short work of the remaining pirates and rounded up the rest of the gold bullion found in the shadowy ruins of the former mansion. Word had already been passed to the men at the office as to the safety of the gold. The Sacramento River was once again safe for transporting cargo.

It took the men in the still-smoldering ruins of Walnut Grove two days to make the necessary repairs to the paddles, and Zac stood on the deck of the refitted *Delta King* with Jenny, Hattie, and the boys as it finally pulled away to finish the voyage to San Francisco.

What had been left of the shipment of gold was safely aboard, and Mamie was secluded in her stateroom. The lady was anxious to visit the doctor and give him some "pleasant nursing," as she put it.

It was a day of bright sunshine, a day when they could make some good time in river travel. What had been obscured by the fog for weeks on end was now bathed in the warm glow of the fresh and sparkling morning sunlight.

Zac put his arm around Jenny and held his violin case. She was a beautiful sight in the morning light, a new yellow dress and hair the color of roses and hay. "I think you boys should go and see how those new paddles work back there," he said. "We put into San Francisco tonight, but tomorrow we're going on to Oakland. We all have a funeral to attend."

"Fer Robbie?" Jack asked.

"Yes, for Robbie."

Jack beamed. "I sure do thank you, mister, I surely do. I think Robbie'd be sure-fire proud of bein' buried like regular folks." The boy dropped his head and shook it slightly. "I can't rightly say what his last name was fer a stone, though. Don't think he ever knew it his ownself."

"A man ought to have a last name," Zac said. "Gives one a sense of belonging. We could give him yours, Jack."

"Nah, don't think so. My last name ain't really mine no ways. Ain't quite sure what mine truly is. The feller my ma's livin' with now has a last name of London. I sorta took it on my ownself, but don't think it'd be right fer Robbie."

Skip put his hand on Zac's arm. "We could call him Cobb."

Jack beamed. "That would be mighty fine. I'm sure he'd like that sure 'nuff. Sounds kinda nice, 'Robbie Cobb.' Kinda has a strong sound to it, it do."

Hattie leaned over the rail and spit into the river. "Why not?" she growled. "Long as you ain't in the business a givin' birth to yer own young, you might just as well fill up the cemeteries with the Cobb name."

"Well, we'll take care of this first," he looked at Jenny, "and the other later."

Hattie wiped her mouth with the back of her hand. "You best

get on with it then, boy. Times a wastin' on yer good years, ya know."

Zac turned around and leaned back on the rail. "All right, enough about that. You boys go back and look at those paddles. You're responsible for them. You might as well see them work."

Skip pulled on Jack's sleeve, and the two boys raced around the deck toward the stern of the boat.

"It's a beautiful day, isn't it?" Jenny said.

"Yes, it is," Zac replied. He glared at Hattie. "It might just be a fine day for gamblin' too, don't you think, Hat?"

The old woman wiped her tobacco-stained hands on her dress and, narrowing her eyes, glowered at him. "Is you tryin' to get rid of me?"

"For a spell," Zac said, "that's exactly what I'm trying to do."

Hattie held up her hands, motioning them toward him. "All right, all right. Woman can't never figure you out no ways. One minute you'ze happy to have me so you don't haf to talk serious like to the lady, and the next you're shooin' me away like a horsefly." She leaned forward. "You just gots to make up that befuddled mind of yourn, boy."

"Well, Hat, that's exactly what I'm trying to do, if you'll let me."

Hattie backed up and spit once again into the river. Wiping her mouth, she grinned a tobacco-stained, toothy smile at Jenny. "All right, girly, he be yours to deal with now." She cocked her head slightly at the young woman. "But if he don't go to makin' an honest woman outta you, you tell old Hat here. I'll split his noggin 'tween the ears with the butt of my pistol."

Jenny smiled. "I don't think that will be necessary."

"Never can tell. Ever' man I ever had that and more had to be done to 'em."

"I don't doubt that in the least," Zac chuckled.

"Hmph." Hattie gave off a grunt, turned on her heels, and ambled her way toward the salon.

"I like her a lot," Jenny said. "There's a raw honesty to the woman that has the name Cobb written all over it."

"That's the Scottish Woodruff you're seeing, too mean to kill and too tough to go peacefully."

Jenny looked down at the rough and beaten violin case. "I much prefer to see you carrying that than I do a gun."

"I shouldn't wonder. In many ways I suppose I'm more suited to the violin. There's a gentleness to it that at times I feel like is trapped somewhere inside of me, aching to get out and be heard."

"I hear it, Zac." She put her hand on his arm. "At times I hear it when you would least suspect. I hear it when I've seen you sleeping, too tired to find a bed." She chuckled. "I see it all over your face when you light up that smelly pipe of yours, so pensive, so thoughtful. But I think I hear it most when you just look off at the horizon, trying to find a peace to your life that seems so far away."

He nodded and then looked deeply into her bluebonnet eyes. "Jenny, I think I feel what it is that I've been looking for mostly when I see you. I'm not very good with words, so I let my music speak the words my mouth doesn't seem to wrap itself around. That's why I brought the violin with me this morning. There's somethin' I'd like to say to you, and this seems to be the best way."

"I'd like to hear it," she said.

He unsnapped the violin case and took the cherry instrument out. Setting down the case, he pointed to a bench. "Why don't we sit over there. It might steady my hand on this here boat."

The two of them took seats on the brightly painted bench, and Zac held the violin to his neck, laying his chin on the polished surface. He drew the bow across the strings and twisted the pegs until he heard the proper tones.

Putting it down he said, "I'm gonna play something I heard some time ago in San Francisco. It made me think of you and your soft spirit the first time it came to my ears, and I haven't been able to shake it since. It's an intermezzo from Act III of Carmen. I hope you like it."

Raising the violin to his chin, he pulled the bow across the strings. The sweet melody rose from the soft wood, floating out over the passing water. There was a charm to the notes that spoke of soft sunlight on fields of flowers and the unmistakable sound of love at its tenderest moments.

Two birds flew beside the big boat. Seeming to listen to the music, they hung in the air, the currents of wind barely rippling the wings that held them aloft. They were two birds that flew as one, side by side, swooping down, only to rise together once again.

Zac continued to play the love song, his fingers expressing what his mind felt deep inside. They ran over the strings, pushing them down and holding them steady, summoning forth feelings of love.

He finished the melody and held the strings down as the last of the notes crept along the surface of the river.

Jenny once again put her hand on his tense arm. "That is you, darling, so strong and powerful but with a gentleness inside that I love."

Zac set down the violin and pushed it aside. "There's something I've been wanting to tell you for such a long time now. I've had it locked away inside of me but just couldn't say the words."

"I think you just did."

He put his hand on top of hers. "Yes, I suppose I did."

"I don't think I'll ever forget that melody nor the way you just played it."

"But I do want you to hear the words too."

He paused, working hard to build up his courage. In so many ways Zac Cobb was a man of action, not words, and Jenny knew that.

"Jenny Hays, I love you. I've never known what the words meant before, but every time I think on you I do."

He smiled and shook his head. "That wasn't so hard, I suppose. Maybe the rest will go a little easier."

He straightened his back, ramrod stiff. "This here is hard to admit, but usually I know what I want the first time I see it." He swallowed hard. "The first time I laid my eyes on you, I didn't even know your name, but I said to myself, now that's the woman I want to marry."

Jenny blushed, ever so softly. She wasn't about to offer him help. This was something he had to do all on his own.

"You know, in times past all I had at night was nightmares about the war. Now, though, when I dream, I dream of you. I dream about you, and I wake up wanting to make those dreams come true. During the day, I have songs in my head that talk only about you and words that call out for me to say them every time I'm close to you."

There was so much she wanted to say, but she remained perfectly still and silent.

"I suppose what I'm trying to say is that I do love you, Jenny. I love you, and I'd be mighty appreciative if you were my wife."

He blushed. "There, now I've said it. There just ain't no more to be said on the matter. You don't have to answer me right off. Take some time and think it over. In some ways it'd be like hitchin' up a pretty filly to an old, wore-out plow horse."

She paused. If there was anything else he wanted to say, she was going to be the last one to stop him. "Do you mind if I answer you right away?"

He gulped out loud.

"I love you too, Zac. I've been desperately in love with you for two years now. A fool could see that. And yes, I'll be your wife. I'll be proud to be your wife."

Zac closed his eyes and clinched his fists tightly. He almost looked as if he were in great pain.

He got to his feet and without explanation walked over to the rail. She watched him, unsure if he would run or just lean over the rail and be sick. Instead he shouted, a bloodcurdling Rebel yell, the likes of which she'd never heard before.

It startled her, and then she smiled.

Stepping back, he lifted her to her feet. "I've never known what it meant before to be the only man ever to see or feel anything, but now I do. There's never ever been a man that felt like I do right now. I'm just about the happiest man that ever lived."

He joined his lips to hers, pressing them softly into a warm kiss that expressed his deep feelings very clearly to Jenny.

They spent the rest of the day together, seeing everything with a fresh new light of spoken love. Zac dressed for dinner, putting on a tie to go with his freshly cleaned suit. He hummed a tune to himself as the boys watched, and then he applied an overly generous amount of bay rum to his freshly shaven face. He picked up his pipe and the bag of tobacco, then laid them back down on the dresser.

All during the evening meal, unspoken words passed between Zac and Jenny. It was something Hattie took great delight in.

"Carn sarn it, boy, somethin' fierce got holt of that tongue of yourn. Don't go to figurin' that you is the first man that's ever been in love, 'cause you ain't."

Zac spooned a bite of the pudding into his mouth and stirred the rest. "It's just a first for me, that's all that matters."

The *Delta King* was cutting its way through the waters of the bay. The boat stopped at the mouth of the river, but now they were underway once again.

Moments later the captain burst into the dining room and walked toward their table. "I understand congratulations are in order," he said.

Zac reached over and patted Jenny's hand. "For one of us, at least. Miss Hays here has agreed to become my wife."

"Well then, congratulations, Cobb, and my condolences to you, Miss Hays." Reaching into his pocket, Van Tuyl produced a yellow telegraph envelope. "Pilot's boat just delivered this telegram for you, Cobb. Figured it might be important, elsewise they'd have waited till we docked. I hope it's good news. I hate these telegrams my ownself."

Zac tore open the envelope and slowly read the message. His face was passive, not betraying a thought as to the contents of the message. Refolding it, he put it into his coat pocket.

"What is it?" Jenny asked.

Van Tuyl leaned forward. "After what this man did, I figure it to be a telegram from the governor giving him half the state."

Zac looked sober. "No, it's from my brother Joe." He looked at Jenny. "The one I told you about in Texas. The one whose wedding I went to in Dodge City."

"Is he all right?" Jenny asked.

"Yes, but he wants us to all meet in Santa Fe. He wants me to come right away. It seems one of the brothers is in great danger."

"Who?"

"He didn't say."

AUTHOR'S NOTES

\+ + + + + + +

When writing my books, I strive to keep every detail accurate to the times—and this includes my use of historical characters. I must confess that in the *Oyster Pirates* I have violated that rule. The book takes place in 1878, and Jack London would have been only two years old. However, the details of his life used in this book are accurate, and I have strived, as I do in all my books, to make his character one that does not disagree with what we do know about his life.

An illegitimate child who later adopted his stepfather's name, London grew up in poverty and deprivation in the Oakland slums and poor farms nearby. As a child, he became an oyster pirate and gang leader on the Oakland docks, experiences that later formed the basis for such boys' adventure stories as *The Cruise of the Dazzler* (1902) and *Tales of the Fish Patrol* (1905). At seventeen, London ran away to sea on a sealing ship bound for the North Pacific.

I think you'll find his character in the *Oyster Pirates* one that adds spice to the book and reveals what life and its pressures must have been like for the young Jack London.